Praise for *Half of What You Hear*

"The ending is neatly constructed, with satisfying redemption for all. Fans of Emily Giffin and Sally Hepworth will appreciate this enjoyable family drama featuring likable characters in challenging situations." —*Booklist*

"Fans of Liane Moriarty will adore the quirky cast of characters, gossip, and intrigue. I thoroughly enjoyed it!"
—Jamie Brenner, bestselling author of *The Forever Summer* and *The Husband Hour*

"Imagine a Liane Moriarty novel served with a tall glass of sweet tea and you'll have *Half of What You Hear*. Kristyn Kusek Lewis' latest tells the story of a Virginia town that may be too small to handle the truth—and the explosive result when several women's secrets manage to come to light anyway. Utterly captivating."
—Camille Pagán, bestselling author of *Woman Last Seen in Her Thirties*

"Incredibly intriguing, *Half of What You Hear* is a must-read that artfully delves its way through the layers of gossip, secrets, and lies of the small and seemingly charming town of Greyhill, where everyone knows your name, and *oh so much more*. Buckle up for a fun ride and one thing is for sure: you won't know who to believe until the very end."
—Liz Fenton and Lisa Steinke, bestselling authors of *Girls' Night Out*

Praise for *Save Me*

"Lewis gets it just right in her examination of how tiny cracks can shatter in a marriage that gets 'cemented in the fable' of what being together is supposed to be."

—*Publishers Weekly*

"Lewis' newest novel is an emotional roller coaster of a read, but in a good way. As fans follow the protagonist's story and journey through one of the hardest moments of her life, they will find themselves feeling every emotion with her along the way—hope, anguish, rage, sadness, and love all emerge. It's a testament to Lewis' great writing and is an absolutely fantastic read."

—*RT Book Reviews*

"Kristyn Kusek Lewis has written a novel that is as thought-provoking as it is thoughtful. From its heartbreaking beginning to its heartwarming end, *Save Me* had me asking myself, 'What would I do?' over and over—and over again. Absorbing, compelling, and a pleasure to read, this book is a page turner."

—Taylor Jenkins Reid, author of *The Seven Husbands of Evelyn Hugo*

"Kristyn Kusek Lewis defines heartbreak with deep understanding and compassion in *Save Me*. I swung from hope to rage, and back again, as I followed Daphne through the shattering after effects of infidelity. Lewis portrays neither angels nor demons, but the aching reality that marriage can become, along with the possibility of grace that love offers."

—Randy Susan Meyers, author of *Accidents of Marriage* and *The Comfort of Lies*

Praise for *How Lucky You Are*

"Fans of women's fiction about enduring female friendships will relate to debut author Lewis's vivid and genuinely written protagonists. A good choice for readers who enjoy the novels of Kristin Hannah."
—*Library Journal*

"Charming and achingly real. . . . I'm certain it will become a book club favorite."
—Sarah Jio, *New York Times* bestselling author of *The Violets of March* and *The Bungalow*

"In this wise and compulsively readable debut, Lewis follows three thirtysomething female friends and tackles even the heaviest of subjects with a restrained and self-assured hand, avoiding sentimentality while displaying an impressive emotional range. . . . If you've ever had a best friend or been a best friend, this is a book for you."
—Meg Mitchell Moore, author of *The Admissions* and *The Arrivals*

"*How Lucky You Are* is a compelling, insightful, and moving tale of the ever-shifting terrain of female friendship and the secrets we keep even from those who love us most."
—Meg Donohue, *USA Today* bestselling author of *Every Wild Heart* and *Dog Crazy*

Half
of
What
You
Hear

Half
of
What
You
Hear

A NOVEL

KRISTYN KUSEK LEWIS

HARPER

NEW YORK · LONDON · TORONTO · SYDNEY

HARPER

P.S.™ is a trademark of HarperCollins Publishers.

HarperCollins books may be purchased for educational, business, or sales promotional use. For information please email the Special Markets Department at SPsales@harpercollins.com.

FIRST EDITION

Designed by Joy O'Meara

Library of Congress Cataloging-in-Publication Data has been applied for.

ISBN 978-0-06-267335-0 (pbk.)

19 20 21 22 23   LSC   10 9 8 7 6 5 4 3 2

For my parents

Being careful is not as much fun as being friends. . . .
Do you want to be careful, or do you want to be friends?

—*A Bargain for Frances*

Half
of
What
You
Hear

❧ ⸻ ❧

PROLOGUE

Susannah

Even with the windows rolled down, the air feels thick and hot. Like "drowning in chowder," Teddy used to say, although he didn't know humidity like this. New York could get warm in the summer, even unbearably so, but it wasn't Virginia. Susannah had forgotten just how bad it could get.

She's sweating in a way that a lady should never admit—that was something she might have said once, in her old life, winking to her well-heeled friends to indicate that she didn't really buy into the stodgy rules she'd been raised with—and her palms are slippery against the steering wheel. Its perforated leather reminds her of the one in the Cadillac that her father had driven. She leans into the open frame of the window and pushes her foot on the gas, encouraging the breeze.

She'd wanted a truck like this her whole life. It's red, a Chevy Fleetside pickup. She'd first seen it in an advertisement in the back of the *New York Times* in 1967. She was nineteen then, living in the Barbizon Hotel on Sixty-Third Street. Occasionally, over the years, she'd mentioned the truck to Teddy, not in any serious way, just in passing, daydreaming aloud, the way you might say that it could be fun to climb the Great Wall someday, or see the northern lights. But because he was Teddy, he filed the nugget away (he was always listening, even when he seemed like he wasn't), and on her sixtieth birthday she found it parked in the circular drive of their summer house, a bow the size of an inner tube tied over the hood.

She remembers the shock of it, the first time she saw the truck and how it filled her with good feelings—warm feelings, loving feelings. This is what he could do to her. It was as if she were one of the precious crystal water pitchers she'd received as wedding gifts, and his actions could fill or empty her, depending. She'd turned to him in the driveway that day, shocked and elated, her fingertips pressed against her lips, and then ran and wrapped her arms around his starched shoulders, just like he knew she would. Her friends commented on how fortunate she was to have this doting and generous husband, but they didn't know the half of it.

That was ten years ago now. Teddy is gone, his body buried in Connecticut beside his horrible mother last year. The summer house is gone, too. She's back in Virginia, living in the house she grew up in, a move some people might describe as *full circle*. She takes a deep breath, the thick air in her mouth like . . . well, like chowder. So much in her life has changed. And yet, she's realized recently, so much hasn't.

Like the radio, for instance, still playing Patsy Cline all these decades later. "I Fall to Pieces." She chuckles to herself, noticing the sick irony of it.

And this lazy stretch of asphalt, Whippoorwill Road. The pines are still densely packed on either side, soldiers marking a path. The mottled metal mailboxes are familiar, the wooden plaques carved with house numbers and nailed to the trees. Even if she doesn't know the people inside them, she *knows* the little houses in her blood. Eyelet curtains hanging in the windows, porches jammed with rusting furniture, the occasional horse slapping at something with its tail, blackberry brambles, the sharp scent of someone burning something in their backyard.

Gone for more than fifty years, she thinks. With all the land and the expansive blue sky, the breeze in her hair, the mountains beyond, she should feel free, released, but she doesn't. Instead, she's anxious, a single leaf floating aimlessly through the air.

She sticks her hand out the open window and feels the liquid warmth of the wind through her fingers. Her eyes dart toward the trees. *Even when you're by yourself out here, you're never really alone*, she thinks, imagining all the things she can't see in the woods, the way she used to when she was a girl, squinting out the window in the back seat of the car. The bears, the deer, the snakes, the foxes. The ghosts.

She rubs a sweaty palm against her skirt—pink, Norma Kamali, bought in 1983 after she saw it on the runway. Her eyes dart from side to side. She realizes she's swerving, kicking up gravel on her right side. *Jesus*, she mutters, shaking her head at herself, and then takes another deep breath, her hands at ten and two. *Maybe it's time to turn around.*

She reaches for the radio dial. She's losing the signal. When she looks up, there's the slightest bend in the road, easy and gradual, like the curve of her hip. A bead of sweat rolls down her temple. She flicks the heel of her hand against the side of her face, runs a finger across her upper lip. There is no AC in the truck. The wind is hot. The sun is beating down on the hood. It's one o'clock in the afternoon, August in central Virginia. What was she thinking?

The static on the radio is getting worse. She reaches to turn it off, and when she looks up—the bend in the road—there's another car. A sort of goldish beige, sleek. Barreling fast.

She hugs her side of the road, but the car is coming faster, right toward her, in fact, the glare from the sun a white streak across the windshield. She lays on the horn, pounds at it, but it barely whimpers. She always meant to mention it to Teddy, how it never worked. *The car! It's crossing* . . .

She opens her mouth and screams.

The wind stops. The air is still. Searing. The locusts buzz in the trees around her, the sound unforgiving, an electric singe that feels like it's coming from inside her. She tastes blood in her mouth. She hears the trill of a bird in the distance—*a pine warbler*, she thinks, remembering. She opens and closes her eyes and wonders if this is the end. She thinks to herself, tries to say it again, over and over (*how many times has she said it?*): *Help.*

ONE

⚬〜───〜⚬

Two Months Later
October
Greyhill, Virginia

"So, Martha, how many people did you turn away today?"

Martha Brown swallows a sip of her third chardonnay and tells herself that it is her final glass. "Take a guess," she says, yelling across the bar to where her godson Tom is mixing a whiskey sour.

"How about seven?" he guesses, draining the cocktail shaker into a glass.

"The final count was *eleven*," she says.

Tom whistles, deep and low.

"Eleven wives!" repeats Jenny Perkins from her usual Saturday-night spot at the bar, wiping ketchup from the side of her mouth with her pinky.

"*E-lev-en*," Martha repeats, lifting her glass again.

They play this guessing game at the bar in Dahlia's restaurant every week. Martha is the owner and sole proprietor of Brown & Brown Realty on Maple Street. Her grandfather and great-uncle founded the office, but now that they're both gone and her parents are, too, she's the only Brown left in Greyhill.

Fall and spring are her busiest seasons, but not because she sells any houses. Instead, she puts aside her usual workday activities—reading her paperback mysteries, watching CNN on the little TV she keeps on her grandfather's desk, *maybe* sipping an occasional afternoon glass from the bottle of wine she keeps in the office fridge—and fields questions from the DC and Richmond women and their husbands.

They come to town in droves this time of year, when the leaves are at their peak, the town seemingly outlined in a garland of reds and oranges and yellows, the scent of wood smoke and cider in the air. They walk up and down Maple in their quilted vests and designer jeans, darting in and out of the delightful little shops, pointing at the hand-painted signs above each storefront and the brass plaques on the brick facades of the buildings on the National Register of Historic Places, and it doesn't take long for the wheels to start turning in the wives' heads. *We could start a simpler life here*, they think, hobbling in their high-heeled boots on the cobblestoned streets. *We could open one of these little shops! We could get horses! Chickens! We could garden!* By the time they walk into Martha's office, they're practically panting. "I'm interested in some property," they squeak, looking down their perky powdered noses at Martha, the gold bracelets clink-clanking on their wrists. They all wear those big bangles now, Martha has noticed. All the way up to their elbows. They look to Martha like handcuffs.

She explains, as she always does, that there is nothing currently available.

"Nothing at *all*?" they say, their mouths open in little O's like in that famous painting *The Scream*. The husbands, in contrast, are barkers—lawyers and lobbyists, she's sure. Little terrierlike men. "You have nothing?" they say, eyes narrowed, not believing her.

"Nothing at all," she coos, placating them by turning to the dusty Dell monitor on her desk and offering to add their names to a wait list.

The wives all want to be reincarnations of Jackie Kennedy, whose escape from Washington was a horse farm an hour from here, on Rattlesnake Mountain near Middleburg. What they don't understand is that while Greyhill has all the charm and timeless beauty of those hunt-country towns farther north—Middleburg and Upperville and la-di-da—Greyhill is no-vacancy. It has never been a weekend-country-house kind of place. Martha, and everyone she knows in town, would like to keep it that way.

She can tell you, having sold just a single property in the past six months, that the vast majority of homes in Greyhill proper are true family heirlooms, passed down from generation to generation or sold by word of mouth to close friends. The last one she sold was the Ammandale house, to Cole Warner and his wife, the chubby woman who used to work in the White House. It's nice for Cole to be back in his hometown, across the street from his parents.

"Would you believe that I had somebody ask me about Esperanza today?" she says. Her voice feels loose and slurry. She pushes her wineglass away.

"You're kidding," Dahlia says from behind the bar.

"It happens once in a while. Lately, more than ever. Everyone wants to know what's happening up in the house on the hill. Dear old Susannah."

"I can't blame them for asking," says Dahlia, stretching to place a clean wineglass on the rack above her. Her tight T-shirt rides up, revealing her navel, and Martha watches, amused, as Tom's eyes travel over her curves. Oh, to be young and naive and not realize that everyone knows you're sleeping together.

"Susannah's brought all that attention on herself," says Jenny. "That's the way she operates, always has. I still don't understand why she came back here after all these years."

Hal, her husband, shifts in his seat. He puts a hand over his mouth, pretending to clear his throat, and says, "*Carpetbagger.*"

"Oh, *Hal*," Jenny says.

"What?" he says.

Martha laughs. "If the shoe fits."

"I don't know, though . . ." Tom starts, putting a hand on his hip. He has that squinty look on his face like he thinks he's about to say something insightful. Martha rolls her eyes.

"Is what she's doing really 'wrong'?" he says, making little quotation marks with his stubby fingers. "If Susannah Lane has all this property to sell, why can't she sell it to whomever she wants? Isn't that her right?"

"*Hell no!*" Hal says, leaning across the bar, a finger pointing to the boy's face, making Martha giggle.

Tom rears back. "Well, why not?"

"Because, Tom," Hal says, "the woman is a *Greyhill*, the last living one, and that land of hers is *Greyhill* land. She has a responsibility to all of us who've been raising our families here for generations to continue the tradition of this town, not turn it into a playground for outsiders. I mean, *damn!* The buses that come through town on the weekends, carrying in all those drunk Northern Virginia housewives for lunch after they've been around to the wineries—that's bad enough."

Jenny pats his arm.

"I heard she listed that plot up north of Little Comfort Road for almost three million," Dahlia says.

Tom whistles again.

"That true, Martha?" Hal asks.

She throws a hand up. "How the hell would I know? You know I refuse to have anything to do with any of this. When she came to my office after she moved back, asking whether I'd be her agent, I told her *exactly* what I thought of that idea."

"And that's why she brought in that guy from New York," Jenny says.

"He flies down whenever it's time to show some land," Martha says. "He got licensed in the state just for this."

"Well, he knows what kind of commission he'll make," Hal says, spitting as the words come out of his mouth.

"Now, now," Jenny says, patting his shoulder.

He shakes his head. "I'm sorry," he sputters. "This infuriates me. It should infuriate all of you! How she can just come back here after decades, thinking she's the queen bee and that she can just start shaking things up!"

"Times change, Mr. Perkins," Dahlia says. "We might not like it, but—"

"Times change!" Hal screams back. "Dahlia, if your father

heard you say that! I mean, come on, you were raised here. And here you are, running the restaurant your parents started. Is nothing sacred?"

"The way you're riled up, Hal, I might start to believe you're the one who tried to run Susannah off the road over the summer," Martha says, laughing and reaching again for her glass.

"Martha!" Jenny scolds.

"Don't think there's not a part of me that didn't wish it *was* me!" Hal says.

"Hal!" Jenny says.

"Oh, I don't mean it," he says. "I saw the pictures the sheriff took afterward. You should have seen the way Susannah's truck was wrapped around that tree." He whistles.

"It's amazing she lived, much less came out basically unscathed," Dahlia says.

Martha nods and looks around the bar. "Nine lives, that one."

"That's for sure," Jenny mutters, her eyes on her plate as she drags another fry through her ketchup. "That's for *damn* sure."

"Anyway." Martha clears her throat. "I told the woman who came into the office today that Esperanza wasn't for sale and probably never would be. I said the owner is very happy to stay where she is."

"Well, did you tell her about all the land she *does* have for sale?" Tom asks.

Martha smiles. "Forgot that part."

Hal laughs. "Here's to ya, Martha!" He raises his glass.

"You think she's really happy being back here, up in that house all alone?" Dahlia asks, rubbing the rim of a wineglass with a white bar cloth.

"I can't imagine she would be." Jenny shrugs. "I almost feel sorry for her."

Her husband huffs and steals a fry off her plate. "Almost," he says. "That's the key word. I, for one, hope she leaves just as quickly as she did when she was seventeen."

TWO

Bess

The invitation from Greg and Mindy Barker arrived in the mail weeks ago, just after Labor Day. I pick it up off the stack on the kitchen counter, flicking the black paper with my finger. It is heavy Crane cardstock, five and a half by seven and a half inches, the same size I'd used for the First Lady's less formal events. Concerts in the East Room. Garden teas on the South Lawn. A televised tour of the White House kitchen for the Food Network.

Mindy had chosen a sparkly silver spiderweb design. Nice. A little cutesy, but it was hard not to be on a Halloween invitation. In silver script, it announced that this would be the twentieth anniversary of their annual masquerade party.

"Tell me this isn't standard invitation etiquette around here," I turn and say to Cole, fanning myself with the card.

"What?" He puts out his hand to have a look.

"Don't get me wrong, it's nice and all, but they could have just done Paperless Post and saved themselves a few hundred dollars."

"Well, it's the twentieth anniversary of this party," he says through a mouthful of potato chips. "It's a big deal to them."

I grab the envelope off the counter and run my finger over the return address printed in letterpress on the back. 46 HONEY-SUCKLE LANE. I know that street. Big, green lawns and manicured boxwoods. Gorgeous oil lanterns flanking the front doors. Ever since the kids went back to school last month, I've been driving around a lot, trying to get my bearings. Most of Greyhill's population lives just outside downtown, on wide swaths of land that in many cases were once working farms. Now, they showcase beautifully renovated homes with equestrian barns, hobby animals, and carefully plotted formal gardens.

I thought finding my way around Greyhill would be easy compared to driving around DC. How could it not be—it's a town of barely seven hundred, with a main drag called Maple Street that runs less than a mile from end to end. Plus, I'm not entirely a stranger. I've been coming here for years to visit Cole's parents.

How naive I'd been. The minute you leave Greyhill proper, everything looks the same. Idyllic, with rolling pastures criss-crossed by old stone fences, the purple-gray peaks of the Blue Ridge Mountains framing the view but also distracting for that very reason, and it's impossible to navigate. It is so expansive, so *empty*, and so different from what I'm used to that sometimes, when I take a moment to really notice it, I feel my breath catch, the space almost startling me. It is hard to believe that we are just eighty miles from DC.

I fling Mindy's envelope onto the counter and reach for the chips. "So this party's a big deal?" I repeat, my hand digging into the bag.

"What?" Cole says, a touch of defensiveness in his voice.

"Nothing." I look across the room and smile at him. He thinks I am criticizing his friends, and he's right, I am. But it's not that I don't *like* them. I simply don't *know* them yet. And the problem is that they all know who I am, or they assume they do—I have cable news to thank for that—and that's what makes me nervous.

I turn and open the refrigerator. "What do you want for dinner?" I ask, scanning the contents of the shelves as I lick the salt from the chips off my fingertips. Another new thing since we moved: I'm cooking again. There is no more sloppy takeout eaten at the kitchen counter while we scan emails, no more bullshit slow cooker gruel, no more racing by the store to "pick up something quick" in the twenty-minute window between leaving work and grabbing the kids from their after-school program.

"Anything," he says, wrapping his arms around my waist. He kisses my neck. "Maybe that?" He points to a parchment-wrapped package I bought at Bully's, the local grocery store, this morning. A cut-up whole chicken. "Heritage breed," the butcher had said proudly from behind the counter. "Killed it myself yesterday."

Cole starts for the door.

When we agreed to take over the inn that's been in Cole's family for generations, Bradley and Diane, his parents, warned us over champagne and cake that the business might surprise us. "You know, this could be every bit as busy as your lives back in DC," Bradley said, a line neither of us really believed, even while we knew there was a steep learning curve ahead of us.

So far, we've been right. It's not that the work isn't hard— Cole's at the inn seven days a week and often heads back in the evenings after dinner just to check on things—but it's *different*.

It's happy work, catering to people, coddling the guests—a welcome change from grinding it out for fifteen hours a day on a laptop or in meetings, the way we used to do.

And the business is stable . . . I think. Let's say I'm 80 percent sure. The only other hotel option nearby is a terrifying motel fifteen miles down the highway that's begging to be a crime scene. It's reassuring that we've been the only game in town for decades, ever since Cole's great-grandfather decided to turn his childhood home into an inn after he returned home from the First World War. Back then, Greyhill was a stop on the C&O Railway, a pass-through between the coal mines of Appalachia and the ports in Newport News and Norfolk, so there was actually a need for a place for people to stay when they were passing through on business. But the railroad is long gone, so now the inn quietly caters to couples on weekend getaways and to guests of Greyhill residents, and occasionally to people who have business in Charlottesville, about thirty-five miles away. It would be nice if it were a bustling business, but Cole assures me that his parents have never had a problem making money. Still, I insisted on seeing all the income reports and spreadsheets before I agreed to jump in with both feet, and I keep reminding myself that I've visited enough over the years that I'd know if we were making a mistake.

I hear Cole collecting his keys, the rustle of him putting on his coat. "Hey," I yell. "You'll be home . . . ?"

"The normal time," he says. "Five thirty or so."

I chuckle.

"What?" Cole says.

"I just can't believe you're home for lunch and then home again at five thirty," I say.

"Are you complaining about it?" he says, laughing down the hall.

"Of course not," I yell back. "That's why we're here, isn't it?"

"Yes," he says. "But if you're going to get sick of me . . ."

"Go to work!" I yell, laughing.

"Bye."

We decided when we moved in that Cole didn't need an office at home, not with the inn just two miles away, so the sunny room at the front of the house, with a big bay window overlooking the yard, is mine.

The Ammandale house, Martha Brown, the Realtor, had called it, after some long-ago former owner. I'd always known the white Dutch Colonial that sat across the street from Cole's childhood home as the Millers' house. They were distant Ammandale cousins, Ms. Brown explained to me, a knowing in her voice that smacked just slightly of condescension.

I'd always loved the house and its pretty white facade, the crisp black shutters framing the windows, the tawny cedar shingles on the roof, an old oak tree just to the right of the house in the front yard, exactly where it should be, a rope swing hanging from one of its limbs. Mr. Miller had put the swing up years ago, for Cole. They'd never had their own children, Mrs. Miller had wistfully told me once, but Cole had been "a joy to them," growing up right across the street, like a beloved godson or nephew who always obliged when they asked if he could haul their Christmas tree out to the curb after the holidays or help Mr. Miller clear the gutters.

I don't want to say that my husband had an ulterior motive when he told me last spring that Mr. Miller had finally convinced his wife to move to a golf community in Sarasota, but he knew that he was starting a conversation. We were sitting in maddening traffic on the Beltway, a panorama of brake lights in front of us, on our way back to DC from Easter brunch at the inn. Livvie and Max were in the back seat, trading candy from the baskets we had given them earlier that morning, and I could feel my body tensing as our car inched farther into the crush of Northern Virginia, a bottleneck of noise and people that made bucolic Greyhill feel like something I'd imagined.

Earlier that day, Diane and I had stood in the archway of the main dining room, watching as Cole's father, dressed as the Easter Bunny, posed for pictures with the guests' children. She mentioned, once again, that Bradley would love to retire, saying it in a hushed tone like this was a secret rather than something she'd expressed a dozen times before. I pretended not to hear her and watched Bradley hop a loop around a crowd of mesmerized toddlers. If I were him, I'd work until the day I died if it would give me a reason to be out of the house and away from Diane.

She'd never liked our lifestyle in DC. When she and Bradley came to visit (which wasn't all that often, because of the inn and also because Diane preferred that we come to her), she complained that it was too noisy, too busy. Our place was too small. The restaurants were too crowded. In the past couple of years she'd become more vocal about her desire for Cole to take over the family business, but Cole and I had made a practice of ignoring her "hints." He hadn't been able to picture leaving his job as in-house counsel at the National Wildlife Federation any more than I could imagine leaving the White House. But when I got fired and started wondering aloud, especially after my sessions with Dimitria, my therapist, whether the hustle-and-strive we had in DC was the life we still wanted long-term, Cole revealed that there was a small, secret part of him that actually liked the idea of stepping in for his dad at the inn. He said he'd never mentioned it before because he didn't want me to have to give anything up. *But now,* he started, measuring his words, *maybe things are more flexible.* . . . He graciously left out the fact that because of what I'd done, nobody in Washington—at least, none of the good people in Washington—would consider hiring me any more than they'd consider employing one of the pandas at the National Zoo.

I looked out at the traffic that night and told Cole what I'd said to him many times before: I had fallen in love with Greyhill the first time he took me there, and had long harbored fantasies about what life could be like for us in his sweet hometown. They were unrealistic, never-gonna-happen fantasies, on par with my dreams of a cottage on the Maine coast and a flat in Notting Hill, but they existed nevertheless.

And the Millers' house: not only was it triple the square footage of our place in DC and easily half the price (Cole had to ask Mr. Miller to repeat himself when he'd offered a number out on their driveway earlier that day), it was also the House, a home like the one I'd held in my dreams since I was a little girl growing up in a forgettable saltbox with peeling paint and rusting gutters in a down-at-the-heels suburb of Burlington, Vermont. I'd gazed longingly at the Millers' house every time we came to Greyhill, and even referenced it when we were house hunting near Capitol Hill: *I'll know it's the right place when I feel the way I feel when I look at the Millers' house.*

That night, we crawled through the traffic. We parked the car. I started the laundry, checked to make sure we had milk for the morning, and looked at my appointment book while I chewed the ears off the chocolate bunny Cole had given me earlier that day.

And then, right before bed, I walked out of our bathroom and announced to Cole through a mouthful of toothpaste that I wanted to make an offer on the house. He looked up from what he'd been reading, looking as stunned as if I had emerged with my hair dyed hot pink. He made me insist that the move was truly what I wanted and continued to repeat the question, dozens of times, over the next few months, right up until the morning the moving truck pulled up to our curb. I assured him, over and over and *over* again, that I was sure. I wanted the house, the adorable town, the backyard for the kids, the promise of a new start—not just for me but for all of us. Our family. This would be our next chapter. This would be our home.

I sit down at the desk and click open my email, scanning a forwarded article from my dad about the lineup for this Sunday's Patriots game, which I've started to believe he sends more out of habit or superstition than a belief that I might actually read it or watch the game. It is so quiet, and I start to feel a familiar uneasiness rise up inside me. It happens all too often lately, when I'm in the house alone. I think of Dimitria and what she said in her gloriously ornate Greek accent during our session when I told her we were leaving Washington: "What if people think you're running away?"

I miss our weekly appointments more than I thought I would. I never pictured myself becoming the type of person who not only needed weekly therapy but craved it. Then again, I didn't picture a lot of things that have happened in the past year. *Weekly.* I play with the word in my head like it's a riddle, a tongue twister I have to practice to understand. Weekly. *Weakly.* Weekly. *Weakly.* I feel *weak.* Like a *weakling.*

Before the move, those appointments had become the highlight of my Monday through Friday, the one thing that broke up the hours after Cole and the kids went off for the day and I sat alone in the house, my teeth unbrushed, watching the *Today* show. (Often all four hours.) Those commercials they play during morning television? The ads for stain remover and cereal? I know them all now. I catch myself singing along to the jingles when they come on, or mouthing the dialogue. The ones that really got to me, though, were the personal-injury lawyer ads that started showing up around ten o'clock, after the rest of the world had turned off their televisions and moved on with their lives. *Have you been hurt on the job?*

Well, yes, actually, I'd mutter to the empty room. *Yes, I have.*

Every time I walked into an appointment with Dimitria and slung my bag down onto the pristine Oriental rug, I said the same thing, the thought that railed at me all day long, neon red letters screaming at me inside my head: "I should be at work."

I know how that makes me sound. Workaholic. Ego-driven. Selfish. All of which was true, to an extent, but you could say the same thing about anyone you pulled off the street in DC. My official title had been White House social secretary and special assistant to the First Lady. Do you know how delicious that was, for a girl like I'd once been?

It's not that I thought I was too good for therapy. Quite the opposite, in fact. That was what had landed me on the Eames lounge chair in Dimitria's sleek office in the first place. We'd actually been meeting on and off for years, whenever I needed a tune-up, someone to help me sort out the usual shit—years ago, the exhaustion of juggling my career and infant twins, and then later the stress of a big, big job and a husband's big, big job, plus kids who were careening full speed toward adolescence.

Just this morning, wiping milk from the corner of Max's lip: *Is that hair?* I'd said, gripping his chin in my cupped hand. *Mom, stop. . . .* He'd shrugged me away with a grimace, and I'd reached for my coffee, taking a deep, long sip so he wouldn't see the way his rejection made my lip tremble.

My hang-up, let's be clear, is not the therapy itself but the reason for it this time around.

What if they think you're running away, Dimitria had said. *What happened to you was a scandal, Bess! A beeg one!*

A big one?! I repeated, sparring with her. *You think I don't realize that?*

My photo had been printed in every major newspaper in the country, my name a punch line on the late-night shows for a week after the story broke.

I'd been to other therapists before. The kind who wore goofy LIFE IS GOOD T-shirts to the office and put their palms on their hearts while they listened to you, the kinds who played new age background music and gave limp advice: *Imagine, Bess, that you're placing your negative thoughts on a cloud. Close your eyes, Bess. Watch them drift away.*

Dimitria wore angular business suits and gave off the impression that smiling was beneath her. She pushed me around, got in my face (not literally, of course, though I wouldn't put it past her). The one time I heard her laugh was when I told her about the clouds. She snorted. "No! *No*," she said, punctuating the words with a pointed finger. "You take your issues to the firing range. You line them up. *And then you shoot them dead!*" Our hour together often felt athletic, physically cathartic in the way that a good cry feels.

People are going to think what they're going to think, I told her right before we moved, and she nodded, pleased with me. That's the big lesson I've learned through all of this. Or learned again, because I've most certainly had it proven to me, like a club over the head, more than once over my forty-two years. Each time, I get back up. That's what I need to keep reminding myself.

I pick up my phone and check my texts. For years, I slept with two smartphones just inches from my pillow—one personal, and the second a federal government–issued BlackBerry. I fantasized about a life where I didn't have to live by their chimes and dings.

So what an irony that now that I'm free I swipe down on the screen dozens of times a day, like I'm playing the slots. Again and then again, watching that little spinning pinwheel and hoping (*c'mon, baby!*) for a message from an old colleague that might—*poof!*—make my life fall neatly back into place. A job offer, perhaps. What I wish for most of all is a missive from FLOTUS. *We made a horrible error, Bess. We need you!* But that will never happen. I am yesterday's news, no longer relevant.

Maybe I did run away, I think. *And so what? What does it matter now?*

I imagine my ex-colleagues back in DC, what they might be doing at 10:00 a.m. on a Tuesday, as I look around the room. The walls are covered in Mrs. Miller's original, timeless grass cloth, with the kids' pictures, which we've taken during the height of cherry blossom season every year since they were infants, hanging in gold frames on one side. I have this beautiful room, a room of my own, all to myself, and I don't have the slightest idea what it is I'll actually *do* here. I will help at the inn, of course, eventually. I'm not sure how, exactly. It's all still sort of murky, but when Diane and Bradley and Cole and I sat down to talk everything over all those months ago, that was what we'd decided. I didn't want to commit to anything formal, and my in-laws, especially Diane, were happy to oblige.

"Take your time," Bradley said. As he reached across their old farm table to squeeze my arm, I'd felt a pang in my chest, remembering his kindness when he called me the day I was fired, and how he'd had William, the owner of the local bakery, overnight a dozen of my favorite shortbread cookies from his shop. The card was signed by both of them, but I knew better, if for no other reason than that Diane would never condone sending me fattening food.

"Yes," Diane had said, her eyes boring into mine despite her tight smile. "You might find that you prefer to just focus on your family for a while." She's never believed in my career. Never approved of it, I should say. Not when I could be home ironing Cole's shirts. The first time she called after I was fired (I got the sense that Cole or Bradley had put her up to it), she sounded relieved. "The kids must be thrilled!" she said, a comment that still stings when I think of it.

It is so quiet. I click on my email again, and a line from that old Talking Heads song pops into my head: *And you may find yourself . . . in a beautiful house!* I love this house, but I miss my old one despite everything. I miss it all.

One afternoon shortly before we left DC, I watched our Realtor from a window seat in the coffee shop across the street from our place. I was armed with a cappuccino and a chocolate-chip cookie, my reward for being a good girl at therapy that morning. The potential buyers were a young couple—the man in the standard-issue blue gingham shirt, the woman in a law-firm-appropriate black sheath. They carried their phones purposefully in their hands, like walkie-talkies.

I hated them. They reminded me of Cole and myself years ago, the midafternoon sun shining on them like its perfect golden glow had been calibrated just for that moment. My stomach burned as I watched them climb the steps to my house, a house we'd bought seven years ago when the world seemed like it was ours for the taking. They looked so . . . *what was it?* They looked so goddamn sure of themselves.

I knew they were the Ones when they got to the landing and the woman bent down to smell the lavender bushes I'd planted the month before in the iron pots that flank the front door. The way she looked at her husband when she straightened up . . . I could tell. I picked up my cookie, and it crunched with a snap between my front teeth.

The buyers—Melinda and Stephen Parker, I discovered—became a brief but fervent obsession, a place to channel the problem of my newly acquired self-loathing. *Melinda and Stephen will have better furniture than us. They'll throw the dinner parties we always meant to. They will have passionate sex years into their marriage, and they will never fight.* I relayed all this to my mother, who laughed on the other end of the phone between sips of her coffee and told me to let it go, to keep my eyes on the prize, which I eventually did: Remember adorable Greyhill, the way my girlfriends moaned when I told them we were moving here—to take over an inn, no less. Remember the row of white hydrangeas blooming along the side of the new house, the family dinners every night, twinkling lights strung over the patio, and the twins chasing fireflies on the lawn. The *quality* of our lives is what matters now, I tell myself, instead of the unruly quantity of everything, the rushing around, the juggling.

We are two months in, and everything is different. Completely so. Except, so far, me.

❧━━━━━━━━❧

My email chimes. "Proposition for you," the subject line reads. The sender is . . .

Noelle Bartram?

We met years and years ago, back when she and I were both fresh out of college and I thought I might want to be a journalist. We were working side by side as editorial assistants at *Government Executive*, a business magazine catering to the federal government, which is exactly as dry as it sounds. Noelle was the only fun thing about working there, and it didn't take long for me to leave the magazine for a job at an event-planning firm. After I left, we remained friendly—in fact, a few years later, she introduced me to Cole—and she had since become the executive editor at the *Washington Post* magazine. I don't think I've seen her in over a year. Maybe two. *Why did we lose touch?* I think. *Did I even tell her we were moving?* I click open the email and start reading.

Hey, old friend. How is life in the sticks? How are Cole and
Livvie and Max? Excuse me for getting right to the point
but I'm on deadline ... remember those?

Typical Noelle. Short on time and pleasantries.

I have a proposition for you. We want to do a story
about Susannah Lane and what she's doing around
Greyhill. A guy in the office says he was down there a
few weekends ago with his wife and overheard something about her selling a bunch of land, trying to make
Greyhill the next Middleburg, flying in some fancy NY
real-estate agent and her zillionaire friends. Is that
true? Didn't she just have a big accident? Do you
want to write the piece?

I squint at the words on the screen. *Susannah Lane?* I think.
Write the piece? I know who Susannah is, of course, though I
haven't laid eyes on her in person. Her late husband, Teddy Lane,
was a banking genius and multibillionaire, a man *Time* magazine once put on their cover with the headline "The Last True
Tycoon." The two of them were often featured together in the
media—or at least, in some of the newspaper and magazine columns I kept tabs on for my old job, like the party-picture pages
in *Vanity Fair*. Teddy Lane was a big contributor to the guy who
ran against President Calhoun in the last election, one reason he
never made it onto a guest list. But Susannah . . . I might like an
excuse to meet her. Originally from Greyhill, she moved back into
Esperanza, her childhood home, just about a year ago, and had

a horrible car accident this summer that everyone around town seems amazed she survived. She's also—fun fact—my father-in-law's high school sweetheart.

I click reply.

Noelle! Good to hear from you. Yes, Susannah crashed her truck right before we moved here. She's fine, as far as I know. And yes, she is a hot topic around here.

I pause, my fingers hovering over the keyboard for a moment before I continue.

As for the assignment, I'm intrigued, but you do realize that I haven't written professionally in twenty years?

Noelle's reply comes back almost instantly.

It will be a fluff piece, three pages or so, you can handle it. We want someone local to the area and apparently there's no newspaper there?! (IS THERE RUNNING WATER?!) I trust you, and I'm a good editor. Come on, do it. I'll pay you well. Or as well as newspapers can pay these days. And what else do you have to do? Forgive me if I'm being blunt, but I thought you might like the idea of doing something different—of recasting yourself, if you will.

I raise my eyebrows.

What else do I have to do? I mutter under my breath. I think of Esperanza, which sits like a cake topper overlooking downtown.

I used to make Cole drive us past the iron gates when we came for a visit, just so I could gawk at the big house on the hill. *Hmm.*

I'm flattered that you thought of me, I type, but then stop myself. I pick up the phone and call Cole.

"Hey, I only have a minute," he says. "About to have a staff meeting."

"Okay, real quick," I start. "You won't believe who I just heard from."

"Shit," he says, sighing into the phone. "I'm sorry, Bess. I didn't realize what time it was. Can it wait?"

"Oh," I say, rapping my fingertips against the desk. "Sure."

"I'm sorry, I'll call you back in a bit."

Before I have a chance to say anything, the line goes dead.

I put down the phone, thinking of Diane, my mother-in-law, and what she'll say if I agree to do this. She has strong opinions about everything, but Susannah Lane is chief among the things she openly disdains, right up there with people who don't send thank-you notes and women who wear exercise clothes in public. I personally think she's jealous that Susannah was her husband's first love, which is, of course, ridiculous, but so is Diane.

What will people in town say? I think, hearing her voice in my head.

I look back at my computer screen, nibbling on the inside of my lip as I think it over, and before I can talk myself out of it, I pick up the phone again and dial the number in the signature line in Noelle's email. She picks up after half a ring.

"So are you in?" she says by way of greeting.

"Well, what are the details?"

"Two thousand words, due in about . . . mmm . . . let's say

five weeks, right before Thanksgiving. That's not too taxing, right? Given that our staff writers do that much on a daily basis?"

"And they're professionals. They win Pulitzers," I say. "Remember, I've spent the last several years throwing parties."

"Throwing parties, very funny. I see you're still as humble as ever. Look, I know it's been a while since you've written anything, but I have to tell you, even all these years later, despite everyone I've worked with, you're still one of the smartest, most capable people I've ever had the pleasure of sharing an office with. I wouldn't ask if I didn't think you could do it."

"Aw, thanks," I tease, though her kind words matter more to me than I'd like. "So you're going to pay me accordingly?"

"I can pay you a dollar a word. This is a newspaper, not a lobbying firm."

"Got it. But a dollar a word, huh? That's fine, but I think I got a dollar fifty back in the day."

"Yeah, well, that was before the King Kong known as the internet started decimating our business. That's the best I can do. And we'll send someone down to do a photo shoot; it'll be fun. Just think about your byline, and all the people in DC who will see it. . . . This could do wonders for you, Bess." My mind zips to my former coworkers opening their Sunday papers and seeing my name. "Well?" she says.

I look around the office again. "I'm in," I tell her. "Let's do it."

THREE

⸙

"I was at the Greyhill Inn yesterday."

"And? How is it looking now? With Cole at the helm?"

"Well, that's just the thing."

"What?"

"The whole Warner family was there, standing in the lobby. Cole, Bradley, Diane, Cole's wife, even their two kids. I think they'd just had dinner."

"Ah. I hope no one had the chicken piccata. Cole has to do something about that menu."

"Agreed. But that's not what I want to tell you. The *interesting* part is that they were all standing there, the whole family, just chatting, you know, with that young kid who works the front desk?"

"Henry, Harry, something like that."

"Right. And in walks—you won't believe it—*Susannah Lane.*"

"*No!*"

"Yup! She had this big scarf wrapped around her head, all these bright colors—"

"God forbid she go unnoticed."

"Exactly! There was a gauzy bandage peeking out from under the scarf. Actually, not peeking—it was clearly visible, like she wanted it to be seen. And she was using a cane."

"I *heard* about the cane! She's really milking this thing, isn't she? I mean, it's been a couple months."

"I wouldn't be surprised if she caused the whole accident herself, you know, for publicity. To get people on her good side over this whole land thing."

"This isn't the first time I've heard that theory."

"Mm-hmm. Anyway, so she comes in, walks right up to the Warners, and says hello to Bradley. She actually walked right up to *him*, put her hand on his arm, and leaned in and *kissed his cheek! Right in front of Diane!*"

"She didn't!"

"Oh, she did! And you should have seen the look on his face. You know, it takes a lot to render Bradley Warner speechless."

"What about Diane?"

"You know Diane, she looked like she was about to explode. But that's not all: Susannah then turned to Cole's wife . . . Bess, I think her name is? And said she was looking forward to their *appointment*."

"Appointment?"

"Yes!"

"What *kind* of appointment?"

"Hell if I know; they didn't elaborate, but you should have seen Cole's wife. Her face turned bright red, like she'd been caught."

"Caught doing what?"

"That's what I'd like to know. Even Cole looked confused."

"Huh. That *is* interesting."

"I *know!* But that's not even the best part."

"No?"

"Nope. So then, Susannah announces to the group of them that she's come to the inn to have a drink."

"A drink?"

"Yup. And then she turns to Bradley Warner, right there in the lobby, in front of everyone, and says, 'Wouldn't it be fun if you could join me, Bradley? You'll have to stop by the house sometime and visit.'"

"*What?*"

"I *know!* Diane walked away then."

"Walked away?"

"Yup. And Susannah started *laughing.*"

"Laughing?"

"Yes! Bradley looked appalled. Cole and his wife pretended not to notice—they turned their attention to their kids, I think they were trying to act like nothing happened, but I saw the two of them exchange a look. Unfortunately I couldn't stick around to see the rest because William pulled up then, with the car."

"Do you think she actually went on to the bar, or was that the whole show? I'm going to ask around."

"Please do! I'd *love* to know more about this."

"I bet she did go on to the bar. And what do you think she's doing with Bradley's daughter-in-law?"

"I can't begin to imagine, but you know, it has to be *something*. The look on Bess's face!"

"That Susannah . . ."

"I know. Shameless!"

FOUR

Livvie

The first thing Livvie noticed about Lauren was the keychain on her backpack. Livvie loved keychains. She had been collecting them forever, at least since kindergarten. Right now, she had nine of them hanging from her backpack: a unicorn; a puffy gumball machine that smelled like cotton candy; an Eiffel Tower; a plastic picture-frame thing of Sara, her best friend in DC; a pom-pom; a hand sanitizer shaped like an owl; a LEGO minifigure; a little notebook; and Stuart, her favorite minion from *Despicable Me*. She used to have a White House keychain, too, but she took that one off and stuck it under some books in her nightstand after her mom got fired.

The one Lauren had on her backpack was an *L*, which was why it caught Livvie's eye. Well, that and the fact that it was big, actually almost exactly the same size as Livvie's hand. Livvie knew this because when she was standing in line behind Lauren to go into homeroom on her second day at Draper Hall, the private school in Greyhill she and Max were going to now, she put her hand up next to the keychain for reference.

Lauren felt her hand and turned around sharply.

"Sorry!" Livvie said, quickly clasping her hands behind her back.

Lauren looked at her, confused, like she was trying to decide whether Livvie looked familiar (Livvie had been getting a lot of looks like that since the move), but then she smiled at her.

"I have an *L* name, too," Livvie said. "Well, it's an *O* name, actually—Olivia—but nobody's ever called me anything but Livvie."

"I got this at Myrtle Beach last summer," Lauren said, cocking her head back toward the keychain. "I won it, actually. Skee-Ball."

"Cool," Livvie said.

"You can borrow it." Lauren slid the backpack off her shoulder and knelt down to take the keychain off. "We could trade for a while."

"Yeah!" Livvie said. "Okay!"

Lauren chose Livvie's pom-pom thing. It was a good choice— it wasn't the yarn kind of pom-pom, it was made of turquoise fur. Max said it reminded him of the Truffulas in *The Lorax*. Or troll hair.

The girls ate lunch together that day, and then the next, and the next. They hung out at each other's lockers between classes and before and after school, and Livvie quickly realized—it didn't take more than a day or two to figure it out—that she might be one of Lauren's only friends. Actually, that she was Lauren's *only* friend. Livvie almost never saw Lauren interact with the other kids, and when she talked about them, which was rare, she had a scowl on her face. When Livvie asked her about a particular girl—what her name was, or what she was like—Lauren seemed to want to blow past the subject as quickly as she could. She mostly wanted to talk about her animals at home—two horses, a goat, two cats, and a dog she called a "yard dog." She lived on a farm out toward Madison. Livvie didn't know where that was, exactly, but she'd seen signs around town that pointed toward there. She knew it was more rural, and she knew that some of the kids at school who were from outside of town got some kind of scholarship to attend Draper. She knew this because she'd overheard her parents talking about it one night while they were doing the dishes. Mom wondering, in that nervous way she got lately, if a private school "like Draper" was the best fit for her and Max. Livvie didn't know what "like Draper" meant, but she knew that the public school out in the country had a bad reputation, at least according to what she'd heard kids say, and that Dad *loved* Draper. He talked about his time there like they were the best years of his life. Livvie had heard all his Draper stories a million times. They usually involved some winning touchdown or home run he'd scored.

She had hoped the kids at Draper would be different from the ones back in DC. Nicer, at least. Less stuck-up. Unfortunately, one morning, not long after she and Lauren traded keychains, she sat down in history class and discovered that things were not going to be better here. They might even be worse.

Class hadn't started yet. She was setting up her stuff to take notes. She put her sharpened pencil (she couldn't stand dull ones) to the left. Her favorite notebook was placed to the right. At the top left, she put her water bottle. *Mise en place*, she always silently whispered to herself. She'd learned the phrase from her mom once when they were making pancakes. *Everything in its place*. Once everything was where she liked it, she bent down and did the thing she always did before class: she unzipped her backpack, zipped it back up, checked her watch, and fixed the strap so it fit snugly against her wrist. *Ready*.

Mr. Billingsley was approaching the smartboard, preparing to speak, when a kid she hadn't met turned around from his seat two rows in front of her and smiled, a certain aggressive glint in his eye that she was unfortunately familiar with. He turned to the boy across the aisle from him—Jimmy, Jamie, something like that—and began to imitate her, making the kind of motions Livvie had seen professional baseball players make when they step up to the mound. *Superstitions*, her dad had explained when they watched Nats games on TV. But it quickly became obvious what he was doing. He leaned down and opened and closed his backpack, all the while looking at her with a rabid grin that was as threatening as if he were opening the backpack to show her a glinting weapon. He played with the invisible watch on his wrist. He adjusted the stuff on his desk. And then the stares started coming. And the laughter. Some looked nervously, some gleefully, a few girls—bless them—with pity, lips closed tightly. Mr. Billingsley turned around. "Class!" he barked, either oblivious to or not caring about the cause of the commotion.

The perpetrator—Livvie thought his name was Evan, maybe—took his time turning around to face the front of the room. One last glance, one last grin. Mr. Billingsley started talking about Jamestown and she tried to pay attention to the lesson, but she felt as if she were aloft, floating above the class on a raft, dizzy and reeling.

So given what she'd seen of the student body, it was actually fine with Livvie that Lauren didn't really have other friends. Who was she to judge? Besides Lauren, her only friend was her brother.

She'd discovered that kids made fun of Lauren, who had a little bit of a limp. One day, when they were at lunch, Livvie asked her if she'd hurt herself, and Lauren seemed almost relieved by the question. She explained that she'd always had it. Her legs were actually different lengths. "It just is what it is," she said. The way she said it made Livvie think it sounded like Lauren was repeating it, like maybe it had been said *to* her a lot.

"Do you know that nobody at this school has ever once taken the time to actually ask me about it?" Lauren said. She grinned. Her teeth were all goopy with the bread and peanut butter from her sandwich.

Livvie shrugged.

Lauren put her sandwich down, and when she did, it bumped against her lunch bag, which pushed Livvie's water bottle aside. Livvie pushed it back, adjusting the bottle so the picture of the cute red fox on the side was facing her.

"Why do you . . . ?" Lauren started.

Livvie put her apple down. "Have weird habits?"

Lauren exhaled. "Yeah."

Livvie shrugged. "I don't know. I just like things a certain way."

"Oh." Lauren nodded. "Like that thing you do with your backpack?"

Livvie nodded.

"And kids make fun of you?" Lauren asked.

Livvie raised her palms up to the sky and rolled her eyes. "What do you think?"

"Yeah. Well, they call me 'Stop and Go,'" Lauren said.

Livvie chuckled, she couldn't help it, and then Lauren laughed, too. "Sometimes they walk behind me—they stand like ten feet back so they think I don't notice it, but I do—and they imitate me." She scrunched her lips together. Her nostrils flared.

Livvie could see the tears welling up in her eyes. She reached across the table and put her hand over Lauren's. "Kids are jerks," she said.

Lauren nodded. "They totally are."

Livvie handed her a napkin to wipe her nose. "Do you want to come over to my house after school sometime?"

Lauren nodded.

"Awesome."

FIVE

Bess

An unwelcome, familiar feeling rises up in my belly as I turn onto the long, meandering driveway that winds up to Susannah Lane's home: *I do not belong here.*

My eyes flick to the name of the house, scrolled into the top of the iron gate at the edge of the property. *Esperanza.* Spanish for "hope."

I take a deep breath, and as I inch closer to the estate, I realize that the formidable view of the house that I have seen from the road doesn't reveal even a fraction of its true size.

According to my research, the limestone mansion was built just before the Depression, on land that had been owned by the Greyhills since even before the founding of the town toward the end of the 1800s. The house itself was a gift from Susannah's grandfather to his wife, who was a debutante and textile heiress from Charleston.

For the past several days, I've spent nearly every minute while

the kids are at school and at night after dinner reading about Susannah Lane. Beside me, in my bag, is a notebook filled with copious notes about her family history, her marriage to Teddy, the
gossip column she briefly wrote—anything I could find, and all
of it, I know, is far more than I will ever be able to fit into my article. And yet still, despite all my preparation and everything I've
learned, despite the fact that I've driven past the property many
times before, I'm awestruck. I can't believe the hulking enormity
of this place. It sits on top of the hill like a fortress, with a grand
staircase in the middle that looks like it belongs outside a concert
hall. The stairs lead to a terrace lined with Doric columns that
remind me of the ones at the front of the Lincoln Memorial. I
count fourteen windows along the top floor. The double door,
where I'll soon be standing, looks like the arched entrance to a
palace.

My heart lurches. I can't begin to imagine what it must have
been like to grow up in a place like this, though I've known plenty
of people who did. My mind flashes back to a familiar memory
from high school, the one that seems to crop up whenever I come
face-to-face with this sort of wealth.

"NOCD."

I'd heard one of my privileged classmates say it to another, the
two of them standing behind me in the hall of the elite all-girls
boarding school I attended as a day student on a full academic
scholarship. When I turned around and asked what she meant,
they both burst into hysterics.

"Not our class, darling," one said, looking me over.

"Not at all," the other agreed.

I look up at the house, thinking of my childhood home and

how visitors who pulled up to it were greeted with my mother's weather-faded, polka-dot mushroom garden ornament in the flower bed, an iron stair railing that rusted into the concrete stairs, and a squeaky screened door.

My parents met at an outdoor concert in Burlington, Vermont, in the mid-1960s. That suggests a certain kind of couple—hippies connected in their mutual pursuit of free love and good hallucinogens—but it actually couldn't be further from the truth. Neither of them can remember the name of the band they saw on the day they met. Both had been dragged to the show by more adventurous friends, and when they found each other, my mom was standing on the outskirts of the crowd, "trying to get a break from the noise." Dad says he noticed her because of her dress. In a sea of cutoff denim and skin, she "looked like a librarian," he says. He knew in that moment that she was the one for him.

My parents are simple people, hardworking and thrifty, and for all I know they now have millions sitting in their savings account at Merchants Bank, but money was tight when I was growing up. Dad was a mailman who worked for the post office his entire career, and Mom still works as a secretary (that's the term she insists on) at a travel agency, an ironic choice for a woman who never takes a vacation.

As a girl, I often felt like I was growing up in the wrong house. I deeply love my parents, but it's perhaps because of the plain and simple way I was raised that I became obsessed with the little luxuries we never had. We didn't do birthday parties or big celebrations. Meals were based on what was on sale and which coupons we'd cut out of the Sunday paper. Our house was clean and bare—*decor* is not a word my parents use. A few years ago, while visiting for Christmas, I asked my mother if she'd ever thought about replacing the old chenille sofa that's been pushed up against the wall in the family room, across from the ancient Panasonic, since my parents were newlyweds. She looked at me like I'd just suggested they install a seesaw in its place. It was a look I knew well.

As a kid, I satisfied my cravings by getting creative. Once, I tried to turn an old bedsheet into a canopy for my bed by attaching it to the ceiling with a combination of duct tape and thumbtacks. In sixth grade, using a craft book from the library, I taught myself how to make scented soap. (I procured the necessary rose petals by furtively plucking them off a bouquet in the floral department at Shaw's.) I wouldn't let anyone use the little squares, instead displaying them, like jewels in a museum, on a saucer next to the plastic bottle of generic hand soap we kept in the bathroom.

In middle school, I was at a friend's house when I discovered her mother's copy of *Entertaining*, the book that made Martha Stewart famous. Mrs. Connor let me take it home to borrow it, amused that a thirteen-year-old would find it so enthralling. I devoured it at the kitchen table after school while Mom and Dad were at work, and then continued under the covers at night, saying the names of the recipes to myself as if I were learning a new language. *Croquembouche. Gravlax. Carpaccio. Coeur a la Crème Fraîche.* Reading Martha's instructions—*how to create ambience, how to make food look beautiful*—was like having the most delicious secret whispered in my ear. I dreamed of the day when I could go to the grocery store with a list that had nothing to do with the sales circular. I dreamed of the day when I would throw parties in my own home. I dreamed of *special occasions*. Special *anything*.

When I became the social secretary for the Calhoun White House, I felt like I had reached the pinnacle of a trek I'd started in childhood. I had learned over the course of my years of event planning that if I wanted to reach the top of the industry in DC, I needed to both do a spectacular job and network with the right people, the latter of which usually stirred up my old inferiority complex and pushed me to prove, to both myself and the people around me, that I was as good as it gets. When I got the White House job, on the recommendation of a former client who had worked with the president in the Senate, I felt that I was *finally* where I was supposed to be. I had succeeded through my own sheer grit and had beaten back the old demons who told me I wasn't smart enough, rich enough, *elite* enough. *Not our class, darling*. And then I fucked it all up. It is amazing to me, now that it's happened, that an entire dream can disappear as quickly as mine did, in the space of a single day. I assume Susannah Lane knows what I did, and there is no telling what she thinks of me because of it.

I pull my car around the back of the estate and I park next to a green Ford Focus, which I assume belongs to Cindy, Susannah's assistant and housekeeper. Setting up the interview had been shockingly easy. I'd simply pulled out the Greyhill directory, a spiral-bound phone book published every spring by the town council that reminds me of the types a school or church or country club might publish, and found Susannah's number listed under the *L*'s. When I called, Cindy answered, listened to the spiel I recited from a piece of paper I held in front of me, and cheerfully responded that she'd talk it over with Susannah and call me back.

I didn't have to sweat it out too long, because my phone rang within the hour. She said Susannah would be pleased to meet with me and advised me to look for the small parking pad behind the house, telling me, "There'll be plenty of room for you next to me. Susannah keeps all her vehicles in the covered garage." She'd started to laugh. "Minus the truck, of course." I wasn't sure whether the joke was meant to put me at ease, but it didn't. Nor did the awkward encounter I'd had with Susannah at the inn after dinner with Bradley and Diane last week. I check my reflection in the rearview mirror, using my pinky to fix a smudge of eyeliner. It's the first time I've worn makeup in months.

As I make my way along a central covered path through the garden that separates the parking area from the house, I'm surprised by how overgrown and untended it is, the ivy a tangled knot that I have to step over to get past. As I get closer, I start to feel the telltale tingling that I get in my fingertips when I'm nervous. My choice that morning to wear heels—another first in a long time—now feels questionable, as they sink into the dirty pea gravel beneath my feet.

I finally make my way around to the front of the house. The stone exterior sparkles in the bright morning sunlight, and before I climb the steps to the front door, I take a moment to collect myself and admire the expansive view of the Blue Ridge Mountains and the rolling pastures. The maple leaves that have fallen on the front lawn—brilliant reds, oranges, and yellows—look like they've been placed by hand. It is *so* picturesque, almost unreal. And it is *so* quiet. The only sounds I hear are the gentle gurgle of the fountain in front of the house, birds chirping, and my heartbeat, pulsing quick and heavy behind my ears.

I shake out my hands, working out the nerves, and start up the stairs, reminding myself that I can do this. I belong here. This is not the first time I've gone to meet a well-known personality in an imposing white house.

I'm searching for the doorbell, thinking as I do that perhaps houses like this *don't have* simple doorbells . . . maybe there's an intercom of some sort, a buzzer, something . . . when the massive oak door swings open, revealing a small woman who must be Cindy.

"Bess!" she says, wiping her hands on a rag before she stretches her right one out to shake mine. "Come in, we've been expecting you."

"Oh—" I stammer, surprised. "Thank you." I don't know what I expected—someone more staid? A dowdy maid in a formal *Downton Abbey*–style uniform?—but it certainly wasn't this. Cindy is maybe sixty, tiny with a youthful face and short, heavily frosted hair. She is barefoot, in bedazzled jeans and a faded T-shirt that has pink palm trees and the word *Miami* printed in a 1980s brush font across the chest.

"Excuse my outfit," she says, looking down at her top after she sees me studying it. "The house and its mistress might be fancy, but I'm not." She winks and laughs, a loud cackle that feels outsized for her teensy frame.

The foyer smells like lemon Pledge. The familiar scent feels out of place here, too *normal* for a room with marble floors and a grand staircase. Though I notice, trying to be subtle so Cindy doesn't see me gaping, that the house has seen better days. The carpet on the stairs, I can see, is frayed. The trim on the walls looks dingy. Honestly, the house looks the way it would if *my* family moved in. There is crap everywhere: a laundry basket—a regular old plastic one—on the floor in the hallway, messy piles of paper on the steps, a book splayed open on the chaise in the formal living room to our right. A sweater threatens to fall off the banister. A pile of junk mail is on the entry table. There's a ballpoint pen on the floor, its cap removed.

"I'm cleaning! I'm cleaning!" Cindy jokes, busting me.

"No, it's—" I start, fumbling for something to say. Noelle had mentioned a photo shoot. We might need to bring in a cleaning crew.

"It's an absolute disaster," Cindy says. "But what with playing Nurse Ratched to Miss Priss, I haven't exactly been prioritizing the housekeeping."

"Understood," I say. *Miss Priss?*

"Come on," she says, heading up the stairs. "She's up here." She turns and leans toward me. "In her *boudoir*," she says, exaggerating the word like *boo-dwaaaah*.

We reach the top of the staircase, and I look up. *How high are these ceilings? Twelve feet? Higher?* Despite the elaborate chandeliers dotting the hallway (one of them crisscrossed with cobwebs), it feels dim. Solemn, even. I notice the open window at the end of the hall, the dust motes in the air. A sheer white curtain dances in the breeze.

Cindy knocks lightly on one of the closed doors lining the hallway, using the same *dun-dun-duhdum-dun* pattern that I do for the kids' bedrooms.

"Come in," a voice says.

I take a deep breath, electric prickles dancing on the surface of my skin, and follow Cindy into the room.

Susannah Greyhill Lane is sitting on top of her made bed, propped up against a pile of apricot-colored satin pillowcases, a pen in one of her hands, which are resting in her lap. Her skirt—voluminous, ankle-length red taffeta—is fanned out around her, covering much of the mattress. The only other time I've seen her in person was at the inn the other night, when she was dressed in an equally memorable outfit: shiny silver pants, a colorful scarf around her head, a fur cape. It didn't occur to me that her eccentric manner of dress was an everyday thing, but what do I know? Maybe if I had spent a lifetime amassing closets full of clothes, as I assume she has, I'd do the same? Would it be weirder to see her in my typical boatneck T-shirts and jeans? (Diane once asked me, in one of her more creative attempts to insult me, why "girls from New England don't fix themselves up more"— referring, I assume, to my minimal makeup and L.L.Bean-heavy wardrobe. I replied that perhaps it was because we didn't need to.)

Her hair is pushed back from her head with a soft band. She has the faintest scar dotting her chin, shaped like a fishhook. She's wearing lipstick. *Maybe* fake lashes. Her beauty is well documented, a mention in every single article I've read about her over the past week, but I'm still surprised how striking she is. It's something about her eyes, dark and gleaming, and how they contrast with her light hair. She looks, even at seventy, like something out of a fairy tale.

She puts down the pen she's holding, placing it next to a gold leather journal on the pillow beside her.

"Bess!" she says, stretching out a dainty, manicured hand. "Apologies for my state. I didn't mean to greet you like this!"

"Oh, it's no problem, of course!" I say, circling around the bed. *Is she not feeling well?* I wonder, eyeing the scar on her face. *Is this a residual effect of the accident?*

"Well, I'm sorry I'm still in bed!" She laughs. "But they say LBJ took meetings on the toilet when he was in the White House, so at least I'm not that bad!" My heart lurches at the mention of my former place of employment, but fortunately she continues on before I have to say anything.

"Regardless, it's so nice to welcome you here! I know we met the other day at the inn, but this feels official!"

"Yes, thank you," I say, shaking her hand. It is cold and bony, but her grip is strong.

"And you!" she says, motioning for me to sit in the upholstered armchair next to the bed. As I do, I take a moment to scan the room. It's smaller than I would expect for a house this large, with faded floral wallpaper, cabbage roses in muted pinks and greens, but there are *actual* flowers everywhere—six vases on the dresser alone—at least half of the bouquets past their prime, in varying states of decay. You can smell the rot in the air.

"So where'd you get a name like that? *Bess?*" she asks.

"My full name is Elizabeth, after my grandmother."

She rolls her eyes. "I was named after my grandmother, too," she says. "My mother, the indomitable Amelia Greyhill, hated her. I always wondered what that meant." She ticks an eyebrow up. "Anyway, *Besssss*," she says, stretching out my name like it's a candy she's turning in her mouth. "I like it. It's cute."

Cute. Hm.

"You know, I have a nickname, too," she says, a gleam in her eye. "Cricket. My father thought it up when I was a toddler, because of my squeaky, little-girl voice."

"Oh, that's—" I stop, realizing she's turned her attention toward Cindy, who is leaning against the threshold with the bored, resigned expression of someone waiting for a bus.

"I hate to say it, Cindy, but all these flowers are giving me a headache," Susannah says.

"How awful for you." Cindy smirks. "To be surrounded by some of the finest cut flowers on the East Coast."

Maybe a week ago, I think. There's a scattering of dried petals on the floor beside the nightstand that sits between Susannah and me.

Susannah laughs. "Don't give me that 'poor little rich girl' bullshit," she says.

"You know, the florist downtown said she's never been so busy in her entire career," Cindy says. "You should be thankful that these bouquets are still rolling in."

Susannah rolls her eyes. "Hannah is a master exaggerator. She always has been."

"That may be," Cindy says, scooping up an oversize vase of lilies and shifting it onto her hip, holding it the way I used to carry the kids around when they were toddlers. "But she made a joke about early retirement when she came by yesterday."

"Well, how lucky for her that I was nearly killed." Susannah laughs. "Shall I plan to convalesce here for a few more months so we can make it happen?" She points to a tight cluster of fresh garden roses and ranunculi in varying shades of pink on the nightstand. "This one's pretty," she says.

"That's the new one," Cindy says.

She reaches for the card, but she can't quite get to it. I lean and hand it to her.

"Oh!" she says, putting her hand to her chest after she pulls the card from its tiny white envelope. "Well, I can't believe this."

"Who's it from?" Cindy asks.

Susannah flicks it aside, and it skitters across the journal beside her on the bed. "This woman who had a little shop near the place we had in East Hampton. You know, she sent me the prettiest bouquet when Teddy died last year. So thoughtful."

"How long were you married?" I ask, even though I already know the answer from my research. I figured on the drive over that her famous marriage might be a good conversational entry point.

She smiles at me. *Thank God*, I think, relieved that the question wasn't too painful. "We married when I was nineteen and I'm seventy now, so . . ."

"Fifty-one years," Cindy says.

Susannah's coral fingernails click-click against each other in the quiet room. "Do you know what we did for our forty-fifth?" She leans toward me like she's about to tell me a secret. "We got ice-cream sandwiches from a street vendor and rode around Central Park in one of those horse and buggies."

"How sweet!" I say.

Susannah grins, pleased at my reaction. "Everyone's always

surprised by that story. They think we'd do something more"—she flits her hand in the air—"*you know*. But that was the thing about Teddy. It was never about the money." She purses her lips and turns her attention to Cindy, then says in an offhand way, "Nope, not Teddy. *Never about the money.*"

Huh. I nod, trying to decipher her emphasis.

"I know you must know about my husband," she says. "Everyone does." She rolls her eyes.

"Oh, of course," I say. "I saw him interviewed on television dozens of times, and in the news, of course—"

"No," she interrupts. "I mean, do you know . . ." She lowers her voice. "About the money?"

"About the . . .," I start, not sure where she's going with this.

"Teddy pledged much of his fortune to charity after he died," she says in a dismayed tone, like she's just revealed that he piled up his billions on their lawn and tossed a match over the stack. *Odd.*

"Yes, I've read about the donations," I say. Just last night, in fact. I'd been somewhat aware of the enormous charity gift back when Teddy died a year ago—there was a ton of news coverage, of course—but I don't recall ever seeing the exact amount, and I don't remember who the recipients were. "He sounds like he was a generous man."

She begins to laugh. "Oh, yes, *so* very generous," she says, looking at Cindy and shaking her head. Now I'm *sure* I haven't misjudged the tone.

Cindy snickers, but then she tips her head against the door and wraps her arms more tightly around the vase she's holding. *Is she just playing along?*

"What about you?" Susannah says. "How long have you and Cole been married? If he's anything like his father, you're a lucky woman."

"Oh?" I say. Now *this* is getting good.

"Back in my day, nobody could *resist* Bradley Warner! Most of all me! He was the most coveted bachelor in Greyhill."

"Is that so?" I say, laughing a little. My father-in-law is a lot of wonderful things—warm, affable, kind—but I've also witnessed him flossing his teeth over the kitchen sink. It is difficult to imagine him as a heartthrob.

"You're not buying it?" she says, studying my face. "He truly was, believe me. The other girls in town were so jealous of me. I assume you know that we dated, Bradley and me?" Susannah says.

"Oh, yes," I say. "I think I'd heard that."

"Cindy," Susannah says. "Give me and Bess a few minutes to talk on our own, if you don't mind. Could you prepare some drinks?" She turns to me. "You want tea? Coffee? A soda or some water? Something stronger?"

Stronger? It's barely ten o'clock in the morning. "Just some water would be nice."

Susannah smiles. "That blue is a pretty color on you," she says, wagging a finger toward my sweater, a cashmere crewneck I'd kept in heavy rotation back when I worked.

"Thank you, Mrs. Lane."

She groans. "Mrs. Lane was my mother-in-law!" she exclaims. "And she was *not* a good one! Maybe you can relate?" She winks at me.

"Oh!" I say, taken aback by her overt reference to Diane. It's not that I disagree, but . . .

"Never mind." She laughs again. "But please call me Susannah."

"What about Mrs. X?" I try, referencing the title of the gossip column she briefly wrote for the *New York Observer* in the early 1990s.

She laughs, dipping her head back. "Oh, you're *fun!* Yes, you can call me that, too." She turns to Cindy, still waiting in the doorway. "So just some water for Bess and coffee for me, please." As the door clicks closed, she exhales, a loud huff, and sinks back into the pillows. "She exhausts me, honestly," she says.

"Cindy?"

Susannah nods. "She's been with me since I moved back, though I've known her for years. She and her husband used to work at the Inn at Little Washington. Teddy and I used to go down there. Have you ever been?"

"No," I say. "Cole and I have talked for years about splurging on a dinner there. In fact, I mentioned to him recently that we should visit and pick up some pointers for *our* inn."

"Your inn?"

"Oh," I say. "I'm sorry. Maybe you don't know . . . we've taken over the Greyhill Inn, from Bradley and Diane."

Susannah laughs. "Of course I know that, Bess."

"Of . . . of . . . course," I stammer. "I—"

"Have you ever lived in a town this small before?" she asks.

"No, not this size," I say.

She tips her head back and laughs. "You should just assume that everyone knows everything there is to know about you," she says. "Trust me, it will make things easier."

Before I can ask what she means, she keeps talking.

"Anyway, Cindy's from Madison originally." She points toward the picture window and the breathtaking view of the mountains behind me. "You know, it's just ten miles or so. She's a lunatic but she keeps me sane, if that makes any sense." She smiles at me. "It's just the two of us here."

"The house is . . . amazing," I say, though it's an understatement, based on what I've seen so far.

"I'll give you the grand tour later," she says. "I wanted to redo a lot of it when I moved back, but I just haven't made the time for it. I'd like to give all the heirlooms to my decorator, Margaret Dunhill. Have you heard of her?"

I shake my head.

"She is this little dark-haired woman from Chicago. Eyes like a cat's! She is *astounded* that I don't want any of this junk—the pre–Civil War mahogany, the precious upholstery, the silver, all the Heywood Hardy foxhunt paintings my father collected. I told her that I want to do an *exorcism*." She widens her eyes and wiggles her fingers like she's telling a ghost story. "Margaret doesn't know what to make of me. There are forty rooms in this house and I want her to redo every single one, except for this one."

"This room is lovely," I say, admiring the curves of the mahogany dresser, which, despite the inch-thick layer of dust and the sad bouquets, is beautiful.

"It was my childhood bedroom," Susannah says.

"This was your bedroom?" I look around and try to imagine a tiny Susannah opening one of the heavy dresser drawers, or climbing up onto the formidable bed. The room seemed crowded and cramped when I first entered, but for a child's bedroom—and certainly compared to the little box I slept in growing up—it's quite grand.

Susannah nods. "I can't sleep in the master suite. My parents slept in two twin beds, like on *I Love Lucy*. And trust me," she says, lowering her voice, "the only heat that ever came off my mother was the angry steam she expelled through her nostrils, like a bull, when *I* was in her presence. I tried sleeping in there once, but it felt too . . ." She shudders. "This is better."

I take the opportunity to really look around. Books—popular hardcover thrillers, a couple of paperback romances—are stacked on the empty side of the bed, next to the gold journal. The nightstand is a jumble of bottles—hand lotions, perfume, a plastic bottle of ibuprofen. There is a nearly empty crystal water glass, a pot of lip balm, and a small silver framed photo of the Lanes in formal dress—Susannah in a long silver ball gown. I know the background immediately. It's the Blue Room at the White House.

"George W.'s inauguration," Susannah says. "You ever meet him?" she asks, smiling like she's in on a secret. "You know, given what you used to do?"

"Yes," I say, my throat suddenly dry.

"I have to imagine that your move is a *big* change for you," she says, peering at me.

I nod, hoping we can skirt past the topic as quickly as possible.

"You know, I've met the First Lady," she says.

"Oh?" I say, my heart pounding in my chest.

"Impressive woman," she says, her fingers laced together at her chin. "At least, so far as I could see." She raises an eyebrow in a way that I can tell is meant as an invitation. She wants the dirt.

"She really is exactly as she seems," I say, choking out the words. It's the truth, in fact, which makes what happened all the more damning.

"What happened exactly?" she says, pointing her chin toward me. "The press really made it sound awful."

"Well . . .," I say. "Yes. They have a way of doing that."

"You can say that again!" she says. "We don't have to talk about it, if you'd rather not. . . ."

"I'd rather not," I say, smiling to soften the blow.

She rubs her palms together, like she's wiping the thought away. "Done," she says, and then something catches her eye. I follow her gaze to where my hands are clasped in my lap.

"Let me see your ring," she says excitedly, wiggling her fingers out at me like a cashier trying to hurry me for change.

"My ring?" I hold my hand out.

"I thought it might be . . . Bradley's mother's ring!" she says, her eyes widening as she tilts my hand in various angles to get a good look.

"Yes," I say, looking down at my engagement ring, a small circle-cut diamond with a sapphire on either side. I've never been much for jewelry—that's one trait I did inherit from my mother—but I happen to love my engagement ring. "You knew her?"

"Oh, yes," Susannah says. "She was the kindest woman. Just the *ultimate* mother, nothing at all like my own. Such a nurturer."

"I've heard she was wonderful," I say, thinking that even Diane has only ever uttered good words about her. "It's a shame I never got to meet her."

"Yes," she says. "You would have *loved* her, everybody did. She was so warm, always thinking of others before herself. . . ." Her voice trails off, and I can't help but notice the expression on her face, like she's wound back to some long-ago moment.

She clears her throat. "So tell me about your move here. And the inn! How exciting for you to be taking over the inn!"

"Yes," I say. "It is."

"And your children?"

"We have twins. A boy and a girl. Max and Livvie. They're twelve."

"Right, I remember," she says. "From the other night, when I ran into your clan in the lobby."

"Yes, of course," I say, as if the uncomfortable moment isn't already imprinted on my mind. We'd had dinner in the back of the inn's dining room—I actually hated eating there with Cole's parents; it was humiliating how Diane treated the waitstaff—and I'd broken the news to my in-laws about my plans to write the story as the kids ate ice-cream sundaes. Diane was *not* pleased, as I expected ("I hate to say it, Elizabeth, but this is among your less intelligent decisions"), but I'd been surprised that Bradley hadn't been more enthusiastic, given how encouraging he typically is. When Diane gets on me about things, he at least usually tosses me a wink, or tamps her down with a *"Now, now, Diane."* The other night, he just stared into his coffee cup and gave me a bland "Sounds interesting."

"Can I ask you something?" Susannah says, cocking her head to the side.

"Sure."

"Did you ever think it was odd that Diane and Bradley didn't have more children?"

"Oh," I say, startled by the question.

She must sense it, because before I have a chance to respond, she says, "Forgive me if that's too forward. It's just that Bradley always talked about having a large family, back when we were teenagers and used to daydream about what our kids would look like." She smiles at me and shakes her head at the ceiling, as if the memory is projected on the plaster above us. It's hard to tell whether she's wistful about Bradley or the thought of children. She and Teddy didn't have any.

"Understood," I say curtly, hoping to convey to her that it's none of our business. My own parents never wanted more than just one child, but Cole has told me what he heard through the walls of their house when he was growing up—that his mother miscarried several times. Despite Diane's obvious feelings about me, I know deep down what the arrival of the twins meant to her, not to mention to Bradley, and to Cole, who would have loved growing up with a sibling. "The Warners have always said the inn was their other child," I say, repeating a line I've heard from Diane.

She raises an eyebrow. "And now it's yours! So tell me again when you moved here."

"August," I say. "Just before school started."

"Yes, yes," she says. "So we both had eventful summers, then."

"I'm so sor—" I start, putting a hand to my chest.

"It's just a joke, dear." She laughs. "Don't worry, I'm fine. But I'm still so pissed about that truck. I *loved* that truck. It was a 1967 Chevy Fleetside, a gift from Teddy, and it was *beautiful*. Damn thing! I still can't believe it happened!"

"How . . . did it happen, exactly?" I ask, venturing the question I've heard people whispering around Greyhill.

She rolls her eyes. "I don't know!" she says, leaning toward me like she's telling me a secret. "That's the thing! I know what people in town are saying, that someone tried to hit me, but that's not it at all! It's not as good a story, but I simply lost control of the wheel! One minute I was driving along, and the next . . ." She sits back and snaps her fingers. "I'd almost rather someone had been trying to hit me!" she says, scowling. "Hate to think I'm getting to an age when . . ." Her voice trails off.

"I'm so sorry."

"Stop apologizing. My God! People never take a woman seriously if she's always apologizing." She laughs. "One thing you have to understand about me is that my filter stopped working a long, long time ago."

"I can respect that," I say, thinking it sounds like something my mother would say.

"I bet you can." She winks. "I know *you* have a sharp tongue."

I feel my cheeks redden.

Susannah laughs again. "Listen, I thought it was hysterical, dear," she says. "I'm not judging you. To be honest, I didn't think it was such a big deal, all that stuff you said. Women say those sorts of things to each other all the time. I don't know why they fired you."

"Well," I say, nodding my head to the side. "It happened."

"Yes!" Susannah says. "It most certainly did! Anyway, my truck!" she says. "I called her Henrietta, after my best friend from childhood. You should have seen me in East Hampton, driving that hulking thing in my Chanel! People didn't know what to make of me. You know about Henrietta, of course. . . ."

"No," I say. "I don't think I do."

Her mouth drops open. "You don't know about Henrietta Martin?"

"I don't think so," I say.

"Bradley's never said *anything*? *Diane?*"

"No," I say, wondering why this is so significant.

She sits back on the pillows. "Huh."

"She was your friend?"

"That's an understatement," she says, stretching her lips into a smile. "She was my best friend! We did everything together. Look . . . ," she says, twisting toward the nightstand. "Open that drawer."

I lean and tug the latch, the bottles and junk on the top jiggling as I do.

"Grab that box," she says.

I hand her an upholstered keepsake box covered in purple calico. "These are some of the treasures Henrietta and I collected when we were girls," she says, opening the cover. "I couldn't believe they were still here when I came back!" She pinches her fingers and pulls out an old arrowhead, then turns the box around to show me. "Is that—?" I say.

"A skull?" she says, taking it out of the box. "Sure is! A rabbit skull! I actually had that with me up in New York. I used it as a paperweight on the entry table in our apartment. My city friends thought that was something!" She latches the box and hands it back to me to put away. "I have to say, I'm stunned you've never heard of Henrietta."

I shrug. "I'm sorry I haven't."

"I'll have to tell you about her sometime," she says, smiling. "But now, let's talk about your article. I have to warn you, you're going to have to be careful."

"Careful?" I say.

She laughs. "I might keep you around here a little longer than you'd like to be," she says. "I get the sense that you and I could have some fun together."

"Oh," I say. "Thank you."

"I like you, and I don't like everyone."

"I'll take that as a compliment," I say, though honestly I'm not sure I should. The past twenty minutes of conversation have felt like being batted through a pinball machine. *What am I getting myself into?*

"So let's get started!" Susannah says, clapping her hands together. "I don't know where Cindy is with those drinks. Let's go find her. Do you want to see the house?"

"Yes!" I say, brightening at the offer of a change of scenery. "Yes, I do."

She swings her legs around, planting her feet on the floor beside the bed, and motions for me to help her up. I hand her the cane from beside the bed, then step aside so she can get past me and lead the way. I'm surprised by how tiny she is—a full head shorter than me, barely five feet. Her presence—and the clothes—makes up for it, I guess.

We start down the worn carpet on the grand staircase, me holding her cane, her gripping the stair rail. "I used to sit right here and spy on my parents' parties," she says. "It was funny what you could learn just by watching people—who finished their drinks the fastest, which men lingered around the wives who weren't their own. It was quite an education."

"I can't imagine what it must've been like, growing up like this."

"No?" she says, leading me down the front hall. I notice

that she doesn't bother apologizing for the state of the house, which makes me wonder whether she notices it. "How did you grow up?"

"More modestly," I say.

"Probably better," she says, but before I can ask her what she means, she turns to me. "I'm so sorry," she says, leaning against the wall and placing her hand against her side, like she has a cramp. "I don't know if I got up too fast or what, but I am suddenly not feeling so well. Can we continue this next time?" She closes her eyes, wincing.

"Oh!" I say, looking down the hall for Cindy. "Yes, yes, of course! Can I do something? Get something for you? Can I get—" My heartbeat quickens. *If Susannah Lane collapses in front of me . . .*

Cindy suddenly appears behind me. She looks unfazed. "I'm right here," she says. "How about I let you out, Bess?" She smiles, motioning toward the front door. It's clear that it's time for me to leave. And it seems like this is something Cindy's used to.

I turn back to Susannah. "I hope this wasn't too much."

"No, no," she says, smiling weakly. "It's just taking longer than I anticipated to recover from that wreck. I'll be fine. Just need to rest."

"Okay," I say. Cindy opens the front door for me, and I start toward it, my heart still pounding in my chest. "Are you sure I can't—"

"She's fine," Cindy says, cutting me off. She nods efficiently, silently telling me to move along.

"Okay," I say, glancing back at Susannah as I step outside.

She's hunched against the wall, holding her stomach. "I hope you feel—"

The heavy door closes behind me before I've finished the sentence. "I hope you feel better," I say again, just under my breath. I start down the stairs, careful, in the blinding sun, that I don't miss a step.

SIX

FRIDAY AFTERNOON
PERKINS VARIETY AND HARDWARE

"Bradley, I hear that your daughter-in-law is working with our old friend."

"Yes, that's true, Jenny. Writing about Cricket for the *Washington Post*."

"Well, isn't that something?"

"Mm-hmm."

"That gonna be strange for you?"

"Why would it be?"

"I remember how you two were. I may be up in years, but my memory's sharp as a tack. The two of you were like . . . well, I'll tell you, I was just fifteen or sixteen, but I could see how in love with you she was."

"Oh, now, Jenny, come on. That was another lifetime ago."

"I guess so. . . . Does Diane ever get—"

"Jenny . . ."

"I'm sorry, sometimes my imagination runs wild!"

"Yes, it does. Now, why don't you let it run off somewhere else."

She laughs. "This all for you? Just the Drano and the gum?"

"Yup, that's all. Here, take this. Keep the change, Jenny."

"Bradley, you don't have to—"

"No, no. Keep it."

"Well, tell Diane I say hello."

"I'll do it. See you next time."

SEVEN

Bess

I'm smiling.

I'm nervous, my stomach all gurgling flutters, but I am choosing—or trying—to ignore it. *This is going to be fun*, I tell myself, using the same cheerful and determined tone that Cole and I did in May when we told the kids that we were moving here. It is the same tone I would use to buoy myself up before the twenty-hour days that preceded state dinners at the White House; the same tone I would use to bolster the enthusiasm of my team in the East Wing, who needed to execute every event flawlessly or my neck would be on the line.

I am smiling.

This is going to be fun.

Cole takes my hand, giving it a little squeeze as we step off the long, winding driveway and onto the flagstone path that leads to the front door of the Barkers' sprawling brick home. He told me on the way over that they inherited it from Greg's parents.

Must be nice to have a house like this passed down to you, I think, taking it all in. Bedsheet ghosts sway from the limbs of the oaks that dot the manicured lawn. Plastic skeletons, their jawbones open in perpetual screams, have been positioned to look like they could rise from the grass at any moment. The spotlights in the shrubbery cast a spooky green glow against the brick. Gauzy spiderwebs are stretched across the windows. Greg and Mindy have gone all out. I'm impressed.

"You said these two have been together since middle school?" I ask.

"Yep." Cole nods.

"Remarkable," I say, though it really isn't, not here. I nibble on my lip.

"What if I can't remember anyone's name?" I say.

"Nobody expects you to," he says.

I grip his hand a little harder. "Okay."

"Are you ready?" Cole says.

"Now or never," I say, waving my hand in front of my face. A machine hidden somewhere in the bushes is pumping out smoke and bubbles. *Very high school prom*, I think, and then immediately scold myself. I get bitchy when I'm nervous, I know that, but I need to get my attitude together. I take a deep breath to settle my nerves. It feels ridiculous to be so anxious, but I can't shake the feeling that I'm going to be under a microscope tonight, a bug splayed on a slide to be examined and picked apart.

We've been to a few other events together since the move—a Labor Day barbecue, a start-of-school picnic on the Draper Hall campus, a happy hour we threw for the employees at the inn—

and Cole's done plenty of socializing on his own, meeting his old buddies for drinks and the like, but this is our first big social event as a couple since becoming official Greyhill residents. Cole can't wait. He's been ramping up for this for weeks, but that's to be expected given that this is his hometown. His homecoming. His people.

The bottom line is that I don't want to be unenthusiastic about my social prospects here. I want to love it here. I *need* to. Because while neither of us has ever said it out loud, it's presumed that this move is meant to be permanent. This is where we're putting down roots. The wagon stops here. And the people on the other side of the Barkers' front door, where I can hear the muffled sounds of party chatter and the refrain of "Purple People Eater" blaring, may very well be the people I will be surrounded by for the rest of my life.

Jack-o'-lanterns flank the front door. But—I notice these details, was *paid* to, once upon a time—there are no janky triangle eyes here, no crooked toothy grins carved with plastic child-friendly tools, no errant pumpkin goop hanging from inside. Each features a carefully whittled Halloween scene—a witch on a broom, a cat with its back arched in fear. Surely Mindy hired someone to do them?

I smooth the front of my blue gingham dress, looking down at my ruby-red slippers. My Dorothy costume is from last year, when we had a masquerade party at the White House for the East Wing staff. The First Lady arrived dressed as Hermione from *Harry Potter*, a nod to her love for children's literature. She's made early-childhood education, and reading in particular, her main initiative while she's in office.

She should have come as the Wicked Witch of the West, I had whispered to Anna, my deputy. I shouldn't have said it, but we had had a long day, and the First Lady had snapped at me earlier that afternoon when our planning meeting ran long and she realized she would have less than thirty minutes to get into costume. The First Lady hated to be rushed, but she also loved to talk and had no sense of time, and keeping her on task was an aspect of my job I had been coming to resent. In any event, I shouldn't have made the Wicked Witch joke. It was one of the many comments that would come back to haunt me, I think now, my stomach clenching at the memory.

Cole is the scarecrow. Livvie had been thrilled to draw two circles of my red lipstick on her father's cheeks before we left for the evening. "Be careful with your mother's lipstick," Diane had directed from her perch on one of the barstools in the kitchen. "Not many women can pull off that color." As usual, it was unclear whether she meant this as a compliment.

Diane is watching the kids tonight. She brought over a tuna casserole, taking tiny steps as she carried the dish across the street from her house in a special insulated tote that zipped up around the dish. My mother-in-law is the kind of woman who has special totes for her casserole dishes. "Do I really have to eat that stuff Grandma brought?" Max had whispered to me before we left. The kids love their grandmother—she reserves any iota of sweetness she has for them. It's a good thing. Of course it is. I just wish that my own parents lived closer, so the kids could see what it's like to have a grandmother who doesn't grumble about their sugar intake or their messy rooms.

I ran my fingers through Max's hair and pulled him in for a hug, whispering for him to do his best. Sometimes he seems like every bit of his twelve years, all giant sneakers and grubby sweat, and on other days, all I can see when I look at him is the chubby toddler who'd slept with his matchbox cars clutched in his fists. He's just four minutes younger than Livvie, but sometimes it seems like there are years between them, especially lately. Maybe this is true for all twins, I've wondered, or maybe it is simply the difference between boys and girls.

Cole presses the doorbell—a glowing button in the middle of a gold fleur-de-lis—and I notice that one of the circles on his cheeks is already beginning to smear, probably because of those bubbles we waded through. I lean to fix it, giving my thumb a quick mom-lick first. "Stop!" He laughs, swatting my hand away. He is in a very, very good mood. The door swings open and the sound from the party rushes out, breaking the nervous chatter in my head. Mindy Barker is dressed as a sort of vampy witch, in a glittery black sheath that is slit to her hip and a wig made of long, tumbling black waves.

"Co-ooo-oooole Warner!" she sings out, somehow stretching Cole's name into three syllables. "And Bess! Look at you!"

"Hi!" I blink. Mindy's costume is . . . well, it's not what I expected. "Thanks so much for having us!"

"Come on in!" Mindy bats her spidery fake eyelashes and wags her long silver nails at us.

"You look great," I say. Cole, his arm around me, pinches my waist, and I nudge him back subtly.

Mindy wiggles her hips in acknowledgment, the drink in her hand spilling a little, and waves us in. The only other time I've met Mindy was at Bully's, the local grocery. Mindy's youngest (*Are there three?* I think now) was tugging at the hem of her windbreaker, stretching with his other hand toward a box of Cap'n Crunch on the shelf. I remember this detail, how I'd felt the pang of nostalgia for that time in my kids' lives like a splinter in my chest. Mindy and I had chatted about teachers. She knew all of them, of course, and not only because of her kids. At least half the staff are alumni who grew up in town.

I look at her now, how she shimmies in her tight dress down two stairs into a sunken living room. I suddenly feel warm in my gingham dress and tug at my skirt

Mindy looks over her shoulder at us. "You two are adorable!" she squeals over the noise.

The room is crowded with goblins and football players, a trio of Pink Ladies from *Grease*, an Elvis, Cleopatra. Cole takes my wrist and links my arm around his, and I notice that he's already beginning to shed the straw that he'd attached with duct tape to the inside cuffs of his button-down.

I squint up at the recessed lights, wishing I knew these people well enough to suggest that they dim the overheads and move some of the guests into another area. When we went to our friends' parties back in DC, they ribbed me for this occupational hazard—my inability to just have a good time when there was a tray of food I could refill back in the kitchen or a drink I could refresh.

Cole carves us a path to the bar, shouting his hellos along the way. *Hey, buddy! So glad to be back in town! Been a long time!*

I grin and smile, grin and smile, noticing how some of the guests' eyes linger on me and how a few, farther back, thinking they're outside my sight line, tilt their heads toward each other and whisper. I keep smiling. I say hello.

The party is in full swing, all laughing and screeching and clinking glasses. It's a little fratty, honestly, especially for people our age. Behind me, someone starts singing along to the opening lines of "Thriller." My heart pounds, and I take a deep breath and then push it out, annoyed that I'm nervous. *I've made polite dinner conversation with everyone from the German chancellor's husband to the Japanese prime minister*, I remind myself. *I've clinked glasses with more than one Supreme Court justice.*

I lean into Cole. "I'm nervous," I whisper.

He puts his arm around me, waving to someone across the room with his other one. "You'll be fine," he says. "Don't worry. Let's get you a drink."

A Frankenstein steps aside to give us room at the bar, and I recognize the bartender, James, from the inn. He's a young guy—maybe twenty-three—and has only been working there for a year or so. Cole loves him, not just for his work ethic but also because of his ideas, which is why he recommended him to the Barkers for their party.

On the night I met him, he made us his latest creation—a

bourbon drink poured in a glass that he flavored with hickory smoke, something James said he and his buddies invented while camping one weekend. It was bizarre and delicious, and it made me think of the president, who loves a good whiskey drink, especially after a long evening. I always made sure to have one sent up to the residence after formal events downstairs.

"Hey, James," I say to him when we finally squeeze into the bar.

"Oh, hey!" he says, wiping the sweat off his brow with his forearm. "Mr. Warner, how are you?" he says, clearly surprised by the sight of his boss in costume.

"Please, James, call me Cole, especially tonight," Cole says. "I don't deserve any respect dressed like this."

"Right on!" he says, the relief evident in his voice. "I guess I forgot you would be here. The costume is pretty sweet. Yours, too, Mrs. Warner."

"Bess," I tell him.

"Right, right," he says.

"So what can I get —" Cole starts.

"Excuse me!" a voice yells behind us. "Excuse me!" When I turn and look, I see a Superman, but a quite short one, with a sizable belly, a bulbous nose, and a ruddy complexion. More Newt Gingrich than Clark Kent.

"Greg!" Cole says. "Hey, buddy! The party's great."

Greg tips his chin at him, but the expression on his face is not particularly congenial. "Cole, what's up!" He puts a finger out before Cole can respond. "Just give me a sec, dude. Gotta talk to my bartender."

I look over at James, who looks like he's going to throw up. Greg leans into him and whispers something angrily in his ear.

Cole clears his throat. "Anything I can help with, guys?" he says.

"No," Greg says. "Think we got it straight now." He raises his eyebrows at James as if to confirm this, and James nods.

Greg rounds the bar and puts his hand out to me. "Greg Barker," he says, smiling in a way that looks like it pains him. He's clearly still worked up about something. "Thanks for coming."

"Everything okay?" Cole says, a little under his breath so James doesn't overhear him.

"Yeah, yeah," Greg says, cuffing a hand around Cole's shoulder. "The guy's fine, but, you know, sometimes you can't trust these guys from out in the country. The kid probably grew up drinking Mad Dog and firewater. I don't know how skilled he is at martinis and manhattans without following whatever recipe book you keep behind the bar at the inn."

"Right," Cole says, and then, unbelievably, laughs a little.

Why is he agreeing with this buffoon? I can't help myself. "Actually, there isn't a recipe book behind the bar at the inn," I say. "And James made me a great drink just a few nights ago."

He turns to Cole, pointing a thumb at me. "She your new GM?" He smirks, and then, unbelievably, Cole laughs along with him. *Again.*

We are crowded against the bar just enough that I am able to subtly, and *mostly* gently, kick Cole's ankle with the toe of my ruby-red slipper.

He shoots a look at me, wrinkling his brow like he's confused.

I smile back at him. I can't believe he's ingratiating himself to this guy, and letting him insult me, too.

"Hey," Greg says to Cole. "I got a bunch of guys over in the corner talking about starting up our weekly poker thing again."

I look across the room to where a group of men—a werewolf, someone in scrubs, a referee—are huddled together and laughing loudly. "We used to play every Sunday night, but then, you know, life got in the way." He shrugs. "We're looking for a place to convene. Hey, maybe the inn? Would you want to join?"

Cole looks at me and shrugs. "Yeah, maybe."

Greg laughs. "You gotta check with the wife first?" he says. "That's not the Cole Warner I remember!"

My mouth drops open, but Greg is moving on, taking a few steps and waving for Cole to follow him. "Come on, let's go talk to them," he says.

Cole looks at me and shrugs. "Sorry, Greg's always been—"

"Go ahead." I pat his shoulder.

He raises his eyebrows.

"Go," I say. "Have fun."

He reaches and squeezes my hand, the straw from his costume scratching against my arm, then leans to kiss my cheek. "I'm sorry about that," he whispers in my ear. "He can be kind of an—"

"No worries," I say, thinking that we'll talk about it later, and then, as he starts to pull away, I hold his hand tighter, hooking my index finger into his. He looks back at me, grimacing in a playful way, and I laugh at myself, covering for the way I feel, my separation anxiety like a kindergartener's on the first day of school. He stops and leans into me again. "I love you," he says. "And everyone here will, too."

"Okay, go," I say, pushing him gently. I watch him cross the room and see how his face lights up when someone in the huddle of men in the corner calls out his name.

After I get a glass of wine from James, I spot Carol, the owner of Fine Feathers, the local women's clothing boutique, sipping a glass of the awful-looking lime-colored punch I'd noticed in a large crystal bowl on the end of the bar. She is wearing a gold leotard, gold tights, gold elbow-length gloves, and a braided gold headband around her forehead. When she catches me looking at her, she waves and starts toward me.

Back when Cole and I used to come here just to visit, Fine Feathers was where I went when I needed a break from my mother-in-law. I was drawn there not so much by the clothes but by Carol, who was five or six years ahead of Cole in school and was always friendly to me, happy to chitchat and greet me warmly even when it was clear I wasn't there to buy anything. Unlike most of the other women in town, who dress in a sort of conservative-rich-bitch casual—Patagonia fleeces, jeans, diamond or pearl studs—she is like a small-town Betsey Johnson, always in some sort of leather or fur, costume jewelry piled on, bright, bright lipstick. "Like a little girl playing dress-up," Diane has said, not in a particularly kind way.

"Did you design this?" I ask, waving my index finger in a circle so Carol will give me a 360.

"Guilty." She twirls cautiously so she won't spill her drink. "I'm a Solid Gold dancer. Are you too young to know what that is?"

"No!" I say, laughing out loud. "Of course not. Watching that show was my favorite thing about Saturday nights when I was a kid!"

"Me, too," she says. "Before I discovered clothes, my life's ambition was to be on it. My poor parents sat through so many of my dance routines in our living room. . . ."

The mention of her parents reminds me of the horrible story Diane once told me about them: how they died unexpectedly when Carol was in her twenties, carbon-monoxide poisoning from a faulty heating system in a hotel room in Key West. "And then the thing with Carol's husband," Diane had said, her eyes widening at the memory of him. He'd run off with someone. "*A woman he met on the internet*," Diane had whispered.

"I *love* your ruby slippers," Carol says, pointing down at my heels. "And you should do braids more often. You can pull it off."

I touch my fingers to one of the ribbons I'd tied to my hair. "I don't know," I say, just as Mindy is bouncing by with a silver tray of crab puffs. We each take one.

"Oh, you have got to be kidding me," Carol says suddenly through a mouthful of food.

I freeze just as I'm about to take a bite. "What? What is it?" I say, dropping the puff back into my cocktail napkin, thinking there must be something wrong with it. But then I follow Carol's gaze, noticing the hush that has fallen over the crowd.

I don't recognize the wearer, but I immediately know the inspiration for his costume. All six-foot-plus of him is squeezed into a blood-splattered, lemon-yellow knee-length dress, and a platinum-blond wig is fastened on his blocky head with an ACE bandage. Fake cuts and bruises have been drawn all over his face, and he has somehow managed to find what is clearly the showpiece of his outfit, attached to a paisley-patterned scarf around his neck: a palm-sized rhinestone pin shaped like a cricket. *Susannah's nickname*, I think, remembering what she told me during our meeting.

He's holding the arm of a woman who is wearing a prim top with a Peter Pan collar and a long skirt. Her hair's pulled back into a ponytail, and there are sticks and leaves poking out from the elastic. And she's holding . . . *what is it? A bottle of whiskey?* It confuses me at first—*is she drinking straight from the bottle?* And then I realize, noticing the XXX label and the skeleton head on its front, that the bottle is just a prop, part of the costume.

"Too soon!" somebody shouts. Laughter fills the room.

"Terrible!" someone else yells.

"Aw, don't be so uptight!" the guy in drag screams back.

Carol turns to me and shakes her head. "Silly."

"Who is that?" I ask.

"Brian White," says a voice over my shoulder. I turn. It is a petite, pale-skinned blonde, at least six months pregnant, in a black leotard and fishnet tights, bunny ears on her head. "Sadly, my first kiss."

"Oh God, Whitney," Carol says, making a disgusted face.

"I know," she says. "I'm not sure why I just admitted that."

She turns to me and puts her hand out to introduce herself. "Hi, I'm Whitney Dickerson. I've known Cole since for-*ever.*" *Whitney Dickerson*, I remember from the quiz Cole gave me in the car, *married to the one who looks like Woody Harrelson. His first name is* . . . I can't remember. "Actually . . ." She pushes her hair up off her forehead and leans into me. "See that scar on my hairline?"

"Yeah," I say, noticing the staple-sized mark.

"Your husband did that."

"*What?*" I say.

She laughs. "He threw a block at me in preschool."

"Oh!" I say. "You scared me."

"What are you dressed as?" Carol asks Whitney.

"Pregnant Playboy Bunny," she says, patting her belly. "It was that or Humpty Dumpty."

I laugh, taking to her.

"Who's that with Brian?" Carol asks, pointing at the woman holding his hand.

"I have no idea," Whitney says. "You know Brian, always hauling in some undergrad from Charlottesville when he can't find a date for something."

"God, he's tacky," Carol says.

"But you have to admit, the costume's kind of funny," Whitney says.

Carol laughs. "Wait," she says, watching as I take a sip of my drink. "You know whom he's dressed as, I'm sure?"

"Of course she does!" Whitney says. "She's writing a story about Susannah, haven't you heard?"

Carol turns to me, her eyes wide. "No, I don't know anything about that!"

They both wait for an explanation.

"Yes, well. I am, it's true," I say. "But it's just a little thing, a couple of pages, mostly about how she's moved back to her childhood home, really."

"Her move back?" Carol says, and I don't know why, but I feel my stomach flip.

"Yeah," I say, playing it off. "Just about her return to town, and about her plans for her land."

"Her plans for her land," Whitney says, lowering her

voice. "And what does she have to say about that? I'd love to know."

"Well, we all would, wouldn't we?" a voice beside me says.

When I turn to look, I flinch, an involuntary *ugh* that I hope nobody notices. It's *Eva*. My husband's high school girl-friend.

She is dressed like a flamingo. It takes me a moment to soak it in, the pink marabou, the tulle, the body glitter. I look up at her. She is one of the tallest women I have ever met—well over six feet, especially in the sparkly stilettos she's wearing. She has a black beak perched on her nose and it looks ridiculous, especially with her peering down at me.

"Cute costume," she says, looking me over. Her eyes are big—heavy, like a camel's—but perpetually watery. *Sick eyes*, I've thought to myself in smaller moments. I am trying to keep an open mind about her, but she doesn't make it easy. Part of the problem is that I know she is the woman responsible for tak-ing my husband's virginity, which is ridiculous for me to care about—it happened, what, over twenty-five years ago?—but some primal, possessive part of my brain latches on to the fact every time I see her.

"Thank you," I say. "You look great."

Aside from the beak and the eyes, she really does. I've actu-ally already seen her costume, having read her post about it on her blog, which I happened upon while googling her shortly be-fore our move. The website mostly chronicles the items Eva buys online, how she decorates her home, and the life of what you might call her designer family, which includes Brittany, a daugh-ter Max and Livvie's age, and her husband, David, who has been the mayor of Greyhill for almost ten years. Eva calls her blog *Belle Luxe*. "Beautiful luxury." It's as awful as it sounds, and yet I never seem to miss a post.

"You know, I ran into Diane the other day downtown and she told me about your story, Bess," Eva says, a saccharine smile blooming on her face.

Oh God, I think. *What is she about to say?*

"It's so . . . *interesting*. I never knew you could write."

"Yes," I say, taking another sip of my drink. "It's something I did a long time ago."

"Ah," she says. "Have you spent much time with Susannah yet?"

"I was at Esperanza just yesterday, actually. We've only met once. Officially."

"Really?" all three say at once, and then look at each other and laugh before turning back to me. It's not clear why, but the questions keep coming before I can answer.

"And how is she?" Whitney asks. "I know she's been keeping a lower profile since the accident." Her eyes narrow, waiting for my reply.

"Oh," I say. "Um . . ." I suddenly find myself woolly-mouthed and unable to find my words. The women step in closer, looming, licking their lips like cartoon snakes.

"She's well."

"How'd she look?" Carol asks.

"As beautiful as ever."

"We should all be so lucky to look like her at her age," Carol says.

Whitney nods. "You can say that again."

"Well . . . I heard," Eva says, lowering her voice and leaning into us, "that after the accident, she whisked herself off to California for plastic surgery." She turns to me. "Do you know anything about that? Did she look like she'd had some work done?"

"She had a bandage across her forehead, but plastic surgery? No, not particularly."

"Who said that, Eva?" Carol asks, looking at her suspiciously. "About her being in California?"

"Don't worry about it," Eva says, waving her hand at her. "You wouldn't believe all the stories we get in the mayor's office."

Ugh. Eva, I've discovered in the handful of times I've run into her around town, is one of those women who talks about her husband's job as if it's her own.

"What was she wearing?" Carol asks me.

"Susannah? Hmm," I say, thinking back. "A big red skirt, ankle length, like something you'd wear to a formal event."

"Lady in red," Carol says, nodding. "I love a blonde in red."

"She has a helper, doesn't she?" Whitney says. "Some sort of assistant or housekeeper? From outside of town?"

"Yes, Cindy," I say. "She's a hoot." I tip my glass to my lips, finishing the last sip of my wine.

"And what *did* she say about the land?" Eva asks, crossing her arms over her chest and looking at me expectantly.

"We haven't really gotten into that yet."

"You'll have to let me know when you do," Eva says. "She has several acres right next to our place. It's not for sale yet, but David and I are on pins and needles waiting to see. He's called that agent in New York several times but can't seem to get him on the phone, which I find suspicious."

"Bess, has she said anything about why she came back here in the first place?" Whitney asks.

"No," I say, starting to feel like I'm sitting on a witness stand.

"But you talked about the accident, I'm sure?" Eva says. "I mean, you *had* to."

"We did, but barely," I say, a sinking feeling starting in my chest.

"And what did she say about how it happened?" she asks.

"Just that she lost control of the truck," I say.

"Well," Carol says. "That may be, but I've heard a lot of rumors at the store about why she lost control . . . that she was drinking, or on painkillers, or that the crash was caused by a stroke or an aneurysm," she says, ticking off each scenario on her fingers. "Someone said she might even be suffering from the early stages of dementia."

"You don't think that's really true, do you?" Whitney says to the group.

"It would explain her selling off her land." Eva laughs "Maybe she's just losing her mind."

The other two laugh.

"So what did you talk about, then?" Eva asks. "If you didn't talk about the land or the accident or why she's back here?"

"She's irritated to have totaled her truck," I say, feeling suddenly protective of her. *All these questions!* "And that's really the only thing she had to say about the accident. The truck was a present from Teddy. And she named it after her best friend from childhood, but I can't remember the name . . . It was something sort of old-fashioned."

"Like Bess?" Eva laughs, and my cheeks redden at the slight. "Oh, I'm just kidding!"

"Yeah, sure," I say, narrowing my eyes just subtly enough that she'll know I don't appreciate the dig. How did Cole date this horrible woman? I know it was one of those typically teenage on-again, off-again relationships, and over as soon as they both went away to college (Cole to Georgetown and Eva to Sweet Briar), but still . . .

"The name was Henrietta, of course," Whitney says.

"Yes!" I say, snapping my fingers. "That's it! Henrietta! We talked about her for a bit."

"You went to Cricket Lane's estate and the two of you talked about Henrietta Martin?" Carol says.

"Yes," I say, scanning their surprised expressions. "Is there something strange about that?"

Eva laughs. "What do you know about Henrietta Martin, Bess?"

"Nothing. Just that she was Susannah's best friend when they were growing up in Greyhill." I'm tiring of their interrogation. "Why? Is there something I should know about Henrietta Martin?"

"Cole's never told you about her?" Eva says.

I shake my head.

"Legendary story! She died tragically during her senior year at Draper," Whitney says, putting her hand on my arm as she explains it. "Right before graduation!"

"Died?" I say. "What do you mean by *tragically*?"

"Oh, don't worry, it was years ago," Whitney says. "Back in the 1960s."

"That's why that woman . . ." Carol says, craning her neck to scan the crowd. "The one with Brian, the guy dressed as Susannah."

"Oh," I say, just able to make out the back of the woman's head on the other side of the room. "The one with the sticks in her hair? And the bottle?"

"Yes," Eva says. "The seniors at Draper used to always throw a party up on the Cliffs the weekend before graduation. The story goes that Henrietta was drunk, wandered off, and fell from one of the lookout points up on the mountain. A hunter found her body in the valley early the next morning."

"How awful," I say.

"I guess it was," Carol says. "Can you imagine if something like that happened now?"

"The lawsuits," Whitney says, rolling her eyes and shaking her head. "And the attention. My parents—Hal and Jenny Perkins, they own Perkins Variety and Hardware downtown? They always thought it was fishy."

"Really?" I say. "Fishy how?"

Carol turns to me. "Do you know what the Cliffs are, Bess?"

"Yes," I say. "Cole took me up there once, years ago, just to see it."

"I bet he did," Eva says. "He used to take *me* there, too."

My ears start to burn, but before I have a chance to say anything, Whitney chimes in: "Is there a woman in Greyhill who Cole Warner didn't take up to the Cliffs?" She slaps her hand over her mouth. "I'm sorry, Bess! I wasn't thinking! That was rude."

"No," I say. "It's fine."

Though it really isn't, because these women are insinuating something about my husband's past that I know nothing about.

I know about Eva, of course—she was his first love, his home-coming date, his prom date. I've seen all the pictures. Diane dragged out the photo albums the first time he brought me to Greyhill, pointing out, in what felt like an aggressive move, what a "gem of a girl" Eva was. How tall and elegant, how feminine, "such a Greyhill girl," she'd said, whatever that means, her finger running over a photo of Cole in a tux with a sapphire-blue cummerbund that matched Eva's dress.

Cole took me up to the so-called Cliffs after dinner during that visit, the two of us laughing over the fact that of course Greyhill would have a cheesy, classic drink-beer-and-make-out spot up on the mountain. Once we got up there, however, the view was spectacular. The sky was full of stars, and the town sparkled in the valley like a scene straight out of the inside of a snow globe. We'd sat on the hood of his car, and it felt silly, like we were playing characters in an old movie, but sweet, too. It feels ridiculous to care—*I'm* his wife—but it somehow spoils the memory to hear that I was just the last in a long line of women who'd accompanied Cole to the same spot.

"I have to tell you, Bess," Eva says. "I find it very interesting that the *Washington Post* would find it remotely worthwhile to write about Susannah Lane and our little town."

"Oh, come on, Eva," Whitney says. "You know people write about Greyhill all the time."

"We're in all those 'best small towns' lists," Carol says. "*Southern Living, Travel and Leisure*. And this is Susannah Lane we're talking about. You know, my father was always going on and on about Teddy, listening to his interviews in the news about the stock market."

"I don't know." Eva shrugs. "I guess I don't see why everyone's so obsessed with her, though. What did *she* do, other than be his wife?"

Huh. If I'm not mistaken, Eva sounds jealous. "She did a ton of charity work and worked with his foundations," I say, referencing what I've researched and what Susannah told me yesterday. "And she was a bit of a fixture on the New York social scene. She was always throwing big parties, and unlike a lot of the other wealthy society wives, she was friendly with a really diverse cast of characters—artists and writers, musicians, fashion people. And she wrote a gossip column for a little while. It's actually funny—she told me that she wrote it because it was an easy way to get the press off *her* case. Beat them at their own game. The media loved her."

"Well, I guess you know better than I do," Eva says, looking down her beak at me. "Given *your* experience." She grins. "With the media."

I freeze, a jolt running through me, but not without noticing the nervous look that passes between Whitney and Carol.

"Yes," I say, mustering my strength and laughing it off. "I guess I do."

Whitney opens her mouth like she's about to say something but then stops.

I raise my eyebrows at her, smiling and willing her to say whatever she was about to. I want someone to take the floor away from Eva.

She opens her mouth again, stretching her lips out, wincing, and I know what she's about to ask because she's making the face that everyone makes before they ask me the question they always do.

"*So what was it like?*" she asks, her voice quiet, leaning in like we all need to huddle for the secret. "Working for her? You were . . . *social secretary?*"

"Yes." I nod. "I was."

"Tell us about it," Carol says. "I'm *dying* to know."

"Oh, ah . . .," I say, hating myself for stumbling over my words. I glance at Eva. She's smirking at me. "It was . . .," I start. "How else can I say it? It was a once-in-a-lifetime experience."

Whitney nods slowly. Carol tips her head to the side. They obviously want to ask about what happened. Of course they do. The words are practically bursting out of their mouths. *Why did you say what you said on those recordings? And how could you?*

"It's a demanding place to work," I say, using the line I always used back when the job was truly mine, in the present tense. The women hum and nod; I know they're hoping for more. "And not for the faint of heart." I look quickly at Eva, wanting her to feel warned. "But it was also an honor, unlike anything I could have imagined."

Their faces go flat, obviously disappointed that I haven't offered them more.

"There must be a lot you can't say," Whitney says, putting her hand on her belly.

"A lot of unusual regulations," Carol adds. "Confidentiality, that sort of thing."

"Yes," I say, clearing my throat. "Working for the First Family is sort of like working for the mafia." I wink.

"Oh?" They tilt their heads toward me.

I fake a laugh. "No, not really."

"So what is the job exactly? When you're social secretary?" Whitney asks.

"It's the event planning, right?" Carol asks.

"Yes," I say. "I was responsible for all the social visits for the president and the First Lady. The state dinners, receptions, even informal gatherings among the First Family and their friends. Traditionally, you work almost exclusively with the First Lady, but you also work with the protocol office, the president's staff . . ."

Eva, beside me, isn't saying a word, but I can feel her eyes crawling all over me. A woman in a Little Bo-Peep costume squeezes by with a tray of chocolate truffles. The other women wave her off, but I stop her and take one.

"It must have been fascinating," Carol says.

"It was," I say, feeling the peculiar swirl of pride and remorse I've become accustomed to whenever I let myself linger on what it was like. "It really was."

"And the First Lady . . . ?" Eva starts, cocking her head at me. I can tell she's trying to bait me.

"She's exactly what she seems," I say, biting into the truffle before it melts onto my fingertips. *Who wouldn't serve these with napkins? Or at least in a little candy liner?* "Incredibly smart and warm. I can't say I ever encountered a single person who didn't feel captivated by her when they met her, even if they were just briefly shaking her hand on a rope line. She is the definition of a magnetic personality."

"People say she should run when her husband's term is up," Carol says, nodding.

"She'd be great," I say. "No doubt about that."

"That's so . . . *interesting*." Eva peers at me, and I know exactly why. She's trying to reconcile what I've just said about the First Lady with what happened all those months ago. The chocolate aftertaste in the back of my throat suddenly tastes off, like watery chalk.

"Are we having fun yet?" a voice behind me screeches, and Mindy, our host, appears at my side. "You look like you're talking about something *good*. Fill me in!"

"We were just getting to know Bess," Carol says.

"We're so glad you moved back. Or, well, that Cole *brought* you back. You know what I'm trying to say!" Mindy says, reaching to give me a squeeze. One of her fake nails digs into my arm, leaving a little half-moon on my skin.

"Thanks," I say. Behind her, I can see Cole standing by the open doors leading out to the patio, talking animatedly, waving his hands, laughing and laughing and laughing. The room feels suddenly, unbearably hot.

"Now, remind me," Mindy says. "How old are your kids?"

"The twins are twelve."

"Same as my Brittany," Eva says.

My Brittany, I think, remembering the way she references her daughter on the blog, like the child is an accessory she picked up at the Neiman Marcus semiannual sale.

"Are your kids enjoying Draper?" Eva says.

"Oh, yes," I say. "So far, so good, I think, though they don't really tell me much. You know kids at this age, they can get a little less forthcoming."

"Really?" Eva says. "Not my Brittany. She just loves school. Always has."

"Well, the kids at Draper are all such dolls," Mindy says. "And the teachers! The best of the best! Aren't we lucky?"

"Uh-huh," I say, thinking that Mindy, nice as she seems, appears to have the substance of cotton candy. My stomach turns— the wine, the chocolate . . . the company. I look across the room at Cole. He looks like he's having the time of his life.

EIGHT

❧

Cole is giddy on the ride home—chatty, almost giggly—telling me stories about the various people he caught up with tonight. I'm driving, which we'd established I would before we even left for the party, and while I expected Cole to have a good time, I haven't seen him like this in a while. A few of his friends tried to get us to stay longer, one of them pulling Cole by his shirtsleeve toward the bar and threatening tequila shots. Fortunately, Cole was just sober enough to recognize that we are not, in fact, despite what he may have reverted to tonight, still in our early twenties.

He babbles on, and I try to pay attention, to keep the names and stories straight so I'll familiarize myself with them, but the truth is, I'm exhausted. I stifle a yawn as I turn onto Old Meadow Lane, a short, dead-end cove populated by just two homes: ours on the right and Cole's parents' on the left. When I turn onto our new street, I often think of my mother, whose first comment when I called her to tell her we were moving here was that she'd rather live next to a slaughterhouse than across the street from my mother-in-law. "But!" I heard my dad cackle in the background. "I suppose it's kinda the same thing!" I've realized that having

Bradley and Diane in our daily lives now just makes me miss my parents that much more. I need to get them down here for a visit, not only because I want them to see Greyhill—all these years later, they've still never been—but also because I know they'll see what I do: it can't possibly be the utopia that everyone here seems so fervently to believe it is.

"What are you thinking about?" Cole asks, unbuckling his seat belt as I ease the car into the driveway.

"Oh, nothing," I say. "I'm just tired."

He reaches for my hand and squeezes.

"Hey," I say, trying to keep my voice light as I pull the key out of the ignition. "Question for you."

"Yeah." He smiles. He has the slightest chip on one of his front teeth—a run-in with a baseball during an attempt to steal home in his senior year at Draper. That, combined with the golden glint he sometimes gets in his hazel eyes, made me swoon when we were first getting to know each other.

"A story came up tonight when I was talking to those women. About the Cliffs?"

He laughs. "Uh-huuuuh . . .," he says expectantly.

I turn in my seat, slapping the console between us. "Okay, that's just it!" I say. "You've answered my question without me even having to ask it!"

"Whoa, what?"

"They kind of made it sound like you had a reserved parking spot up there. And that you were giving out 'frequent customer' cards to all the girls in your class."

"Oh, come on." He rolls his eyes. "Please, Bess."

"Well," I say. "How much truth is there to it?"

He lifts his palms to the air. "What does it matter?" he says. "It was a billion years ago."

"Uh-huh . . . ," I say.

"What?" he says. "You're going to hold my teenage years against me?"

"So it's true, then?"

"I don't know." He shrugs. "I might have gone through a phase."

"Right," I say, laughing at him now that he's squirming. At least he admits it. "And what did Eva think of all the other girls? How many came before her? How many after?"

"Bess." He rolls his eyes.

"Actually!" I start. "What did your *mother* think?"

"Come on," he says. "First of all, she never knew anything—"

"Well, of course she didn't. And even if she did, she wouldn't fault *you*. We both know her perfect princely son can do no wrong."

"Jesus!" he says. "Really?"

"I'm sorry," I say, reaching over to squeeze his shoulder. "But you know it's true. *I* know firsthand."

"Yeah, well . . ." He grabs my hand. "She is who she is."

"Yes, she is." I lean across the center console and kiss the spot on his cheek where the lipstick dot has now officially smeared off. "Anyway . . ."

"Anyway," he repeats.

"I'm glad you had fun tonight," I say, wanting to make up for giving him a hard time. I *am* glad he had fun. I'm just a little jealous, too, is all.

"Thanks," he says. "I did. And you? Seems like you were talking to that same group for a long time."

"Yeah," I say, swallowing against the lump in my throat. "It was nice."

"Uh-oh." He manages an awkward laugh. "You're not exactly convincing."

"No, no," I say, patting his hand, wanting to reassure him even if it's not entirely true. "It's just different, that's all."

I look up at the house from where we're parked in the driveway and see Diane standing in the living room, a mug in her hand. She likes all those "Zinger" teas, so I bought a stash for when she's over, not that she's ever bothered to thank me. Not that I'm keeping score. At least, I'm *trying* not to.

I can feel Cole watching me. "Do you still love the house?" he asks. "Despite the neighbors?" He playfully pinches my leg.

"I *love* the house," I say, looking up at it.

We get out of the car. I start to pull the braids out of my hair and Cole yawns, saying something about how we're too old to stay out this late. Diane opens the front door before we're halfway up the walk. "Oh, Bess," she says, her arms crossed over her chest. "You should have *told* me about your floors. I couldn't find your mop. Do you have one, dear? You know I would have brought mine. All you have to do is ask."

NINE

～⚬————⚬～

"Did you see her costume?"

"I mean, Cole looked great, but the Dorothy getup wasn't exactly flattering."

"Why does it not surprise me that you think Cole Warner looks great even when he is shedding hay all over my house?"

"Oh, stop it, Mindy. We are ancient history. A million years ago. Ancient!"

"I know, I know, you're *happily married*. Cole's even better with age, though, I'll say that."

"He is, isn't he? But she's bigger than I remember, don't you think?"

"Yes! Did you see how she was shoveling those truffles into her mouth?"

"I swear, every time I looked over at her, she was wiping chocolate from her face."

"She's less . . . I don't know . . . I guess I thought she'd be more poised or something. More *polished?* You'd think so, wouldn't you? With the job she had . . ."

"Speaking of, you should have seen how she squirmed when I brought it up."

"Brought it up! You're evil."

"Well, I find it really telling. You can see what kind of woman she is. And now . . . to hear that she and Susannah Lane are spending time together!"

"She's definitely not someone to be trusted. I wouldn't *dare* tell her anything I don't want repeated. And she doesn't seem particularly friendly anyway. Let her go sit up in Esperanza with Susannah."

"Agreed. She's kind of an ice princess, no?"

"You mean 'ice queen.'"

"No, I don't! *I'm* the only queen around here!"

"I know you like to think so! And you better be careful. She seems to have it in for first ladies."

"You're sweet, but I would hardly compare myself to Candace Calhoun."

"I wasn't—"

"Anyway, her kids seem cute, I'll give her that. Brittany seems to like the girl, though have you seen her?"

"No, I haven't."

"She seems a little . . . I don't know how to say it. Just a little awkward, I guess. But the boy, Max, is apparently a doll. Kind of quiet. Not the athlete type, but really nice, Brittany says."

"They must take after their father."

"Let's hope, for their sake."

TEN

Bess

Draper Hall occupies eight acres of land on the east side of Maple Street, anchoring one end of downtown. It is an idyllic campus, made up of a collection of charming ivy-covered brick buildings that sit on a sloping blanket of plush green grass dotted with colorful flower beds kept up by the grounds crew, who get very specific instructions from the Greyhill Gardening Club about what to plant and how to do it. I know this because Diane is a member. The women—all of them older, all of them with too much time on their hands—take themselves very seriously, and Diane gripes about the constant back-and-forth between the club and the workers like they're negotiating arms deals. Every time I spot one of the guys at the school mowing the grass or wielding a leaf blower, I feel an empathetic pang in my chest, knowing what they must deal with.

The first time the kids saw the campus, they said it looked like something out of a movie, and compared to the cheerful but 1960s-industrial public school they'd attended in northeast DC, it did. *Too good to be true*, I'd thought, especially once we embarked on our tour of the buildings' interiors. We were led around by the headmaster, an eager bespectacled redhead with the trim frame of a cross-country runner, who Cole said had been poached from some elite school in Tennessee several years back. The floors of the main building were covered with Persian rugs. Oil paintings hung on the polished mahogany walls. "This place is nicer than the inn!" I said, realizing as I caught my husband's eye that he did not appreciate my joke. Neither did the headmaster, who was so embarrassed for me that his cheeks turned the same shade as his hair.

I could tell when we left that Cole was pissed, but he was trying to keep it together for the kids. He wanted them to be as enthusiastic as he was about his alma mater, and who did I think I was, he said later, to criticize our family's business in front of school leadership? When I admitted that I was worried about sending the twins to a place like Draper— private, exclusive—he accused me of projecting from my own experience.

I still maintain that the joke was no big deal (and only stung because it's the truth), but he's right about my projecting. The private school I attended for high school was beautiful, too, I said to Cole when we fought that night, and an absolute nightmare. I also didn't love the idea that almost the entire student body was composed of a certain kind of kid—all the posh ones, really. They were mostly from Greyhill but there were also some from Charlottesville and Culpeper, plus the handful of kids from out in the country who attended on scholarships. "Fine, then, what do you want to do?" Cole barked. He happened to be wearing a navy-blue Draper Hall baseball cap as we fought, a fact I found sickly comic as he grumbled. "Do you want to send our kids to the shitty public school on the other side of the county, just to make a point?"

"Maybe I do!" I'd yelled, and I had meant it, but then later that night, after we'd gone to bed and Cole was asleep, I'd looked up the school's state ranking on my phone. Draper it would be.

I arrive in the parking lot just before the kids will emerge from under the arched doorway of the school's main building. I've spent most of the day at home, outlining ideas for my article and unpacking some of the boxes I keep putting off dealing with, and as I walk up the lawn to the spot where the students exit each day, I run my hand through my hair, wondering whether I even remembered to brush it today. Back in DC, I'd picked up the kids at five o'clock from their after-school program, even on the days I would have to go back to work after they'd eaten dinner. The other parents I saw when I arrived at the school felt like members of my tribe, all of us in the conservative suits our jobs demanded, all of us still moving at work-speed, the go-getter stride, brows knitted, arms swinging.

This is different. I wave to the mothers I've chatted with at pickup, all Greyhill natives, naturally, who talk in a familiar shorthand that reveals their long ties and, by extension, seems to emphasize just how far I have to go. I'm starting to believe that I'm like Jane Goodall, cast down among the chimps, having to learn an entirely new set of customs and behaviors.

One of them turns to me and smiles, a friendly gesture I'm so unaccustomed to that I actually feel my heart start to swell.

"You made it in the nick of time," she says, lifting her wrist like she's checking her watch.

I think she's kidding and start to laugh, until she whips back around and smirks at the woman standing next to her, who's dressed in full equestrian gear, like she just tied up her horse next to the cavalcade of luxury SUVs in the parking lot.

Maybe *not* so friendly. Sometimes, when I'm standing at school pickup trying to make conversation—actually, just trying to make eye contact—with the other moms, I think of the irony of the sign that greets visitors at the town line: WELCOME TO GREY-HILL: WIDE, OPEN SPACES. SMILING FACES.

The doors start to open, and the kids begin spilling outside, just as a woman in the huddle of moms turns and calls my name. "I thought that was you!" she says. "I saw you walking up."

"Mindy!" I say, pleased to see her. "Hi, how are you?"

"Exhausted!" she says. "Still! There's a reason Greg and I only throw that party once a year. Have you and Cole recovered yet? I told Greg that punch was too strong. I swear, I'm still not right!"

I think of her buffoon husband, how he grilled our bartender and was less than charming to me.

"We had a great time," I say, my eyes scanning the crowd for the twins. "It was really lovely."

"Well, good!" she says. "That means a lot, coming from you. I know *you* know how to throw a party." As she winks, two of the other women turn around. To watch, I can only assume.

"You and Cole were adorable!" Mindy says. "I told Greg we

should reinstate our costume contest. You two would have won for best couple."

"Oh, you're being generous," I say. "There were a lot of great costumes."

"No, it's *true!* You both looked so great. We should have dinner sometime! Greg and I used to double-date with Cole and Eva all the time, back in the day!" She laughs. "Sorry. I hope that's not uncomfortable for me to say!" she says, her eyes rolling back toward the women standing behind her.

"No, no, of course not," I say. *Tactless, maybe.*

"Of course! How silly of me! Why would it be awkward?"

"Why would it be!" I repeat, just as—*thank God*—I spot Max and Livvie. I start toward them. "There are the kids." I wave. "See you soon, Mindy."

The twins slump down the steps, slouching under the weight of their backpacks, their arms dangling in front of them like they're little zombies.

"And how was your day, dear children?" I ask, my irritation with Mindy melting off me as I reach my arms around them. Max gives me a half-hearted squeeze, but Livvie doesn't even make an effort. She just stands there in front of me, her arms hanging at her sides like overcooked noodles. "Livvie—" I start, but she pulls away from me before I can read the expression on her face and starts toward the car.

I follow her, and as we cross the parking lot, the sound of soccer practice starting on one of the sports fields across campus, Max catches my eye, tilts his head toward his sister, and makes a slicing motion across his neck with his hand. I raise my palms at him. *What the . . . ?*

"Max, *God!*" Livvie screeches, catching us.

I break into a little jog and hurry next to her. "What happened?" I say. "Livvie, what is it?"

Her eyes stay pinned to the parking-lot asphalt. I look at Max, who immediately jerks a thumb at Livvie. "I dunno," he says. "Maybe it's that time of the month."

"Max!" I yell, my heart lurching in my chest. Livvie hasn't had her first period yet, though—oh, no—*did she get it today? Is that it? No*, I think. *Please, no.*

Livvie speeds up, marching toward the car, her arms crossed tightly over her chest like she's holding something to it. As I'm hurrying after her, I notice Eva and Whitney across the parking lot, both of them watching us, shading their eyes with their hands over their heads like soldiers standing at attention.

"Livvie, *honey.*"

"Mom!" she wails. "Just leave me alone!" The desperation in her voice is unlike anything I've heard out of her before, and I've heard *plenty*, especially over the last year or so.

"Livvie!" I stage-whisper toward her. I don't want to make a scene—for either of our sakes, but especially Livvie's. An old feeling I haven't had since the kids were toddlers comes flooding back, from when they threw temper tantrums in public—at a restaurant or in the checkout line at Safeway—and my adrenaline would suddenly spike as I desperately tried to get things under control, *immediately*, before they completely fell apart. I look back at Max, who is ambling behind me, staring up at the sky, oblivious. After a lifetime of practice, he has no trouble tuning out his twin.

I take a few quick hop-steps to catch up to Livvie and reach her just before we get to the car. "Honey." I carefully touch my palm to her back, feeling the strap of her sports bra beneath her clothes. She doesn't need to wear it, but all her classmates back in DC did, so . . .

She jerks the door handle, waiting for me to unlock the car.

"What happened?" I whisper, my eyes canvassing the parking lot. Fortunately, we are just boring enough that nobody's paying attention anymore. The lot is emptying out.

Livvie shakes her head, and her long, single braid bounces against her back. This morning, I'd watched her tie the elastic around the base as she was walking up the green into school. Her hair had still been wet from her shower, and I'd thought about all the nightly bath times I'd missed when she was a toddler because I was racing around the East Wing. I'd hear her splashing through the phone, singsonging along with Max and Cole as they recited, "Rub-a-dub-dub, three men in a tub" before they told me good night.

I squeeze Livvie's shoulder. "Talking about it will make you feel better," I say.

"Can we just go?" she says, pulling on the door handle again.

"Of course," I say. I punch the button on my key fob and walk soundlessly around to the driver's seat. Before I get in, I look over the roof to Max, who's shrugging off his backpack. "What happened?" I mouth.

"No idea!" he mouths back.

"Olivia, let's talk about this," I say once I get in the car, twisting around in my seat to face her.

She rolls her eyes and slumps against the window. She has never been a forthcoming kid. Even in preschool, I relied on Max and one of their talkative classmates, a kid whose parents had dubbed her "Katie Couric," to get the dish on what was happening in her classroom.

"Honey . . ." I reach back and try to squeeze her leg, but she jerks away.

"Mom, would you please just . . ." She shakes her head, and then the tears start. Big, gulping sobs that suddenly come out of her in a rush, like she's been holding them in all day. I reach into the back seat again, my chest aching for her, but she just turns more toward the window.

Fuck! This is the one thing I didn't want to happen here. The *one* thing. Livvie hadn't had the easiest time at school the past few years in DC. She can be an idiosyncratic kid—it was her habits, her little tics, like the way she arranged her desk—and this was what we loved about her. They were the things that made her *her*. But kids are cruel.

Max looks at me, a bereft expression on his face, then shifts in his seat toward his sister. That thing they say about twins? How they can feel each other's every pain and emotion? I absolutely believe it, having seen the way my two interact. Max puts his hand out to touch Livvie's arm, gingerly, like he's touching a pan to see if it's hot. "Liv, what is it?" he says. *Sweet Max*, I think, our eyes meeting.

She glares at him. "It's nothing!" she snarls. "Just . . . just *stop!*"

"Livvie, it's obviously not *nothing*," I say, my voice as soothing as I can make it. I hook a finger into the top of the tissue box on the passenger seat and pass it back to her.

Several slow, agonizing seconds pass. "Honey, please talk to us."

"Can we just go?" she says.

"*Honey*," I plead. "Let me help."

"It's just these stupid girls, Mom," she finally says, taking a tissue to dab at her eyes. "Nothing new. You wouldn't get it."

My chest tightens, a swell of anxiety blooming in my chest. "I think I would," I say. *I know I would.*

"Was it Brittany?" Max asks.

"Brittany?" I say. *Eva's Brittany?*

"She's like—" Max wiggles his fingers, trying to come up with the words. "She's like the most popular girl in school, I guess. She's like the queen bee or whatever."

"Oh." I raise an eyebrow. "I see. Livvie, is something going on with you and Brittany?"

She scowls at me like this is the most ridiculous thing she's ever heard in her life. "No!" she says. "It's just . . . it's really stupid, Mom." She takes another tissue from the box and wipes her nose.

"It can't be stupid if it's upsetting you this much," I say. "Tell me what happened."

She purses her lips and looks at me, her big brown eyes rimmed in red. "You know my friend Lauren?"

"Of course," I say. "The one you've told me so much about."

She frowns, looking out the window like she'd rather be anywhere but here.

What did I say? I think, watching her, my heart thumping behind my ears. *What should I say?*

"You promise you won't say anything to anyone?" she finally says, her gaze still focused on the parking lot.

"Of course," I say.

"Brittany and her friends walked by me and Lauren this morning when we were sitting in the hall before homeroom. Brittany's friend Margo has a locker across from ours, and they were stand-ing there together, and they said very loudly how appropriate it was that 'the new girl'—that's me—would become friends with Lauren." She starts to tear up again.

"What do they mean?" I ask, trying to keep my voice gentle despite the frustration building just under my skin. It figures that Eva's kid would be a jerk.

She starts to cry again. "They called us the Outcast Society, Mom! That's what I heard her say!"

"Oh, honey." *Those little bitches*, I think, reaching back to rub her leg again. She hides her face, as if she doesn't want me to see her hiccuping sobs.

"They don't like Lauren because she . . . well, her family's a little different. They live outside of town, not in some big fancy house like the one Brittany lives in—I know because it's all she ever talks about. Being the 'mayor's daughter' or whatever."

"Lauren's an Other," Max adds.

"A what?" I ask.

"An Other," Max says innocently. "It's what people call some of the kids who don't live in Greyhill. The ones who are bused in from outside of town."

"They mean the poor kids," Livvie says. "The scholarship ones."

"Oh, really?" I say, the heat starting to prickle along my ears. *Others, huh?*

"Those girls are stupid," Livvie says. "They make fun of any-one who's not exactly like them."

"I see," I say.

"I really don't care what they think. It's just so . . ."

"It's frustrating," I finish for her. *So, so frustrating*, I think. *I remember it like it was yesterday.*

She nods.

"I'm sorry, honey."

She looks out the window, my words falling flat. Saying "sorry" has so often been my default with the kids when I don't know what to say or do, but *sorry*, sincere as it may be, isn't proactive. It doesn't help. If anything, my wobbling *sorry* just puts an exclamation point on the problem. *I'm sorry kids are assholes, honey. I'm sorry I have to work, honey. I'm sorry we moved here, honey, and that I didn't have the foresight to realize that this kind of thing would only be amplified in a smaller place.* That's all the *sorry* says. We both know it. I think of Susannah, who was right when she told me the other day that . . . *what was it* . . . that people never take a woman seriously who's always apologizing.

Livvie looks down at her lap, picking at her fingernails the way she does when she's upset.

"Honey, you know what we've always said when people are mean, right?"

"Kids act mean when they don't feel good about themselves," Max says.

"That's right," I say.

"But," Livvie swallows. "Brittany doesn't feel bad about herself. I'm sure of that. She's a total bragger."

"Yeah, well." *So is her mother*, I think.

"Can we please just go?" Livvie says. "I really don't want to be here anymore today."

"Yes," I say. "Of course."

I turn around and start the car. Why can't things be as easy as they were when they were little, when the things that hurt them could be fixed with a Band-Aid and a kiss and the promise of a cookie? *What are the words that will make this all better?* I look at Livvie's face through the rearview mirror.

"There's nothing to say, Mom," Livvie says, as if reading my mind. "It just is what it is."

The car is silent, both kids staring out their windows, and I get a sinking sense in my stomach that feels remarkably like regret. *What's going on in there?* I think, watching Livvie stare blankly out the window. *What are you thinking?*

We are just pulling into the driveway when out of the corner of my eye, I see Diane and Bradley's front door fly open. My mother-in-law emerges from the house, waving her hands.

She has such a knack for showing up at the most inopportune moments that it wouldn't surprise me to discover that she's put a GPS tracker under my Subaru.

"Max?" Livvie's voice finally punctures the heavy silence that accompanied our ride home.

"Huh?" I hear the soft thump of him closing his book, a huge hardcover compilation of Far Side cartoons that he's been carrying around everywhere lately.

"Do you want to play Xbox later?" she says, her voice back to its normal timbre. I look at her in the rearview mirror as I turn off the car. She seems . . . *fine-ish?* I sit back in my seat. "After we finish our homework?"

"Yeah, sure," he says, opening the car door.

"Hell-o-*ooh!*" I hear Diane's greeting, cheery and light, the voice she reserves for Cole and the kids.

"Hi, Grandma," the kids call out.

When I get out of the car, she walks right past me. A more generous person would say that she's just so excited to see the kids, but I know better.

"Hi, Diane," I say.

"Livvie!" Diane says, looking up at her on the front stoop. "Honey, are you coming down with something? Your face is all red."

Shit.

"No, Grandma, I'm . . ."

I see her face start to crumple.

"Excuse me, Diane." I hurry up the front steps and stick my key in the lock, then push open the door so the kids can escape.

"Is she okay?" Diane calls after me.

"She's fine," I say. "Normal tween drama."

"Are you sure about that, Elizabeth?" she asks. "What happened?"

"I have it under control," I say, putting my hand on the doorknob to indicate that I'm done.

She lowers her chin, nodding like she's deigning to give her permission. "Okay," she says. "Fair enough."

I take a step into the house.

"Listen, I just wanted to tell you . . . ," she says. "The crows . . . they can get really bad this time of year, and they love to get into the garbage. Go to Perkins and pick up a few bungee cords to secure the lids to the trash cans before you pull them out to the street. Remember, the trash collectors come every Monday."

"Got it," I say, waving as I start closing the door. *We've been pulling the trash cans to the curb every week with no problem*, I think. *Don't exactly need the reminder, thank you very much.*

"And by the way," she says, starting down the driveway. "You might be the only person in Greyhill who locks their door when they leave the house, do you know that?" She chuckles. "What is it you have in there that's so valuable?"

"Your grandchildren," I say, and take another step inside before I can be tempted to tell her that she's the real reason I lock the door. "Have a good evening, Diane."

"You do the same, Elizabeth," she says.

Later, after the kids are in bed and Cole has his feet up in the family room watching a Thursday-night college football game, I retreat to my office with a second glass of wine, intending to check email and maybe distract myself by working on my questions for my meeting with Susannah tomorrow.

But instead, just a minute or two after scanning my email inbox, I find myself typing an old, familiar name into Google. *Tilly Robertson.*

I was fourteen when I started as a day student at the Oak Hill School, the exclusive private boarding school two towns over from mine. I'd won a full scholarship, given annually to two kids in our county who showed "significant academic achievement and tremendous promise." I remember the words exactly because they hung over our kitchen table. When Dad handed me the acceptance letter that night over dinner, the envelope was already torn open. He confessed he couldn't help himself. He'd picked it up off the dashboard of his mail truck and read it several times over the course of his route that day. Mom jumped up from her chair and promptly took down the bronze-gold frame that held a picture of a wildflower bouquet I'd ripped from *Good Housekeeping* many years earlier. She stuck the letter inside, hanging it between the pictures of Ted Williams and JFK that were displayed over our table as if they were members of our family.

The one good thing about Oak Hill, aside from the fact that the education I got there helped get me into Dartmouth, was the uniforms. I loved the uniforms, and not because there was anything special about them. They were plain navy-blue sweaters, oxford shirts, and khaki skirts, but they gave the impression that we were all on an even playing field. My classmates were the children of senators and bankers, ambassadors and CEOs. They came from the Upper East Side and Beacon Hill, Greenwich and Darien, the Main Line. I knew this because they told me.

The uniforms helped me blend in, at least a little bit, at first. Everyone knew that I was local and didn't board, but I could at least pretend it didn't matter. The crest on my shirt felt, in a weird way, like proof of my belonging.

And then came Tilly Robertson.

It was my freshman year. Early November. I was sitting at the end of one of the long wooden tables in our beautiful oak-paneled dining hall, the portrait of the school's founder looking down on me. I opened my brown paper bag, pulled out my ham sandwich, and took a bite.

"Oh my God!" Tilly screamed like somebody had just dumped a bucket of water over her head. She was the heir to the Isadore Robertson cosmetics company fortune. Dad had slipped one of their lipsticks into Mom's stocking one year, and she'd hemmed and hawed over keeping it. *Eighteen dollars for a lipstick?!* She ultimately kept it but never actually used it. I know because I snuck into the bathroom sometimes when she was at work, dug it out of the plastic cosmetics case she kept under the sink, and tried it on. It was called Sugarspun.

"Oh my *God!*" Tilly repeated. She of the long, shiny hair, coltish limbs, and acid tongue. "That is *so fucking disgusting.*"

"What?" I managed, swallowing the glob of ham and mayonnaise and American cheese that had caught in my throat.

Her eyes were on my sandwich. At first I assumed she must be talking about the ham itself—maybe ham was wrong. Or maybe it was the zit that had bloomed on my chin overnight that I had tried for twenty minutes that morning to cover up but had done a shitty job because I couldn't resist popping it first, so it was weird and crusting and oozy.

"Are you *actually* eating that?" she said. The entire room was silent, people smirking, some laughing. I was burning up, a knot twisting inside me from my neck to my toes.

I dropped it onto the table as soon as I saw the offending edge, the crust frosted with green mold, which I obviously hadn't noticed when I made the sandwich under the dim glow of the light above our kitchen sink the night before. My mouth hadn't touched that part of the bread (thank God), but even so, and all these years later, looking at Tilly's picture on my computer screen, I can taste it. Acrid, sour, nauseating.

I shift in my seat and take another sip of wine. Tilly is the creative director of Isadore Robertson now. Her husband runs a hedge fund. She has three beautiful children. They live in Manhattan. And she made me an outcast, an *other*. I take another sip of my wine. My face feels as hot as it did when it happened, almost thirty years ago.

I click away from her picture and type a web address into my browser. I don't have to dig deep to know that everything I've done since Oak Hill—the degree from Dartmouth, the fancy job, the homecoming-king husband—I've done to prove to the world, and myself, that I am more than those kids thought I could ever be. I would never admit it to anyone, but one of the worst aspects of my career falling apart in such a public way was the knowledge that those Oak Hill girls would probably see it. And say, *I always knew she was a loser.*

The page loads. Eva's post for today is about side tables. She just got a new one for their living room. It is acrylic—"Our room needed a *MODERN* edge," she has typed. She does a lot of all-caps and italics to emphasize her points. "And when I saw this one, I knew it would pair *PERFECTLY* with the rest of our decor." The table is $1,900 (of course she mentions this), from Restoration Hardware. It looks to me like nothing special.

I scroll down the page to where Eva has a short bio, along with a family picture. Brittany is an adorable girl, with freckles across her nose and the kind of natural highlights that could make a hair colorist a star. *Please be kind to Livvie*, I think, squinting at her smile. *Please be good to my girl.*

ELEVEN

My phone rings as I'm walking out the door to go to Esperanza for my second meeting with Susannah.

"Hey. It's Cindy," she says, smacking her gum. She talks to me like we've known each other for years, a quality that I like an awful lot.

"I was just heading over there," I say. "Is something wrong?"

"Nah. I'm glad I caught you, though. Her Majesty's sweet tooth is acting up. Can you meet at William's instead? I'll drop her off and do her grocery shopping while y'all chat."

"Sure," I say, though the truth is I'm disappointed. Since Susannah cut our house tour short last time, I was looking forward to seeing the rest of the estate.

When I get to the coffee shop, William is standing in his usual spot at the espresso machine. I scan the tables in the back. Susannah has not yet arrived. In fact, the place is empty.

"Well, if it isn't my favorite new regular," he says, wiping his hands on the cloth hanging in a neat rectangle from his waistband. "Do you want your usual?"

"Yes, please," I say, scanning the bakery case, which is loaded with his inventive pastries. A scone catches my eye: APRICOT AND PISTACHIO WITH VANILLA CRÈME DRIZZLE, the card reads. There are cupcakes and tarts, cookies of all shapes and sizes, and rows of beautiful, artfully made candies. The first time I came in here and started chatting with William, I couldn't believe it when he said he makes everything in the shop. He has help, of course—a young guy who William says he knows is just killing time until something better comes along, and a PhD student from UVA who comes in on the weekends—but his hands are in everything. I eye the sample plate on top of the glass display case—a dainty china platter of tiny, sticky squares—and take one for myself, popping it into my mouth like I don't want to be caught.

He turns from the espresso machine and hands me my latte in a paper cup. "What do you think of those?" he says, nodding toward the sample plate.

"Delicious," I say. "What is it?"

"It's a classic cheesecake," he says. "But I did a toffee-studded shortbread crust and drizzled it with caramel, some sea salt. What do you think? Too passé? Are we over caramel–sea salt as a combination? I mean, I feel like if there's a Starbucks drink with the same flavors, it's a sign I should stop."

"No!" I laugh, closing my eyes as I finish the bite. "*No*. We're not over it."

"Hey," he says. "The torte you were telling me about the other day . . . Where did you say it came from? I wanted to look it up the other night but couldn't find it."

"Dorie Greenspan," I say, sneaking another sample off the plate, rationalizing to myself that I didn't have breakfast. "Chocolate amaretti. You *have* to make it."

"Done," he says.

Of all the people I've met in Greyhill so far, William feels the most familiar. When I come into the shop, our comfortable chitchat feels like relief. So many of my social interactions in town involve explaining who I am, or where I'm from, or how I met Cole, or how our family is settling in. With William, I never feel like I'm being sized up, even when he's asking me questions about the parties I used to throw at the White House. He has no ulterior motive—he just wants to know what kind of food I served, how I set the tables, whether it's true that the president has an aversion to yellow foods (yes, with the exception of potato chips). In fact, he treats me as if I still have the job —or at least as if I still have some expertise—and getting to exercise that part of myself, a part I love and recognize, makes me feel so good that it practically brings tears to my eyes. It's like I'm carrying a secret, treasured thing in my pocket—a precious-to-me seashell, a sparkling piece of rock—and William is the only one who gets to see it.

"So what are you up to today?"

"Actually," I say, raising the coffee cup in my hand, "I should have told you before you gave me the paper cup. I'm meeting someone here."

"Oh?" he says.

"Yes," I say. "And I think I want a treat." I scan the display case. "One of the scones," I say, tapping my finger against the case. "Oh!" I put my hand out to stop him. I've noticed a tray of classic peanut-butter cookies—the kind with the fork-tine crisscross—in the display case. "Let me take two of those to go, too," I say, bending and pointing at them. They're Livvie's favorite.

"So who's your date?"

"Date?"

"Who are you meeting here?" He hands me the bag of cookies and I tuck them into my tote.

"Oh," I say, clearing my throat. "Susannah Lane."

"Mmmmm," he says, in a way that appears to mean something.

"What?"

"Oh, nothing," he says. "Just that my grandmother would roll over in her grave if she knew I was serving a Greyhill in here."

"What?" I say, my eyes going to the photo next to the cash register of his grandmother, Estelle, who founded the bakery. "*Why?*"

"Do you know how she and Teddy got married?" he asks, turning back to his coffee machine. I watch him dump a batch of used grounds into the canister he keeps on the counter, and remember how he told me a few weeks ago that he uses them for his garden.

"They eloped at city hall in New York," I say, remembering the photo I saw online of Susannah in a simple white minidress with elbow-length sleeves, a single gardenia tucked behind her ear.

"Yes, but they were going to get married *here*," he says. "At Esperanza. And then Susannah changed her mind at the last minute because she didn't want to come back. My grandmother told me all about it. She worked for them for a while, before she opened the bakery."

"What did she do? Cook, I assume?"

"Yes." He nods. "Now, I don't want to say anything ugly—Susannah has been pleasant enough the few times she's come in here—but the Greyhills, from what I know, were awful people. So *stingy*, despite all their money, and they treated their help like trash."

"Ugh," I say, thinking of the way Susannah spoke of her mother when we first met and how she wanted to get rid of all her parents' old furniture, calling it an *exorcism*. "That's too bad."

"Oh, yeah. They employed plenty of people up at Esperanza—Susannah's parents threw a ton of parties up there, for every little occasion—and everyone said it was the worst place to work." He glances at the door and leans across the counter to me. "They were drunks, both of them. *Bad* ones."

"How have I not heard this?"

"It's just common knowledge, m'dear. People around here know about the Greyhills the same way they know not to speed on the stretch of Twenty-Nine between here and Culpeper. You just *know*."

"Hmm," I say. "Let me ask you something, William, since you and I are the only ones in here. Why do *you* think Susannah stayed away from here for so long? Could it be because of her relationship with her family?"

"Oh, who knows," he says. "Probably a little bit of that, and a little bit because of Henrietta."

"Henrietta Martin," I say. "Yes. That must have been difficult, losing her best friend."

He laughs. "Oh, Bess."

"What?" I say.

"Sometimes I forget how new you are here."

"What do you mean?" I say, a little miffed by his tone. "What am I missing?"

"Something you ought to know before you start writing about her."

"So you know about the article, then?" I say, certain I haven't told him about it.

"Of course I do, Bess," he says. "Carol was in here yesterday with Eva. They told me all about it. *Washingtonian* magazine?"

"No," I say, feeling prickles on my skin at the mention of Eva's name and the fact that she was talking about me. "The *Washington Post* Sunday mag. So what is it that I need to know?"

"Just that there are lots of people in and around Greyhill who've always thought that Susannah might have had something to do with how Henrietta died."

"What?" I say, feeling a flutter in my stomach. "No! She was her best friend."

"Well, they were quite different. Susannah was the mayor's daughter, Henrietta came from a broken home. Her mother—" He glances toward the door. "She *killed herself* when Henrietta was just an infant. And then, after Henrietta died, her father spent years trying to convince people around town that it was some sort of foul play."

"And nothing happened?"

"Well, nobody was going to listen to him," he says, like this should be obvious.

"Why?"

"Well, his wife had died, then his daughter . . . Tragic, right? I think people wanted to keep him at arm's length, like he had some kind of disease. And also, he was just some mechanic, lived out of town, toward Madison."

"What does that have to do with anything?" I ask, not liking this side of William.

"Oh, nothing," he says. "Anyway, I'm just telling you what people say. Doesn't mean there's any truth to it."

The bell chimes over the door.

"Any truth to what?" Susannah herself says, stepping inside.

My heart lurches. *Has she heard us?* Through the storefront window, I see Cindy standing by her car. She waves to me and I wave back, plastering a smile on my face.

"Any truth to the rumor that Bess and Cole are going to turn the Greyhill Inn into a dance club. Lots of drugs and hookers. Very provocative, very permissive," William says, laughing at his own joke.

"God, I wish you would," Susannah says. "Breathe some life into this dusty place."

She hobbles toward me with the cane. "Good morning, Bess," she says, removing the purple fedora that matches her coat and handing it to me. As I take it, I hear William laugh to himself. Underneath her coat, she's wearing a lilac silk shirt, lavender pants. *Feeling purple, apparently,* I muse, scanning her outfit and thinking that she almost looks like a member of the Red Hat Society, albeit a couture version.

"Let's find a quiet place to sit," she says, walking toward the back of the shop. "William, do you have Earl Grey?"

"I do."

"Bring me one of those and a cookie of some sort. Please."

"I will. Any particular flavor?"

"Something like a gingersnap. No chocolate. Teddy only ever ate chocolate desserts, and I swear, if I never see another one, that will be fine with me."

Once we're seated at a table in the far corner, I take my notebook from my bag.

"Oh *no*," Susannah says, scowling at it. "We don't have to jump right into homework, do we?" William sets a china cup of tea and a cookie in front of her and she nods at it, then reaches up to pat his arm. "Thank you, dear."

I put down my pencil. "No, of course not."

"So what did you and Cole do last evening?" she says, resting her chin in her hand. "Let me live vicariously through you two."

"I hate to disappoint you." I laugh, remembering how I'd gone up to bed shortly after my web search, leaving Cole to finish watching his game. "We didn't do anything. School night for the kids." I think of Livvie, who will be heading to lunch before too long, and feel a tug in my chest, worrying for her. She barely touched her toast this morning, and she hardly said a word when I dropped her off at school.

"Of course, the children," Susannah says, dropping a sugar cube, and then another, into her tea.

"I would imagine that you and Teddy had a lot of exciting nights out together?" I say.

She laughs in a way that surprises me. "Yes, *lots* of them." She rolls her eyes. "I had to make my own fun, honestly. Teddy was too busy making money."

I glance over at William, who is back behind the counter and busy humming to himself, though I have a feeling he's listening to our every word.

"How did you and Teddy meet, anyway?" I ask. "I'm trying to remember what I read, but I can't seem to recall . . ."

"Now that's a story," she says, pushing her plate toward me. "Have some." She turns in her seat. "William!" she shouts.

"Yes, ma'am?" he says, walking down the length of the counter.

"This gingersnap is to die for!" She pushes the plate toward me again.

"Oh, that's okay," I say, gesturing to my scone. "I have plenty here."

"Oh, come on. I can't stand a woman who doesn't like to eat."

"In that case . . ." I lean over and break off a bite.

"So," she says. "To answer your question . . . Teddy."

"Yes."

"Well, I ran off to New York right after I graduated from Draper. Just days after. Surely you already know about that from Bradley?"

I didn't, but I nod, playing along.

"My parents didn't speak to me at *all* for almost a year after I left. I was supposed to attend Sweet Briar that fall, marry your father-in-law, have his babies." She smiles at me, her expression turning wistful. "But what could I say?" She sighs. "I wanted *adventure*."

Or escape? I think, wondering about what William just told me. If my father-in-law was truly in love with Susannah, he must have been heartbroken about her leaving him—if that's the way it really went down, and if what she's told me about the plans they made for their future are accurate . . . Bradley has always been so open and easy with me, but we've rarely discussed anything particularly personal about his life. Could there be a tactful way for me to ask him?

"So off to New York I went!" she says.

"And I think I remember that you became a flight attendant shortly after you got there?"

"No, honey, I was a *stewardess*. That's what they called us. For Pan Am. Fortunately, I got fired after just two months."

"Oh no!" I say, trying to imagine her pushing a beverage cart. "Why?"

"They had ludicrous rules. I wore an unacceptable shade of lipstick once—Wine and Roses, I *loved* it, a *gorgeous* deep red—

but they wanted me in demure pink. And then—get this—I had the audacity to work a flight without a girdle."

"How did they know?" I ask.

"They checked!" she says.

"No!"

"Yes, it's true. They employed people to fly on the planes and spy on us. I guess I leaned over to pour someone a drink! Those uniforms were *so* short! And the guy who figured it out—he must have been looking *very* closely—wrote me up. I also wore a black bra under my uniform once. A big no-no."

"You've got to be kidding me."

"I'm not," she says. "So I got fired, which was fine. Good riddance. And my roommate—her name was Marcy, she was from Philadelphia—she had a cousin who worked at the Oak Room at the Plaza. They needed a cocktail waitress, and I remembered reading in *Life* magazine that Truman Capote and Gore Vidal lunched there. That was good enough for me."

"So you got a job there?"

"Yes. A life-changing one. When I went for the interview, I offered to make the bar manager my perfect martini. I'd been making them for my parents every night since I was thirteen. Gin, straight up, extra olives for my mother. Served daily at precisely six o'clock. In the garden if it was spring or summer, in the library in fall and winter."

"Thirteen?" I say, imagining Max and Livvie wielding cocktail shakers.

She shrugs. From the look on her face, I can tell she's enjoying my reaction to her story. She knows it's a good one, and it's obvious she's told it many times before.

"I almost had to beg that manager to let me make him a drink.

'We need a cocktail waitress, not a bartender,' he said. He had a craggy face, the kind of greasy skin that almost looks plastic, you know? Anyway, it didn't matter to me that they only really expected me to be able to balance a tray and bat my eyelashes at the customers, which was child's play after accomplishing the same at forty thousand feet. I knew I would get the job if I could make him a drink."

"And you did."

"Of course," she says. "And a week later, on my second shift, I walked across the room to deliver a bottle of Coca-Cola to a corner table." She smiles and pauses, picking up her spoon to stir her tea. "The customer had on a beautiful navy suit. Custom-made, I knew, because my father wore custom-made suits by Georges de Paris, that legendary tailor in Washington who did all the politicians for decades?"

"I don't . . ." I shake my head.

"Oh, he did LBJ, Gerald Ford . . . I think he even made the suit that Reagan was wearing when he got shot . . ." She stops and shakes her head, looking like she's just remembered something she wishes she hadn't. "My father . . ." She grimaces, like saying the word burns her mouth. "He was just the mayor of this dinky town, but he had quite the *superiority complex*." She flares her nostrils, and I sneak a look at William across the room, wondering whether he's heard her more or less confirm what he just told me about the Greyhills.

"Anyhow, I walked across that room with that Coca-Cola, the tray balanced just so on my hip, and I could tell that the customer I was serving was handsome before he even turned around. He was broad shouldered. Smelled *fantastic*. Like leather and money, you know what I mean?" she says, giggling. "He was a *man*."

I start laughing along with her, totally amused. None of my friends ever talks this way about men. In fact, now that I think about it, we usually just complain about them. *You won't believe what my idiot husband did today . . .*

"As I put the drink down, bending from the knees, just as I'd been taught to at the airline," she says, pointing a finger at the sky, "he shifted toward me and we locked eyes—he wore those big tortoiseshell glasses even then—and I knew, *immediately*, that my life was about to change."

"It was Teddy Lane."

"The one and only," she says. "Not that his name meant a thing to me at the time."

"That's a great story."

"It was *meant to be*," she says, mocking a dramatic tone like the voice-overs in movie trailers.

"I would say so."

"And the bonus," she says, now deadpanning, "is that once my mother found out who he was, she acted as if I had just summited Mount Everest. She was so proud of me." She lowers her chin. "She'd never been before, I can tell you that."

"Proud of you?"

She breaks off a piece of her cookie and dunks it into her tea. "My mother was the kind of woman who considered marrying a rich man an accomplishment. A *supreme* accomplishment. My older sister, Margaret, was the focus of my mother's attention up until that point, but marrying Teddy! It was the one thing I did right."

"Tell me about your sister," I say, remembering how I'd scrawled a reminder to myself to ask Susannah about her after I saw a brief mention of her online the other day. "Were you close?"

Susannah rolls her eyes. "She was six years older than me, did everything exactly the way my mother expected. Always had her nose stuck in a book, graduated from Hollins, enjoyed *embroidery* and *polite conversation*." She sticks her tongue out like this disgusts her. "But then we found out she had ovarian cancer. She died shortly after I married Teddy."

"I'm so sorry," I say, though I don't seem to need to be. Susannah's acting as if she's talking about the death of a pet frog she kept in a shoebox for a few days, not her only sibling.

She shrugs. "It was a long time ago," she says.

"She never married?"

"Margaret?" She laughs. "Oh, no!"

"What?"

"This is terrible to say," she says, looking up at the ceiling, almost as if she's speaking to someone up there. "But I got the looks in the family. Margaret . . ." She shakes her head. "Anyway, that's how we met, Teddy and I. I never would have expected it. My original plan, of course, was to marry Bradley. Would have been *quite* a different life." She laughs in a way that feels like a slight. *Does she mean it to be?*

"The money with Teddy was, of course, a nice side bonus," she says. "Very nice. But all of that . . ." She pops the last bit of cookie in her mouth and chews quickly, like she's trying to choke it down. "Easy come, easy go." She busies herself brushing crumbs off her lap, and when she looks up at me, I notice that her eyes are shimmering with tears.

"You must miss him."

"Teddy?"

"Yes," I say, wondering who else she'd think I meant.

"I do, I do," she says strangely, like she's trying to convince herself. "I really do.

"Anyway, enough about me!" she says, pushing away her plate. "Tell me about you and Cole. I want to know how *you* met."

"Oh," I say, shifting in my seat. I don't know how much time we have, and I'd like to get to the questions I'd prepared, or at least keep the focus on her. "Well . . . We met on the banks of the Potomac River," I say, laughing at my half-witted attempt to make my story sound as colorful as hers.

"The banks of the river?" she says, her *river* sounding just slightly like *rivah*, the way Bradley says it. "That sounds . . . rustic. Not what I pictured for a metropolitan girl like you."

"Ha!" I say. "You have a lot to learn about me."

"Even better," she says, rubbing her hands together like she's warming them up.

"So a mutual friend—actually, as a matter of fact, the woman who assigned me this story—introduced us. She arranged for a group of us to take a kayak tour of the Potomac one night after work, for her birthday."

"How outdoorsy," she says, smirking.

"I suppose," I say, remembering how Cole, whom I'd known for all of four minutes, had offered to help me clasp my life preserver, and how Noelle had rolled her eyes and laughed at him when I told him, quite pointedly, that I didn't need any help. He redeemed himself when we started talking out on the water, and I discovered that he was actually quite sweet. He took me to dinner a week later. He was so old-fashioned—pulling out my chair, waiting for me to sit before he would—and I was smitten by his charm, sure, but also found it a little funny, because I'd never met anyone who acted that way before. Most of the guys I'd dated up to that point thought that being gentlemanly meant not spilling their beer on you. Cole was so earnest and mannered, in fact, that my girlfriends and I joked that he seemed like the kind of everyday hero Tom Hanks might someday play in a movie.

"So why did you marry him?" Susannah asks, as if reading my thoughts.

"Why did I . . . Oh." I shrug. "Well . . . I guess it's hard to articulate. I just knew he was the one. We were best friends . . . *are* best friends."

"And how did he propose?" she says, nodding toward my left hand as I take a sip of my coffee. "I want to hear what you thought when you saw that ring! Did he tell you it was his grandmother's right away?"

"Honestly," I say, my mind casting back, "I don't remember if he told me it was hers at that moment. Actually . . ." I laugh, trying to decide whether to be honest. "When he proposed, I'd just vomited on the sidewalk."

"What?" she says, loud enough that out of the corner of my eye, I see William turn to check on us. "*No!*"

I nod. "We'd just eaten at a little Greek place in Old Town Alexandria and we were walking along the water. I don't know if it was the smell of the Potomac or the souvlaki I'd just eaten that set me off." *Everything was making me throw up back then.*

"Oh my!"

"He took it in stride," I say. "In fact, he helped me clean myself up. With the sweater he was wearing, no less! And I figured, if he still wanted to marry me after that . . ."

"He sounds like he's quite the gentleman."

"Yes," I say.

She gestures for my hand again, and I hold it out to her. As she examines it, studying it like an appraiser in a jewelry shop, I think back to a sweltering August night a couple of weeks before Cole proposed. Nervous doesn't begin to explain how I felt. My legs were so jiggly that I thought I might sink into the linoleum floor outside Cole's apartment. The hallway reeked from the Chinese place on the ground floor, and I could hear the *ER* theme song coming from somewhere in the building. He opened the door in a sweaty T-shirt and gym shorts. He'd just gone for a run. I hadn't called ahead to tell him I was coming.

"I'm pregnant," I said, the words barely out of my mouth before I started sobbing.

He didn't say, "What?" or "How?" or anything like that. He put his shock and alarm aside, and instead, right in character, he smiled at me gently and held out his arms. "Come here," he said, pulling me close. He brought me inside and sat me down on his saggy couch and got me a glass of water. That's the real moment I fell in love with his Boy Scout goodness. That's when I knew I would marry him.

Three months later, we did, in a small event space on Capitol Hill. The fear had faded, the excitement of what we were about to embark on taking over. I was barely showing (my belly was probably smaller than it is now, if I'm being honest), but all night Diane kept putting a glass of champagne in my hand, as if it might lead people off the trail. Everyone knew, of course. My dad kept telling everyone his joke about how he'd tried to convince me to put little shotguns on the invitations.

Susannah releases my hand. "I remember the first time I met your father-in-law," she says suddenly.

"Oh?" I say.

"I was maybe five or six," she says, smiling at the memory. "At the church? Just across the street from the inn."

I nod.

"We were standing side by side, singing 'Jesus Loves Me' in a fidgety row in front of the altar. I was wearing a starched crinoline dress, my hair in waves because Margaret, my sister, had been tasked with pinning it up with rags the night before. Isn't it funny what you remember?"

I nod

"Anyhow, Bradley and I pretended to ignore each other all through elementary school. He was obsessed with whatever boys are obsessed with—baseball, fishing—and I was rattling around in that big silent house. But then! When I was fourteen, well . . . the world flew into high relief. Do you remember what that felt like, becoming a teenager? Children one day, and then . . ." She snaps her fingers. "It was like a bomb went off! Things were finally *happening*, you know?"

I nod my head again, but I'm thinking that I was never enthusiastic about the transition into my teen years, particularly once Tilly Robertson entered my life. The sandwich incident was the beginning of four long years of her treating me like a second-class citizen. I'd put my head down and prayed to get through it as quickly as possible.

"On the day that Bradley and I began," she says, her voice more animated than it's been all morning, which throws me off a little, "he was walking out of the inn. I had been at the library all afternoon with Henrietta, and I was carrying my shoes in my hand. They were new—patent-leather Mary Janes that my mother made me wear—and I had angry blisters all over my heels. He asked me if I was okay. I was crying."

"Crying?"

"Who knows why, but *he* was a gentleman, *too*—your Cole, he learned from one of the best—and he offered to drive me home. He had his father's car—some big boat, an Oldsmobile, something like that—and I remember waiting for him to come around the car and get in, smoothing my skirt over my knees and placing my shoes on top of my satchel in the space on the seat between us."

"It sounds like it's still very vivid for you," I say, wondering if it's the same at all for Bradley.

"Oh, yes!" she says. "How could I forget my first love? I asked him where he wanted to go as he started to pull away from the curb, and the question surprised him. He thought he was driving me home, of course, and said something about it being five o'clock. Wouldn't my mother wonder why I wasn't home for dinner?" She laughs. "I told him that my mother never wondered about me at all, for dinner or anything else.

"Well, he didn't know what to say to that! His own mother slapped him on the top of the head with her kitchen towel if he wasn't sitting at the table, his hands and fingernails scrubbed, ready to receive his plate when she set it down in front of him. I learned *that* soon enough. We were *often* late for his mother's dinners."

She laughs again, leaning across the table toward me like we're two gossiping girlfriends. I don't know what to think—it is awkward and, I'll admit, a little fascinating to listen to her talk about my father-in-law like this.

"On that first day, though, I told him to take me to the swinging bridge. He looked across the seat at me, and I could tell he was weighing his options. He flipped the car around and took that right onto Church Street. He's *never* been able to tell me no. Never, *never* could." She pauses now, looking at me with a steadiness that suggests that this is something she wants me to remember.

"So after that first day, Bradley and I were together every day, usually going to the bridge at first, wading in the creek, catching tadpoles and peeling those slick, loathsome leeches off each other's calves. The first several times he took me there, we hardly talked at all. We just walked across the bridge, over and over, me first and then him, back and forth, back and forth. I could tell he liked being with me. I certainly liked being with him. He was all I thought about from the moment my eyes popped open in the morning until I put my head on my pillow at night."

"Ugh." I can't help it, I shiver, and she laughs.

"Oh, don't be so childish!" she says. "These are some of the best memories of my life! We were *so* in love. It was like something out of a fairy tale! It really was."

"I'm sorry," I say, amused by her doggedness about this. "It's delightful to hear about, but it's just hard to picture my father-in-law . . ."

"Oh, I know," she says, putting her hand over mine. "I get it. Especially with a wife like Diane." She widens her eyes. I keep a straight face, though there's a part of me that wants to shake my head along with her. "Anyhow, I don't mean to make you uncomfortable," she says. "But it's important for you to understand, Bess, if you're going to write about me and my relationship to Greyhill, that I had a *very* strange upbringing."

I nod. *Now we're getting somewhere.* "How so?"

"Well . . . I was the mayor's daughter, so people in town were always watching me. At least, that's the feeling I had. I'm sure I was made more insecure by the way my mother treated me. My hair was so white, even lighter than this thing I do now with a bottle," she says, pulling at the ends. "And my eyes were so dark. My grandmother in Richmond was always saying, *'Those eyes are not from our side! Is that girl part Gypsy?'* What a bitch she was. No wonder my mother became who she did."

"What do you—" I start, wanting to know more about this apparent mommie dearest.

"No, no," she says, tapping the table. "Here's what I want to tell you." She leans in. "People were always watching me, but Henrietta and Bradley were the only ones who *saw* me, you know? Once Bradley and I were together, I became more myself. You're not supposed to say that now about a man, not when you're a woman like me who's lived long enough to see some things, but it's the truth. Those two were the first people in my life who behaved as if I was someone worth loving, and there was something specific about Bradley's validation that gave me a confidence I hadn't had before. You're not supposed to say that, either, but it's also true."

"No, I understand," I say, thinking that it's both sweet and sad. Heartbreaking, in a way.

"Coming back here hasn't been easy, because . . . well . . ." I see her start to tear up again. "The memories are everywhere, and Henrietta's gone, and your father-in-law—well, he might as well be, too. We haven't really known each other in years, you know. *Years.*"

I nod as if in agreement, but the way she says it, it's strange . . . it's a little too angry, almost like an incrimination.

"One of my favorite memories of Bradley and me—I was thinking about it just a little while ago, as we were driving here to meet you—is of the two of us throwing coins in the fountain. We made up these silly rules. We said that the wish was especially likely to come true if we were able to hit my great-grandfather's face." She laughs.

"Your great-grandfather's—?"

"The statue of him, in the center of the fountain."

"Ah, of course," I say, laughing, remembering how Max says that Clement Greyhill looks like Teddy Roosevelt.

"We made so many wishes, Bradley and me. Henrietta, too. He really *never* mentioned her to you? Not *once*?"

"Nope," I say.

"Hmm," she says, and starts stirring her tea. I look over at William, thinking of what he told me a little while ago, the rumor about Susannah being somehow involved.

"Can I ask you something?" I say, emboldened by the candor with which she's been speaking for the past few minutes.

"Of course," she says. "Anything at all."

"Your move back here hasn't been easy. You had the accident. There's the drama with the land. I have to ask, given the . . ." I pause, trying to find the gentlest way to say it. "Given everything I've read about the life you had back in New York, are you happy you returned to Greyhill?"

She sits back in her chair, a solemnity falling over her face, and I worry that I've misread our newfound chumminess and crossed a line. "What does it matter?" she says finally. "There was nothing left for me in New York. In a way, there had never been anything."

"What do you mean?" I say. From the looks of it, she had everything anyone could possibly want in New York.

She stares at me, long and hard, more pointedly than she has yet. "Have you ever seen the dioramas at the Museum of Natural History, in New York?" she says. "The Hall of North American Mammals?"

"No," I say, curious to see where she's going. "But I've been to the natural history museum in DC, of course. The Smithsonian."

"Yes," she says. "Well, then, you know what I'm talking about. Our apartment was across Central Park from the natural history museum. There was a time when I used to visit there quite often, sometimes twice a week. The dioramas are really something spectacular—I'm sure it's the same in DC. They *enthralled* me, for some reason. The habitats looked so real, you know? There was such detail in the way they were curated, and it was exciting to me that someone had been able to re-create each scene with such precision."

"I didn't know you had an interest in animals," I say, still confused.

"Well, I didn't. I *don't*," she says. "I never even had a pet. But I figured out after I'd been going there for a while—the security guards in those halls must have thought I was crazy, standing in front of the exhibits for hours on end in the little pastel suits Teddy liked me to wear—that I was so captivated by those dioramas because I felt a kinship with them."

"I'm sorry, I'm not following," I say.

"My relationship with Teddy was a textbook case of having

everything and nothing, Bess. It *looked* a certain way. It *looked* perfect, down to the last detail. But if you'd looked closely at me, you would have seen that behind the jewelry and the clothes and the houses and the parties, I was every bit as dead behind the eyes as the taxidermied wildlife in the museum."

"Oh, that's horrible," I say. "I never would have thought—"

She puts her hand out. "Of course you wouldn't have." She twists her lips to the side, as if she's considering something. "Things aren't always what they seem," she says. "But I'm here now, and I have to make the most of it."

"Well, that sounds like the right attitude," I say, though I know it's pat and though what I really want to do is ask her to tell me more.

"Forgive me, Bess. I know we're new friends, but I have to say this."

"What?"

"Couldn't *you* stand to learn the same thing?"

"I'm sorry?"

"We both have to make the most of it here in Greyhill, don't we?"

I nod, slowly, wondering what she's getting at.

"I don't want to offend you, dear. Please don't take it the wrong way. I just mean that you're new here, too. And maybe there's a reason we were brought together."

"Maybe," I say, though I'm not sure I believe her.

"One thing Teddy always said—one of the things I agreed with, at least—is that there are no accidents. Do you believe that?"

"I don't know that I do," I say, thinking of what happened to me at work. I'm also starting to notice that with only a few exceptions, Susannah's portrayal of her deceased husband is not exactly a flattering one, and she doesn't appear to be shy about it, either.

"Well, I believe it," she says. "In fact, at this point in my life, given everything I've been through, I might believe it more than anything." She smiles at me. "But who knows?" she says. "Maybe I just *have* to, because otherwise . . ."

"What?"

"Well, otherwise . . ." She looks up at the ceiling, shaking her head, and I can see the tears welling up again. "Otherwise, it's just a sad, sad story. Pathetic, really." She starts to laugh. "I mean, it all has to mean something, doesn't it?"

"Yes," I say, thinking that of all the things I expected Susannah Lane to be, pensive and melancholy was not among them. "I guess it does."

"I hope so," she says, dabbing at the corners of her eyes with her fingertip. "I really do."

TWELVE

After I help Susannah into Cindy's car, I stand on the curb and wave goodbye, smiling to hide my frustration with myself. I suppose it doesn't hurt for us to get to know each other, but over the course of the two hours we spent together *(two hours!)* I asked Susannah fewer than half the questions I'd written down ahead of time. I'd planned to get down to business, to ask her specifically about the land she's selling and why she's doing it, and also more about the house and what it's really like to be back here after so long.

I puff out my cheeks and pull my phone out of my coat pocket to check for . . . what, I don't know. An email. A text. A missed call. Something. I scan my inbox, where there's nothing new since I checked a few hours ago, and in the sun's late-morning reflection on the screen, I can just barely make out the dour scowl on my face. Immediately, I think of the First Lady.

"You're making that face," she would say, always startling me with her uncanny ability to see the frustration I tried my best to hide when some detail of our day was stressing me out.

I shove the phone back into my pocket and decide to walk

down the block for an impromptu visit to see Cole. We almost never saw each other during the workday in all our years in DC. *But this is the advantage of living in a small town, isn't it?* I think, lightening at the thought of it. Why not pop in on someone you love, just for fun, just because you feel like it? It's like living in Stars Hollow, the charming small town on *Gilmore Girls*, which Livvie has been watching on Netflix. Although, honestly, so far Greyhill feels a little more *Desperate Housewives*. The star character being me.

I turn the corner toward the inn, a blocky, moss-green Victorian home just off Maple Street with a wraparound porch studded with rocking chairs and a little brass sign by the front doors that reads EST. 1919. I eye the rocking chairs as I cross the porch, thinking that they need a coat of paint, and then squint at the mottled light fixtures on either side of the double doors, making a mental note to start bookmarking new options online. Cole and I have had lots of late-night conversations about the various ways we might modernize the inn, once he gets used to the business. My first priority once we're both ready, I've told him, is going to be the decor.

"Good morning!" I say to the woman at the front desk. Shawna, I think her name is, and make a mental note to confirm later. Like much of the staff who works at the inn, Shawna lives just south of downtown, in an enclave of small, sweet houses between Greyhill proper and Madison.

"Is it still morning?" she says, turning to check the time on the old chiming wall clock behind her.

"Oh, I guess not," I say, cursing myself again for the unproductive meeting with Susannah. "Is Cole around? I was just popping in to say hello."

"I believe he's back in his office with Mr. and Mrs. Warner," she says. "Go ahead back."

I can hear Bradley's distinctive, deep-belly laugh in the hall behind the lobby before I'm halfway to the office.

"Well, hello!" he bellows as I appear in the doorway. Cole is sitting behind the desk his father used for years, a huge, hulking oak thing that I'm glad will never come home with us, and his parents are sitting on the couch to my left where, I've been told, Bradley used to take a daily nap after lunch. "Isn't this a nice surprise."

"Bess!" Diane says, her eyes trailing over my outfit. I'm a bit more dressed up than usual today, in a casual dress and boots, though you would think from the way she's looking at me that I just slunk in wearing a beaded Diana Ross number. "You're looking . . . sharp. How was your meeting with Susannah?" she whispers, her voice low, like she's asking about a painful medical condition.

My eyes dart quickly to Cole, who smiles at me behind his hands, which are folded at his mouth, his elbows on the desk.

"Fine, fine," I say, deciding in the moment to leave it at that. I start to pull out the chair across from them and sit down, but Bradley hops up, insisting on doing it for me. He squeezes my shoulder after I sit.

"I heard you laughing, Bradley," I say, watching him settle back in next to Diane and thinking about what he must have looked like on the day he drove Susannah to the bridge. I imagine him the way he looks in the wedding photo that hangs in his and Diane's living room. "Must have been something good."

"Oh, it was!" he says, chuckling again. "Cole was telling us about some of the hotel trends he's been reading about in the trade magazines! Would you believe there is a hotel chain out of San Francisco that has psychotherapists on call for their guests?!" He slaps his knees. "*Therapists!* Like a room-service item! Can you believe it?"

"Did he tell you about the *pet* masseuses we read about?" I say, referencing an article Cole forwarded to me last week. "That was at a boutique hotel in Dallas, I think. They're available for a meager two hundred fifty dollars an hour, if your pet's nerves are shot from all the luxury. I looked at the hotel's website, and they have a separate in-room dining menu. *For pets.* It actually looked delicious."

"Ridiculous," Diane says, shaking her head and squeezing a small tube of hand cream into her palm like she's angry at it.

Cole clears his throat and taps out a few beats on his desk with his fingertips. "So . . ." He looks at me. "Those sorts of things obviously wouldn't work in Greyhill," he says, picking a pencil up and twirling it. He's so fidgety . . . *Is he nervous?* "But I do think we want to talk before too long about some ways we might, I don't know . . ." He looks at his dad. "Freshen things up around here."

"Freshen up?" Diane says.

Ah, I think. *So we're doing this now.*

"Well, yes," he says. "The inn is a well-oiled machine, Mom. It obviously works. But we might think about making some small changes, here and there, just to . . . *update* things a bit."

"Cole," his dad says. "I know what you're getting at. No need to beat around the bush with us. It's like we said when we gave you this job: the inn is yours, to do with what you'd like. No need to ask for our approval." He looks at me and winks.

"Thanks, Dad," Cole says.

"Just remember, this is a traditional place in a traditional town. We don't need any . . ." He shakes his head and throws his palms up into the air. "*Sushi bars* or things like that going up in the dining room."

I laugh a little. *Whoa . . . sushi bars!* But when I look over at Diane, she's making a face like we're sitting at a funeral. I look at the two of them, thinking that although I've always found it surprising that the two of them ended up together, it's even more so now, now that I've learned about Susannah.

"We wouldn't do anything crazy, of course," Cole says, meeting my eyes for a minute. "Understood."

"We just mean little things," I say, jumping in to help him. "Like, maybe, one idea Cole and I talked about was the possibility of finding ways to bring more of Greyhill into the inn."

"More of Greyhill into the inn?" Diane repeats in suspicious bewilderment. "What on earth does *that* mean? Why would people in Greyhill want to stay at the inn?"

"Well," I say. "We don't necessarily mean as guests. The inn could be"—I look to Cole, expecting him to take over, but he doesn't—"more of a gathering spot for people in town. We could host more regular events, like the ones you do at the holidays, for instance. And we could also showcase more of Greyhill in the way the inn feels," I say, referencing a conversation Cole and I had not long ago. "Like, what about, instead of those little chocolate coins the maids put on the beds at turndown, we used little candies from William's?"

"Oh, Bess," Diane spits. "You and the desserts! You really are *obsessed* with that place, aren't you?"

"*No . . .*," I say, feeling my face start to flush. *Why isn't Cole backing me up?* "But, okay, if you don't like that particular idea, what about, instead of the generic shampoos and soaps, we feature some of those handmade ones that woman sells at Persnickety, the gift shop down the street?"

"Linda Booth, you mean?" Diane deadpans, her mouth hanging open. "She is one of my closest friends, Elizabeth, and trust me, the woman can barely get her teeth brushed in time to open that store four days a week. Relying on her to supply all our guest rooms with her little dinky soaps would be a catastrophe." She looks at Bradley and shakes her head like I've just suggested we burn down the building and start over.

"Are you certain about that, though?" I say, feeling a sudden need to win this one. "It's not as if we have dozens of rooms," I say, glaring now at Cole to back me up. "It's just twenty-five. It's hardly the Ritz-Carlton."

"I beg your pardon!" Bradley jokes, putting a hand to his chest.

"*We . . .*" I say, pausing for effect for Cole's sake, "just thought it might be nice to give the inn a stronger identity attached to the town."

"Well, I think we showcase Greyhill just fine," Diane says, looking from Cole to Bradley. "But what do I know? I've only lived here for the past forty-nine years. And Bradley, well, he's only done this his whole life. But, Elizabeth, don't let us stop you. With all your experience . . ." She shakes her head disapprovingly and starts rifling through the handbag in her lap.

"Mom," Cole says. *Finally.* "You have to admit, the place could use a little sprucing up."

She rolls her eyes in a put-off way that reminds me of the twins.

"Well, I'm all for a fresh coat of paint on the place," Bradley says, slapping his knees before he stands up. He's clearly not interested in this conversation, and after decades running this place, I can see why. He retired to *retire*, not listen to his wife squabble with his daughter-in-law about work.

"But maybe even a little more than just paint, Dad . . . ," Cole says, eyeing me. "Like maybe we could do some more with the lobby."

I smile at him. This is his way of making it up to me. He knows that of all the things that bother me about the inn, the lobby is at the top of the list.

"Like what?" Diane says. "What's wrong with the lobby?"

"Nothing, exactly," I say, trying to moderate my tone to appease her now, though what I really want is to tell her that the lobby looks straight out of 1983, with the hunter-green trim, shiny honey-hued wood, and rose-patterned salmon carpet. All that's missing is some plastic ivy plants dangling over the top of the furniture. "But we could look through some design magazines together. We might find something a little—"

She stands, cutting me off. "Oh, Elizabeth," she says, waving her hand at me. "That's enough, really."

"Diane." Bradley snickers, reaching out and tugging at the hem of her sweater. She swats his hand away, scowling back at him, but then as soon as she looks away, he does it again, a little twinkle in his eye.

"Bradley!" she scolds, but this time she's grinning, looking at him like he's her untrainable puppy. "Cut it out!" Cole says they're a simple case of opposites attract—Bradley is like the valve that keeps her from exploding. "Elizabeth, it's clear you have plenty of opinions and that you've been giving a lot of thought to all this," Diane says, scooching past me toward the door. "I just had no idea that the inn we've devoted our entire lives to was in such disrepair."

"Disrepair? Oh, come on. I don't think I—" I turn to Cole, who, maddeningly, isn't coming to my defense. If this is how his mother reacts to these nothing suggestions, there's no telling how she'll feel about some of the bigger ideas we've talked about, like completely revamping the menu in the restaurant and adding a Sunday brunch with live music to bring in more weekend business. I glare at him. *What the hell?*

"Diane, come on," Bradley says, stepping in where my husband apparently can't. "The kids are entitled to do what they want. That's what we—"

"Enough!" she says, slicing her hand through the air. "Really." She adjusts her purse in the crook of her elbow. "I really have to go now. Bradley, I'll see you at home."

After she's gone, I turn back to my husband. "Cole," I say. "We'd talked about all of this stuff. Why didn't you say anything?"

"Oh, don't mind her, Bess," Bradley says. "You know how she gets. I must have forgotten to sneak her tranquilizer into her coffee this morning." He pats my shoulder as he passes my chair.

I turn back to Cole, giving him one more chance—it is *so* infuriating that he still, all these years later, does not have the nerve to stand up to his mother when it comes to me.

"We just might need to take it a little slower with her, that's all," he says.

Ugh. Here we go. I've heard this "treat her with kid gloves" argument a million times before. It's as if his mother is a wild animal we're trying to catch, and we have to approach her very, very carefully, not looking her in the eye or making any sudden movements, to avoid getting mauled.

"I barely said anything," I say, standing. I've had enough.

He shrugs. "She is who she is."

"All right," Bradley says impatiently, tapping the side of the doorframe with his hand. "Let's continue this later. Bess, you wanna walk out with me?"

"Yes," I say, looking back at my husband before I go, just to be doubly sure he knows how irritated I am. "So glad I stopped by to see you, Cole. This was lovely."

"Bess, come on— " he starts, but I walk off before he can continue.

"So, you headed home?" Bradley says, once we're out on the front steps. An older couple in windbreakers and thick-soled tennis shoes sit in rocking chairs to our left. Bradley waves and smiles at them, and I follow suit, thinking that I need to get used to the idea of being a hostess once I start putting in more time here. *If* I decide to start putting in more time here.

"I am," I say. "I have a few more hours until the kids are done for the day."

"Well, listen," he says. "Just for the record, I think your ideas are great. It's not lost on me that you have an expertise that could really be put to good use around here. If you want to, of course."

"Oh," I say, touched by his acknowledgment. "I appreciate that, Bradley. I really do."

"You'd be good at it," he says. "I'm sure of it. Diane, you know, she never wanted to be tied down to the business. She kind of made up her role as we went along, which suited both of us just fine. That's the beauty of this thing, you can do it however you want."

"Well, thank you, Bradley," I say. "That means a lot to me."

"I really mean it, Bess. Do this your way. Hell, don't do it at all if you don't want to!" he says. "But don't let Diane bother you. She's just never been good with change."

"Right," I say, thinking that that may be true, but I think the problem is more that she's never been good with me.

"Well, I'm off—" he starts.

"Wait!" I say, encouraged by our little heart-to-heart just now. "Can I talk to you about something?"

"Depends," he jokes.

"Another topic," I say. "Not about the inn . . ." I pause and swallow, suddenly nervous. "Somebody told me something . . . about Susannah . . . I'd never heard it before."

"Oh, lordy," he says, pursing his lips like he has a bad taste in his mouth. "Well, when it comes to her, it could be anything. What is it?"

I inch a step closer to him and lower my voice. "I'm sorry if I'm overstepping here. I know you two were involved—"

"Ha!" he interrupts, throwing his head back. "Bess, we were *involved* over fifty years ago. And I can hardly remember what I ate for breakfast this morning, so . . ."

Wow, I think. *Bradley's memory of their romance is a stark contrast from the way Susannah's carried on about it to me.* "I know, I know, which is why I feel silly saying anything, but . . ." I shift my weight from side to side, trying to find just the right words.

"What is it?"

"Do you think there's any truth in the rumor she had some-thing to do with what happened to her friend?"

"Her friend?" he says. "You mean Henrietta?"

I nod, feeling sheepish now. "Yeah."

"Oh, who knows?" he says, pulling a pack of cinnamon gum from his pocket and offering me a piece. "I certainly never bought all that."

"And you and Henrietta were friends?"

"Oh, sure," he says. "You know, town this small . . . It was horrible when she died. Real sad."

"I'm sure."

"But you've seen by now, Bess, how rumors fly around here. People just like to talk. Whether it's true or not really doesn't seem to matter much."

"I'm definitely beginning to see that," I say.

"And you thought the gossip mill was bad in Washington!" he says, reaching out and patting my shoulder.

"Yeah," I say, thinking that if almost anyone else said that to me, I would take it personally. "I sure did."

"How is she, anyway?" he asks.

"Susannah?" I say.

He nods.

"Honestly, between us, she seems pretty lonely," I say, think-ing of our conversation that morning, how she kept tearing up. "I feel kind of sorry for her."

"Mmm," he says. "You know, Bess, I'll be honest with you. She's always kind of been that way. Sort of a lonely person, with the way her family was."

I watch as he folds his gum wrapper into a tiny rectangle. "I could tell she was feeling nostalgic today," I say. "She told me a bunch of old stories."

"Is that right?"

"Mm-hmm," I say. "I heard all about how the two of you used to go to the swinging bridge. And about you tossing the coins in the fountain."

"Oh, my goodness!" He chuckles and gazes out toward the road. "Cricket . . ."

"*Cricket?*" I say. "You call her that?"

"Oh, it's just . . ."

"She told me about it!" I say, putting my hand to my chest. "The nickname from her dad!"

"Yeah . . . I guess . . ." He looks at me for just a split second before he looks away. I've never seen Bradley, unlike his wife, get ruffled about anything—he's steady as the beat on a metronome, one of the many reasons I've always found him so easy to talk to. But if I'm not mistaken, watching him now . . . he's flustered. And rather than make me uncomfortable, it's endearing, almost . . . adorable, discovering this part of him that I've never known anything about.

"She enjoyed telling me about all of it," I say. "I could tell."

"Well," he says, clearing his throat and pulling his Greyhill Grain and Feed ball cap out of his back pocket and squeezing it down onto his head. "It's good that you're there for her to talk to."

"You mean that?" I say, genuinely curious. "Because I've wondered what you thought about this whole thing. Diane clearly doesn't like it."

"Don't worry about her."

"I just worry about what . . .," I start. "I know that people around here aren't particularly fond of Susannah, and I don't know, with me being new, and now I'm spending time with her . . . Do you think it's a bad idea?"

"It probably won't help you around here," he says. "I'll be honest about that. But people will give you the benefit of the doubt. And if they don't, let me tell you, as someone who's lived here my whole life, you just can't worry about it too much."

"Okay, I just don't want to make anyone uncomfortable," I say, hoping he realizes that by *anyone*, I mean *him*.

He reaches around me, hugging my side. "You'll be fine, girl," he says. "You will."

"All right," I say, remembering what Susannah said about him earlier, how he made her feel so good about herself. "I'm sorry if this is weird for you, that all this stuff from your past is coming up. I didn't anticipate it."

He laughs as he starts down the front steps. "Ancient history, Bess," he says, waving goodbye over his head as he walks away. "Ancient history."

THIRTEEN

I'm spying.

I didn't mean to, but I am.

I came into the kitchen intending to make a cup of tea, but then I heard the girls talking through the open window over the sink. I am standing crouched over the basin, lifting my head just above the windowsill every few seconds to sneak a peek at Livvie and her friend Lauren, who came home with her from school today. I twist around to check the time on the clock on the stove. I told her mother, when we emailed the night before, that I would drop Lauren off at Bully's, where she works in the bakery department, around five thirty.

I take another look at the girls. Livvie sits straddling the bench next to the picnic table on the back patio, leaning on one elbow, watching as Lauren draws a curved line along her page of notebook paper. Somehow, when she curls her pencil up before she pauses, the line materializes into the top of a dolphin's back.

"You should totally be an artist when you grow up," Livvie says.

"I totally plan to," Lauren jokes back, smiling as she catches Livvie's eye.

"What should I draw next?" Lauren asks.

Livvie shrugs. "I don't know," she says, taking a sip from her water bottle. "How about a mermaid, to go with the dolphin?"

Lauren nods, her eyes widening a little at the sound of an idea she likes. "Okay," she says, starting to draw. "Wait! I have an idea! I'm going to make it, like, an evil mermaid!"

Livvie looks away, toward the back of the yard, where a squirrel is hopping along the rocking limb of one of the elms. I can tell that she is starting to tune out. She has that vacant, spacey look she sometimes gets at dinnertime, when Cole and I are talking about something grown-up and boring or Max starts going on about the intricacies of whatever sci-fi book series he's currently engrossed in.

My eyes fall back on Lauren's page. From what I can tell, it has morphed into a full-fledged sea battle scene, the mermaid with a pitchfork like the one carried by Neptune, the Roman god of the sea.

"So which evil sea witch should this mermaid go after first?" Lauren asks.

Livvie sighs, considering the paper. "I don't know."

"What?" Lauren says, lifting her pencil.

"Nothing," Livvie says unconvincingly.

"Let's make it Brittany," Lauren says.

"Whatever," Livvie says, a surliness in her voice. *Uh-oh.*

Lauren turns in my direction, and I feel my heart jump, thinking she's seen me. I duck down, my eyes level with a bottle of Mrs. Meyer's hand soap.

I hear Livvie sigh. "You know she's really not that bad," she says.

Lauren laughs.

"What?" Livvie says.

"Do you hear yourself? Have aliens taken over your brain? Earth to Livvie! Earth to Livvie!"

"Whatever."

"Did you eat something weird at lunch?" Lauren jokes. "Was the pizza radioactive? Maybe it fried your brain."

"Come on," Livvie says. "Don't be ridiculous."

"Fine," Lauren says. "If you're so desperate to be friends with them."

Friends with them? This is new.

Livvie gasps. "You know, you saying mean stuff about them isn't any better than the way that they act."

Attagirl, I think. *Stand up for yourself.*

"Give me a break," Lauren says.

"I just don't want to be on anyone's side, okay?" Livvie says. "Why can't I just be friends with everyone?"

Yes! I think, wishing I could run outside and hug her for the way that she is handling herself.

I peek back over the windowsill. Lauren shakes her head. "You're so naive."

"*Naive* is not a word I would use to describe myself," Livvie says, a sudden haughtiness in her voice that sounds too affected and beyond her years, like makeup on a little girl's face.

Hmm.

"Anyway," she says, rising from the table. "Let's go in. It's getting cold." I take a quick step toward the refrigerator and open it, pretending to look for something.

"Hi, girls," I say. "Everything good? You guys want a snack?"

"Nope," Livvie says, walking past me toward the front hall. "We're going upstairs."

"Okay," I say, watching them, Lauren behind Livvie, her notebook clutched to her chest. "Let me know if you need anything."

"Yup!" Livvie yells, already midway up the stairs.

Max comes into the kitchen, his hair hanging in his face.

"Hey, bud," I say, reaching to push it out of his eyes before he weaves away from me.

"I'm starving!" he says, leaning over my shoulder to look into the open fridge. "What are you up to?"

"Me?" I say, putting my hand to my chest, pleasantly surprised. "You want to know about me?"

"Ha, ha," he says. "Yes, *you*. Are you busy with something? Want to watch a show? Play chess? Something?"

It's as if he's just handed me a rare and precious artifact that he dug out of the backyard.

"What?" he says.

"I didn't say anything."

"No, but you have this super goofy smile on your face."

"Oh . . ." I laugh. "It's nothing, Max. You just sometimes know exactly what to say without even realizing you're doing it."

"What?" he says, squinting at me as he pulls the wrapper off a piece of string cheese.

"Never mind," I say, walking toward the door that leads into the family room. "Let's play chess. Feels like it's a good day for you to get smoked."

FOURTEEN

❦

TOWN & COUNTRY

"Mouth from the South"

JUNE 1998

"I got you something," she says, greeting me at the door of her apartment. Susannah Lane is holding her hands behind her back like a child playing a trick, but this is obviously not a joke. One of the first things you must know about Susannah Lane is that she doesn't say anything she doesn't mean.

She looks tiny standing in the open doorway, like a doll, the familiar white-blond bob tucked behind her ears. She ushers me into the marble foyer of the Fifth Avenue penthouse she shares with her husband, Teddy, owner of the eponymous investment firm Lane Capital. Her hands are still behind her back. "Here," she says, revealing the surprise. It is a vintage silver key, with a crown carved into the top that resembles the Imperial State Crown worn by Queen Elizabeth. Attached to it with a pink velvet ribbon is a small envelope. It's an invitation to Ms. Lane's fiftieth birthday party, to be held later this month at the Four Seasons. "The theme is Pandora's box," she says, raising an eyebrow.

"Pandora's box?" I ask.

"Come dressed as one of your dirtiest secrets. Something that might be dangerous if it got out."

It is a fitting theme for one of the city's most unlikely gossip columnists, a woman equal parts quirk, glamour, and mystery. From her post atop Manhattan's society scene, she could devote her time to the usual pursuits: philanthropy, international travel, the couture shows. But Susannah Lane is not like other society wives. There's the gossip column, for one, and her eclectic mix of friends. She is difficult to define, a fact that she seems to revel in. Says her husband, "Among a pool of swans, she is the peacock."

"Why gossip?" I ask her, sitting in the plush living room overlooking Central Park. It is almost noon. Chopin plays softly in the background.

"I hate that word," she says, sniveling. "*Gossip.* It makes what I do sound so underhanded. And what I do is not mean-spirited or conniving." She laughs. It's a mellifluous laugh, the kind that's pleased with itself. "In fact, most of the things that end up in my columns are things that my friends are already talking about. Old news, really. And occasionally, say, when I break the story of a cheating husband? You could say that I'm helping the poor woman who's married to him. Anyway, it's harmless girl talk."

The subjects of her work might disagree. Take Randall Lloyd, the world-famous restaurateur and, ironically, star of the Food Network's *Family Man* series. After Ms. Lane wrote about his affair with a twenty-year-old aspiring model, Lloyd banned the Lanes from all his restaurants.

Ms. Lane shrugs. "I don't think I did anything wrong there. His ex-wife is a friend. She's better off with the son-of-a-bitch out of her house. And as far as his restaurants go, que será, será. I've had more inspired meals at the fast-food places on the side of the New Jersey Turnpike." She smiles. "Listen, I grew up in a small town, and you know what they say about small towns. If there is one skill I honed growing up the way I did, it's talking."

Before Ms. Lane met her famous husband, she was Susannah Greyhill, raised in Greyhill, Virginia, a quaint hamlet in the Shenandoah Valley founded by her great-grandfather Clement Greyhill, who was involved in the formation of the C&O Railway. Susannah's father, like all the Greyhill men before him, was the mayor. Her mother threw the parties. "Our house was always full of bustle, very busy," she says.

"And you didn't want that life?" I ask her.

"I wanted something bigger," she says, the twinkle in her eye competing with the Cartier diamonds in her ears, a gift from Mr. Lane for their tenth wedding anniversary.

"Understand, I love Greyhill, you won't find a prettier spot in the nation, but the people in town . . . they didn't know what to do with me there. And neither did my mother." She winks. "I suppose I've always been a bit of an iconoclast, in my way. That's why Teddy and I are such a good fit. We're both a little kooky, you know? Though you'll never catch me climbing down the side of a skyscraper," she jokes, referencing the time her husband rappelled down the side of his company's Park Avenue building to raise money for a children's charity.

The Lanes' apartment reflects Susannah's one-of-a-kind taste. While the decor is what one might expect for a family of their means and a woman raised in the South—a lot of brightly colored florals, an impressive silver tray overflowing with hors d'oeuvres ("My mother would roll over in her grave if I didn't offer my guests an array of refreshments," she says)—there is a touch of the offbeat. The lady of the house is dressed in Chanel, but she is barefoot, and a thin band of diamonds adorns the second toe on her left foot. She uses a stainless-steel straw to sip from a can of Sun Drop, a popular Southern lemon-lime soda that the Lanes have shipped up in cases from Charlotte. There are hot-pink feather pillows on the Queen Anne wingbacks. Over the buffet in the dining room, a framed T-shirt, sweat marks and all, worn by Robert Plant during Led Zeppelin's first show at Madison Square Garden hangs next to the trophy that Mr. Lane's grandfather won at the Royal St. John's Regatta.

"Let me show you my favorite piece of art in the home," Ms. Lane says, leading me to another sitting room off the kitchen, this one done up in lavender and emerald green. It's a Magritte, one of the paintings from *The Lovers*, the disturbing series believed to have been inspired by the artist's mother's suicide. It is a disarming piece: a couple locked in embrace, kissing through the heavy white veils that cover their heads.

"What is it about it that appeals to you?" I ask her.

"It reminds me of someone I used to know," she says, her

mouth agape, marveling at the artwork like she's seeing it for the first time.

"What do you mean?" I ask. "Who does it remind you of?"

"It's a secret," she says, turning away from the piece and inviting me into the kitchen for lunch. "We're having egg salad," she says. "And rum and Cokes."

"*Wow*," I mutter to myself, dropping my pen next to the legal pad where I've just absentmindedly scrawled and underlined *iconoclast*. I first read this article right before I'd gone to Esperanza for the first time. Now that I know her, I can see her in the story, the way she almost flirts with the author, with her jokes and one-liners, like the way she is with me. I stand up from my desk and stretch in front of the bay window that looks out over the front yard. All day, the wind has howled hard and fast, rattling our old windows, the bitter cold announcing the season that's on our heels. I think of the kids, wishing that today of all days wasn't the one we finally decided to let them walk home from school. This morning, as they were slouching into their backpacks, I'd begged them to put on their hats and mittens. "*Mittens*, Mom?" Max had said, laughing with his sister. "We haven't worn mittens since, like, third grade." So hats, I'm hoping for. Hoods, at least.

I, meanwhile, wore out my tolerance to the cold during my first twenty-one years of life in New England, so I have spent the day huddled up inside. The past few days around here have been tense, and my mood reflects it. I'm still irritated with Cole for the way he didn't back me up in front of his mother, and despite his apology in the moment, I just don't want to be around him right now. I was thrilled a couple of nights ago when he texted to say he was going to meet Greg Barker and his poker buddies for drinks, and when he told me he was meeting his dad for an early breakfast this morning, I practically pushed him out the door.

All afternoon, I've been salving myself by poring through the online archives of Mrs. X's Diary, Susannah's old gossip columns that ran once a week in the *New York Observer*. Now that I know her a little bit, I can't help but notice how much the writing sounds like her—and I'm glad I was never on the receiving end of the pen she wielded like a skewer. When I read them, I picture her sitting at a gleaming antique writing desk in front of a window framing the Manhattan skyline, a fountain pen, like the kind my parents gave me on the day I graduated from Dartmouth, in her dainty hand.

. . . A supermodel supermama wore a Gaultier minidress to the Sloan Kettering Gala at the Met—a bold choice for the Upper East Side, not to mention a new mother, though not nearly as bold as her decision to forego her undergarments! Ladies, if you drop something in public and there isn't a gentleman nearby to retrieve it for you (and let's be honest, is there ever these days?), BEND AT THE KNEES, NEVER THE WAIST!

. . . A certain silver-haired actor—we all know he's far more entertaining in those three-hour cowboy movies than he is at a party—was seen ducking out of Da Silvano with a woman who was not his saintly wife. Maybe she'll finally divorce the bore and make it official with that young director who's her meant-to-be.

. . . A pint-sized Broadway powerhouse was dining
at THAT downtown bistro with not one, not two, but
THREE yapping furballs stashed in her purse. Sources say
the canines enjoyed the steak frites more than their mother
did, which, if you've had the displeasure of dining there,
isn't hard to believe . . .

When Noelle called this morning to ask how the article was going, I told her it was hard to explain. I don't know what to make of Susannah Lane, which is making it difficult to decide how I'll approach writing about her. What I do know is that trying to explain her in two thousand words is going to be like trying to stuff an elephant into a paper lunch bag. I only have a few weeks, and as easy as it would be to stick to the surface-level stuff that Noelle mentioned on the phone—the nuts and bolts about her land sales, a sugary mention of some of her favorite sights in town—I feel like I want to say more.

Despite everything I'm warned about around town, where everyone from the moms at school to the cashiers at the grocery store seem to regard Susannah with a mix of apprehension and intrigue, the expressions on their faces when her name comes up like they've just swigged from a bottle of vinegar, I find myself simply drawn to her, and at the most basic level really enjoying her. In fact, I look forward to seeing her more than most anyone else I've met in Greyhill. So what does that say about me? Susannah is a character, there is no doubt about that, but I'm starting to believe that the critics in Greyhill are just tough and that she is, in large part, misunderstood. Maybe if I write this story in just the right way, I could help her with that.

The flip side is that I could be entirely mistaken. Maybe she is as awful as everyone says. What I do know for sure is that I'm gun-shy about my instincts, especially after the past year. You can pay a heavy price for trusting the wrong people.

I turn away from the window, and my eyes land on the stack of boxes in the corner that we still haven't unpacked. Every time I look at them, I feel a sense of dread, and it's all because of the box that sits second from the top, WORK scrawled across the side in black Sharpie.

Nine months ago, I'd had to pack the box quickly, gritting my teeth to keep from crying, a Secret Service agent looming behind me while I emptied the contents of my desk. Later that evening, a courier dumped the box on our front stoop, ringing the bell and driving off before I'd even answered the door. I shoved it into the bottom of the hallway closet in our rowhouse, behind the vacuum and the bin of cleaning supplies, as if I could forget about it.

It's time to rip off the Band-Aid. I drag the box into the center of the room and pull the tape, wincing as I do it. When I open the flaps, my heart feels like I'm squeezing it in my two fists.

And just like that, there it is, the massive binder that I lived and died by for the three years that I was social secretary. We called it the bible, and inside is a chronicle of every event I executed, an itemized retelling of every detail, from the food that had been served to the fabric we'd used for the table linens to the names of the musicians who had played. The memories are so ingrained and so much a part of me that I can remember what I wore on each occasion, what the weather was like, whether my nose was stuffy or I was feeling especially stressed. I pull the binder out of the box, thinking of how we joked in the office that it held the same importance in the East Wing that the "football," the briefcase containing the nuclear codes, did in the West.

I open the front cover and run my fingers along a sample of the stunning multicolored embroidered linen we'd used as a runner for the state dinner for the Mexican president, one of my favorite events. The guests had eaten under the stars on the South Lawn, and the chef, a noted expert on Mexican cuisine who had a series of restaurants around the country, had kept the three hundred plates warm on the long walk from the White House kitchen to the lawn by having the waiters carry each plate in a custom-made insulated wooden box. A pergola drenched in twinkling white lights and a blanket of dahlias, Mexico's national flower, canopied the president's table, and after dinner, a twenty-year-old Mexican American jazz impresario provided the entertainment.

I sit back against the love seat and unfold the press clipping I'd saved that had run in the *Washington Post* the following day. Pamela, the Style section writer who covered these events, had done a beautiful job in her usual way of explaining my vision for the decor—the lighting, the sophisticated menu, and the interesting and varied guest list, which included everyone from the president and First Lady's close friends and advisers, to military personnel, to notable Mexican Americans, including a recent Pulitzer Prize winner, a hugely popular comedian and his talk-show-host wife, and a renowned architect. I study the photo of Candace, the First Lady, standing beside the Mexican president's wife. She was impeccably dressed, in a long gold column by an up-and-coming Mexican designer.

I crumple the newspaper clipping and toss it toward the trash can. It hits the edge and lands under my desk. I can feel the anger building up inside me, a burning pressure that feels like carbonation spilling over inside my chest. It's not fair, what happened to me, but it's still my fault—that's what makes this so hard to get over. I had done good work, *superior* work, that I loved, and it had all disappeared in a snap. Or, to be precise, a few slips of the mouth. *My* mouth.

I wasn't thinking when I did it, that was my big mistake. *Not thinking* when you work at the White House is on the same level of stupidity as not thinking when you're performing open-heart surgery. But the truth is that I didn't even remember any of it until I heard the recording, which ran ceaselessly on the cable news shows over the course of a few days as a funny aside, a thirty-second "get a load of this" that the stations used to lighten the reel of tragedy that made up the daily broadcasts.

The first couple are beloved by the country. Just a few days ago, I read that the president's approval rating is almost 65 percent, nearly unprecedented in modern times. The Calhouns are young and good-looking, frequently compared to both the Kennedys and the Obamas, and they had run and won on their image as down-home "real folk" who'd been raised in the same "bitsy town" (Candace's phrase) on the Georgia-Florida line. They'd married a month after their high school graduation and had three babies, each more adorable than the last, all now grown.

But the thing about them, the exceptionally rare thing, is that they are also the real deal, each of them oozing genuine good-heartedness and brainpower. Candace may capitalize on her image, which, despite her long legs and long blanket of hair ("I'd be working in my momma's beauty salon if I wasn't up here in the White House!"), is "just a regular gal, trying to balance work and family!," but she's as smart as they come—chiming in on policy debates, writing op-eds for the papers. That said, what really wins people over is her demeanor. She makes jokes about her junk-food diet and her Spanx, teases her husband for leaving his socks on the floor, and laughs at herself frequently, like when she tripped on the tarmac outside of Air Force One or was photographed at a state dinner with lipstick on her teeth. "America's Best Girl-friend," *People* magazine called her. And I, unfortunately, became the unwitting mean girl. All thanks to Anna, my deputy, who was also my work wife and closest friend on staff. On late nights or particularly grueling days, we vented to each other, sometimes about our boss, who, despite her pleasing charm, could also be quite finicky and difficult to please. At any given time during my conversations with Anna, one or both of us would be typing on our phones. The usual multitasking, I assumed.

How wrong I had been.

While typing away with her thumbs, texting vendors and schedulers, communicating with staff, Anna was also swiftly hit-ting that bright-red button on her phone's voice recorder. She re-corded little things, like when I joked that the First Lady should make skin care her administrative priority since her collagen in-jections were the thing she was most passionate about, and she recorded bigger things, like the time I lost it after the First Lady tried to back out of a formal tea for veterans' families because of a scheduling conflict and I said I wanted to give her a one-way ticket to Mosul.

Anna filed these little snippets away. Quietly. Connivingly. And then she knitted them together into one poisonous forty-five-second piece of audio that she attached to an email and sent off to David Dunson, a bottom-feeding producer on one of the cable network shows whose sole mission in life is to find ways to embarrass the Calhoun White House. He aired the clip the next morning, and as Candace Calhoun herself would say, *It spread like honey on a hot biscuit.*

I was in the back of an Uber when I found out, heading to work after dropping the kids at school, something Cole usually did, but I was enjoying the rare leisurely morning. I'd had a late night the evening before—the president's fiftieth birthday—and we'd hosted a few dozen of their closest friends and supporters and a smattering of celebrities for dinner and dancing. I was buried in my phone, answering emails and checking messages, when my driver exclaimed, "Oh, shit!" and turned up the volume on the radio, which was tuned to a local news station. What I heard when I tuned in to see what he was laughing at was my own voice.

I panicked. I told the driver to pull over, worrying illogically in the moment that he would somehow know I was the voice coming out of his speakers--and ran into the bathroom of a Starbucks, where I promptly vomited before calling Cole. He talked me down, calming and consoling me in the same way that he would continue to do for the next several months. We both knew that there was nothing for me to do but deal with the consequences, so that's exactly what I did.

The First Lady herself fired me. She called me up to the residence shortly after I arrived at work, where Anna was nowhere to be found and the rest of the staff was doing their best to avoid me.

Candace explained to me, over coffee and tea, that she had no other choice. She was incredibly gracious, given everything I had said, and I was completely humiliated, which she knew. "I know that we all say things we don't mean when we're frustrated, and I know that this isn't who you are," she said, before delivering the final blow. "But I am so *disappointed*." The big *D*. There wasn't anything worse she could say.

I felt about two inches tall. I started to grovel, my hands shaking in a fist against my lap (I didn't dare pick up one of the china teacups), desperately asking for forgiveness, although I knew they couldn't keep me. Optics are paramount in the White House, and I no longer looked like a team player. She hugged me on my way out, telling me as she did that Anna would be leaving, too, a fact that should have made me feel better but didn't.

As Bruce, the chief usher, walked me back to my office, I tried not to cry. I loved my job. I reveled in it. And I couldn't believe that a bit of private gossip with my formerly favorite coworker—jokes, venting—had cost me all of it. Bruce stood with me, his brow knitted, as I removed the lanyard with my badge from my neck. We shook hands, he bowing slightly, ever the gentleman.

I close the binder and hold it in my hands, looking at the trash can across the room. *You have to move on!* Dimitria's voice rings in my ear.

I can't do it. I stand up, walk to the closet, and shove the binder onto a high shelf. I know it's hopeless, like keeping an ex's T-shirt supposedly for the nostalgia of it when you know, deep down, that you're really clinging to the possibility that you might get back together.

I shut the door, pick up my coffee from my desk, and look outside. The light is changing, filmy brightness through the trees. The kids will be home any minute now.

Those months after I was fired were the toughest of my life. It wasn't just the public humiliation and the knowledge that I would go down in White House staff history with an asterisk beside my name. It was my disappointment in myself. Cole was unbelievable—he lay next to me in bed for hours, just holding me while I cried, and took on all the responsibilities around the house despite his own demanding job. My parents came down for a week—no small feat, given how they feel about taking time off from work—and told me every day that no matter how proud they'd been of me for landing that gig in the first place, they had worried privately about the pressure I'd put on myself. My new goal, they told me, should be to simply be happy.

So why couldn't I see it? Why couldn't I do it? The thing about that job was that for the first time in my life, I felt like I really belonged somewhere. Not in the White House itself, of course—that was an absolute privilege—but in the role. I still don't know who I am without it. I hate to admit that, but it's true. I miss the charge, the fight, the big picture, the way I used to be.

I miss that feeling. I miss it so, so much.

Twenty minutes later, I'm folding laundry when I hear the side door open. "How was your day?" I say, stepping over the kids' backpacks in the hallway and meeting them in the kitchen. The refrigerator door is wide open. Max (in his hat!) has his hand in a bag of Doritos. Livvie is cradling a bowl of leftover pasta salad in one arm and digging a fork out of the drawer with her other hand. They haven't removed their coats.

"Earth to Warners, I asked you a question," I say. "How was your day?"

"Fine," they both respond, with the enthusiasm of toll collectors.

"Wow," I say, sliding into the banquette beside the breakfast table in the corner of the room. "Just fine?" Max walks over and reaches for Bradley's old copy of *The Hobbit*, which he was reading before school this morning. "Don't get any of that radioactive nacho dust on your grandfather's book," I joke, noticing his bright-orange fingers.

"I won't," he singsongs, walking out of the room, the bag of chips tucked under one arm.

"So, Liv," I say, watching her spoon pasta into a bowl. "I noticed your backpack. Where are all your keychains?"

"Oh," she says. "Just not into it anymore."

"Oh," I say, frowning at her.

"What?" she says. "It's not a big deal, Mom."

"Yeah, sure," I say, caught off guard by my own sentimentality over such a tiny thing. "I know. So . . ." I clear my throat. "How are the girls at school?"

She shrugs, her sharp shoulder blades rising and falling under her uniform shirt like little bird wings.

"Have things been better?"

"I guess." She sighs, and then, to my delight, pulls out the chair across from me and sits down. I watch her eat for a minute, shoveling pasta into her mouth in big forkfuls. "Brittany," she says, through a mouthful of food. "She did something today that was pretty rude . . ." She pauses to swallow. "But in character, I guess. Now that I'm getting to know her."

"What was it?" I say.

"Well, she's been nicer to me, sort of. Saying hi or whatever. But then today, totally out of the blue, she came up to me at lunch, while I was throwing out my stuff. First . . ." She raises her fork in the air. "She told me that Dad and her mom used to be boyfriend and girlfriend, which I knew, of course, but . . . gross."

"Agreed," I joke, picturing Eva telling her daughter some old story about Cole, her eyes all gaga the way Susannah's look when she talks about Bradley.

"Then she invited me to sit with her and Ainsley and the rest of her crowd."

"Well, that was nice."

"Yeah, but she said, 'Don't bring her,' and motioned back to Lauren."

"Oh," I say. "I see what you're saying."

"I don't know . . ." She shifts in her seat. "I kind of want to sit with Brittany and her friends. A couple of them actually seem cool. But Lauren . . ."

"That's tough," I say. "Could you just take Lauren with you? See what happens? If the other girls are truly good people, they'd probably be welcoming, wouldn't they?"

She drops her fork to her bowl. "Mother," she says, giving me a deadpan look.

"Never mind," I say, putting out my hands. (Mother?) "Well, if they're not nice, you probably don't want to be friends with them anyway," I say, knowing that this is at least the four thousandth time she's heard this from me. "But if they're the kind of quality people you want in your life, they won't care."

"Yup." She stands, and I feel a yearning come over me, not

wanting our conversation to be over just yet. She takes her bowl to the sink and I watch her face, looking for signs that something I've said registered. At this stage more than ever, motherhood is starting to feel like throwing darts in the dark.

"I know you'll figure it out, Liv. You're a smart kid. Just spend time with people who see you for everything you are." The moment the words are out of my mouth, I realize that as much as I'd like to believe it's that easy, I know better. Sometimes, despite your best efforts, people only see what they want to.

"Thanks," she says, the corner of her mouth turning up just slightly before she walks out of the room.

Is she okay? It takes all my willpower to stop myself from following her. She's not even a teenager yet. She's still here, just down the hall, and already, somehow, I miss her so much.

FIFTEEN

A couple of days later, on Friday afternoon, Max and I are lying on either end of the couch, watching *American Ninja Warrior* and sharing a bowl of popcorn that I have doused in copious amounts of Old Bay, when Cole arrives home and announces that he's taking me out to dinner.

"Is it our anniversary?" I say in a dopey, joking voice, feigning shock. "My birthday?"

"Oh, geez, Mom." Max tosses a throw pillow at me, hitting me right in the face. I throw it back and it bounces off his chest and onto the floor.

"Really, what's the occasion?" I say, twisting my body to face Cole, stretching my arms over my head and moaning like a dog lying in the sun. I actually know exactly why he's doing this. It's his mea culpa for his behavior at the inn, when he didn't back me up in front of his mother.

"No occasion, just go get dressed," he says. "Or don't. But let's go soon, I'm starving." He starts loosening his tie as he walks out of the room. Bradley keeps trying to tell him he doesn't have to wear one anymore. *Gotta purge that lawyer out, son*, he keeps joking.

"What about the kids?" I nudge Max with my foot and he nudges back.

"Mom said she'd keep an eye on them," he yells from the foyer. I look at Max to see what he thinks of this, but he's turned his attention back to the TV, where a highly sculpted twenty-something in a sports bra is straddling a swinging, padded tube over a pool of water. *Great.*

"Okay!" I yell to Cole, hoisting myself off the couch. "Max, time to turn the TV off."

The Herringbone is a little brick house across from the Greyhill Inn that looks like it belongs on the cover of a children's book. Ivy winds up the facade, window boxes spill over with flowers and foliage, and the bright-blue front door matches the shutters. Just inside the entry, in the vestibule that separates the front door from the rest of the restaurant, there is a framed black-and-white photograph of its first incarnation: a tack shop, with piles of horse blankets and saddles lining the walls, a man with a bristle-brush mustache standing in the threshold. As I stand in what looks like the very same spot, Cole holding the door open behind me, a grid of horseshoes on the far wall—iron, gold, and silver—catches my eye. There is a fire roaring in the fireplace, and the room smells like heaven, assuming heaven is bathed in butter and garlic. This is my very favorite restaurant in all of town, infinitely better than the dining room in the inn my husband and I now happen to own across the street, and there's no way we'll ever compete if Diane holds fast to the same dusty decor and menu they've been churning out for decades. I start to say something to Cole about it but then stop myself. We need a break. Not tonight.

We take a seat at the bar and order our drinks—a manhattan for Cole, a glass of pinot noir for me—and have just opened our menus when I hear a voice calling our names behind me.

"Happy *Fri*-day!" Whitney says, her hand on her belly as she squeezes into the narrow space behind our stools.

"Whitney!" I say, turning over the paper menu on the bar. "How are you?"

"Oh, you know," she says, looking down at herself. "Counting the minutes now! Isn't it cozy in here?" She hunches her shoulders up. "I *love* coming here in the fall."

"It is cozy," I say, glancing around the room to see if I recognize anyone else. Sure enough, two of the mothers I've seen at pickup are sitting in the corner.

"Cole, I haven't seen you in forever," she says. "How are you? How are things at the inn?"

"Good," he says. "Getting busy. I thought I knew the business, having grown up around it, but running the show's a little different."

Whitney makes a sympathetic face. "Well, I'm glad you're stealing a little time away together. So important, isn't it? Jeff and I are doing the same." She turns and points to a table by the window, where her husband is cutting into a steak with the cautious deliberation of a surgeon. Whitney waves her hand, trying to get his attention.

"Jeff!" Cole calls out, one hand cupped to his mouth like we're standing on a football field. The other diners look up from their tables, and I slap his leg. It's not particularly quiet in here, but it isn't a sports bar, either. Jeff starts to stand, resting his napkin on the side of his plate as he rises, but Whitney waves him off with her hand.

"Sit and eat!" Cole stage-whispers to him.

He nods, sitting and raising his steak knife toward us. He looks relieved not to have to come over.

After she's walked away, I turn back toward the bar. "I win," I say, tapping his glass with my own.

"But we didn't bet on anything." He laughs.

"I still win." We'd joked in the car about whether it was actually possible to spend an evening together within the city limits of Greyhill without running into anyone, and made predictions about how long it would take to see someone we knew. Cole had said twenty minutes and I had guessed five, just to make a point. I didn't think I'd actually hit the nail on the head.

"Fair enough," he says.

Our bartender walks down the bar to check on us—he's about our age, nice-looking in a rugged way—and I wonder, as I often do around town, about who he is and where he's from. I know I'm not the only nonnative here—Diane herself grew up in Richmond—but it feels like it a lot of the time. I'm certainly the only person from the Northeast. After we order our dinner—a bacon cheeseburger for Cole, crab cakes for me—I ask Cole whether he knows him. Cole squints at him, watching him pull a tap behind the bar, and decides that he doesn't. "If he grew up around here, he might have gone to the other high school," he says, referencing the public one, and I think again about the kids—especially Livvie—and whether we made the right decision sending them to Draper.

"You didn't socialize with the kids at the public school at all?" I ask, although I know I've asked it before.

"Nope," he says. "Not really."

"Hmm," I say.

"Hmm what?" he says.

"Nothing." *But why?* I wonder. I take a sip of my wine and look over at the bartender, thinking about how his experience of this town might be entirely different from Cole's, and then peek over my shoulder at Whitney, who's bopped over to another table. I think I'd assumed that when you move to such a tiny place, everyone's just lumped in together, swimming in the same pond, but really, I'm starting to see, it can be as segregated and stratified as anywhere else.

"So this is nice," Cole says, interrupting my train of thought. "Besides the Barkers' party, I can't remember the last time we had a night out."

"I know," I say, thinking that I wouldn't exactly call our night at the Barkers' a date, given that we barely spent any time together. "I can't, either. When you were growing up here, where did people go on dates?"

"Dates?" he says, making a perplexed face like I've just asked him where he used to go in town to shoot heroin.

"Yeah, *dates*," I say.

"I don't know," he says, looking up at the beams crossing the ceiling like they might provide him with a clue. "I guess we went to William's occasionally, though it wasn't William's back then, it was his grandmother's place.

"And we went to the inn, but only before a special occasion, like prom or something. We had to drive all the way to Culpeper to go to the movies, so that didn't happen very often." The bartender arrives with our plates and I move our drinks out of the way, making room. "Honestly, I think we mostly all just hung around the fountain in town square, or at people's houses, or, of course, the Cliffs."

"Oh right, the Cliffs." I roll my eyes.

He smiles. "You wanna go later?" he says, elbowing me.

"Is that *it*?" I laugh. "Was *that* your move?"

"Very funny."

"But speaking of the Cliffs," I say, "I can't stop thinking about how I never heard about Henrietta Martin before I moved here."

Cole shakes a bottle of ketchup over his plate. "I don't know," he says. "It just never came up, I guess."

"Do *you* think Susannah Lane had anything to do with Henrietta's death?" I ask.

He picks up his burger and takes a bite. "I don't know," he says. "I guess she could have."

"Your parents never talked about it growing up?"

"No," he says, the corner of his lip turning up. "Why would they have?"

"I don't know," I say. "Your mother has an opinion on everything else. . . ."

He makes a face like he's conceding my point. "But why does it matter?"

"I don't know, it just bothers me," I say. "I just want to know if my first profile for the *Washington Post* is of a murderess, and if I should be pitching her story to *Dateline*."

A confused expression materializes on my husband's face, and I start to laugh. "I'm kidding, Cole!"

"Obviously." He smirks at me.

"But I do want to understand her, you know?"

"I get it."

"I asked your dad the other day, when we left the inn. He said it was just a rumor. I mean, he would know." I turn my glass by the stem, thinking about it.

"He would," Cole says. "But why don't you just ask her?"

"Susannah?" I say, giving him a look. "Really? *Did you murder your best friend when you were a teenager and have to leave town?* I'm sure that would go over well."

"All right, all right," he says. "By the way, I meant to tell you: we had a guest at the inn last night who was here to look at her land."

"Really?"

He nods. "Lisa . . . you know, who manages the dining room?"

I nod, though the truth is I can't picture her.

"She said she thought he was from Silicon Valley. Some tech guy wanting to build a farm on the East Coast."

"Oh, great," I say. "People will love that."

"Tell me about it. But it did make me think that we really ought to start working on our plans for the inn. If that's the kind of clientele we might be looking at hosting. . . ."

I put down my fork. "I'm pretty sure . . . ," I say, closing my eyes and tapping my fingers on my forehead as if I'm trying to remember something, "that *someone* might have said something like that the other day when we were talking to your parents. . . ."

"I know," he says, threading his arm into the space between my shoulders and my chair so that he can give me a conciliatory pat on the back. "I'm sorry about that. I really am. I just didn't want to get into a whole *thing* with her."

"So you let me take the fall?" I say, stealing a potato chip off his plate.

"I'm sorry," he says. "It shouldn't have happened, and I won't make a habit of it, I promise."

"Okay," I say, not wanting to spend any more of our evening on Diane. I feel myself start to relax, enjoying the comfortable ambience of the room, the soft jazz playing in the background. I watch a couple in the antique mirror over the bar; they're a little younger than us, I'd guess, holding hands while they talk. "So get this," I say. "The other day, Livvie called me *Mother*."

Cole laughs. "Mother?"

"Yeah," I say, sticking out my bottom lip. "I wish I was still *Mommy*."

"They're growing up fast," he says.

"Too fast," I say.

Before I can continue, I hear the telltale rasp of a voice behind me. *Fuck. It can't be . . .* I glance quickly over my shoulder. "Are you kidding me?" I murmur to Cole.

"Well, look who it *isssss!*" she slurs, wedging herself between our stools and slinging an arm around my husband. She is swaying like a tree in the wind.

"Hi, Eva," he says, a little too happy to see her, if you ask me. I stare at him, wanting to make eye contact so I can maritally transmit how annoying this is, but his focus has shifted to Mindy, the perpetual sidekick, it seems, who has just appeared behind me. Both women have had a bit to drink. Or a lot to drink. If I'd known these two were going to show up, I would have agreed to go sit at the bar at Dahlia's, like Cole wanted to.

"Our newest residents!" Mindy says, hip-checking Eva farther toward Cole so she can throw her arms around the backs of our chairs like we're all old friends.

"Ooh, *Bess*," Eva says, looking down at my nearly empty plate. "I see you liked your meal!"

I smile at her, if only to keep myself from lunging at her with my knife. "I did, Eva."

"Lucky you," she says, in a way that is clearly meant to be poking fun. "If I ate a big dinner like that, I would hardly be able to move for the rest of the night!" She pats her middle.

"Yes, you strike me as quite delicate," I say. I hate this woman. *I hate her. I hate her. I hate her.*

She smiles at me, but I see right through it. I can tell by the eyes, gleaming with the haughty scorn I'm beginning to expect from her.

"So what are you two up to tonight?" Cole says, shifting in his seat to face the women.

Ugh!

"Oh, Greg's out of town," Mindy says, her breath a putrid mix of alcoholic berry something or other. "He took the kids down to Blacksburg for the game tomorrow with his parents. Eva came over to keep me company, but we got bored sitting at home." She giggles.

"So we thought we'd come be bored here," Eva says, leaning her elbow on the back of Cole's chair in a proprietary way that I *swear*, from the way she's looking at me, feels like a challenge. I look around the room, wanting to see if anyone's noticed that the mayor's wife is buzzed out of her mind, but sadly, I appear to be the only one who's offended by her presence.

"Sounds like fun," Cole says, and then, like watching an accident in slow motion, I see him put his finger up to signal to the bartender for another drink. I want to strangle him.

"You should join us next time, Bess!" Mindy says.

"You should," Eva says. "You really must be bored to death since you moved here. Your lives must have been much more exciting back in the city. The museums, the restaurants . . ."

"Unfortunately, the downside is that we didn't have time to take advantage of all that while we were there," Cole says.

"Oh, I'm sure," Eva says. "Especially with Bess's job."

"No, it wasn't that," Cole says. *Finally! Look at him, acting like a husband!* "I mean, Bess was very busy, of course. But it was really just the pace of everything."

"Things are soooo much easier here," Mindy drones, her eyes all googly. "I don't know how or why anyone could live in a place like that. Just the traffic alone! And the crime!"

"Oh, sure!" I say, knowing she won't catch my mocking tone. "See other places? Why would you want to?" Cole raises his eyebrow at me. I smile back, then reach across the bar and take a sip of the drink the bartender just set down in front of him.

"You just missed Whitney and Jeff," Cole says.

"Oh," Eva says, widening her eyes at Mindy, who starts to laugh. "That's too bad." They both start giggling.

"What?" I say.

"Whitney's just . . . ," Mindy starts.

"She's a *lot*," Eva says, and then looks at Mindy, her eyes widening, realizing her joke. She puts her arms out in front of her, as if she's cradling a massive belly.

They both burst into hysterics.

"She is huge, isn't she!" Mindy says, nudging me.

"I didn't even mean it that way!" Eva says, her hand on her chest as she laughs.

Wow. My mind reels back to Tilly Robertson and company back in high school, who used to make horrible jokes about me, mostly about the disgusting things they were going to leave in the mailboxes on my dad's route. Bags of dog shit. Rancid food ("We know it's your *favorite*, Bess"). Used pads and tampons.

"Well," Mindy says, barely lowering her voice. "Whitney ought to be careful. With her body type, she's the kind who can go from curvy to fat in the span of a few pounds."

"Oh, Mindy!" Eva says, laughing like Mindy's starring in her own HBO comedy special. This bullshit infuriates me. Grown women making fun of a friend's size.

"Aren't you all close?" I say.

They both look at me, perplexed, like I've just asked them to recite the Pythagorean theorem.

"Of course we're friends!" Eva says, admonishing me. "Why would you think otherwise?"

"It's pretty brutal to talk like that about someone who's—"

Mindy cuts me off. "Come on, Bess, we're just having some fun. She does look like she's having twins."

"Bess, *you* had twins!" Eva says, snapping her fingers like it just occurred to her. She flashes the smile again, but this time her eyes dart to my shoulders and then my chest, and down to my toes and back up again.

I'm sure I'm not imagining it. I look down at myself, as if I might have spilled something on my shirt, and then back up at Eva.

"What?" I say, so she knows that I know what she's doing.

She ignores me. "God, *twins*," she says, turning to Cole. "That must have been something!"

"We were busy!" he says. When he reaches across to pat my leg, I want to twist his arm off his body and chuck it into the fireplace across the room. *Why doesn't he see how awful these people are? Why is he being so fucking friendly to these monsters?*

"But, God, even *before* that, when you first found out Bess was pregnant! Wasn't that the surprise of your life! I remember . . ."

My ears start ringing as I realize what the insinuating expression on her face means.

"How did you tell him, Bess?"

"Excuse me?" Surely she's not going here. Cole's face, when I look at him, is rigid with alarm. I narrow my eyes at him, trying to discern . . .

He looks at me, just for a split second, and then looks away, the guilt as evident as if he could scrawl it on his forehead.

"I just remember when you came home to tell your parents." Eva puts her hand on Cole's shoulder and throws her head back at this apparently hilarious memory. "You were so nervous, you didn't even *touch* your key lime pie at William's! And you know that's his favorite pie," she says, bending a wrist toward me as if I need to be filled in on the likes and dislikes of the man I am married to.

Angry pressure starts pulsing behind my ears. I look at Cole, hot prickles coursing over my body. *He told Eva I was pregnant before he told his parents?* I didn't even know they were in touch at that point.

"He was *terrified!*" She keeps laughing. "Remember—" She elbows him. "Neither of us could agree on whether your mother would ever speak to you again!"

"Neither of you could agree?" I say to Cole, my heart hammering like I've just sprinted across a finish line.

"What are you guys talking about?" Mindy says. "She was about to become a grandmother! Why would Mrs. Warner never—"

Cole finally mans up and looks me in the eye. I can see his tongue poking the inside of his cheek, the way his lower jaw shifts. He knows how badly he's fucked up.

"Oh, Mindy," Eva laughs. "I'm sure Diane was *thrilled* once she got used to the idea, but I don't think she ever planned for Cole to become a father in the way he did."

"The way he—?" Mindy says.

I cut her off, putting my hand out. "Eva, you're out of line."

She just smiles at me and continues. "Mindy, they weren't married," she says, looking at me the whole time. "They'd hardly even been dating. Right, Cole?"

Mindy claps her hands to her mouth. "Nooo!" she squeals, looking back and forth from me to Cole. "So, what, were you pregnant when you got married?" She puts her hand on my arm like we're friends and I jerk it away.

"I can't believe you don't remember this, Mindy!" Eva says. "We all talked about it!"

"We had actually been dating for a while when it happened," Cole says, reaching across and grabbing my hand out of my lap. I let it sit like something limp and lifeless in his grasp. "We just got started earlier than we planned. Best thing that ever happened to me."

Nice try, I think.

Eva laughs. "That's not what you said at the time!" She looks at me. "You really scared the shit out of him, Bess! You really, *really* got him!"

"*Jesus*, Eva!" Cole finally—*finally*—spits out. The woman sitting behind Cole jolts at his voice. "It's not like Bess was the only one responsible. Believe me, nobody was more surprised than her. It isn't any of your business, for the record, but it also isn't a big deal. The twins are almost thirteen." He squeezes my hand a little harder. This time, I squeeze back. Just a little. "And, you know . . ." He laughs, a lame attempt to lighten the mood. "We're living happily ever after."

"That's right," I say, a clip in my voice. I want to throttle him, but I can't, not in front of these two. I don't want them to ever for a minute think they can get to me.

I also remember when Cole drove down to Greyhill to share the news with his parents. My own parents had met Cole just a couple of times, and adored him, but even so, when I'd called them that week to tell them I was pregnant, convincing my mother to relay it to my dad so I wouldn't have to, there was some yelling ("With all the education, all the scholarships, you somehow forgot about birth control?" she had screamed) and some tears, mostly on my part. But by the next day, things had settled. My dad called, and when I picked up, the first question out of his mouth was whether he should go by *Grandpa* or *Gramps*.

I had no idea what to expect from Bradley, but I was terrified about Diane. She had made it obvious from the start that I wasn't what she had pictured for her son, and now that *I'd* gone and done this . . . When Cole went to tell them, I spent most of the weekend in bed, alternately worrying and throwing up from the severe nausea that characterized most of my pregnancy. When he got back to DC, he came straight over. He said it went well, or as well as we could have expected. *"My dad's really excited."* I didn't know it at the time, but over the course of the weekend, Bradley had given Cole his grandmother's ring. Diane called me a few weeks later, treating the whole thing like it was a business matter. She wanted to make sure I was taking proper care of myself, that I was seeing a good doctor . . . essentially, that I was a sufficient incubator for her grandchildren.

Eva clears her throat. "Speaking of the kids," she says, putting her hand on her hip. "Brittany told me that she and Livvie sat together at lunch today."

"Oh, really?" Cole says. "Well, that's sweet."

Adorable, I think, fuming. *Just what I want for Livvie.*

"Actually . . .," Mindy starts, and I catch the flicker of recognition on Eva's face, like this is exactly what she wanted to happen.

"What?" I say.

"I guess she was kind of rude."

"Livvie?" Cole says, giving me a wary look.

"I guess she made a joke about something that Brittany had done incorrectly in math," Mindy says. She wrinkles her nose. "She was being . . . *kind of a mean girl.*"

"*My* daughter?" I say, my mouth dropping open.

"Brittany struggles in math," Eva says, with a somberness that would suggest she's revealing that her Brittany has terminal cancer.

"Livvie would never do that," I say, angry heat rising up my back and neck. "Trust me, that's just not who she is."

Eva raises her eyebrows and tips her head to one side.

"Well . . ." She shifts her weight. "I hate to say it, but that's not all. Brittany said she completely froze out some of the other girls, that she just wasn't being very . . . inclusive."

"I don't know, Eva, that doesn't sound like Liv," Cole says. "And you know kids, how they say things . . ."

"I'm just saying maybe you should talk to her," Eva says, looking solely at me. "I know she's a darling girl. Maybe she's just having a little trouble adjusting. With the move and all?" She smiles, her watery eyes glinting in the dim light. "I know she's befriended that Lauren . . ."

"Who?" Mindy asks, hiccupping as she says it.

"You know," Eva says, starting to laugh. "The one with the walk? I think her mom works at Bully's."

Mindy raises her eyebrows. "Oh, right!" She snorts. "I know exactly who you're talking about!"

We haven't even pulled out of the parking lot before I start screaming.

"I can't *believe* you told her before you told your parents!"

"I ran into her, Bess, and I was terrified," he says, his voice so low and measured that he sounds like a hostage negotiator trying to reason with a crazy person, which only pisses me off more because that means the crazy person is me. "She was the first person I saw on my way into town and I confided in her. I shouldn't have, I knew that in the moment, which is why I never told you. I never thought it would matter, in the grand scheme of things. It *doesn't* matter."

"Of course it matters!" I scream, my balled fists hitting my lap. "Did you see how she acted just now? Did you see how she held it over my head?"

"She didn't—"

"How can you defend her?" I shout. "How can you keep letting it go and expect me to be friends with a woman like that? With people like that?"

"Eva isn't any particular way, Bess. She's . . ." He shakes his head. "And I'm not defending her."

"This is what you don't get!" I say. "And it's baffling to me! It's like you're clinging to some weird, utopian vision of this place, Cole! How do you not see what I see?"

"Bess, come on!" He pulls over to the side of the road, turning on his hazards just outside the business district at the end of Maple. "Why is it so bad?" he says, his voice rising to meet my volume. "What is the problem? Why is it so hard for you to just play along? To not *care* so much?"

"Because of the way these people are, Cole! Superficial! Stuck-up! Materialistic! I shouldn't have to 'play along' at anything!"

"Do you hear yourself?" he says. "*You* sound every bit as judgmental as you say we are!"

"*We?*" I say. "So it's me against all the rest of *you* now?"

"No." He gasps and closes his eyes for a moment. "Come on, Bess! To be honest . . ."

"What?"

"I think you're projecting a little bit."

"Projecting?" I say. "What? About how I grew up? Comparing?"

"Well . . ." He shrugs.

"That's beside the point!" I say, though I know it's a little true. "And if I am, it's because I don't want what happened to me to happen to our kids. And to Livvie! I mean, did you *hear* that bullshit tonight?"

"I know," he says, reaching his hand out for mine. I flick it away.

"So Eva's lying about our daughter now, too!" I shout. "And that's okay with you? I should just let it go? Play along?"

"No, Bess," he says. "Of course not. It's just . . ."

"What?"

"You just have to be careful about the way you approach things around here," he says. "People talk."

"Oh, I *know*," I say. "Believe me, I know." I laugh. "And I'm starting to understand why Susannah Lane hightailed it out of here all those years ago."

"Well, that's great."

I sigh, my shoulders dropping, and put my hands over my face for a moment, trying to settle myself down. "Don't you see how hard I'm trying?" I say, tipping my head back onto the headrest. "I'm making an effort, you know. But sometimes I feel like this is a square peg, round hole kind of situation. Maybe it's just not right for me here."

Before he has a chance to answer, a shadow falls across the car's dash and I jump, yelping as the knock comes on the passenger window beside me.

Cole rolls down the window. It's Martha Brown, our Realtor. *Wonderful.*

"Everything okay, you two?"

"Fine," we say in unison, both of our voices a bit more charged than to be believable.

"Okay," she says, taking a tentative step back. "If you're sure."

"Good night, Ms. Brown." Cole rolls the window back up. "Do you see what I mean?" he says, gesturing as we watch her walk off. "Eyes and ears everywhere."

"Yeah," I say, though I really don't want to. "Believe me, I see."

SIXTEEN

The next day, Cindy barely greets me before she turns and screams into the dark foyer behind her.

"*Susannah!*" she yells, her voice echoing into the cavernous house.

The sun is out, but despite my heaviest winter coat I'm shivering on the front landing. It's colder than it should be for this time of year, though when I spoke to my mother this morning, she laughed at me for whining about the weather in Virginia. She said she'd already had to use the ice scraper on her windshield this week.

"You really don't have to yell for her—" I start, looking down at my feet. I'm standing on top of a massive, scrolling *G* that decorates a doormat the size of a twin bed. But Cindy keeps on, the power of her voice a stark contrast to her diminutive size, like Tinker Bell wielding a bullhorn. Under the arch of the imposing doorway, she looks like a child, a little elfin thing in the home of a giant.

A gust of cold wind blows, and Cindy hurries me in. "Come on, come on," she says, trying to shield herself with her arm, and

I stifle a laugh as I watch the wind push her hair off her forehead in one softball-sized hair-sprayed clump.

"You like my shirt?" Cindy asks, pinching it at the front and then letting it go. She's caught me staring again. It's bright aqua, with LEADER OF THE PACK written in a feathery modern font across the front.

"I do," I say, thinking that I'm sure I saw it in the girls' section at the Old Navy in Charlottesville when I took Livvie shopping before school started in August. "It's cute."

"Just want ol' *Miss* to know where she stands!" she says, laughing. "*Susannah!*" she screams up the stairs, both hands cupped around her mouth. "Bess is here!"

"It's okay," I say, stepping onto the scuffed marble floor. "I'm not in any rush."

Let me just hide out here for the rest of the day, I think. I've been in a horrendous mood all weekend, and dinner last night didn't help. Bradley and Diane came over, the last thing I wanted after the way my night with Cole ended on Friday, but Diane would have been even more unbearable if I'd tried to cancel, wanting to know the reason for the change of plans and almost certainly taking it personally.

The problem is your son, I could have said, though I know that's not really true. It's not his fault, but I'm realizing how resentful I am of how easy the transition here has been for him. It's like we've moved to a remote country on the far side of the world, and he's the only one who speaks the language.

It didn't help that when we sat down to eat, Diane managed to both criticize the sauce I'd made for the pork roast ("Bess, we can never accuse you of being stingy with the sugar, can we?")

and recount how she'd run into Eva at the grocery store that week ("So chic, that girl. So elegant!"). The one bright spot was Bradley, who ate like he hadn't in days, exclaiming that we ought to put the dish I'd made on the menu at the inn.

My eyes land on a portrait on the wall that I didn't notice the last time I was here, just past the entry to the front sitting room.

"That's Susannah and her sister," Cindy tells me. The portrait is all soft colors—peaches and pinks, muted soft greens—and the girls are in pastel dresses. Baby blue for Susannah, yellow for her sister.

"It's beautiful," I say, studying the picture. A portion of it, mostly the left side, has faded, presumably from the sunlight streaming onto it from a window across the hall. Susannah and her sister look to be about Livvie and Max's age, just on the cusp of their teenage years. They clearly sat for the portrait, and I try to imagine what that must have been like, given that the twins can barely hold still for the few seconds it takes for me to attempt to snap a photo of them with my phone. Susannah's hair is pulled back at the top, a white ribbon tied at her crown. Margaret's waves are tied loosely to the side, cascading down one shoulder. Pinkish-red paint, a color that reminds me of the stain that a cherry Popsicle leaves on your tongue, blooms off the apples of the girls' cheeks. A strange contrast, I think, to the solemn expressions on their faces. I notice the gold crosses hanging from both girls' necks.

"Were the Greyhills a particularly religious family?" I ask Cindy, pointing toward the pendants.

"In general? No, not any more or less than any other family around here. But Susannah's mother? That's another story. At least, that's what I've heard. She was *real* pious. Always down at the Methodist church."

"Susannah herself, though?"

Cindy looks at me and laughs. "I think the church would burst into flames if Susannah stepped foot in it." She glances up the grand staircase, a puzzled expression on her face. "I don't know where the hell she is. Come on."

She starts down the long hallway that leads from the foyer, and I attempt to get a peek at what I missed when I was here the last time. We pass by another formal sitting room full of faded furniture, and then an empty ballroom. I catch a glimpse of a massive, shimmering chandelier through the open sliver of a pocket door before I take a quick step to keep up with Cindy's purposeful pace.

"So are you here every day, Cindy?"

"Yup," she says. "Three days a week I clean, though it's really not as much as you'd think." (*I didn't think much*, I want to say, given the state of the house.) "Susannah only uses three or four rooms. The rest of the time it's just a little bit of cooking, helping her with her correspondence when she needs it, and driving her to her appointments, which I have a feeling I'll be doing for a while."

"Why? Does she have a lot of them?"

"No, it's just that she's a little skittish in the car now. I'm starting to wonder if she might have a phobia. PTSD, in a way. I have a nephew with that," she says, turning back to me. "Was an army ranger, two tours in Iraq. Anyway, you should see the way she grips the armrest when I'm driving."

"How do you think she's recuperating?" I ask. "I noticed the last time we met that she wasn't wearing that bandage around her head. But she still needs the cane?"

"Yes, her hip bothers her," she says, continuing down the hall.

"Is she seeing anyone for it? Physical therapy, or . . ."

Cindy stops, pursing her lips for a moment before she speaks. "No, no doctors." She takes a tiny step toward me. "Between us, I think there's more damage here." She taps her finger on the side of her head.

"Her *brain*?" I say. "What do you mean?"

"Oh, no, not like . . . Don't take me the wrong way. I don't mean anything serious," she says. "More that . . ." She bites her lip, trying to find the right words. "I think she's fine, Bess, but I think . . . she needs some attention. She's lonely."

"So you think she's playing it up? Is that what you're saying?"

She holds up her hand and sticks out her thumb and index finger, leaving an inch of space between them. "Maybe just a little."

"I know she must feel lucky to have you, Cindy."

"Well, she's enjoyed doing this with you, too. I think it's helped. It's hard being alone after you've lived with someone so long. Trust me, I know. I lost Gerald three years ago this December."

"I'm sorry."

She nods. "Mr. Lane *loved* my husband. He was . . . well, you could tell he was a harsh man. Especially the way he spoke to her. But he loved Gerald, he really did. I think he was one of those men who's just uncomfortable talking to women, you know?"

"I do," I say, thinking of the president's chief of staff, who fit that description to a T.

"They came down to the Inn at Little Washington for dinner every couple of months—flew down to the private airport in Leesburg from New York and then drove fifty-some miles from there. And would you believe that sometimes, they turned around and went right back after dessert? Susannah called me just a few weeks after Teddy died and asked if I would come work for her full-time. I like her company, crazy as she is." She laughs.

"Can I ask you something?" I say. "Don't you think it's strange that not once, in all those times you say they came to Virginia to go to the inn, that Susannah never came to Greyhill to see her family?"

She shrugs. "Not really. Susannah's mother was pure evil, from what I've heard about her. You know a mama's bad if her daughter spends most of her life just trying to forget about her. Anyway, it isn't any of my business." *Or yours, either*, her tone seems to say.

She pushes open a swinging door at the end of the hall and leads me into the massive kitchen. It is industrial, the kind of room you might see in the back of a catering hall, and it occurs to me that when this house was built, its residents weren't hanging out in the kitchen or cooking for themselves. The one bright spot in the gloomy room is a wall of floor-to-ceiling windows that frames the extensive gardens and grounds behind the house. I notice the snowflake-shaped crack in one of the panes and think that it looks like it was caused by a baseball, or even (*maybe? Is my imagination getting the best of me?*) a bullet.

Cindy marches to a pair of French doors on the far side of the room and pulls one open, the hinges creaking like a sound effect in a low-budget horror movie. Cindy starts down the steps and I follow, the wind still gusting around us, and as I turn the corner onto a stone patio past a boxwood hedge that I can tell was once trimmed into a sharp spiral, I see the top of a wide-brimmed hat and a hand doing its best to keep it on the owner's head.

"Dammit, Susannah!" says Cindy. "Why didn't you tell me you were coming out here? Didn't you hear me calling you all over the house?"

"Oh, I'm sorry, Cindy," Susannah says and laughs. She's sitting at a wrought-iron table with a tartan plaid blanket wrapped around her shoulders, with the gold journal that I noticed at our previous meetings. Her cane rests against her chair.

"I needed some fresh air this morning, Bess, I hope you don't mind," she says. "It's a little breezy, I know. Here, I'll come inside." She stands, and Cindy hurries down the steps to meet her. I take the opportunity to peek at the gardens, and it pains me to imagine how magnificent they could be. Rows of overgrown hedges mark gravel paths that are pocked with weeds and fan out for what feels like a football field's length from the property. In the middle, I can just make out a marble fountain like the one in front of the house, this one stained with some type of algae or mineral deposit and encircled by a mass of weeds that must once have been flower beds.

"Some garden, huh?" Susannah says, meeting me at the top of the steps. "You should have seen the one I had in East Hampton. I had a gardener, this gorgeous kid from Sweden." She makes a motion like she's fanning herself. "I loved to watch him work."

She looks out at the view and I wonder just how hard this is for her, to have had such a different life. She must be in a constant state of comparison. "See just beyond the fountain, to that row of hedges?"

"Yes," I say, looking beyond a leggy, ruffled mass of green.

"That is where your father-in-law and I had our first kiss," she says, chuckling. "We drank our first beer together back there. It was *my* first beer, anyway. I stole it out of the stash my father kept at the back of the icebox. I don't drink beer anymore—never liked it, really—but whenever I've tried it, that salty, bitter taste has always reminded me of kissing Bradley. You should see the expression on your face when I mention him, by the way. You look like you want to sink right into the ground!"

"Can you blame me?" I say, shivering, from the cold or the conversation or both.

Susannah leads me to a room in the back of the house that she says was her father's office, and my mood lifts at the prospect of getting to see more of Esperanza. "I know we need to get down to business," she says, leaning her cane against a table and walking—fairly easily, it seems—across the room. "And I talked your ear off last time, so I'm ready to be a good sport and just answer your questions."

As we enter, I have to squint against the blinding brightness of the room. It's more of a sunroom than an office, with floor-to-ceiling windows that look out over the fields behind the house, and a worn Persian carpet that reminds me of the ones I see in design magazines, though this one doesn't look "antiqued" in a trendy way. One of the corners actually looks like some kind of animal might have gotten to it. A side table to my left is crowded with a collection of dusty silver-framed photos, and over them there's a painting I instantly recognize. It's *The Lovers*, the Magritte painting that was mentioned in the *Town & Country* article I read recently, and it is every bit as tense and disarming as the author had described, especially in such a rarefied room. Inside the gold frame are a man and a woman, in an ordinary black suit and red dress, kissing through opaque white veils that cover not just their faces but their entire heads.

"That used to hang in the Museum of Modern Art," Susannah says. "But then Teddy made a big donation so we could *borrow* it."

"Oh?" I say.

She laughs. "I don't know how much he gave, but nobody's asked for it back yet. I should try to sell it on the black market!" She begins to remove her wrap and the wool coat beneath it. "I just love the surrealists, don't you? This one . . . it makes you *feel* something."

"Yes," I say, remembering what Susannah said in the article. "I have to confess, I read an old *Town & Country* profile of you that mentioned it. The author quoted you saying the painting reminded you of somebody. Do you mind telling me who?"

"Look at you, girl reporter!" she says. "I'm impressed! But it's not important."

"All right," I say, sneaking another look at the painting as I move behind her to help her out of her coat. Today's ensemble is a winter white cashmere sweater and matching pants, with Ferragamo flats nearly identical to the ones I'd splurged on when I got my White House job. I'd never spent so much on a pair of shoes before—not even half as much—but I reasoned to myself that I should adhere to the old adage that you should dress as well as the people you work for, and my boss had been on the cover of *Vogue* four times, a record for a First Lady.

"So how was your weekend?" she says, sitting on a saggy brocade sofa and motioning for me to join her.

"Good," I lie, thinking back over the past couple of days.

"You sure?" Susannah asks, an amused expression on her face. "You don't look like it was good."

"I'm probably just tired," I say.

"Oh, come on," she says. "I can see it all over your face."

"Really," I say, feeling myself start to flush. "It's nothing."

She reaches over and pats my knee. "Bess . . ."

I sigh. "It sounds silly when I say it out loud, but I'm just having a little trouble in town. Adjusting, I guess."

"Adjusting?"

"Some of the women . . ." I wrinkle my nose.

"Ooh!" She claps her hands together. "Now, this I can relate to! What happened?"

"I really don't—" *Don't lump me in with you*, I want to say.

"Come on!" she says. "It will make you feel better."

"All right," I say, giving in. "I guess it's a conflation of things. Just getting used to a new place, mostly, and I'm worried about how my kids—well, my daughter—is adjusting."

"You're a wonderful mother," she says. "I can tell by the way you speak about your kids."

"Thank you," I say, warmed by her acknowledgment. "It definitely doesn't feel that way lately."

"No, no! I can tell you're one of the good ones. And Bradley has told me as much."

"The two of you are in touch?" I say, shocked to hear her say it.

"Oh, some . . . ," she says, smiling like she has a secret. "I call him every once in a while, just to say hello." She leans toward me, lowering her voice. "I'll confess, sometimes when I call the house and Diane answers? I hang up! Once, though . . ." She starts to laugh. "I pretended to be a telemarketer! I went on and on. To tell you the truth, I was surprised by how polite she was!"

"Did you really?" I say, completely alarmed.

She nods.

But Diane and Bradley have a landline with caller ID, which I know because when I call them for something, not that it's often, I've noticed that Diane likes to let my calls go to voice mail, even though I can look right out my front window and see that she's home. I wonder why she'd answer Susannah's calls and play along . . . "What do you . . ." I'm almost afraid to ask. "What do you and Bradley talk about?"

"First of all, don't worry. I'm not trying to break up anyone's marriage. Believe me, the last thing I need or want is another husband!"

"Okay," I say, thinking that it's funny how she assumes it would be that easy.

"Even though we were out of touch for all those years, Bradley still knows me better than anyone around here," she says. "I know how much people love him in town. I feel like . . . given my reputation . . . or lack of one . . ." I notice how her voice sounds suddenly tinged with irritation. "His word could go a long way in terms of helping how people see me around here."

"Well, I can relate to that," I say, thinking of Cole's reticence with Mindy and Eva the other night.

"How so?" she asks, tucking her fist under her chin.

I wave a hand at her. "You've heard enough about me."

"Oh, come on," she says.

"All right, all right," I say. "Well, like I said, there are some women in town . . ."

"That's not a good start, you know," she says, though with the way her mouth is hanging open in delight, as if I'm about to pop a treat into it, I can tell she's very pleased by the turn our conversation is taking.

"Well, it's *one* woman," I say, and then tell her what happened at the Herringbone the other night. Susannah's right—by the time I get to the end, to when Eva started criticizing Livvie, I do feel better.

"If this Ava is draping herself all over your husband—"

"Eva."

"Whatever!" she laughs. "I know who you're talking about, of course. She's so *tall!*" She makes a face like the fact offends her. "Bess, you have to do something about it!" she says. "Take it from someone who knows."

I sigh. "I'm hoping if I just ignore her long enough, she'll stop," I say. "Or I'll just get used to it."

"Oh, honey," she says. "No, no, *no!* Trust me, if there is something I know about, it's how to deal with other women."

"What do you mean?"

"Try being married to a billionaire! The women were *everywhere*, circling around Teddy like surgically enhanced sharks, looking for any 'in' they could find! They were in the obvious places—openly fawning over him at parties, coddling him at work—and the less obvious ones, too. I always had suspicions about his dermatologist, for instance, who seemed like she was always making house calls to his office. It was quite an education, learning how money could make people behave."

"Huh," I say. "I guess I never thought about what that might be like."

"Oh, you wouldn't believe it! It amazed me how women—even my ostensible *friends*—would abandon any sense of propriety they had around him, all in an effort to get their hands in the proverbial cookie jar!"

"Did you have any reason to worry?" I ask.

"Of course I worried! I never let on, but I worried all the time. I kept my ears and eyes open, you can be sure of that, because the vultures were everywhere. But here's what you should know: It actually gave me *deep* satisfaction to find them and winnow them out. As excruciating as it was, you can be sure I made them pay."

"Made them pay?" I ask, noticing the way she seems to be getting more and more animated as she talks. She's hinted plenty about how her marriage wasn't how the press portrayed it, but this vengefulness . . . surely she's playing this up for my benefit . . .

"Oh, yes. I should've written a book! *Getting Back!: How to Root Out the Social Climbers Who Are Trying to Steal Your Husband!* Ha! Can you imagine? I could have been on *Steve Harvey.* That's Cindy's favorite, I watch it with her sometimes."

"It couldn't have been that bad, though," I say. "You don't really mean it, do you?"

"Oh, I really mean it!" She closes her eyes, a smile on her face like she's recounting some delicious memory. "I'll give you an example, but you have to promise not to hold this story against me."

"Of course not!" I say. *What on earth could she possibly be about to say?*

"All right," she says with a smile. "I trust you.

"Teddy had a hairdresser come to his office to cut his hair on the second Monday of every month, and I discovered that she had slipped a note with her phone number into his pocket. I had long sensed that she was somebody I needed to watch out for. Teddy told me how she pressed her torso against his back while she cut his hair, about her low-cut shirts and how she'd lean over to give him a peek."

"At least he told you."

She rolls her eyes. "Please. He was just trying to keep me on my toes."

"Oh," I say, thinking that I like Teddy less and less every time she speaks of him.

"When I found that note—I won't tell you what it said, but it was *graphic*—I could have just had her fired. It would have been a cinch. Teddy, for all his wonderful qualities, was quite vain, and all I would have had to do was tell him I didn't like his latest haircut. But—this is what I'm trying to tell you, this is why you have to do something about that Eva: It's one thing to send a message to your husband, but nothing will end if you don't get to the source of the problem. It's like pest control, Bess. If you want to get rid of her, you've got to go for the big guns. Use the off-label toxic stuff! Make the problem go away so you never have to deal with it again."

"But the hairdresser," I say, trying to direct the conversation back to her. "What on earth did you do?"

"First . . ." She claps her hands together. "I made an appointment at the girl's salon on Madison Avenue. Just for a blowout, and not with *her*, of course. Even if she was the owner of the salon, with a line of products in her name that they sell at every high-end department store in America, I wasn't stupid enough to let her within five feet of *me*. I arrived at my appointment a little early and asked to use the ladies'. Once in the loo, I locked the door and did a little investigating. I had to make sure my plan would work."

"Your plan?"

She nods. "I got the blowout, which was just okay, but I made a big deal about how much I loved it. I went on and on, oohing and aahing at myself in the mirror. I made another appointment, and when I returned a week later, I again asked to use the restroom first."

"What did you do?" I put my hands to my face. "I'm almost too scared to know," I say into my palms.

Her eyes widen. "Oh, it's awful, Bess. I almost can't tell you."

"What?" I say, dropping my hands into my lap and clenching them together. "You can't hold back on me now!"

She bites her lip. "It was a trick I'd heard about years earlier, in a smutty paperback mystery I'd read on vacation." She takes a deep breath. "I went to Citarella before my appointment and asked the fishmonger to wrap up a couple of beautiful, bright-eyed whole fish. I think they were branzino."

"*Fish?*" I say.

She laughs with excitement, her eyes wide. "Once I was in the ladies' room at the salon, I retrieved the screwdriver that I'd put in my purse the night before. It was one of those tiny ones, the kind you might use for tightening the hinges on your glasses? I wasn't sure it would work, but . . . *oh, Bess*, it did! It worked perfectly!" She sucks in her lips before she continues, making a face like she's about to plunge into a freezing pool of water. "Well, I unscrewed the air vent from the wall next to the sink, unwrapped those two beautiful fish, dropped them just inside the wall, and reattached the air vent!" She widens her eyes at me. "As one does."

"No!" I say, starting to laugh, though I'm thinking that she's actually crazy. I've heard a lot of outrageous things over the course of my life, but *this* . . .

"Oh, I *did*! I really did. And when I went back out to my stylist, I made sure to complain a couple of times about the temperature and asked if they could turn the heat up."

"Oh!" I clutch my hand to my chest. "That's so . . . It's awful! It's so . . ."

"Brilliant?" she says, laughing so hard that tears are rolling down her face.

"What do you think happened?"

"Well, I don't know when they started to notice the stench of a couple of whole fish rotting behind the wall, but I can't imagine that it was good. A few weeks later, there was an item in my column, called in 'anonymously,' of course, about the *unfortunate, mysterious rotting odor* at the venerable salon."

"You are . . .," I begin, my face hot with alarm. "Susannah, I am both horrified and amazed. Did Teddy ever find out?"

"If he did, he never let on, but the item in the column certainly tipped her off, because Teddy came home and complained to me that she'd called to say she was *shrinking her client base to make more time for other business opportunities*." She laughs.

"Wow!" I say, shaking my head slowly from side to side. "Now I know never to cross you." She's even more off-balance than I had thought.

"Bess, you're too smart to cross me," she says, winking. The words hang in the air between us, and I clear my throat.

"I'm sure I'd never have a reason to even consider it," I say, and she smiles at me, pleased, like she believes the words I've just said. I'm not lying—not exactly—maybe *hoping* is the right word. . . .

"Listen, not everything I did was so theatrical. I did smaller things. We had some couples over for cocktails once and I put a few drops of Visine in one of the women's vodka tonics after I saw her grab Teddy's knee under the table. Do you know what Visine does to the digestive system?"

"No."

"She called two days later, saying in a roundabout way that she'd been in the bathroom for the past forty-eight hours. She wanted to know who my caterer was, and whether anyone else had fallen ill."

"Susannah, that's terrible!"

"No," she says. "Just proactive. Those women deserved it for making a move on a married man. *Eva* deserves it. Just think, if you'd Visine-d her drink on Friday night, you'd feel better now, trust me."

"Oh, no," I say. "I don't have that in me."

"Well, maybe you should," she says. "Don't come crying to me when something happens."

"Oh, Cole would *never*," I say. "Trust me, I know my husband."

"Yeah, and I knew your father-in-law, too." She grins.

"What?" I say, not sure at first that I've heard her right.

She shakes her head, stopping herself, like she's finally gone too far.

"What do you mean, Susannah?"

"I shouldn't have . . ." She waves her hands at me. "It was so long ago! It doesn't even matter."

"What?"

She takes a deep breath. "Just keep it between us?" she asks. "Of course."

"He and Henrietta . . ."

"Your best friend?" I say. "No, not Bradley! I can't believe that!"

She purses her lips, dismayed. "Well, I never knew for sure, but they got very close. It got very uncomfortable. Bradley always denied it, but listen, Bess, I knew what was going on. You know, women's intuition."

"I don't know, Susannah." I think back to what William said in the coffee shop that morning, about her sudden departure after Henrietta's death. *Everyone in town thinks . . .*

"Believe what you want to believe." She shrugs. "And forgive me for saying anything about your marriage. I'm sure you're right about Cole, Bess," she says. "I never should have been so forward. I didn't mean—"

"No, I know," I say, still fixated on Bradley and Henrietta. "But it's just . . ."

"What?"

"I guess I don't understand. If what you're saying is true, it must have made things difficult between you and Henrietta? Not to mention you and Bradley, of course."

"Oh, I never let on that I knew," she says.

"Really?" I say. "But why? You just told me about all those other women and Teddy . . . I can hardly believe you wouldn't confront her."

She laughs, but it's not convincing this time. "I didn't have the nerve back when I was younger, Bess. And I couldn't do anything to Henrietta. She was my best friend! Although, well . . . she wasn't always such a good one."

"I guess not, if you thought she—".

"As much as I loved her, Henrietta was one of those friends who, when you parted company, didn't leave you feeling better about yourself. Do you know what I mean?"

"Yes, I do," I say, thinking of Anna from work. "But, Susannah, I just don't get it . . . If you and Bradley were so close, planning to get married and all . . . why didn't you confront him?".

"Did Bradley tell you we were planning to get married?" she says, her eyes brightening in a way that, honestly, frightens me a bit.

"Well, no, Susannah," I say. "You did."

"Of course." She laughs. "Of course. So why didn't I confront him?" She shrugs demurely. "Well, I can't really explain it . . . First loves, you know. You forgive so much. And it was a different time back then. Men got away with that stuff. Women turned a blind eye. Look at JFK and Jackie."

"How exactly did things end with you and Bradley?" I ask, daring to tread a little deeper than I maybe should.

"Oh!" she says. A stunned expression appears on her face, almost like I've just slapped her.

It surprises me, how the question seems to upset her. "I'm sorry," I say. "I shouldn't have—"

"No, no," she says, a tautness in her tone. "It's a legitimate question. There wasn't a specific moment it ended, to be honest."

"What do you mean? Surely you had a conversation . . ."

"Bess, when Henrietta died, it should have brought us closer together. You know," she explains. "Because we shared the horrific loss."

"Well, of course," I say, wondering what else she could possibly mean. *Surely not because Henrietta was now out of the picture . . .*

"But instead, I just sort of disappeared into myself. I didn't want to be around anyone. The day we graduated from Draper, I was like a zombie. I hardly remember it. Bradley's parents threw a party. My parents came, pretended to care about me . . ." She shakes her head. "Bradley tried to get me to talk to him, to tell him what I was feeling, but it was all just too painful, Bess. I couldn't handle being in Greyhill without her. As complicated as our friendship was, we were always together, always, and after she died, I felt her loss in a physical way, like her ghost was hovering just beside me, wherever I went."

I suddenly feel guilty for bringing it up. "It must have been so difficult," I say, reaching out and placing my hand over hers. She turns her hand over underneath mine and wraps her fingers around my palm.

"It didn't help that when people in town looked at me, they saw her. Or her absence, I guess. I had to get out of here. A few days after our graduation, I left. It wasn't this grand plan. I just woke up one morning, packed a bag, and left. Henrietta had talked about joining the airlines, so I decided that's what I would do. In her honor, I guess."

"What did your parents think?"

"They didn't know until after I'd gone. I'd bribed one of the maids to take me to the train station in Charlottesville."

"And Bradley just accepted it?"

"He had no choice but to. I called him from a pay phone that first night. I was terrified. I'd read about the Barbizon, and they took me right in—I had the money, I'd taken some from my father's office—but I felt like I was in another country. Honestly, when I told him I didn't know how long I'd be gone and to move on with his life, to forget about me, I think he was relieved." She wipes a tear from her cheek. "I'd burdened him enough."

"I'm sure he didn't feel that way."

"Well . . . like I said . . . he'd already moved on from me, in a way. . . ."

Despite what she's just accused Bradley of, I ache for her. She sounds so bereft, like the things she's talking about happened just recently, not years and years ago. The pain has obviously never subsided. "You really miss her," I say.

"I always think of what we might be doing if she'd lived," she says, her voice vibrating with pain. "The places we might have gone together, the things we might have done." She looks at me, her blue eyes rimmed with red. "Everyone thinks I've had this extravagant life, but Henrietta was the far more adventurous spirit of the two of us. If things hadn't turned out the way they did, I would have just stayed here. Henrietta would have done something big with her life," she says. "I'm sure of it.

"Now," she says, pulling her hand from mine and wiping her eyes. "That's enough. We should really move on from all these sad stories. Why don't we get to your questions?"

"Okay." I open my bag and take out my notebook, trying to ignore the somber energy that's fallen over the room. There is, of course, one question I'd love to ask her now, before we move on. It's the perfect moment. *What does she think about the fact that people in town say she had something to do with Henrietta's death?* But I can't do it. Not now. Not after everything she's just revealed to me.

She's quiet, waiting for me as I flip through the pages.

"So," I say, running my pen down my list of questions.

"Ask away, honey," she says, the ease in her voice obviously trying to compensate for the dark turn our conversation has taken. "Really, go on."

I stop and look at her, slumping a little into the needlepoint pillow behind me as I do. "I'm sorry," I say. "I'd prepared some trickier questions this time, and it feels a little strange, asking them now."

"Just ask already," she says. "Go for it." She reaches out and pats my leg again.

"All right," I say. "Well . . . You said . . . a little while ago . . . that you and Bradley talk occasionally."

She nods.

"And that you'd like Bradley to help you with your reputation around town, so let's talk about that."

"Shoot," she says.

"The land," I say. "We need to talk about the land, since that was the initial focus when my editor assigned the story. They want to know how you hope that selling it might change Greyhill. Do you really want the town to become like another Middleburg? I heard your Realtor brought someone to the inn last week. An exec from Silicon Valley."

"So you heard about that, then!" she says, seeming pleased.

"I did."

"I do have some interested buyers from out of town. Several buyers. But as far as my hopes go . . ." She pauses. "You know, people seem to think I don't care what happens with the land. They think that because I haven't been here, that I don't have Greyhill in my blood, but I do. I don't want this place to change any more than anyone else does. What people don't give me credit for, you know, is that I could have just sold the land to one of those builders—that's what my agent advised me to do, by the way—but I wasn't about to have it all subdivided into a bunch of little tacky houses. I am being particular about who I sell to, based on what they want to do with it."

"That's good to know," I say, writing it down. "Because people in town, I hear, are worried that you're just going to sell to whomever . . ."

"Oh, please!" She rolls her eyes. "You know, I never anticipated that this would become such a *thing*. I should've known better. People around here need something to have an opinion about, and I'm an easy target."

"You have a point there, too," I say. "But you could clear it up easily enough, couldn't you? If you want so badly to be accepted here—"

"Bess," she says, putting her hand out to stop me. "I don't want anything *so badly*."

"No, you're right," I say. "I stand corrected. But what I'm getting at is, if you want your life to be easier here, if you're settled here, then why sell the land at all?"

"Because I don't have any use for it," she says, like it's as simple as that.

"That's all?" I say.

She nods, her lips in a tight line.

"Susannah," I say, noticing how her expression has changed. She looks like she's hiding something. "What is it?"

"Well, I've told you enough today," she finally says, and I notice how her voice is shaking. "I may as well tell you the rest."

She sighs and presses her fingers to the corners of her eyes.

There's a box of tissues on the old trunk in front of us, and I reach to hand it to her. She takes one, pats it in dainty taps under her eyes, and continues. "I'm going to tell you a *real* secret now, Bess," she says. "But I have to know I can trust you. I don't want you to say anything to anyone about the things I'm telling you today. This is strictly off-the-record."

"Of course," I say, wondering what on earth this could be about. "You can trust me with anything."

"I know that I've alluded a bit to the kind of man my husband was," she says. "You know, like when I told you that story at William's, about how I used to go to the museum? How things weren't what they seemed?"

I nod.

"The truth is . . ." She sniffs. "I thought that when I left Greyhill, I was escaping for a better life. The life I was meant to have. But my life with Teddy was awful. A *nightmare*."

"Susannah . . . ," I start, my heart sinking.

"No, no," she says, her voice suddenly stern. "I'll tell you all of it, but I don't want your pity."

"Of course," I say.

"Teddy controlled me. It was his belief that if you didn't earn the money yourself, then you didn't get any of it. He had me on an allowance, like a child. He picked the clothes I wore, the parties we went to . . . He expected me to be a certain kind of wife."

"Why didn't you leave?" I ask. "You're such a strong woman. You had all those friends . . ."

"I know," she says. "I know. And I ask myself that same question all the time, especially now. But, you know, as much as I suffered, my life was . . . it was a gilded cage, really. I'll tell you one thing: it's a blessing that I couldn't have children."

"I'm sorry, Susannah. I didn't know that," I say, though the truth is, I was curious about why they'd never started a family.

"Don't be sorry," she says. "He would have been a horrible father, and I know a thing or two about bad parenting."

"Susannah . . ."

"It would have been a good distraction for me, though. The only thing I did for myself during the course of our entire marriage was writing that silly newspaper column. Is it any wonder to you, now that you know, that I was so focused on other people's lives?"

"I never thought of it that way."

"Well, I think I thought that if I could just keep myself busy, everything would be fine. But then Teddy died, and . . ." She starts to cry.

"What is it, Susannah?"

She's silent for a moment, wringing her tissue in her hands. "You know how, in his will, he gave all that money to charity?"

"Yes," I say.

"Oh, the media!" she moans. "How generous of Teddy Lane! How saintly! To give away his millions and millions!" She rolls her eyes. "Well, what those articles didn't say, because they didn't know, is that Teddy left me with nothing."

"Nothing?"

"Nothing," she repeats through her tears. "Zero. I left New York, Bess, because I had no other choice. I had my clothes, the furniture, a little bit of money that was left in our bank account, and that truck. He had stipulated in his will that everything else was to be given away or sold. The apartment, the house in the country, all of it—gone."

"But why would he do that?" I say. "That is so . . ."

"Cruel?" she says, her sobs growing heavier. "Believe me, I've tried to figure it out. Why he would do it, how I couldn't have seen . . ." She reaches for another tissue. "Bess, I'm selling the land because I have no other choice. Along with the house and the little bit of money I have, which is going to run out before too long, the land is it. I won't be able to pay Cindy much longer, not unless I start selling things. And I think she's starting to catch on."

"I see," I say. "I never would have . . ."

"No, you wouldn't have," she says. "That's just the thing. Everyone thinks they know everything there is to know about me. Everyone thinks I'm this horrible, out-of-touch bitch up on the hill. The truth is, I'm just trying to keep my head above water."

"Susannah, I'm so—"

"Don't," she says.

I nod.

"The reason I agreed to do this story with you, Bess, was that I thought the publicity would be good for the land. It has to sell."

"I get it," I say. "Believe me, I do."

"So will you help me, then?" she says. "Write something that will make people come. Make it *wonderful*. It's been eight months, Bess, and we can't find a single buyer. I'm starting to think I'm going to have to do something else. This house . . ." She waves her hand around like a hostess introducing the prizes on a game show. "It takes a lot of money to run a place like this."

I nod. My head is reeling from the past hour with her.

"Can I ask you something?" she says, crumpling her tissue in her hands.

"Yes, of course."

"Do you think this is karma, Bess? Is it the world's way of getting back at me for all the horrible things I've done? Those things I told you?"

"Susannah, no," I say, an uneasy tingle on my skin at the mention of her revenge schemes. "It won't help you to blame yourself. Nobody deserves to be treated the way he treated you."

"That's right," she says, and for the first time since I've known her, she looks old. Worn out, weary. "Nobody does. Nobody, it seems, except me."

SEVENTEEN

‚ô≠‚ïê‚ïê‚ïê‚ïê‚ïê‚ïê‚ïê‚ïê‚ïê‚ô≠

"Who was that who just walked out of here?"

"Somebody staying at the inn. From Virginia Beach, I guess."

"Speaking of the inn!"

"What?"

"I heard that Martha Brown saw Cole and his wife having it out the other night."

"Really?"

"Mm-hmm. I didn't talk to her directly, but from what I heard, they were screaming at each other on the sidewalk, right in the middle of town! And she heard the wife say something about Eva."

"Eva?"

"Yup."

"Didn't Eva and Cole date back when they were kids?"

"They *sure did*."

"You know, now that I think about it . . . When was this?"

"Over the weekend."

"Wait . . . We had dinner at the Herringbone on Friday. I saw Cole and Bess sitting at the bar."

"Did they look happy?"

"Sure. She seemed to be doing most of the talking."

"I'll tell you what, I don't know what Cole's type is now that he's grown, but she's nothing at all like Eva. Doesn't seem to be, at least."

"You don't think Cole and Eva . . ."

"No, I don't think Cole would . . . But Eva, on the other hand . . ."

"Oh, no way! The mayor's wife? She loves that husband of hers."

"Come on! What she loves is being the mayor's wife."

"Well, I read Eva's blog, and it looks to me like she is perfectly happy. She's got a nice little life. I don't think she'd screw that up."

"Yeah, but . . ."

"What?"

"I guess I just see it differently. I read Eva's blog, too, and *nobody's* life is that perfect."

"I don't know. If anyone's messing around, I might put it more on Cole."

"Really? Why?"

"I shouldn't say anything."

"Oh, come on."

"I heard that the reason Cole and Bess moved back here is that they don't have any money. She's a real spender, I guess. Or *was*."

"Huh. Now *that's* interesting."

"Isn't it? And you know, I was thinking, maybe that's why she's spending all that time with Susannah Lane."

"You think she wants in on Susannah's money? Trying to get herself written into the will?"

"I mean, if what people are saying is true, it would make sense."

"Yes, it sure would, wouldn't it?"

EIGHTEEN

Bess

"If that came in a brighter color, it would already be in my closet," Carol says, looking at me over the top of her leopard-print reading glasses from her spot behind her vintage cash register, where she's twirling a pencil in her hand and marking up a stack of invoices on the counter in front of her.

"It's pretty," I say, checking the price tag on a soft gray cashmere cardigan before I release it from my grip. I turn to the rack behind me. Carol's shop feels like the well-appointed bedroom of an adored older sister, warm and feminine, with scented candles perfuming the air, but somehow I can't relax. I'm not looking for anything in particular, just came in to kill time this afternoon before I meet the kids.

I ran around town all day like a second-string Nancy Drew, trying to dig up information about Henrietta, whom I can't seem to get out of my mind since my last meeting with Susannah. The more time passes since that meeting, the more I think how odd it is that she segued from crazy revenge stories about the women who tried to seduce Teddy into this whole thing about my father-in-law and Henrietta. I know it's probably my imagination getting the best of me (too much time on my hands, my mother would say), but it makes me wonder about how Henrietta died . . . And then how she threw in the fact that she's broke, to boot? Every time I think of it, I feel a pang of sadness for her. She's just so complicated, so difficult, so eccentric . . . I don't know what to make of her, and after everything that happened to me in Washington, I'm scared of trusting her too quickly. How this will all play into the actual story I need to write, I don't know, but I'm feeling the pressure. I don't want to leave a single stone unturned. I want this to be perfect.

I went to the library today to research, which proved incredibly frustrating. Aside from a short, three-sentence obituary, I couldn't find a single news story about Henrietta's death. I don't know what I expected to find—some buried article revealing Susannah's true nature, some missive explaining it all—but I do think it's strange that when I asked the librarian why there wasn't anything in the old *Greyhill Times* about the incident, she looked at me as if I'd asked her to exhume Henrietta's body from the little graveyard near her family home where she's apparently buried alongside her parents.

I'm starting to realize that there are certain things people talk about in Greyhill and certain things they don't, and Henrietta Martin, all these years later, appears to be on the *don't* list, no matter what those women might have said to me back at the Barkers' Halloween party. When I stopped at William's after the library, I asked him why he thought this was. "It's just not good manners, Bess," he explained. "Nobody wants to admit that anything bad could ever happen in Greyhill, even if the something bad happened fifty years ago."

⤜⟿————⟾⤛

"You okay?" Carol says.

"What?"

"You're just slapping those hangers together like they've offended you," she says.

"Oh, I am?" I say, pulling my hand away from the rack like it's just burned me. "I'm sorry, I didn't realize." I turn and run my finger along the embroidery on a white blouse. "I badly need to upgrade my wardrobe," I say. "I don't know what to wear for my life around here." *Now that I no longer need work clothes,* I think.

"That would look nice on you," she says, nodding her forehead toward the white blouse.

"I don't know," I say, looking down at my uniform of navy sweater and jeans. "I feel so . . ." I shrug. "It might have something to do with all this time I'm spending with Susannah. Her outfits . . ." I shake my head. "I wish you could see. She had on these shoes the other day . . . little embroidered slipper things that she said she got in Casablanca in the seventies."

"And I bet they're worth more than everything in here put together," Carol says, stepping down from her perch and coming around the register.

Good point, I think. *Why doesn't Susannah sell some of her couture items, too, if she's so desperate?*

"How's that going, anyway?" Carol asks.

"Fine," I say, weighing whether to say more. "You know, to be honest, I quite like her. She's really funny, and deeper than I think anyone gives her credit for. She's actually been through a lot." I watch Carol's expression to see how she'll react.

"Oh, *yeah*," Carol laughs. "Must have been difficult, being married to a gazillionaire. I'd take that tough life."

"You'd be surprised," I say, running my hand down the side of a long blue skirt.

"What do you mean?" she says.

"Just that looks can be deceiving," I say.

"Seems pretty straightforward to me," she says. "Superrich, born with a silver spoon . . ."

"Yeah, but . . ." I bite my lip. "Do you know her?"

"No, not really." She shrugs. "I did feel bad for her after the accident. But, you know, my neighbor said she had that coming."

"What do you mean, *had it coming*? She lost control of her car."

"I still don't believe that."

"Carol, she told me herself that's what happened."

"Okay, okay. Suit yourself," she says, straightening a pile of sweaters on a table. "Hey, Eva was in here earlier. She said she ran into you guys last weekend."

"Uh-huh," I say, turning away from her. I don't need her to see the residual anger on my face, the evidence of Eva's effect on me like a fading bruise.

"I guess she and Mindy were having a big night, huh?" She laughs. "She said she barely got out of bed the next day."

"Doesn't surprise me," I mutter.

"You know, though . . . ," Carol says, leaning against the rack of clothing I'm pretending to be more interested in than I actually am. "It's good for Mindy to blow off some steam, after everything she's been through."

"What do you mean?" I say.

"You don't know?" she says.

I shrug. "Nope."

Her eyes dart to the door, and then she takes a step toward me. "She found out that Greg was sleeping with someone else."

"How terrible," I say, feeling suddenly guilty about how I'd discounted Mindy as an oblivious ditz. "How many kids do they have?"

"Three," she says. "Three under six."

"Was it recent? The party was just—"

"Oh, noooo," Carol says. "It was last year."

"Oh," I say. "So she stayed, obviously? They're working it out?"

"Well, *of course* she stayed," Carol whispers.

"What do you mean *of course*?"

Carol looks surprised. "Where else would she go?"

"Right . . . ," I say, thinking that it's a funny way to look at it. I try to work it out in my head: I suppose if you marry someone from town, and you have always lived in town, and your families are all in town . . . "God, how did he think he'd get away with it, in a place as small as this?" I say before I can stop myself.

"*Exactly*," Carol says. "And you'll die when I tell you who it was."

"I don't need to know," I say, though the truth is, I very much want to know.

"*Dahlia.*"

"Like, from Dahlia's, Dahlia?" I say, thinking of the restaurant's stunning owner. "But she's so . . ."

"I know!" Carol says.

"And he's so . . ."

"I *know!*"

"Wow," I say.

"A bunch of guys used to have a monthly poker night there, and I guess Greg tended to stick around at the end of the night and hang out with her. Mindy figured it out once she heard from the other wives that their husbands got home at a reasonable hour, and Greg did not. She caught him herself. Drove over there in the middle of the night and found them in a *very* compromising position behind the bar."

"Oh, yuck," I say, wincing at the mental picture. "I don't need to hear any more."

Carol laughs. "Makes you think twice about wanting to eat a burger at the bar there, doesn't it?"

"Yes," I say. "Are you guys close?"

"Me and Mindy?" she asks. "I used to babysit her. I've known her my whole life."

"Right," I say, thinking also that this is another prime example of why I'm never going to be able to confide in any of the women I've met in Greyhill so far—except, it seems, oddly enough, Susannah. Everyone else *talks* so much, I think, remembering how Eva and Mindy went on and on about Whitney the other night. It's like a competitive sport.

"Well, I'm glad Mindy got out and had some fun," Carol says. "She deserves it for putting up with that asshole."

"I guess so," I say, lifting a green dress from a rack.

"Why don't you try that?" Carol says. "The color would be great on you."

"Hmmm," I say, looking at the dress and considering whether

a gathered waist is a good move for me right now. "Why not?" I take the dress and start toward the dressing room in the back of the store.

"Hey," Carol says suddenly.

"Huh?"

She points toward the storefront window. "Isn't that your daughter?"

"What?"

I weave around a rack of clothes and look out the picture window in the front of the store. Sure enough, there is Livvie, walking with a group of girls from school, all of them moving together in one skipping, giggling blob. "Aww," I say, my heart swelling at the sight of her having a good time. *Take that, Eva and Mindy*, I think, remembering how they accused Livvie of being a bully. There's Lauren, of course, easy to spot because of her cautious gait, and Brittany (hmph) behind them, with three other girls I don't recognize. "Yes, that's Livvie," I say. "She asked if she and some friends could walk down to William's together after school today. I'm supposed to meet her and her brother at the inn at four thirty."

"It doesn't look like they're going to William's," Carol laughs, as we watch the girls pass by the front door of the coffee shop.

"Wait," I say. "Where are they . . . ?"

Livvie's friend Lauren is walking slightly in front of her, and before I know what I'm seeing, Livvie is reaching out, grabbing for Lauren's ponytail. At first I think it's a friendly tug, two kids kidding around. Lauren laughs as her head dips back.

But then—I can't believe what I'm seeing—Livvie suddenly lets go, but she's not laughing. She has that intense, almost pained look on her face that she gets when she's working on a challenging homework assignment. She glances back at Brittany, as if to make sure she's watching, and then she grasps the handle on the back of Lauren's backpack and jerks it. *Hard*.

Lauren falls backward onto the sidewalk, her feet splaying out in front of her like an ice-skater who's just flubbed a landing.

Lauren's not laughing anymore. She's hurt. But Livvie—

No. *No, no, no, no, no*.

Livvie is. *Livvie* is laughing. Even louder now. So loud, in fact, that I can hear it as clearly as if it was the tinny melody of an ice-cream truck coming down the street. The other girls start laughing, too. Brittany is *howling*, clapping her hands—no, *applauding*. My heart starts to thrum. My mouth goes dry.

I watch as Livvie steps over Lauren. She *steps over* her friend and keeps walking, *laughing*. Brittany catches up to Livvie, taking a little hop-step. And then Livvie circles her arm into Brittany's and keeps walking. She doesn't even look back.

I do. My eyes dart back to Lauren. She is struggling to get up, her heavy backpack weighing her down. Her hair is falling in front of her face. She's brushing dirt off the side of her leg. A woman walking out of William's stops, her paper coffee cup in her hand. She stoops down and Lauren shields her face, trying to make herself disappear. I know that feeling. I know that feeling *exactly*. The woman looks down the street at Livvie and the other girls, screams something after them.

Livvie is still laughing.

"I can't—" I drop the dress and race out of the store and across the street, careening past a Volvo station wagon that stops short when the driver sees me.

"Livvie!" I scream. "Olivia Warner, you stop right there!"

Lauren is up on her feet. "Lauren, honey!" I stretch my arms out to her. The girl turns and scrambles away in the other direction. Her face is splotched with pink. There are tears streaming down her face.

A vision pops into my head. The cafeteria at the Oak Hill School. *"That is so disgusting. You are so disgusting."*

Livvie isn't moving now. Or laughing. She stands frozen, her face pale.

"Olivia Warner, I can't believe what I just saw!" I wail, my voice warbling with rage. The other girls stand behind her, but their expressions are amused, and it's that very fact—their incongruous reaction—that makes it clear: I know who these girls are, this type. They *love* this. They are *pleased* by this, deliciously so. But Livvie . . .

Oh, Livvie.

"Mom," she says, barely able to get the word out, the panic evident in her voice. *Mommy.* The word flashes in my head. *Mother.*

"Why on earth would you do that?" I shout, my voice trembling and panicked. "Why would you do that to your friend?"

She looks down at the ground, her face hard, my questions bouncing right off her.

I take another step forward, so close that I can see the tiny mole just beneath the collar of her shirt.

"Livvie, you need to come with me. Right this minute!" I say, trying and failing to keep my voice measured. I will grab her by the scruff of her coat if I have to. I'm not above it. "This is unacceptable," I say through gritted teeth.

"Mom, stop!" she says, her voice barely a whisper. "Mom, people are . . ."

I scan the street. Sure enough, a crowd has gathered. A family holding their leftover containers outside the café across the street. Carol, outside her shop, the green dress in her hands. William, just a few feet away, standing in the threshold of the bakery. The other girls have scattered, like cockroaches in the light.

"Livvie." I lower my voice. "Livvie, what's gotten into you?"

"Mom," she pleads. "Can we just . . . Can we *go*?" The look on her face is pained, like *she's* the victim. I am so angry at her. I have never been this angry at her. I have been irritated and frustrated, worried, like after that day in the parking lot, when she wouldn't talk to me and it scared me about what was yet to come. About moments like this. I grab her arm and yank her in the direction of the inn.

As we start down the street, I feel like we are walking across a stage. Eyes on us. People whispering. Out of the corner of my eye, I see the Volvo that I nearly collided with pull up to the curb. The driver rolls her window down. *Mindy.* Of course. What a coincidence—except, no, there are no fucking coincidences in Greyhill. How *could* there be?

"Everything okay, Bess?" she says, a soppy smile on her face like the last few minutes have disappeared, a lightning flash swallowed into the dark sky.

I look at her, her cheeks sucked in as she sips something from a monogrammed Tervis tumbler. *What's the smile for?* I wonder. Is this her way of letting me know that she saw what just happened, that she was right about my daughter? *Kind of a mean girl*, she'd said the other night. The words ring in my ears.

"Fine, Mindy," I say, my voice shaking as I grip Livvie's arm. "Everything's totally fine."

NINETEEN

"Brittany made me do it!" Livvie wails as I drag her into Cole's office. "It was all her idea!"

I close the door, resting my palms on the back of it for a moment to collect myself and slow my pounding heart.

"What is going on?" Cole says, standing up from his desk. His gaze goes from me to Livvie.

"Go ahead, Liv," I say, my voice still trembling with anger. "Go ahead and tell him."

She looks at me, her eyes pleading, and then her face crumples again. She stands there, her shoulders shaking from her sobs, Cole and I watching her from opposite sides of the room. He comes around his desk and puts his arm around her, catching my eye when I shake my head at him, telling him to stop.

No, I think. *No, she does not get a pass on this. If we coddle her through this, she'll never learn.*

"What happened?" Cole says, his voice gentle. "Livvie, what is it?"

"Go ahead, Liv," I say, my voice like a sergeant's. "Go ahead and tell your father about the scene you just caused in the middle of town."

"Scene?" I knew that would get his attention. He shifts a half turn toward her, putting his hands on her shoulders so he can look directly into her eyes. "What scene, Livvie?"

"It's *her* fault!" she screams, her right arm flailing in my direction. "She's the reason there was a scene!"

"Oh, *no, no, no*," I say, taking a step toward them. "You do *not* get to put this on me, Olivia." I look to Cole. "I was in Carol's shop and happened to look out the window just in time to see your daughter push her friend down in the middle of the street."

"Livvie," he says. "Is this true?"

I roll my eyes. I want to kick the earnest, even-keeled, Mr. Brady–style reasoning right out of him. "*Yes*, Cole, of course it's true!"

"It was just a joke, Mom! You're the one who freaked out and started screaming in the street!" she wails.

"Livvie, lower your voice," Cole says, looking from me to her.

"It wasn't a joke, Livvie. Don't you dare lie to me! I saw the whole thing, and I saw the look on Lauren's face when you *pulled her onto the sidewalk and stepped over her, and then kept walking while you laughed with your friends!*"

"I didn't mean it!" she says, snot running down her face as she speaks. "I didn't mean to do anything!"

"Oh, Livvie, enough with the act," I say. "I saw you with my own two eyes, and you clearly meant to do exactly what you did. Why on earth would you do something like that? This is *not* who you are! This is *not* the girl we raised you to be!"

"I don't know," she says, her eyes on the floor as she cries. "I don't know why I did it."

"Because Brittany told you to?"

"Oh, Bess," Cole says. "Come on."

I gasp. "Really, Cole?" I put my arm out to Livvie. "Look at this! Is this the kid you know? You didn't see what I just saw out there. It's these kids she's hanging out with! Eva's daughter!"

"Come on, Bess," he says, pulling a chair out for Livvie to sit down. She does, wiping her nose with the sleeve of her shirt. "It might not be . . ." He looks at Livvie. "Is what your mom said true, Liv? Was it because of the other kids?"

She nods her head, her eyes still on the floor. "Brittany dared me to do it," Livvie says. "She dared me to." She starts to cry again. "I don't know why I agreed, I just . . ."

"Livvie, you know better than that," Cole says.

"We taught you how to treat people," I say. "You know better than to hurt someone like that."

She finally looks at me. *Finally.*

"Like you can talk, Mom."

My stomach drops. I suddenly feel dizzy. *"What?"*

Her chin starts to wobble. "Like you can talk!" she says, her voice gaining strength. "Look at what you did! You got fired because you were mean to someone! And it was the *First Lady!*"

I'm stunned. I look at Cole, the pressure in my chest like the wind's been knocked out of me. Of course, the kids knew what had happened with me. We'd talked about it—how kids at school would probably say things, how they might hear things that might or might not be true—but we said it was a more complicated situation than we could really explain, and they seemed okay with that reasoning.

"Livvie," Cole says. "What happened with your mother's job has nothing to do with this situation."

She looks down at her lap. "How could it not?" she says. "I heard you on the tapes, Mom. What did Grandma say when she heard them? Was she proud of how *she'd* raised *you* then? What do you think people are going to think of you now? Now that they've seen you screaming at your daughter in the middle of town?"

My mouth falls open. I look to Cole, whose shocked expression matches my own. She's never talked back to either of us this way. "Livvie," I say, trying to keep my voice steady. "Livvie, what happened with me, once again, has nothing to do with this. Now, here's what's going to happen: We are going to go home, and you are going to get on the phone and call Lauren's house and apologize to her. And then you are grounded. Your father and I will think of an appropriate punishment."

Cole's eyes meet mine and he nods, just slightly, in acknowledgment.

We sit there, all three of us silent, but I can feel the anxiety and sadness swirling in the room as plainly as if we were sitting in the center of a storm. I don't want her teenage years to look like this. I *can't* let her teenage years look like this.

"Mommy," Livvie suddenly says, her voice small. "I'm sor—" She starts to cry before she can get the words out.

I go to her. I am so angry, so confused, but I know what it's like to be her age, and so I put my arms around her and shush away her sobs. "I know you are," I say. "And I know you know better."

"I didn't mean it," she says. "I really didn't."

"I know," I say. "But you need to think about Lauren now. There are consequences, Liv. You have to make this right."

She nods into the crook of my neck. Suddenly the door creaks open, and Max steps in, a baffled expression on his face. "They told me you were all back here," he says, hitching his thumb toward the hall. He looks at Livvie. "What's going on?" he says. "Did something happen?"

"It's okay," Cole says. "We'll talk about it later. Let's let your sister collect herself and then you guys go out front. I want to talk to your mom alone for a minute."

Livvie looks up at us like a cowering, orphaned animal. She stands, wipes her hands across her face, and then follows Max out to the hall.

"So which one of us is going to call Eva?" I say, once the door has closed behind the twins.

"What are you talking about?" he says, moving back around his desk.

"One of us needs to," I say. "Mindy saw the whole thing, too, you know." I shake my head. "This fucking town," I say, muttering under my breath.

Cole rubs his hands over his face. "What exactly happened out there?"

I gesture toward the door. "You heard her. Just what we said. I saw her push Lauren down and start walking away and laughing with Brittany and those other kids, and then I ran after them."

"Why did you run after them, Bess?" He sounds tired, a fact that only incenses me more. He doesn't get to judge how I handled this, not when he's sitting back here in his little office, drinking iced tea and getting his ass kissed by his staff while I'm out doing the hard labor of raising almost-teenagers.

"You're kidding, right?"

He sits down and threads his fingers through his hair,

scratching at his scalp. "Listen, I don't know what happened. I didn't see it—"

"No, you didn't," I say. "Of course you didn't."

He sighs. "Bess, at a certain point, we're going to have to let her figure this stuff out on her own."

"You think I should just mind my own business? Just turn my back while our daughter carries out Brittany's orders?"

"I don't think she's doing anything she doesn't want to do," he says.

"And that's a *good* thing? When she's making these kinds of decisions?"

He sits back, his palms flat on the desk pad in front of him. "And it's better for you to fly into the fray and start screaming at her in the middle of town?"

My stomach starts to burn. "Oh my God," I say. "How did I not get it? I should have known. You're more worried about how this looks than about what actually happened."

"Oh, come on, Bess," he says. "Come on. It's just, like I said the other night—"

"Don't get me started on the other night. So what is it, Cole? On top of everything else, now I'm a bad mother?"

"Bess, don't be ridiculous."

"You're the one who's being ridiculous!" I say, starting for the door. I put my hand on the knob before I turn around. "So make a decision," I say. "I'm not backing down. Are you going to call Eva or am I?"

He closes his eyes. "Fine," he says, throwing a hand up in the air. "I'll do it."

"And what are you going to say?"

"I don't know, Bess," he says. "But I'll do it."

"Tell her what I saw, and tell her what Livvie said—that her daughter was the one who made Livvie push Lauren. Tell her we won't stand for her kid to treat ours like one of her minions. Tell her that Livvie is not going to do her dirty work."

He looks at me across the silent room, my words reverberating in the air. They sound silly and childish now that they're hanging out there between us.

"Okay," I say, leaning back against the wall and rubbing a hand over my mouth. "Maybe it's not the solution."

He looks at me, his eyes aching and sympathetic. It's a look I know well after this past year.

"Did you hear how she spoke to me?" I say, the tears welling up in my eyes.

He hops up from his desk. I meet him in the middle of the room and bury my head in his chest. "I just don't know what I'm doing, Cole. I don't know how to handle her growing up."

"I know," he says. "This is new for all of us."

"How will we get through it?" I say. "I just want everything to be easier. And calm. I just want her to be okay. I want all of us to be okay."

He doesn't say anything. He rubs my back, his chin resting on top of my head. "I don't know," he says. "But it's going to work out. It's going to get easier, I promise."

"Right," I say, but the truth is, I don't believe a word of it.

TWENTY

"Well, it sounds like you've had a shitty few days," Susannah says, staring at me from across the table in her breakfast room. She's invited me over for lunch, and I've just unloaded on her about what happened with Livvie yesterday. I'm apparently so fed up with everything that I've lost my will to care about whether it's wise to confide in Susannah.

"I didn't even tell you about how my mother-in-law laid into me," I say, my mind zipping back to the night before, when Cole and the kids and I were eating our spaghetti dinner in silence, Livvie pushing her food around her plate, and Diane started knocking on the front door, her telltale staccato *bang-bang-bang*, the sound like a lunatic woodpecker. I'd locked the door before dinner, anticipating this, and felt a swell of justification when I heard her start jiggling the doorknob.

Cole offered to go deal with her, but I met her out on the front stoop, closing the door behind me so the kids wouldn't hear, and listened to her go on for an easy ten minutes about how her phone was ringing off the hook with people calling to ask about my quote-unquote *outburst*. "She acted like I'd walked down the middle of Maple stark naked," I say now.

Susannah moans. "That woman." She shakes her head. "What is it about you that bothers her so much?"

"I can't tell you how many hours I've spent trying to figure that out," I say. "I'm simply not the kind of person she pictured for a daughter-in-law. I am the embodiment of the hardest lesson she's probably ever had to learn, which is that she can't control everything, including who her son chose to marry."

"That's a good way to put it," she says, pointing a finger at me. Her lipstick is bright pageant-girl pink. "Teddy's mother was similar. She was like a wax figure in a Chanel suit. No pulse, no personality, no opinion."

"I think that's what Diane would prefer me to be," I say. "I think I'm *too much*, if that makes any sense. Too focused on my work—or used to be—too independent, too Northern . . . Too much *not like her*, essentially."

"I saw her walking into the Parlour the other day," Susannah says, referencing the local hair salon.

"She gets her hair set and pressed every other Tuesday." I laugh. I know I shouldn't, but it feels good to vent about Diane— like sneaking a second cookie at night after everyone else is in bed.

Susannah makes a face. "She's like an old woman! Goodness, her taste . . ."

"I know," I say. "You should hear how she's fighting me on updating the inn."

"Updating the inn?" she says, waving hello to Cindy as she comes into the room.

"Yeah," I say. "Cole and I have a lot of ideas. Bradley's receptive to them," I say, conscious of how her eyes flicker at the sound of his name. "But Diane . . . she acts like we want to turn the place into a carnival."

"If you don't mind me asking, Bess . . ."

"Shoot."

"What is it like, running it?" she asks. "Wasn't Cole a lawyer back in DC? This is a big change."

I nod. "He was. And he's happy to not be one anymore." I look at her and smile. "I *think*. Anyway, the inn is good. It's always been a stable business, but Cole and I would like to do something to shake it up."

"Great idea," she says. "I know people in town shudder at the thought of it, but Greyhill has real potential to be a destination. You know, it's so beautiful, and with the wineries that have popped up everywhere, I really think something could happen around here."

"Maybe," I say. "Though, to be honest, after the week I've had, I have a bad taste in my mouth about everything about this place."

"I get it," she says, twisting in her seat to call for Cindy, who's walked through a swinging door into the kitchen. "I have an idea," she says. "Something I was thinking about this morning. It's a beautiful day, so much warmer than it should be. Are you up for eating outside?"

"Sure," I say.

And just when I think Susannah can't top her ability to surprise me, I find myself helping her out the window of her childhood bedroom and onto a terrace that I didn't even know existed.

"Susannah!" I say. "This is crazy." I noticed when she got up from the table that she didn't use her cane, and I thought of what Cindy whispered to me in the hall the last time I was here—that Susannah's problems since the accident might be more in her head than in her body. Even though she'd asked for my help, she didn't have any more trouble crawling out the window than I did.

"Perfect!" she says, brushing the dust from the windowsill off her hands.

"*This* is where we're eating lunch?" I say, shielding my eyes from the sun. The view is glorious, mountains in all directions, lit up in vibrant shades of orange and red. I take a step in the direction of town, watching the cars move up and down the tiny grid of streets, the buildings looking, from here, like the ones in a train set, with their boxy shapes and sweet, shingled roofs. It looks so quaint. And, I think, like lots of things viewed from a distance, so harmless.

"Come and sit," she says, walking across the tiled floor to where a couple of rusted old camp chairs are set up against the wall.

"Susannah, are you sure you want to eat here?" I say, scanning the dirty floor, the piles of dead leaves that have collected in the corners.

She sits in one of the chairs.

"This is comfortable for you?"

"I came out here all the time before the accident," she says. "It's been ages since I've done it. Come, sit." She pats the seat of the chair next to hers.

"Are you sure?"

"Please," she says, lifting the silver scarf from her neck and wrapping it over the top of her head. "I'm only seventy, Bess. Don't treat me like I have one foot in the grave."

I sit down next to her.

"Henrietta and I used to spend a lot of time out here," she says, a wan smile passing over her face.

"I have to confess something to you," I say, acting on what I'd resolved to myself on the drive over.

"Ooh, good!" she says. "A confession!"

"I did some digging around town the other day, trying to learn more about her."

"Henrietta?" she says, like this puzzles her.

I nod.

"Why?" she asks, clearly surprised.

"Well," I start. "Forgive me for saying it, but every time her name comes up, a funny expression falls over your face. I feel, in a way, that if I want to understand you better—or, at least, your relationship to the town—then I need to understand her." I decide to leave it at that, even though I promised myself that today would be the day I finally asked her about Henrietta's death.

"Mm," she says, looking out at the view. "How insightful."

"I'm sorry if that's too . . . personal. I hope that isn't insulting."

"No, no," she says. "You're not off the mark. In fact, you're right on the money. The memories I have of her have never left me. She was such an essential part of my childhood. But since I moved back here, it's all come rushing back in a way I didn't expect."

"It must be difficult."

"Yes, it is," she says. "Sometimes. But there are a lot of good memories, too. Like now, us sitting here . . . I've told you how my parents threw all those parties?"

"Yes."

"Henrietta and I used to hang around in the kitchen during them—lurk offstage, if you will—and Bonnie, one of my mother's cooks, would have this long wooden table in the center of the room covered in trays of party food. Canapés and finger sand-wiches, tarts and petits fours. Always a ham with this Montmo-rency cherry sauce my father loved. We would wrap yeast rolls in these stiff cotton napkins my mother used and slip little blocks of cheese into the pockets of our dresses, pastries and petits fours, too. And then we'd bring it all up here and have a feast."

Cindy suddenly appears in the window, bearing a basket wrapped in cloth. "Your lunch," she says, holding it out for me to grab. As I do, she gives me a look that says she thinks our eating out here is as peculiar as I do, and maybe I'm just imagining it, but it suddenly seems like something between us shifts, like our eyes meeting is a silent acknowledgment that perhaps there is more to Susannah's behavior than simple eccentricity.

I take the basket from her and place it between Susannah and me.

"Ah," Susannah says, taking out two sandwiches wrapped in parchment. "Here we are. Cindy is good at following directions."

"What is it?" I ask.

"Egg salad, with lots of dill and capers, just the way Henrietta liked it. I should have asked her to bring some champagne."

"Champagne?"

"Yes," she says. "Once, Henrietta and I stole a bottle from the butler's pantry and drank it out here. What I didn't tell Henri-etta is that I had been stealing alcohol from those parties for years, usually drinking from the glasses that came back into the kitchen—you could count on the minister and his wife to not touch their wine, and the Perkins family, too. Anyway, the time Henrietta and I stole that bottle . . . We got so sick! We didn't know it was meant to be sipped!"

"How old were you?"

"Fourteen maybe? The other day I was lying in bed, just up from a nap, and I called for Cindy to get me a glass from the bottle I always keep in the refrigerator. That's one good thing I learned from Teddy—he required that we always have a bottle of champagne at the ready. Anyhow, Cindy brought the flute to me and I drank it down in two gulps, watching the sky turn pink, missing the feeling of Henrietta's head on my shoulder, tears running down my face."

"You miss her," I say, noticing her flowery description of the memory, how it's almost as if she's rehearsed the lines. *Has she?* Something about all this—her nostalgia, the spot where we're eating—feels too orchestrated.

"It's hard to be here without her. She loved those nights, and as much as I hated my parents' parties—they were a reminder to me that I was not their priority—I loved that time with her."

She takes a tiny bite of her sandwich and looks out at the mountains. "All my childhood memories include her," she says. "All my good ones, at least. Though she was there for the bad ones, too."

"What do you mean?" I say, wondering if this is my opening.

"Oh . . .," she says, a shadow falling over her face. "Just my mother . . ." She shakes her head. "There was this one time . . . Henrietta and I must have been ten or eleven . . . we found this stash of candy my mother kept in a storage closet in the basement. My father used to bring her boxes of chocolate when he traveled, probably to make up for whatever he did while he was gone." She gives me a knowing look. "But my mother, being as rigid and regimented as she was, never touched them. So one day,

Henrietta and I did. We would eat a bite out of one, then put it back, then take a bite out of another . . . We were like Lucy and Ethel, in that scene in the chocolate factory?"

"Yes," I say, laughing a little.

"But my mother . . ." She shakes her head slowly, thinking about it. "We didn't hear her coming. I think that was the first time Henrietta saw her hit me."

"She hit you, Susannah?"

"Oh, yes," she says. "All the time, Bess."

"That must have been—"

She puts her hand out before I can continue. "It was," she says. "It was as bad as you can imagine. But now you see why I clung to Henrietta. And later, Bradley."

"It sounds like Henrietta was more like a sister to you," I say. "It must have been awful for you when she died." It feels cheap to do it, given how genuinely sad she seems recounting these stories, but I watch her face as I say it, searching for some clue.

She nods, her eyes half closed, as if she's sunk back deep into some memory. "I was a fool to think that by running away, I could forget her. Still now, all these years later, my first thought when I wake up in the morning, when I'm still in that space between sleep and conscious thought, is of her. That sounds outlandish, I know, but it's true."

"Why do you think that is?" I ask, putting down my sandwich.

She looks down at her lap. "I just wish there was something I could have done. It is the regret of my life that I didn't somehow stop her that night. Henrietta had so much life ahead of her." She stuffs a hand into her pocket and pulls something out, a pink ribbon. It's a dusty-rose color, shiny in spots, worn, like it's been handled many times over the years. I wonder about its special significance for Susannah, if it's a kind of lucky charm.

"This is one of her ribbons. She treasured her ribbons. She wore one every day," Susannah says. "And with good reason. They reminded her of her mother."

"How so?" I say.

"It's a horrid story." She pinches her mouth shut before continuing. "Her mother killed herself."

"How terrible," I say, remembering how William had told me this.

"Oh, it was gruesome." She looks at me for a beat, as if considering whether to go on. "Bess, she hanged herself from one of their home's rafters. She used an electrical cord that she'd cut off the iron. The ironing board and basket of clothing were right next to her when Mr. Martin found her. Henrietta was only ten months old. It was *obviously* postpartum depression, but of course nobody diagnosed those things back then. People just thought she was crazy. Honestly, she probably chose the better option."

"The better option?" I say, unnerved by the way she's put it.

"What?" she says, reading my expression. "You don't understand how it was back then. She would've ended up in a mental hospital otherwise, receiving *God knows* what kind of treatment. Electroshock therapy, lobotomy . . . But the ribbon." She hands it to me and I run it through my fingers. "Before she died, she made Henrietta the most beautiful christening gown. I saw it once. Henrietta had it folded up in the bottom of a drawer, where her daddy wouldn't come across it. It had hand-sewn lace, the sweetest smocking across the chest, and a ribbon, just like this, running through the ruffle at the hem. When Henrietta was—*hmm*, let me think," she says, tapping her finger against her chin. "Maybe about eight? Nine? She found the roll of ribbon in the bottom of her mother's old sewing things when her father asked her to patch a hole in a pair of his pants. It was nice ribbon, you can see." She holds it up in front of us, turning it like a precious artifact. "Imported velvet from France. The Perkinses used to carry that sort of thing in their store, back before they started selling Rubbermaid containers and Crystal Light or whatever it is they sell now. When Henrietta got up the nerve to ask her father about it, he told her that her mother had saved for her entire pregnancy to buy it."

"That's so touching."

"Yes," she says, taking the ribbon from me and coiling it around her finger. She seems more pensive suddenly.

"What is it?"

She grabs my hand, her fingernails digging into the fleshy pad of skin beneath my thumb. "On the morning when they found Henrietta's body . . .," she starts. A gulping sound escapes from her mouth, and when I look into her eyes, I see tears beginning to well up. "I went to the family's house, to give my condolences. He was . . ." She waves a hand and turns away from me. "I'm sorry," she says.

"No, please," I say. "I don't want you to talk about it if it's too painful."

"*Painful!*" She takes a deep breath, then exhales, blowing like she's extinguishing a candle. "Henrietta's father was . . ." She pauses again. "You know, he was a hard worker. He'd been a handyman here at the house for years, and then he started working as a mechanic at the gas station next to the house that he and

Henrietta lived in. He'd already been through so much, losing a wife, and then to lose Henrietta . . ." She looks up at the sky and shakes her head, like she still can't accept it all these years later. "When I went to see him that day, we sat at their kitchen table and cried together and told some old stories."

"And what happened to him?" I say, wondering whether she'll confirm what William said, how he spent years trying to convince people that Henrietta's death was suspicious.

"He died maybe twenty years ago," she says. "And he died a lonely, bitter man, a horrible way to die." A tear begins to fall down her cheek, and she swipes it away quickly.

"You shouldn't beat yourself up." I put my hand gingerly on her arm. "It's a terrible thing that happened . . .," I say, measuring my words. "But she simply wandered off, didn't she? What could you have done to stop her?" I ask, my eyes searching her face, waiting for her answer.

"I should have said something to her," Susannah says, her voice dropping to a gravelly pitch.

"What do you mean?"

She starts to laugh, a low, deep, *I can't believe I'm doing this* kind of ripple. "You said you wanted to learn more about Henrietta . . . Let me tell you, honey. You're not going to get the real story down at the library. Or *anywhere* downtown, for that matter!"

She suddenly stands, with a strength and urgency that confirms my suspicions about her physical condition, and walks to the edge of the terrace, where she places her palms to either side of the ledge and stands there for a moment, the wind blowing her hair as she looks out into the distance. It's as if she is standing against the railing on a ship, her eyes searching for some lost horizon.

"Bess, we'd had a fight that day," she finally says, turning to me. "On the day she died. I said things to her . . ." She dabs at the tears falling from her eyes. "We had never argued like that before."

"But you were just kids," I say. "Surely it had nothing to do with it." *Right?*

"Oh, but I think it did," she says. "She never would have . . ." She looks at me, her eyes landing on mine just for a moment before she turns away again. "Bess, I know what it is you want to ask me. I can see it all over your face."

"What?" I say, feigning ignorance. My heart starts to pound in my chest.

"You want to know if I had something to do with it. I know that's what people say about me. I know it's part of the reason they hate me so much."

"No, Susannah. I—"

"Bess," she says. "I know it's the truth. I'm sure somebody told you about the rumors as soon as it got out that you were doing this article. Don't insult me by pretending otherwise."

I nod.

"The truth is, her death was my fault," she says, the words making my chest seize as they leave her mouth.

"*What?*"

"But not in the way people say. More in the way that the things I said before the party affected her state of mind. I'd wanted to hurt her that day, and wouldn't you know? I did!" She puts a trembling hand to her mouth, closing her eyes as if it pains her to say it. "Words can be vicious, as dangerous as the deadliest weapon."

The thought rings in my ears, remembering how it felt to listen to the recording that cost me my career. "Believe me, I know," I say. "But . . . Susannah . . . for her to have died . . ."

She glances at me.

"What did you say?" I ask. "What were you fighting about?"

"I told you those stories the other day," she says. "About getting revenge, about those women in New York who had threatened my marriage."

"Yes," I say.

"Well," she says. She rests her forehead against her clasped hands. "I left one story out. The one that started it all, I suppose."

"Susannah," I say. "I'm not following."

"Henrietta and I . . . We were arguing about your father-in-law."

Oh, I should've known. My stomach drops, a dread-induced hollowness building inside it. "You said you had suspicions about—"

She cuts me off. "It wasn't just *suspicions!*" she says, a ferocity in her voice like I've never heard before, and I'm taken aback, that *this* is the thing out of all of this that gets to her. She shakes her head. "If they had only . . ."

"But you were so young," I say. "You can't blame yourself for the things you said when you were just a teenager. And you were in love. If you really believed that something was going on between the two of them, you can't punish yourself for having stood up for yourself. It's a horrible coincidence that she happened to have the accident that day, but you can't blame yourself for it, Susannah. Especially after all this time."

"But everybody else still does," she says. "So why shouldn't I?" Suddenly she spins around and pitches the top half of her body over the railing, as if she's going to jump.

"Susannah!" I yell, heaving myself toward her, wrapping my arms around her tiny middle. "Susannah, stop," I say, feeling her shake underneath my arms and then melt against me, like she's giving in. Or giving up. "You're okay," I say, shushing her like she's my child. "You're okay."

"I'm sorry, Bess," she says, her back against me. "Sometimes it's just . . ."

"I know," I say, wishing to myself that Cindy would suddenly appear. *Has she been this far gone all along and I'm just now seeing it, or is she falling apart in front of my eyes?*

She lets go and shuffles back to where we were sitting. She moves slowly, like she's been walking for miles. When she turns to me, her eyes are glassy. "I didn't mean to scare you," she says, a dazed look on her face as she leans back against the chair. Her eyes scan the scenery behind me. "Sometimes it's just . . . sometimes it all comes rushing back. And sometimes it's just too much."

TWENTY-ONE

Diane would like us all to have Sunday brunch together at the inn every week after church. That was the way she phrased it. It wasn't "*Would you* like to all have brunch together on Sundays?" or a cheery "*How would you all like to* have brunch together on Sundays?" but, instead, a terse, definitive, Chairman Mao–like proclamation, which she threw down just yesterday morning while Cole and I were in the front yard, planting mums and pansies in the flower beds.

She tit-totted over from her house, where she'd probably been watching us from behind the drapes in her living room, waiting for the moment our defenses were down: *I would like us all to have brunch together on Sundays.* Cole stood up and wiped his hands on his running shorts, and instead of saying something reasonable (maybe, perhaps, "*Sure, Mom, Bess and I will check the calendar and talk about it*"), answered, "*All right, great! What time were you thinking?*"

We started fighting about it the minute Diane disappeared behind her front door. I stomped around to the back of the house and hurled the spade back into the box of gardening tools that Mrs. Miller had left for us and marched into the house, Cole

following, letting the screen door slam behind him, telling me I
was overreacting and being unreasonable. And maybe it's true.
We have been fighting all week long, over everything, and I can't
say I can explain why, or tell whether it's justified, except to think
that the mood in our house just sucks.

Livvie is grounded. She has been forced to rake leaves and
clean bathrooms and come right home after school, and the mis-
ery is catching up with her, and by extension the rest of us. All
weekend she moped around the house, enduring her punishment
like a surly prisoner, and begging, a few times, for me to let her use
the computer "for homework," even though we both knew she just
wanted to use a screen, another luxury we told her was off-limits.

What Livvie doesn't realize, given the way she glares at me
as she passes me in the kitchen or answers my questions with
one-word mumbles, is that her punishment is a drag for me, too,
even if I'm the one who imposed it. Even Max seems off, declin-
ing my offer yesterday to take him to the comic-book shop he's
been wanting to check out in Charlottesville. Cole is the only
one who seems unaffected. Or maybe just oblivious.

I push my scrambled eggs around my plate. They are over-
done, browned at the edges, a rookie mistake that I want corrected. A chef at an inn needs to be able to handle scrambled
eggs. Cole, meanwhile, is laughing with the cute college-aged
waitress who's refilling his coffee cup. "Keep it coming, Steph!"
he smiles up at her.

Ugh. Give me a break.

I look across the table at Livvie, whose expression, I fear,
matches my own. She is sulking into her pancakes, drawing de-
signs in the pool of syrup on her plate with the tines of her fork.
I sit up straighter in my chair, take a deep breath, and resolve in

the moment to improve my attitude, if only for the kids. My own mother's voice rings in my ears: *If you can't get out of it, get into it*, she'd say, shooing me off to school or to do my chores or some other obligation I didn't want to fulfill.

Bradley is telling a story about the fox he saw earlier this week during his early-morning walk. It trotted right down the middle of Maple, he says, and then stopped at William's—"*I swear on my mother's grave!*"—and sat by the front door like it was waiting for the coffee shop to open so it could get itself a cappuccino! Our eyes meet as he looks around the table. I can't look at him now without thinking of what Susannah has revealed to me. *Did he really cheat on his first girlfriend with Henrietta?* I wonder. *Does he feel responsible at all, the way Susannah does, for the way their best friend died? Has he carried this guilt around for decades, too?*

"So, kids," Diane says, putting down her teacup. "How are things at school?"

Livvie squirms in her seat. As far as I know, Diane doesn't know she's grounded. I purposely didn't mention it, certain she'd use the information to opine about my parenting.

"Good," Max says, through a mouthful of French toast. "There's a kid in my math class." He starts to laugh. "You won't believe what he did on Friday! He came into class giving everyone high fives. But not me, fortunately, because he'd covered his hand in Vaseline first!"

"Oh my goodness, whose child is that?" Diane says, looking to me, like I should have the names of every Draper student some-how committed to memory.

"No idea," I say.

"Max, I've known kids like that," Cole says, laughing. "Take it from me, that sounds like someone you might want to steer clear of. We had a teacher when I was a senior who always drank Diet Coke. She kept a bottle on her desk all day. This kid in my class replaced it with another bottle, and when she took a sip . . ." He shakes his head.

"What, Dad?" Max says. "What did he do?"

"He'd replaced the soda with soy sauce!"

"Ugh!" Max screams. Livvie starts to laugh, and I sink back into my chair, surprised by how the sound of it makes me feel so relieved. "That's disgusting!" she says, giggling.

When she notices me watching her, she smiles back at me. I've been waiting for that all week.

"Speaking of people to steer clear of," Diane says, patting at the corners of her mouth with her napkin. "How is your story about Susannah going, Elizabeth?"

"Great, actually," I say, pushing my plate forward and leaning my elbows onto the table, which I know will make her crazy. "We've actually been talking a lot about the past." My eyes dart to Bradley, to see how he'll react, but his nose is deep in his coffee cup.

"The past?" Diane says.

"Yes," I say. "We spent a lot of time this week talking about her relationship with Henrietta."

"Who's Henrietta?" Max says.

Diane squirms in her seat. I wait for Bradley to say something, pausing to give him the invitation, and when he doesn't, I start in. "She was a woman who grew up with Susannah Lane and Grandpa. She was in their class. She and Susannah were best friends. She and Grandpa were friends, too."

I know that this is bold, and it pains me to second-guess him, a person I adore so much, but I can't just sit here. I watch him, waiting for him to say something, but he is acting as if I am speaking in a vacuum and he hasn't heard a word I've said. He reaches past Diane for the butter, having just rifled through the bread basket for a slice of raisin bread.

"Elizabeth, I have to know. If you are writing a story about Susannah selling her land, why are you talking to her about Henrietta?" Diane asks.

"Just getting to know her better," I say. "And Henrietta's death is a big reason why she didn't come back all those years."

"Well, that's what everyone says," Cole mutters.

"What?" Max asks.

"Never mind," Diane says.

I clear my throat. "Actually," I say, looking at the kids, "your dad's right. A lot of people say Susannah Lane left Greyhill and never came back because of . . . well, it's a sad story . . ."

"Elizabeth!" Diane says, her cheeks pink with alarm.

"They're nearly thirteen years old, Diane. It's fine," I say, my eyes still on Bradley, who's chewing his bread with the vacant expression of a cow chewing its cud. *The longer he sits there silently, the more I start to think there's a reason for it . . .*

I press on. "So, kids, it's a sad story, but Henrietta Martin actually died in an accident."

"No, no, I've heard about this!" Livvie says, with a burst of enthusiasm. "She's the one who fell, up on the mountain!"

"The Cliffs!" Max said, wagging his finger in acknowledgment.

"How do you know about the Cliffs?" Cole asks, looking from me to the kids.

Max hums something that sounds like "I don't know."

"Everyone knows about it," Livvie says, her face rearranged back into its more typical scowl.

"But what does that have to do with Mrs. Lane?" Max says. "What did you mean, Dad—"

"Really, nothing," Cole says.

"No, no," I say. "It's not nothing." He glares at me, signaling me to stop.

"*Elizabeth* . . ," Diane mumbles, shaking her head in disapproval.

"This is an important lesson for the kids to know," I say, my focus now on Bradley. *Is he not chiming in because of the way Diane feels about Susannah? Or is it because he fears I know something* . . . "Especially Livvie."

"What?" she says, her eyes widening. "Why me?"

"People in town, as you have probably heard, don't particularly like Mrs. Lane. She has all this land that she's selling, and people think it might change Greyhill if outsiders start moving here, or building big, fancy vacation homes."

"But we're outsiders," Max says.

"Exactly right—" I start, but Cole cuts me off.

"You're not outsiders," he says. "You come from a long line of Greyhill natives who—"

Now I cut him off. "Come on, Cole, it's not like they've become members of the royal family. It's just a town. Give me a break." I pause, realizing from the expression on his and my in-laws' faces that I may have gone a *touch* too far. "Anyhow, people around town also say she had something to do with her best friend's death, which is awful, as you can imagine."

The kids nod. "Like she pushed her or something?" Max says, his mouth dropping open.

"Well, yeah," I say, my eyes darting around the table. "Or something . . . Anyhow, the point is that people say that's why she left town and didn't come back until now."

"But you don't think that, Mom?" Max asks.

"Absolutely not," I say, my eyes landing on Bradley, who is *still* behaving as if I'm recounting something innocuous and irrelevant, like the plot of a nighttime soap. "Now that I've had the chance to get to know Susannah, and actually become friends with her, I think she's misunderstood. She hasn't had the easiest life, and people around here think the worst of her. Imagine what that's like . . ."

"Not fair," Livvie says.

"Exactly," I say. "But being around her, I've learned how strong she is. How loving and warm. You should hear how she talks about her friend. And what I want to tell you both is that people might say things about you as you go through life, people might believe you're a certain way—not as extreme as in Susannah's case, of course—but it should never dictate what you believe about yourself in your heart, or the way you behave toward others." I smile at Diane. A *big* smile. *Extra* satisfied. *Extra* warm. She looks, more than she ever has before, like she wants to strangle me.

"What do you think, Grandpa?" Livvie asks, in the tentative way she sometimes speaks to adults now. "What do you think about what people say about Mrs. Lane? You probably know her as well as Mom does."

"Ohhhh . . ." He wipes his mouth brusquely and tosses his napkin over his plate. "Well, me and Mrs. Lane haven't been close for a long, long time, but I think your mom's right. People say things that aren't true."

But Susannah says you've talked on the phone recently, I want to say. So many questions are running through my head.

"You don't think Susannah Lane knows something about Henrietta's death?" Max asks.

"Nah," he says, reaching over and rustling Max's hair.

"But you knew Henrietta, right?" Livvie says.

"Oh, yeah," he says, leaning back and shifting in his chair like he wants to loosen his belt. "Small place like this, you know everyone you grow up with."

"It must have been sad," I say, finally getting him to look me in the eye.

"Yup, it was," he says, standing, declaring that the conversation is over. *Why is he so ready to have it end?* I look across the table at Diane, who's narrowing her eyes at me, like she's trying to figure out what I'm up to. "But enough of all this," Bradley says. "Max and Livvie, what do you say we go check out the fish in the koi pond out front?"

The kids jump up and Diane follows suit, her anger so obvious it's practically vibrating off her.

"This brunch was a great idea, Diane!" I say, my voice as merry as I can muster.

She walks off, not bothering with goodbye.

Cole looks at me. "What was all that about?"

I stand. "What?" I say, pushing the chairs into the table so I can scooch through. He is the last person I feel the need to explain myself to right now. "Didn't you think it was fun? That Steph! She was great. Make sure to leave her a big tip."

TWENTY-TWO

⁂

My mother is laughing.

"Oh, Bess! Bradley? The Bradley Warner *I* know?" she says through the phone.

I am lying on our bed, still in the dress I wore to brunch even though the kids and I got home hours ago, leaving Cole at the inn to do some paperwork. "I know. It's ridiculous to think he could be hiding something, but you should have seen how he was acting at brunch this morning. I almost feel like I have no choice but to believe Susannah's story about their past. He was cheating on her. And when she confronted Henrietta . . ."

"That may be, but like you said, it's all just a case of bad timing for Susannah."

"I know, but can you imagine the guilt you would feel?"

"Well, sure. But honestly, Bess, I can't stress it enough: From what you've said, she sounds nuts!" I can hear her rustling around in the kitchen, taking a pot out of the corner cabinet next to the sink. "That whole scene on her balcony the other day! You said in your email that she practically threw herself off the side of the house!"

"You have a point," I say, feeling tiny prickles on the back of my neck as I remember how I lunged after her.

"Bessie, just focus on getting that story written and move on," Mom says, the sound of her turning on the faucet in the background.

"You're right."

"Of course I am!" She laughs. "Listen to your mother. Okay, doll. Gotta go. I'll talk to you this week."

"Thanks, Mom." After the line's gone dead, I hold the phone in my hands for a second and then turn onto my side and close my eyes. I'm just about to drift off when something brushes against my foot and I startle awake.

Cole is standing at the foot of the bed, his mouth set in a hard line.

"Cole! You scared me!" I say, sitting up.

He doesn't say anything, just stands there sulking.

"What?" I say, though I know exactly why he's pissed.

"Do you want to explain to me what it is, exactly, that you were trying to do at brunch?"

"Nothing," I say, feigning innocence. "I was just making conversation."

"Bess."

"All right, all right," I say, my voice dripping with a sarcasm that I'm too frustrated to restrain. "I was just filling the kids in on the history of their new hometown. Don't you think it's important, Cole, for them to know the way things are around here?"

"The way things are . . ." He stops and closes his eyes, putting his fingertips to his skull like our conversation is physically hurting him. "Bess, why did you do that?"

"Do what?" I say.

"Come on, Bess. The way you brought up Henrietta Martin at brunch. Do you know how uncomfortable that was for my mother? For my father?"

"Since you mentioned him, your father seemed suspiciously quiet, don't you think?"

"Suspiciously . . ." He shakes his head. "Give me a break, Bess."

"What?"

"Well, let's think about it: you're the *only* person in Greyhill who trusts Susannah. Why do you think that is?"

I laugh. "Maybe because I'm the only one who's dared to give her the benefit of the doubt. Maybe the problem is not Susannah but all the hang-ups these assholes in town seem desperate to hold on to for some reason." *There. I've said it.*

"Wow," he says.

"What? Is that too strong an opinion for you?"

"No," he says. "Not at all. But what I think is that you're wearing blinders because of what happened back in Washington," he says.

I feel like he's just punched me in the stomach. "What did you just say?"

He crosses his arms over his chest. "Maybe you're clinging to her because you need to, Bess. Maybe you're scared of getting let down again. Or maybe you so badly want to make up for what happened with Candace that you're determined to do right by Susannah."

My mouth starts to water. I swallow, staring at him, waiting for him to take it back, but he doesn't. "I can't believe you just said that to me."

He doesn't say anything. He stares back at me, eyebrows raised, like we're on opposite sides of a chess match and he's waiting for me to make a move.

I swallow. "The reason I am, to use your word, *clinging* to Susannah is that she's the only person around here who tells the truth."

"Mom!" Max's voice suddenly calls out from the hallway. "Someone's at the door."

I narrow my eyes at Cole. "If that's your mother . . ."

"And what if it is, Bess?" he says, starting out of the room. "She's my mother. And she lives across the street. How did you think this would be?"

"Not like this," I say, my voice shaky with anger. "Not at all like this."

I'm still sitting on the bed when I hear her voice.

"I do not want to make anything uncomfortable between us, Cole, you know that," she says. "But I was just across the street, dropping off some papers for your mother for the holiday fair— Mindy and Whitney and I just met about it—and, well, I just can't let it go."

I tiptoe to the top of the stairs, where I can hear them better. I can't face Eva today, not after everything else. I peek around the wall, just enough to see the pointed toe of Eva's high-heeled boot in the threshold of the front door. At least Cole hasn't invited her in.

"Listen," she says, her voice not quite a whisper. "My Brittany . . . well . . . she says that Livvie made her cry at school." *Oh, give me a break!*

"Made her cry?" Cole says.

"Yes," Eva says. "I don't know what it was about, Brittany wouldn't tell me. And she tells me everything, Cole, so it must have been bad." I see her reach out and touch his arm.

"I don't know, Eva," Cole says. "Livvie's really not the kind of kid who would make another girl cry."

"I'm sure under normal circumstances, that's true," Eva says, her hand still on his arm. "But with your move and all . . . it's a big change for a girl her age. Maybe it's just a temporary thing. You know, a phase she's going through . . . Anyway, I wanted to tell you. I need to protect my child, surely you understand that."

"Of course, Eva. It's just—"

"Please, let's not let this get in the way of our long friendship," she says. The hand is *still* on his arm. "I just wanted you to know. Because if things don't change, I just don't know that I can allow Brittany to be around Livvie."

We can only hope, I think.

"Eva, I don't think that's going to be a concern," Cole says, adopting what I used to call his *lawyer voice* whenever I overheard him on a work call. At least he's standing up to her, sort of.

"Oh, I'm sure it won't be any problem," she says. "I know you'll handle it." There's silence then, and I peek around the wall just in time to see Eva releasing Cole from a hug. As I hear him closing the door, I hurry down the hall to Max's room, where the kids are supposed to be doing homework.

"Hey," I say, knocking as I enter. *I just need to clear this up*, I think. *Just need to ask her real quick and move on.*

They are both reading. Max is at his messy desk, which is covered with books and papers, Star Wars figurines, half-completed LEGO projects. Livvie is lying on Max's bed, her head nearly hanging off the side and her feet resting on the wall in front of her, the latest Sarah Weeks book in her hands.

"Liv, can I talk to you for a sec?"

"Huh?" she says, sitting up. I can't tell if her cheeks are red because she's been lying with her head nearly upside down or because she thinks she's in trouble. *Should she be in trouble?*

"Come here?" I say.

She swings her legs around and stands. I close the door behind us after she's joined me in the hall. "Did you make Brittany cry at school? Did something happen?"

As soon as the words are out of my mouth, I see Cole coming up the stairs.

She rolls her eyes toward the ceiling. "No, Mom. Of course not!" She glances from me to Cole and then back again.

"I swear!" she says, her voice high and her eyes wide, the way they get when she's lying. "There is nothing for you to worry about. Everything is fine at school."

"Okay," I say, looking quickly at Cole. "But you'll tell me, right? If there's something you need to talk about? I'm here, you know, Liv."

"I know, Mom," she says. "There's nothing for you guys to worry about. Really."

"Okay," I say. Cole nods.

I twist the doorknob and open the door to Max's room, where he's turning back and forth in his chair, his book in his lap, seemingly oblivious. *Is he, though?*

I close the door after Livvie escapes inside and then press my ear to it, listening to see if they'll say anything telling.

"What was that about?" Max says.

"Nothing," Livvie answers.

"Nothing?" Max says.

"Just some stupid stuff about that idiot crybaby Brittany."

They're quiet then. I turn around to Cole.

"Anything?" he mouths.

I shake my head. I can hear the rustling pages of one of their books, the sound of Livvie clearing her throat. I want so badly to trust her, though a sinking feeling in my stomach tells me, loud and clear, that I should know better.

TWENTY-THREE

"She waited on them at brunch."

"Who? Stephanie?"

"Yeah. She said it was the whole family, all of them. The kids, too. She also said that Bess barely touched her food. She even made a face at her plate when Stephanie set it down."

"Made a face?"

"Like she wasn't pleased with it."

"Well, excuse me! Not good enough for her, huh?"

"I guess not."

"You know what? I've heard the daughter's a real terror."

"Her daughter? Who said that?"

"Eva. She said she's been picking on some of the girls at school."

"Well, that's too bad. Maybe the girl's just getting adjusted."

"That's what I said. I didn't want to tell Eva what I really thought, which is that her daughter is the one who's always been the instigator of that sort of thing."

"'*My Brittany*,' you mean?"

"Ha! Exactly! Maybe Eva's just trying to shift the blame off her kid."

"Could be. Though you know Cole's wife spends all that time with Susannah Lane. That says something to me about her."

"Have you met her, though? She's perfectly nice."

"Maybe so, but then I saw her on the street that day, screaming at her daughter."

"Oh, I'd forgotten about that! Was it as bad as it sounded?"

"I could hardly watch. I was so embarrassed for her! She just seemed kind of out of control."

"That's not good."

"I know."

"If she's willing to show all that in public . . ."

"Ooh, good point! *Very* good point."

TWENTY-FOUR

❧───────❧

Bess

You must be kidding me.

I look at the clock. It is eight fifteen in the morning. *Eight fifteen!* Even if she knows we've all been up since 6:00 a.m., Cole and the kids already off for the day, who bangs on someone's door at eight fifteen in the morning?!

"One minute!" I screech from upstairs, tying my robe around my wet body.

Bang! Bang! Bang!

"One minute!" I hurry down the steps, worrying for a split second that it's Cole and the kids, that maybe something happened after they left the house a little while ago. But no, he has keys, so . . . And really, *who else* could it be?

Bang, bang, bang!

"*One! Minute!*" I scream again, though I'm just on the other side of the door. I don't know how much longer I can take this.

"What is it, Diane?" I say, the cold wind whooshing into the house as I throw open the door. We haven't spoken since brunch the other day. I assume that's what this is about.

And then, I see it. Worse, I smell it.

"Oh no!" I hurry past her, knocking into her side.

"Elizabeth! You're in your robe!" she yells after me. "Your hair is wet!"

The wind is strong, so cold and raw that it feels like ice against my cheeks. It has forced the lids off our trash cans, which I asked Max to drag to the bottom of the driveway this morning before school, and now our garbage is strewn across the front lawn and is making its way across the street onto Diane and Bradley's property.

The crows, I realize. It's like a scene straight out of Alfred Hitchcock. There must be a dozen of them, feasting on the innards of our garbage bin, which is turned on its side, one of our trash bags ripped open like a carcass, this morning's coffee grounds and toast crusts spilling out of it along with the mountain of tissues that Max has been using on an early-winter cold.

And the shrimp. *That's* the smell. I'd made shrimp and grits last night, and now the crows are in heaven, poking at the pink, translucent shells like seagulls descending on a beach picnic. *What had she told me to get . . . bungee cords?* I will never hear the end of this.

"Elizabeth!" she yells.

Dammit! I hurry down the driveway, chasing after a crumpled wad of papers that's blown out of the recycling bin.

"Oh, *dear!*" Diane calls behind me. She is fully dressed, of course, in wool trousers and a turtleneck sweater, a glittering rhinestone pin fastened to the lapel of her coat. "*Elizabeth!*"

I lunge for an empty black-bean can (evidence of last week's

Taco Tuesday) as it rolls toward the mailbox, then rise and turn to her. I know better than to think she's actually going to help, or at least commiserate with me. She came over here not so much to alert me to the disaster in my front yard as to celebrate it. I can see it in her eyes. She's like a child who's just discovered the Christmas presents hidden under the bed.

She starts down my front stairs. "Now, I'm sure I mentioned the crows to you, didn't I?" she yells. "They're scavengers! Horrid creatures!"

"Takes one to know one," I say under my breath, leaping to catch a piece of notebook paper decorated with Livvie's handwriting in purple ink.

"What?" Diane says, her flats clap-clapping against the asphalt.

"Nothing." I right the garbage bin and walk up the driveway to meet her. "Diane, I'm sorry, but I'm just going to have to leave some of this," I say, looking around at the mess. "I have an appointment and I'm going to be late."

"Well, that's too bad, isn't it?" she says, a definitiveness in her voice that tells me she's still angry about yesterday.

"Diane," I say. "Forgive me." I muster a smile. "But I really have to go."

"Are you heading over to Esperanza?" she asks, her penciled-in eyebrows ticking up in a way that reminds me of the Joker.

"I am," I say, starting past her. She grabs the sleeve of my robe.

"Diane!" I pull away. She rarely touches me, one of the many ways I know how little she cares about me. I see her air-kiss people all over town, squeeze my poor kids into her chest, bear-hug my husband. With me, she doesn't even fake it.

"Elizabeth, before you go over there, we need to talk."

Ughhhhhhhh. "Diane, I know that you are not pleased with me about brunch yesterday and I know that your opinion of Susannah is not a positive one, but I'm writing this article, and I don't know how to get it through to you that—"

She puts out her hands, closing her eyes and shaking her head like I've just given her terrible news and she can't tolerate hearing anything more.

I sigh. "Diane, we're just going to have to agree to disagree on this one."

She keeps her eyes closed. For such a long time that I start to wonder if what I said might actually be sinking in. Is this a sign of a compromise? Is she actually going to see things my way?

"Please," she says, finally looking at me, her whole body shivering in the cold.

Please? Wow. It has to be the first time I've ever heard her say it to me.

"Please, Elizabeth," she says. "Just listen to me."

"Okay, but—"

"Bradley got a phone call."

"A phone call?" I say, balling my fists into my sides as I shiver against the wind.

"From Susannah."

"Oh," I say. *Oh.* My mind starts whirring. I picture Susannah pleading into Bradley's ear, pelting him with her sad nostalgia. That's why Diane is acting so strange.

"I know that you and I feel quite differently about Susannah Lane, Elizabeth," she says. "But I have to tell you this, and I'm hoping it might sway your opinion. All I can ask is that you give it some consideration before you continue on with this story that you're doing."

"Diane." I have to stop her. "Listen. I know this is awkward, but I've made a commitment to the maga—"

"Elizabeth!" she yells, reaching out and gripping my arms.

I freeze.

"Listen to me!" she yells.

"Okay!" I say. *Wow.* "Okay."

"She called Bradley to tell him that she is considering turning her home into an inn."

"What?"

"Or a resort of some kind," she says, shaking her head help-lessly. "She says she already has investors!"

"But I can't—" *An inn? Esperanza?*

"Did you know about this, Elizabeth? Please, be honest with me. We have to do something," she says, her voice racked with worry. "We can't let her do this to us. It could ruin our business."

"I don't . . . Of course I didn't know about this! Are you sure that's what she said?" *Out of everything Susannah's told me, she chose to leave this out? Why wouldn't she tell me? And why would she call Bradley first? Something about this feels like a ploy . . .*

Diane wrings her hands, her eyes pinned on me like I should have an answer for her.

"I don't have any explanation for this," I say. "I swear to you I didn't know anything . . . But . . . actually . . . now that I think about it," I say, realizing something, "she did tell me something in confidence." I look at her, weighing whether to trust her. "She told me that she's in financial trouble."

"She told Bradley that, too!" she says. "She told him Teddy left her with nothing."

"So she told him, then?"

Diane nods. "Is it true?"

"I don't know what to believe anymore." I shake my head. "She never said anything about a resort. . . ." And then I remember the other day, during our lunch up on the terrace, when she was asking me about what Cole and I plan to do with the inn, and how Greyhill has such *potential*. That's the word she used, *potential. Could she really?*

"Bradley just told me this morning. She called yesterday and he's been up all night, worrying over it. He's at the inn now, talking to Cole."

"Okay." I start up the driveway, my confusion and anger building as the seconds pass and the news settles in. "I'm going to call Cole now. Don't worry, Diane, we'll figure it out."

"The inn is just so small, and Esperanza is so big . . . What if the investors are one of the big hotel chains? What worries me is that I can see how it might work, Elizabeth. Esperanza is beautiful. It's perfectly suited to—"

"Let's try to think of the bright side, Diane."

"Bright side!" She throws her head back. "Really! What bright side?"

"I don't know. I really don't. But let's say Susannah goes through with this. The inn is entirely different. A totally different kind of thing. Maybe a resort would simply draw more people to the area, and maybe it could be good for us both?"

She shakes her head violently, slicing her hands through the air. "No, no, no!" she says. "That would never work! It would draw business away, Elizabeth! It would squash us! I know you think you know everything, but we've been running this business for decades. Trust me on this!"

"Diane, I don't think I know . . ." I sigh. *What's the use?* "Listen, after I call Cole, I'm going to go see Susannah." I start toward the house.

"Call one of us as soon as you finish with her!"

"I will," I say, turning on the stoop. "And, Diane, listen, Susannah says a lot of crazy things. A lot."

She nods like this reassures her.

"This might just be one of them."

As soon as I'm inside and have closed the door behind me, I sprint for my phone and race up the stairs to throw on some clothes.

"Hey," Cole says, answering halfway through the first ring.

"I just talked to your mother."

He moans. "Esperanza?"

"Yes," I say. "I don't know whether to believe Susannah, Cole, she says so much ridiculous shit, but like I told you, she says she's broke. And the land isn't selling . . ."

"Dammit!" he says. "This isn't good."

"Let's not get ahead of ourselves, though," I say, tapping my hands nervously at my sides. "It could mean nothing, couldn't it? It could just be Susannah being Susannah. Your mom said she told your dad she has investors. I find that hard to believe, Cole. I feel like I would've known, or someone would've known, if she's had people in town to look at the property."

"She *has* had people in town, Bess," he says. "That guy a few weeks ago?"

"Yeah, but still. That was just to look at the land."

"I don't know if that's the case, Bess."

"Why?"

"Because I just got a phone call from Eva."

"*Eva?* What does Eva have to do with anything?"

"Susannah called the mayor's office," he says. "She insisted on talking to David himself. He told Eva that Susannah wanted information about permitting. About licenses and inspections, for turning her home into a hospitality business."

"Shit!"

"Yeah."

"I don't . . . ," I say. "I don't want to believe this quite yet."

"But, Bess . . ."

"I feel like she might just be up to something. I'm going to go talk to her now. I'll find out what's up."

"Okay, but Bess, if what Eva said is true . . ."

"Yeah?"

"And if she already has investors . . . She may have been working on this for a while."

"Right," I say. "And therefore, she's been lying to me. Or at least, hasn't been entirely truthful. You don't think she's been playing me somehow, do you?"

"I don't know," he says. "But this could really hurt us, Bess."

"You honestly think so?" I say.

"I do," he says. "It could be a massive problem." He sighs. "Listen . . . ," he says, his voice taking on a darker tone.

"What? What is it, Cole?" I say, my heart banging in my chest.

"I haven't wanted to say anything . . ."

"What? What is it?"

"The inn . . . ," he starts. "I think we're going to need to start making a bigger investment in the business if it's going to be viable in the long run."

"*Viable in the long* . . . Cole, what are you talking about?" I sit down on the bed, grasping the edge like I'm steadying myself on a raft. "I saw all the financials before we signed everything! The inn is perfectly stable!"

He takes another deep breath, and the sound of it—his worry, his frustration—is like sandpaper on my skin. I feel like I might throw up. "Now that I've been here a few months, Bess, I'm starting to see just how much work there is to do. Stuff my dad either never saw or decided to ignore. The building is so old, Bess. It's not just cosmetic stuff that needs to be upgraded. The plumbing system is ancient, the HVAC is totally inefficient . . ." His voice trails off.

"Why didn't you tell me any of this?"

"I was going to," he says. "Soon. I've been trying to wrap my head around all of it. And, you know, we have some money saved. I just have the feeling that once we start fixing things . . ."

"It might snowball," I say.

"Exactly."

I close my eyes, rubbing my forehead like I could wipe this away. I stand up and walk across the room.

"Okay," I say, shoving my feet into my shoes. "I'm going to go talk to her. I'm going to go figure this out."

TWENTY-FIVE

"Honey, we weren't expecting you this early!" Cindy says as I enter the house.

"Well, here I am."

She takes a step back. "Well, well," she says. "Aren't you full of spit and—"

"Cindy," I interrupt, peeking into the parlor off the hall for Susannah. Music's playing. Billie Holiday, "I've Got My Love to Keep Me Warm." "Forgive me, I don't mean to take this out on you, but I just got some news."

"What is it?" she asks. "Is everything okay?"

"I need to ask you something."

She nods, businesslike, clearly suspicious of my attitude. "Shoot."

"What do you know about Susannah turning this place into a resort?"

"Ohhhhh," she says, taking another step back. "That."

"Uh-huh," I say, a hand on my hip. Now I officially feel like I've been duped. "That."

She looks at me for a moment, clearly weighing her words. "All

I can tell you is that she's hard up, Bess. Worse than she lets on. Desperate times, desperate measures. She hasn't said anything to you because she didn't want you to take it the wrong way."

"Right," I say. The whole drive over, Cole's statement about my having blinders on when it comes to Susannah rang in my ears. "Well, I've officially taken it the wrong way." I start down the hall, and Cindy hurries behind me. "Where is she?"

"She's just down here," she says, giving me a look that feels like a warning as she slides open the pocket door that separates the foyer from the ballroom. "And, listen," she says, lowering her voice. "She's gotten into something today."

"Gotten into . . . ?" I step into the room, and I gasp.

"Good morning!" she says, as sunny and sweet as a kinder-garten teacher welcoming her students to class. She's wearing a lilac taffeta ball gown and a starched men's oxford shirt, diamond earrings the size of golf balls dangling from her ears. She is bent at the waist, leaning over a gold cane dining chair. On the chair is a painter's palette, and there is a paintbrush in her hand. Lemony-green paint splatters dot her freckled chest.

I walk across the Persian rug that covers most of the par-quet floor. On the fading damask wallpaper, between two floor-to-ceiling windows dressed in heavy blue silk drapes, are the beginnings of a mural. It is not good. It looks like the sort of well-intentioned gloppy student art you might see on a cinder-block wall in a high school. There, it would seem cheery and fitting, almost folksy. But here, in this grand room . . . There are bushy green trees, the leaves made up of bubbly loops, and a winding brown stripe that I think is meant to be a dirt road. And . . . Wait a second . . . I squint, trying to make out a little red rectangle, four black circles for wheels, one of them gone rogue.

"Is that—?" I point to it.

"My truck!" she says, giggling. "Isn't it funny?" She stands back, marveling at her work. "If my mother could see me now!"

The front of the truck is flat—a thin red line pressed against one of the brown trees, the trunk dark in the middle because the paint is still wet. Little specks of red paint fan out from the truck, the way a cartoonist might draw sweat flying off someone's forehead. *Is it meant to be blood?* I wonder.

"I don't know if *funny* is the word I'd use," I say, turning to Cindy in the doorway. She gives me a helpless look.

"Years ago, Teddy got me a bunch of blank canvases for Valentine's Day," Susannah says, dipping her brush into a bold green and then drawing a line across the foreground of her picture with a flourish. *Grass.* The paint is too thick. It starts oozing onto the baseboards. "I'd taken a painting class the summer before, out in East Hampton, where I had very lonely weekdays, with Teddy in the city working." Her voice sounds loose and loopy. *Did she take something? Is she drunk?*

"I know I'm not very good," she says, shrugging. I nod, chewing my lip as I notice that a thick swath of blue paint—a stripe of sky—is dripping into the tree line. She swirls a big yellow orb above the smashed truck, and the edge of her brush catches in one of the red splatters, sending an orange streak through the yellow paint. "But this morning I woke up early—*so* early, before the sun came up. I'd had a dream about Teddy. We were walking in the woods together. Up by the Cliffs?" She points toward one of the windows with her brush, as if we could see the spot from here. "We were walking there, Teddy and I, so strange . . . ," she says, seeming to puzzle at the thought. "And it was such a *real* dream. You know the kind? Where even when you're waking up, you're in this funny in-between, not sure where you are and whether it really happened?"

I nod, watching her brush move across the wall, a wobbly line dripping onto the floor because she is looking at me instead of at what she's doing.

"So I woke up very sad, missing him. Despite everything, I *miss* him, Bess. And I remembered how painting made me feel. Calm and happy. Teddy—he was a monster, I've told you all that, but he could be sweet when he wanted to, that was part of his ruse. He hung my canvases all over our summer house. He acted like my little pictures could rival the work of the greats."

"I see," I say.

"So what's got you all . . ." She swirls her paintbrush in a circle in the air, as if she's outlining my face.

I swallow against the sour taste in my mouth.

She cocks her head at me. "Something's wrong."

"Yeah," I say. "Something's wrong."

She laughs hesitantly. "Well, are you going to tell me what it is? What's got you so worked up?"

I gesture toward the mural. "Susannah, what are your guests going to think about this? Or is it for their benefit?"

"My guests?" She narrows her eyes at me.

"Will your investors like it? Have you been courting some of the big hotel chains? I have to say, this doesn't look very Marriott to me. Not sure this will fly if you sell to Hilton or Hyatt."

"Mmmm," she says, her smile flattening out. "Well, I see you haven't lost your sense of humor, at least." She turns to the doorway. "Cindy, we're good."

"You sure?" Cindy says, her eyes on me.

"Well, you could turn that music up," Susannah calls to her. She waits until we're alone to continue. "I was going to tell you, Bess. Of course I was going to tell you."

"When?" The inside of my mouth feels tacky, like I've eaten glue.

"Today, actually."

"Really?" I say. "You expect me to believe that?"

"Well, yes," she says.

"Susannah, I'm not sure I believe anything you've told me now."

She laughs and rolls her eyes. "Oh, don't be so dramatic!"

I turn away from her. I need to collect myself. And I want her to feel how disappointed I am. "On the way over here," I say, my eyes on the view out the window, "I was thinking about what I might say to you, how I might approach this." I turn back to face her. "The first question I have is, why? Let's start there."

"You know why, Bess," she says, dropping her paintbrush in the crystal bowl she has balanced on the chair. "I have no other choice."

"Really?" I say, my eyes darting to the gleaming diamonds hanging from her ears. "No other choice?"

"Did you think I was lying to you when I told you that Teddy didn't leave me with anything?"

"As far as I'm concerned, you could be lying to me about everything."

She sucks in her lips.

"Why did you call my father-in-law and tell him? What was your reasoning there?"

"So is that how you found out?" she asks.

I take a deep breath to calm my nerves. "What I want to know is why I didn't find out from you."

"Bess," she starts, and when she folds her arms over her chest, I see how her hands are shaking. "I have no one to depend on. You realize that, right, after everything we've talked about?"

"Of course I do," I say. "But I had also thought that after everything we've talked about, that we'd built a certain level of trust. Do you know how many times I've stuck up for you over the past few weeks, Susannah? How many times I've told my husband how misunderstood you are, and that I'm going to use this article to help you? I told you things about what it's been like for me here that I haven't shared with anyone. I opened up to you, and although, I'll be honest, I wasn't entirely sure I should, I had confidence in you. I thought we were becoming friends."

She turns away and, unbelievably, picks up her paintbrush and starts painting again. Little brown flecks on the dirt road. Mud.

"Hey!" I say, willing her to respond. "Do you hear me, Susannah? Did you hear anything I just said to you?"

She whips around. "You think your life is hard because you're new here, Bess? Give me a break. You have no idea what it's like to be me! You have no right to judge me!"

"This decision you've made could destroy my family's business, Susannah," I say, my stomach churning, thinking of what Cole told me earlier.

"I'm sure you'll be fine," she says. "You're overreacting. What my people and I are talking about is quite different from your quaint sidewalk inn. We're thinking high-end resort. A beautiful spa by the gardens. Cooking classes. The land—*that's not selling*, let me repeat that again so you hear me—could be a golf course."

I close my eyes, trying to will my anger from exploding out of me like the air in an overinflated balloon. "Susannah," I say, my heart racing. "You're not listening to me."

"I hear you loud and clear."

"I don't think you do," I say. I pause, weighing whether to say what I'd thought of on the drive over. "I could use this article in a different way," I say. "You wrote a gossip column, Susannah. You know. I could reframe the whole story."

She starts to laugh. "Are you threatening me?"

I feel my cheeks start to burn, angry heat cascading up the back of my neck, prickling behind my ears and into my scalp. "I could do it, you know . . . ," I say.

"Oh, I *know* you could," she says. "I heard the way you spoke about the First Lady."

My throat starts to tighten. "Good, then." I choke out a laugh, though nothing about what she's said is funny. "Then you know what I'm capable of."

I see the subtle way she gnaws at her lip, how her chest is rising and falling under the bodice of her ridiculous dress. Suddenly I see a flash of the lonely little girl she says she was, and for a second, I feel pity. *No*, I tell myself. *Don't let her—*

"You want to know why I told Bradley first?" she says, walking across the room to a curved settee next to a window. She flops down, her hand gripping the upholstered arm of the piece like she needs to steady herself. "Because he owes me."

"*Owes you?*" I say.

"*Yes!*" she says, the word coming out in a breathy gasp. Suddenly, she starts to sob, the cries coming out in angry huffs. She reaches into the front of her gown and pulls out a crumpled tissue. "He owes me everything!"

"Susannah," I say, telling myself to stay calm, to not let her *crazy* start to affect my ability to stand my ground. "What do you mean?"

She looks at me, her eyes like two blue disks rimmed in red, her mascara trailing down her cheeks like soot.

"He is the only person in Greyhill who could help me, Bess, and he hasn't. Like I've told you, he could easily do it! All he would have to do is start talking, Bess. But he won't do that, will he?"

"You can't expect one person to turn things around for you, Susannah. You have to steer your own ship."

"*You have no idea what you're talking about!*" she screams, startling me so much that I take a step back. "*Listen to me!*"

"Okay," I say, waving a hand in acknowledgment. "I'm listening."

"I thought he might help *me* now because of how I helped *him* when Henrietta died."

"When Henrietta . . ." I shake my head, not understanding. "What are you talking about?"

"All these years, everyone has whispered . . . *Susannah Lane was involved in Henrietta's death! Why else would she run off?* And what did Bradley do? *Nothing! He let everyone assume the worst!* I came back here with my tail between my legs, with nothing, begging for a second chance at my life. Hoping I could right what had gone wrong. But he is just like everyone else, treating me like a pariah. *Listen to me*," she says, pushing herself to the edge of the seat. "And listen closely. You think your father-in-law is so wonderful? So righteous and kind? He was with me when Henrietta died, Bess. We were arguing about *her*. I knew about the two of them and I couldn't stand to be made a fool any longer, not by the two people I'd trusted most. You can say a lot of things about me, Bess. I have enough faults that if you stacked them one by one, they would reach the top of the Empire State Building. But if there is one thing I know about myself, it's that I am loyal. One hundred percent. It is my greatest quality and my biggest handicap. It's what kept me with Teddy, and it's what made me cover for Bradley."

"Cover for—"

"When she died, I could have told my father the whole story. The sheriff was in his office, I was in the hall just outside. I could have told him how I'd confronted her and Bradley, and how she stormed off. I started after her, but Bradley screamed at me and grabbed my arm. He threatened me. He told me that if I went after her, I would regret it."

"I don't . . . ," I start. "I don't know if I can believe—"

"Oh, *believe it!*" she spits. "I kept his name out of it! I didn't say a word! Now, I don't know what happened to her. I don't know if she had drunk too much and slipped, or if she was angry and . . ." She shakes her head. "But Bradley went after her, ostensibly to help her, and I never saw my best friend again." She leans forward. "Let me repeat that," she says. "*He went after her, and I never saw my best friend again!*"

"I don't believe you," I say. *Not Bradley.* "I don't believe you anymore."

"Oh, I covered for him!" she says, her eyes two angry slits. "I never said a word about him, even when her father was here, day after day, begging my father to look into her death! Mr. Martin wouldn't let up, Bess. And he was right, it didn't make sense. How could she stumble and fall off a mountain path she'd been walking her whole life?"

"Then why didn't you say anything?" I ask, looking for holes in her story.

"I've been asking myself that question my entire life," she says. "And so . . . to get back to your initial question about what I plan to do with this place: My family may have had more than everyone else in Greyhill, but we were small town–wealthy. There wasn't some giant nest egg. I have this house and the land. A few things from my marriage." Her lip starts to tremble again. "Bradley knows all this, Bess. He *knows* how my reputation has taken the fall for his. He's left me no choice but to be resourceful, and if the one idea I've come up with that might work happens to hurt him a little in the process . . ." She shrugs. "Well . . ."

"But, Susannah," I say, "I still don't . . ."

"You don't believe me?"

I clear my throat. *There's no reasoning with her.* "I know that getting revenge isn't going to change how you feel about yourself, Susannah. It's not going to make things better. You're just going to hurt people in the process. You're going to hurt me."

She smiles. "You don't have it in you to see that your wonderful father-in-law might not be so wonderful after all."

"No," I say, my anger ratcheting up again. "I don't."

"Well, then, how about this: When I came back here a year ago, the first thing I did was contact Bradley. I asked for his help.

I knew that selling the land wasn't going to go over well, and I knew that he could help me soften the blow around town. But he refused, he said he didn't want anything to do with me. I assume I can blame your mother-in-law for that. So I told him that I could go another way . . . that I could start talking about my dear old friend Henrietta, maybe even to the press . . ."

"Susannah—"

"You know what's funny, Bess?" she says. "This summer, when I lost control of my truck and it hit that tree? It was the damnedest thing." She shifts in her seat, inching herself up. "Now, I might have been imagining it—after all, my brain had just been shaken in my skull like one of those Magic Eight Balls. But I was able to lift my head up just a little bit from my position on the steering wheel, just enough to see a sliver of the reflection in my driver's-side mirror. . . . I remember the car, Bess."

"The car?" I say. "What car? You told me you lost control of your truck."

"There was another car," she says. "It was a goldish color. Sort of a goldish beige . . ."

Bradley's car, I think.

"He was trying to scare me, Bess." She nods her head slowly. "He didn't think he'd run me off the road, but he was trying to scare me."

"That's ridiculous," I say, my heart pounding in my chest. "If you know Bradley at all, you know how insane that sounds."

She purses her lips, making a clucking *tsk-tsk* sound. "You know what?"

"What?" I ask.

"The beauty of being so desperate at my age is that nothing

scares me anymore. I have nothing to lose. He *can't* scare me."
She laughs. "So when you see him today—because I'm sure you
will, resourceful little bee that you are—ask him about what I've
told you, and tell him that I'm not afraid of him anymore. Make
sure you say that, Bess. Tell him I'm not afraid. Tell him that
he should've seen this coming. Tell him it's my turn."

TWENTY-SIX

⁂

"I'm going to call Noelle and tell her I'm not going to write the story," I say to Cole, standing with him on our back patio later that night.

"I just can't believe she would actually concoct this whole ridiculous scheme," he says, taking a swig of the whiskey he poured the minute he stormed through the door from work. "I can't believe she would actually implicate my father . . . She basically accused him of murdering Henrietta, and then threatening her, too. It's ludicrous!"

"Well, she didn't say that outright, but . . ." I meet his eyes. "Yes, more or less. What did your dad say when you told him?"

"Honestly, he shrugged it off. He said it didn't surprise him, coming from her. But he's apoplectic about the hotel thing."

I nod. I'd called Cole as soon as I left Esperanza, right from the parking pad behind Susannah's house. I didn't care if she saw me. I didn't care if she heard me.

"How much do you think it might hurt us if she goes through with it?"

"There's no way to tell yet," Cole says. "But the fact that we're the only option is what has always made the inn work."

I close my eyes, rubbing my fingers along the bridge of my nose.

"You okay?" he says.

I tilt my head from side to side. "I just . . . My mind is . . ." I stop and sigh. "She's told me so many crazy stories about her life, and I believed most of them. I really felt sorry for her. And now . . ."

"I know."

"I just feel like I've been conned," I say. "Again."

He reaches out and I step toward him, wrapping my arms around him and resting my head on his chest. I close my eyes, listening to his heartbeat, trying to steady my breath in time with it.

"This hasn't exactly been the smooth and easy transition we had anticipated, has it?" he says, his breath tickling the top of my head.

"No," I say. "No, it hasn't. Remember when we thought our lives were messy in DC? Everything was good, in retrospect. We just worked too hard."

He laughs. "Do you want to go back?"

My body tenses against his, and he notices it and starts to rub his hand across my shoulders.

"We can't," I say.

"But would you?" he says.

I think back to what our lives were a year ago, before I lost my job. "I don't even know what our lives would look like there," I say. "It seems like another lifetime. And we couldn't, Cole. We couldn't do that to your parents."

"They'd understand."

"Your mother?" I raise an eyebrow. "Honestly, Cole, I don't feel like it's an option. In some ways, the past feels more like a movie I once saw than it does my own life, like the people we were are distant acquaintances and not our former selves. Does that make any sense?"

"Yes," he says. "It does. Listen, I know this hasn't been easy for you. And I haven't said it outright, but I really appreciate the effort you've made here, Bess. I know it hasn't been the most welcoming . . ."

"Thank you," I say. "It means a lot for you to acknowledge it."

"I do believe that despite the past few months, it's going to get easier."

"I can always count on you for that."

"What?"

"To see the silver lining, to be the positive to my negative."

"Bess, you're not like that."

"I don't want to be," I say. "It certainly hasn't done me any favors."

"So what are you going to do about the story? When are you going to talk to Noelle?"

I groan. "I don't know. My fear is that if I tell Noelle about Susannah's plans, she'll want me to write about that, too. I guess before I do anything, I need to go back to Susannah to find out whether this is real or a scheme she's cooked up."

"Do you really think she'd lie about it? I feel like if she's already called the mayor's office, she's moving forward."

"But I wouldn't count on her to be that rational, Cole. You should have seen her today," I say. "She's not okay."

I turn back toward the house, where I can see Livvie and Max through the kitchen window, getting ice cream from the gallon of mint chocolate chip I bought a few days ago. Livvie hands the scoop to Max, and I watch as he licks it before digging it back into the container. *Oh, Max.*

"You know, the one bright spot about this move is that I think Max has adjusted well," I say, watching as he retrieves the whipped cream from the refrigerator and hands it to his sister.

"That's true," Cole says. "And I think Livvie's starting to have an easier time."

"Do you?"

"Yeah," he says. "Did she tell you? She and some of the other girls in her class are going to dress up together after school on Friday for the fall festival. She said she'd come find us somewhere on Maple. I told her it was okay, as long as she was at the inn around five o'clock."

"The festival!" I say. "I'd completely forgotten about the festival."

"Yeah," he says. "Excellent timing. Just what we need, to have the whole town gathered together in one spot to pelt us with questions about Susannah's plans."

"You think Eva's already told people?"

"Bess . . ."

"Right," I say. "Stupid question. Did Livvie say anything about who the friends are?"

"No," he says. "But I assume it's the usual crowd."

I roll my eyes at him.

"Bess . . ."

"Don't," I say. "I know. I know she needs to make her own friends, and I know I can't control who they are. I just *wish* I could."

"I know," he says. "But she's got a good head on her shoulders."

"Do you think so?" I ask. "I mean, I know she does. I just sometimes get stuck on what Mindy said that night, calling her *kind of a mean girl*, and this phase she seems to be going through. I worry that we're not seeing everything we should."

"I think she's going to be fine," he says. "And even if she makes mistakes, which she will—we both did—we'll be here to catch her fall."

"You're right. I know you're right," I say. "But it doesn't change the fact that I wish I could go back in time and freeze her at three or four, when things with her were so much simpler."

"Remember the things she used to say?"

"*Fridge-a-later* for 'refrigerator,'" I say.

"How she'd say *it's winding* when it was windy."

"*Last year yesterday*," I say.

"I'd forgotten about that one!" he says. "Everything in the past was *last year yesterday*."

"Yes," I say, wiping a tear from my cheek, feeling the bitter-sweet ache in my chest. "I miss last year yesterday." Cole wraps his arms around me again. "I miss everything about that."

TWENTY-SEVEN

The Greyhill Fall Festival on Maple Street is an annual tradition as old as the town itself. It's a typical harvest celebration—lots of apple cider, candied apples, bobbing for apples, and apple desserts, plus pumpkin-carving contests and hayrides. The town tradition is to block off the main artery through town, and all the local businesses participate.

When I arrive at the inn, Cole is already standing behind a skirted table out front, doling out cups of apple cider and mulled wine while his mother, standing next to him, offers bags of caramel popcorn. Bradley is sitting in one of the rocking chairs on the porch, his cap pulled low over his face.

I take a quick hop up the stairs toward him. "Hey," I say, tapping his arm.

He looks up at me, grinning, his eyes half-lidded like he just woke up from a nap. "Hey, Bess," he says, sitting up in his chair. "How's it going?"

"Trying to take a little snooze?"

"Yeah, you know, gotta sneak it in when I can."

"I'm impressed that you're able to out here," I say. From the porch, I can see hordes of people, masses of families, and kids running zigzags through the crowds. "This is crazy."

"Always is," he says. "Every year."

"So, listen, Bradley . . . ," I start, taking a step closer to him so we can have a little bit of privacy.

"You don't have to say anything, hon," he says. "Cole told me everything Susannah said. I'm just sorry you had to deal with all that."

"Thanks," I say. "You haven't heard from her, have you?" Every time I've called the house over the past few days, nobody's picked up. Today, when I broke down and went over there, no one came to the door and I didn't see Cindy's car in the lot. The more time goes on, the more anxious I get—about the article, about the hotel plans, about Susannah . . . all of it.

"No, I haven't," he says.

"I think she's . . . I don't know how to put it."

"She's troubled," he says.

I nod.

"To a certain extent, Bess, she always has been. I always thought it had to do with the way she was raised, I really did, but now . . ." He shakes his head. "I just hope that a few weeks of listening to whatever she laid on you hasn't changed *our* relationship in any way."

"No, of course not," I say, my eyes on the crowds because it's easier that way. I never want to admit, even to myself, that there was a moment when I considered taking her word over his.

"We're going to be okay," he says. "Stop worrying about the inn."

"I'm not," I say, though of course I am.

Cole catches my eye, waving me over to join him.

"Looks like the boss is calling," he says.

I give him a look, and he starts laughing. "Just kidding," he says. "I know who's really in charge when it comes to you two. Same way it goes in my marriage."

I lean down and punch his arm playfully before I start to walk away. "I'll see you in a bit."

The air smells like cinnamon and cider, and a live band is playing bluegrass music in front of Dahlia's. I recognize lots of familiar faces—Carol passing out candy in front of her shop, the agonizingly slow bag boy from the supermarket, a group of sleek moms from school huddled together with lattes from William's. Whitney steps out from behind the group, one arm cupping one side of her belly like she needs to hold it up, and waves.

"Hey, Bess!" she says, waddling over.

"How are you feeling?" I say. "Aside from being tired of answering that question? I'm sorry, I should know better."

"Oh, it's fine," she says. "I'm okay. How are you? Is this your first festival?"

"It is," I say, spotting Max dashing out of the bookstore.

"Max!" I yell.

He turns and sprints up to us. His cheeks are flushed. He takes a second to catch his breath. "This is the *best day*! Look at what I just got from the bookstore!" He holds out two big handfuls of candy. "Mom, you can have some of my chocolate."

I laugh and reach out to rub his shoulder. "That's generous, buddy. Thank you. Have you seen your sister?"

"Yeah, she's somewhere over . . . There she is!" he says, pointing.

Livvie suddenly darts out of the post office across the street. She's dressed in a sweater and jeans, with one of the silk scarves

I used to wear to work tied artfully around her neck, the way that I've noticed the models in the J.Crew catalog are wearing them. To be honest, I'm bothered more by the fact that she looks so grown-up than I am by her swiping my scarf.

"Is that Lauren with her?" I ask, shading my eyes with my hand so I can get a better look.

"Uh-huh," Max says. "Bye!" he yells, sprinting off.

"Do you think it's wise for us to let all the kids run wild like this?" Eva says, wrinkling her nose at Max as she approaches us.

"You sound just like my mother-in-law," I say.

Whitney giggles. "Lighten up, Eva. They're having fun," she says. "When did you become such a downer?"

"God, Whitney!" Eva says, making a face at her. "Hormones getting to you?"

"I don't think so, Eva," I say casually, rocking back and forth on my heels. "I think it's just you."

Both of their heads whip toward me.

"Damn, Bess," Whitney says, breaking into a laugh. "I didn't know you had it in you."

I smile at them both. Eva rolls her eyes and walks away.

Almost two hours later, Cole and I have ladled out what feels like a thousand cups of hot cocoa, which we switched to when we ran out of cider, when Max comes racing down the street toward us.

"Mom! Dad!"

He's running through the crowd, knocking into people like he's being chased, his cheeks flushed like he has a fever. "Mom, Dad!" he pants. "Come with me!"

He gestures for us, waving his hands. "Come on," he says, his eyes darting around. "It's Livvie! Now! Come on!"

Livvie.

"What's going on?" I yell, Cole jogging alongside me as we follow Max to the parking lot behind the inn. The crowd thins the farther we move from the center of town, but I'm aware that people are stopping and staring, and I can hear the murmurs.

"Max, where are you taking us?" I say. "What is going on?"

"Listen," he says, his breath heaving. He slows down, breaking into a fast walk. "We need to get in the car!"

"Buddy, just take a minute and tell us what's going on," Cole says.

"A guy in my class . . . I don't know if it's true, but he just came up to me . . . He says those girls, they're going to do something to Livvie."

My heart flips in my chest. "Do something to . . ." I look at Cole. "What girls? What are they going to do to Livvie?"

Cole puts his hand out to me. "Bess, it's okay," he says. "It's going to be fine."

"He said they were taking her up on the Cliffs, Mom. He said they were going to try to scare her."

"Scare her?" I say, my eyes meeting Cole's. "Scare her how?"

"I don't know, Mom," Max says, his voice wobbling. "But, those girls . . . I think we need to get up there."

We barrel up Old Vine, the road behind the inn that leads out of town and toward the Cliffs. "How much farther is it?"

"Just a couple of miles," Cole says.

"How did they even get up there?"

Max clears his throat. "I think Brittany got one of the older kids to drive them."

My heart starts banging in my chest. I feel like I'm going to throw up. "I hadn't seen her in a while, Cole! I was looking, and I hadn't seen her! I should have been—"

"Stop, Bess," he says, pushing his foot on the gas as we turn onto a wooded incline.

"Mom?" Max says from the back seat. "I have to tell you something."

I turn to face him. "What, Max? What is it?"

"Whatever those girls are doing to try to scare Livvie . . ."

"Yes, Max, what?"

"I know why they're doing it."

"What do you mean?" Cole says, looking at him through the rearview mirror.

"Livvie . . . ," he starts. "I didn't want to say anything. I've been trying to tell her to stop."

"Stop what, Max?" I say, rolling down the window to get some air.

"She's sort of . . . developing a reputation. She's been picking on a lot of kids. I don't know what's going on with her—if it's her friends or whatever—but she's become sort of a bully."

My stomach drops. Cole's eyes meet mine. And then, just as we're pulling into a clearing at the top of the hill, I see her.

The minute the other girls see me, they let go of her. She comes sprinting toward me, tears streaming down her face. "Mom!" she wails. "Mom!"

She collapses into me, her sobs racking her body. "Shhh," I say, running my hand over her head. "It's okay, honey," I say. "I'm here. Everything is going to be okay."

TWENTY-EIGHT

"We didn't mean for it to turn into anything crazy!" Brittany yells, screaming at her mother in the parking lot behind the inn, where Eva and Mindy were waiting for us after Diane told them we'd taken off after the kids.

"But what exactly happened?" Eva says, grabbing Brittany by the top of her arm and jerking her toward her in a way that surprises me. "You have a responsibility to act like a young lady around here," she says into Brittany's ear, her voice low and angry. "You are the mayor's daughter!"

"I just wanted to show her—" Brittany says, breaking down. "I wanted her to stop acting like she could push all of us around!"

I look at Livvie, who is standing next to Cole, slumped into his side like we've given her a dose of painkillers. "Explain it to me," I say. "Brittany, what were you trying to do?"

Lauren bites her lip, her eyes darting around. "It was Brittany's idea," she says.

"Lauren!" Brittany screams.

"Brittany, stop!" Eva warns her.

"Go ahead, Lauren," I say.

"It sounds so stupid now," she says. "But Brittany said we should all go check out the spot where Henrietta Martin died. You know, that stu—"

"Yes, we know," I say, looking at Cole. "Go on."

"We thought we were just going to see it. Just for fun, I guess. That's what I thought, at least, but when we got up there, Brittany pushed Livvie toward the edge. That's when I grabbed Brittany and pulled her away, but then the other girls grabbed Livvie. And then you guys showed up."

Eva looks like her eyes are going to pop out of her head. "Brittany! Why on earth . . ." She looks at Cole, her mouth wide open like it's being held that way. And then she looks at me. "Well, she must have been provoked!" she says, her eyes narrowing. "Brittany, you have never done anything like this before! Why on earth would you—"

"Actually," Lauren says, "Brittany's always been . . ."

Eva rolls her eyes and puts her arm around her daughter. "I'm taking her home," she says. "I've had enough."

"We were just going to hold her there!" Brittany starts sobbing. "We just wanted to scare her a little! That's all we were going to do!"

"Cole," I say, watching the two of them walk off, "I think it's time for us to go, too."

We walk through the back of the inn, leaving Max and Livvie in Cole's office while I grab the things I left under the table out front. But when we make it down the front steps, we discover that what we've just been through might not be the end of today's drama.

Susannah is mere feet from our table, in a full mink, with a sparkling cane in her left hand—a sympathy prop, I'm now convinced, having seen her walk without it more often than not. She's greeting people like this is a party that's been thrown in her honor.

"Oh, *Christ*," Cole says. "My mother's not going to be able to—"

"I'll handle Susannah," I say. "I can pull her away."

"Elizabeth! Cole!" Diane says when we walk up. She fortunately hasn't seen her nemesis. "Where's Olivia? Is she okay?"

"She's fine, Mom," Cole says. "But Bess is going to take her home."

"What happened?" she says.

"Eva's daughter took her up to the Cliffs," I say, as matter-of-factly as I can muster. I'm aware I'm speaking a little louder than I should, but I can barely contain my anger. I need to get out of here. "She was just going to hold her at the ledge, apparently," I say. "To scare her."

"Eva's daughter?" Diane says. "What? Why on earth? I thought she was such a sweet girl!"

"I know," I say. "Imagine that."

"But Olivia!" Her hand flies to the scarf at her neck. "She's okay?"

"A little rattled, but she's fine."

"Bess, did I just hear you say . . . ?" Susannah says, appearing beside me. "Is Livvie okay?"

I close my eyes. *Oh no.*

She's smiling at us, and I can tell from the moment I look at her that her apparent concern has nothing to do with Livvie. This is about putting on a show. "She's fine, Susannah." *Now move along and get out of here.*

"Oh, thank God!" she says, putting a hand to her cheek.

Diane is standing behind me, but I can feel her presence like an approaching storm. She takes a step forward, so close to me that she is practically hovering over my shoulder. "You stay away from my family," she says through gritted teeth. My only comfort, in this moment, is knowing that my mother-in-law would never lose her composure in public, not even now.

Susannah eases in closer to us, seeming to glide over like she's dancing, like this is fun, casual chitchat. "Or what, Diane?" she says, smiling and leaning in so close that I can smell her lemony perfume. She pauses and looks up onto the porch, where Bradley is leaning against the banister, a stern expression on his face like he's physically guarding the property. "Oh, hey, Bradley!" She wiggles her fingers, then looks back at Diane.

I notice that a hush has fallen over the crowd.

"Susannah," I whisper. "Whatever it is you want to say? Now is not the time."

"Bess, I'm not doing a damn thing," she says, all the while looking at Diane. "Not a damn thing but finally, finally, getting my life back."

"What on earth is that supposed to mean?" Diane says.

Susannah looks back at Bradley and smiles. "I warned you, Bradley!" she says, the smile on her face like she's teasing him.

Oh God, I think, noticing how she looks around to make sure she has the crowd's attention. *What is she doing?*

Bradley just stares back at her, hands in his pockets, like she's no more a nuisance than a fly buzzing around him.

"I know you think you're untouchable, Bradley Warner, but I have proof! Trucks don't just crash themselves! And you know I'm a good driver! You were the one who taught me to drive, after all, and on Whippoorwill, that very road! Was that supposed to mean something, Bradley? Running me off right there?"

Oh my God. My throat feels like it's swelling shut. I glance around the crowd. People are whispering, their eyes on Susannah and Bradley, waiting to see what will happen next.

Diane suddenly takes a step toward her. "You have some nerve!" she screams, her voice shaking. "To accuse my husband of such a thing! After everything you've—"

Cole appears behind her. "Mom," he says, gently grabbing her arm. "Come on, let's go inside. No good can come of this."

For all of our benefit, she agrees. She turns and follows him, and I watch as they meet Bradley at the top of the steps and go inside. I want to follow, but I can't. I need to manage this, to make this stop.

I turn back to Susannah. "My goodness!" she says to me, gasping like we've just escaped something together. She reaches out for my arm like I'm on her side, and I jerk it away. Her eyes widen.

"What are you trying to do?" I whisper. Much of the crowd is politely moving on, but I can feel a few lingering stares.

"Those Warners!" she exclaims, looking around like she's talking to the crowd. "You're going to thank me one day, Bess," she says, shuffling a step closer to me. "Let me tell you, you're going to—"

"Susannah, stop," I say, taking a step away from her. "I don't want to hear it." And then I say the thing that I know will hurt her most. "I have to go, Susannah. My family is waiting for me."

TWENTY-NINE

I press my finger against the sticker on her door. It came inside the shoebox with the new sneakers we bought before the first day of school. It's a cartoon character shaped like a peach, wearing pink high-top sneakers and purple sunglasses shaped like stars. LIFE'S A PEACH!, it reads in bubble letters above its head.

I knew this day was coming, I knew she'd eventually grow up. I just hoped that as we edged toward it, I'd be able to put it off somehow, like her adolescence was a tennis ball that I could hit back over the net whenever it got close to me.

I twist the knob in my hand.

"Livvie?" I say, knocking on the door as I ease it open. "Livvie, honey, we have to talk about this sometime."

Last night when we got home, she was too hysterical to reason with. I tried to talk through it with her, to understand her point of view and address whatever culpability she might have had in the whole thing, but she was too far gone, bawling, her back heaving under my hand while she lay facedown on her bed. Something in that moment propelled me right back to when I was her age, my teenage grief bubbling up like a latent virus that had never really left me. And so I let her be. It was seven thirty when I left her room. Forty minutes later, when I went to check on her, she was sound asleep on top of her covers, her cheeks still mottled from crying.

"Livvie?"

She is wide awake, staring at the ceiling, the light from the window across the room streaming over her in ribbons. She glowers at me, looking not quite angry but more like she does when she is sick: drained, morose. She turns toward the wall, her mattress squeaking underneath her as she turns away from me, curling herself up into a snail shell under the covers.

"Do you remember that game we used to play at dinner?" I say, sitting on the edge of the bed and resting my hand on her hip. She doesn't move. Her eyes stay pinned to the wall in front of her like she's in a trance.

"Two truths and a lie?" I say. "I'd read about it in a parenting magazine. Sometimes it was the only way Dad and I could get you and your brother to tell us anything detailed about your school day."

A flash of recognition passes over her face, the slightest twitch in her eyes. "Remember Max?" I say, attempting the lighthearted tactic I thought up earlier. "He always tried to trick us by telling three lies. Remember how crazy they were? He'd say that he learned how to fly in science, something like that . . ."

"Yeah," she says, and shifts her weight, her hands in a prayer pose under her cheek. "But a lot of times when we played it, you were on the phone, calling from work."

"That's true," I say, feeling the slight like a punch to the gut. I lean closer to her, wanting to run my hand along her hair, and she jerks away, startling me. *I can't touch her now?*

"So . . ." I pause, swallowing against the lump in my throat. "I'm going to tell you three truths." I wait for her to protest, but she doesn't. "First, when I was your age, I was teased constantly, mostly because my family didn't have money. Second, I know how much it hurts when someone betrays you, especially someone you thought was a friend."

"Are you talking about Anna?" she says suddenly.

"Anna?" I say, repeating the name of the coworker who killed my career. "Honey, how did you know—"

"Of course I knew who she was, Mom," she says. "Everyone knew."

"Yes, honey," I say, "I'm talking about Anna," though the truth is, I was thinking of Susannah, too.

"And . . . the third truth: I know this move hasn't been easy for you, honey. I know it's hard to find your place in a new town. Believe me, I know."

She flops over on her back, looking at me like I've offended her. "You have no idea!"

Shit.

She sighs and rubs her fingers in a frustrated circle just above her temples, the same way her father does when he's irritated.

"You have *no* idea!"

"Then, honey, tell me. I can't understand what you're going through—I can't help if you don't talk to me."

She glares up at the ceiling. Seconds pass, then minutes.

"I have to ask you something, Livvie," I finally say. "Max said that those girls did what they did yesterday as . . . well, as retaliation. I hate that it happened to you, Livvie. If I could take it away, I would, but I have to ask you about it. You know I have to."

"I know!" she says, her voice suddenly thick. "I know!"

"Honey, what do you mean, you know?" I say.

"I mean, I don't need you to tell me that what I did was wrong. I know!" She starts to cry.

"Livvie," I say, "you have to help me out here. What do you mean, what you did?"

"I just thought . . . You have no idea how bad Brittany was, Mom! The things she would say! Even about you!" she says. "She said that I was just like you—that I wasn't going to have any friends here because nobody could ever trust me. She used to follow me around in the halls at school, holding her phone up to my ear, playing the YouTube of you on those tapes."

"What?" I say, feeling my anger start to ratchet. *Tick-tick-tick,* like the whistle on a teakettle. I take a deep breath.

"She said that because I am your daughter and because I'm new here, she'd make sure to 'protect' everyone from me. And when I started hanging out with Lauren, it didn't help because they just don't like her or whatever." She shakes her head like she wants to will it all away. "I just thought . . ."

Tears start to roll down her cheeks. I reach out to brush them away. This time, she doesn't stop me.

"I just thought . . ." She gulps. "After the kids were mean to me in DC, and then Brittany started with everything . . . I thought if I was more aggressive . . . if I showed them I couldn't be bossed around . . ."

"I get it, honey," I say, motioning for her to sit up. "I really do."

She sits, and I wrap my arms around her. I rock her gently

from side to side, the way I did when she was younger. "Here's what I want to tell you," I say. "And I want to be totally honest with you. Life is going to get messy. Things are sometimes not going to go your way. Sometimes, you'll feel like nothing is going your way. And people—even well-meaning ones—are going to disappoint you. But the only thing you can control is yourself." I feel my voice start to break, realizing how much I need to follow my own advice.

"Mom?" she says. "Are you okay?"

I wipe a tear from my cheek. "It's really true, Liv. You just have to do your best, stand up for what you know is right, and forget about the rest. The less time you spend worrying about whatever Brittany is going to throw at you—"

"I know," she says. "I know it's not worth it. And I knew I wasn't getting anywhere, acting the way I did." She starts to cry again. "I felt awful, Mommy." I keep holding her tightly, hooking my chin over her shoulder. "What am I going to do on Monday? What am I going to do when I see her?"

"It will be hard, I know," I say, thinking of what happened yesterday—the scene on the Cliffs with Livvie, Susannah's accusation in front of the inn—and the past few weeks . . . "But all you can do is be yourself, Liv. Stand up for yourself if you need to. Ignore her if you need to. But don't change who you are because of her, Liv. Promise me you won't do that."

A while later, when I come downstairs, I am startled to discover Diane sitting at the kitchen table.

"Is she okay?" she says, her hands cupping a mug of tea.

"She will be," I say. "I hope." I pull out the chair across from her and sit down.

"Cole and Max just left for William's," she says. "They said they're going to pick up peanut-butter cookies for Livvie."

I smile. "That's nice."

"I told them to get you something, too."

I cock my head to the side, wrinkling my brow at her.

She looks at me quickly and then back down at her hands. "You're an excellent mother, Elizabeth," she says, as if she's speaking to her teacup. "I'm twelve years too late in telling you that."

I nod, stunned by the words I hear coming out of her mouth. "Thank you, Diane."

"I see everything you do for those kids. I see how you care for my son. I know that this move is a difficult transition, and I should have done more to help you. I remember being new here once, too, and I remember what it was like, trying to find my way in and make this place feel like somewhere I belonged."

"Diane, I—"

"No need to say anything." She stops me, her eyes finally meeting mine. "But I owe you an apology."

"Accepted," I say.

"I also want to apologize for how I reacted to your writing the story."

"Diane, you don't have to. I'm not going to file the article. Not after everything that's happened. You were definitely right about her."

"Well, I don't know about that, actually," she says.

"What do you mean?" I say, not sure I've heard her right.

"I might have been unfair," she says, wiping her hand across her mouth like she is thinking something through. "You know, nobody's entirely good or bad."

"Okay," I say, nodding slowly.

"Even her." She shifts in her seat, tapping her fingertips against the side of her mug, and I get the sense she's weighing whether to say something more.

"What is it, Diane?" I say.

Her eyes flit toward the ceiling. "Is Livvie . . . ?"

"I don't think she's coming down anytime soon," I say. "She was falling asleep again when I left her."

"Okay." She takes a breath. "I need to talk to you about something, Elizabeth. I should have explained it several weeks ago, but my pride . . ." She shakes her head. "Sometimes I let it get the best of me."

"What is it?"

She pushes her teacup to the side and clasps her hands on the table, a grave expression on her face like we're sitting across from each other at a conference table and she's about to tell me I've lost my job. "Elizabeth . . ." She clears her throat. "When I first came to Greyhill, your father-in-law was a different man. He was . . ." She twists her lips to the side, trying to find the right word. "He was . . . between us . . . a little broken."

"Broken?" I say.

"By what had happened here, with Henrietta." She glances at me quickly, as if she's peeking to check my reaction to the name. She pauses again to sip her tea.

"You're going to have to explain more," I say, thinking of Susannah's claim that he'd run after Henrietta right before she died.

"The thing is, Elizabeth, Susannah's coming back here has dredged up the most painful memories of Bradley's life."

I curl my fingers into my hands. "Most painful?" I say. "What do you mean?"

"After he and I settled here, he explained what had happened with Henrietta," she says. "How he and Susannah were the last people who saw her before she died. What he went through was horrible," she says, her fingers tracing the wood grain on the table. "He and Henrietta, well . . . they were in love, Elizabeth, that's the only way to put it, but Susannah couldn't have that. I don't know what sort of lies she's been spoon-feeding you, but she was intensely jealous of Henrietta. She was the one who was drunk and crazy that night."

"She told me that Bradley was the last one who saw her."

"Just Bradley?" she says, her voice rising. "So she made it sound like . . . ?"

"She was implicating him? Yes."

"You didn't believe her, of course?"

"No," I say. "I couldn't imagine Bradley doing anything to hurt someone. But, Diane, I'll be honest. I still wonder what actually happened. I've been wondering."

"They both saw her wander off. She was angry. Susannah had been harassing her about Bradley. And then what everyone says happened, happened. She fell or slipped or . . ." She shakes her head. "Anyway, my point is that Susannah has been a thorn in our sides for decades."

"Decades?" I say, the aftertaste from the coffee I drank earlier starting to sour in my mouth. "What do you mean?"

"She has been sending us letters for years. To the inn, to our

home . . . And the phone calls! We had to change our phone number once, Bess. She was incessant."

"But why?" I say, alarmed. I want to believe her, especially
after the incidents over the past few days, but Diane is . . . *Diane*.
"What did she want?"

"Bradley," she says. "She's never been able to let go."

"Are you sure?" I say, my mouth dropping open. "I mean, she
talks about him. She talks about him a lot. But I didn't think . . ."

"Honestly, Elizabeth, when you first told me you were doing
that story, I thought she had somehow rigged it."

"You did?" I say, remembering Susannah telling me about the
vengeful ways she would retaliate against women in New York
when they got too close to her husband.

"Yes," she says, looking resigned. "Our only saving grace
during all these years was that she never visited Greyhill. Her
relationship with her parents was—"

"I've heard."

"They were strange people. When they died, we thought she
might come back. At least for their funerals. We braced ourselves
for it. Bradley couldn't sleep. But she didn't. I was surprised, until
we got a phone call from her husband."

"Her husband?" I say. "You mean . . . ?"

She nods. "Teddy Lane himself. He called Bradley's office.
I'll never forget it. Cole must have been at Georgetown by then.
Teddy made it sound as if he thought Bradley and Susannah were
having some sort of long-distance affair, and he told Bradley to
stay away from her. Which was absolutely no problem, of course,
and it also explained why we never saw them in Greyhill."

"He wouldn't let her."

"That's right. She said as much in the letters she sent. She said he kept her on a very short leash."

I think back to all the ways that Susannah's told me he controlled her. "That's what she's told me, too." I put my head in my hands for a moment, letting all this settle over me. "What's most disturbing out of all this, Diane, is that it doesn't surprise me, now that I'm hearing it."

"She's out of her mind, Elizabeth. And I'm telling you, when she came back here last year, it got worse. When he wasn't responsive to her, she said she was going to reveal that he had actually killed Henrietta. She said she'd been working on her plan for years."

"Why didn't you tell me all this?" I say. "Before I started the story?"

"I couldn't," she says. "Honestly, Elizabeth, I didn't think you'd believe me."

I probably wouldn't have, I think. "Then why didn't Bradley?"

"You know him," she says. "I think he thought that it might pacify her in some way for you to do it. He kept telling me that we needed to learn how to live with Susannah, whether we liked it or not, now that she is back in Greyhill." She puts her face in her hands for a minute and then drops them to her sides. "I just couldn't." Tears start to well up in her eyes.

I freeze. I have *never* seen Diane cry before. To be honest, I don't think I believed she was capable. "Diane?" I say, leaning into the table. "Are you okay?"

She winces like my question physically hurts.

"Bess," she says, her eyes still closed, "I . . ."

"What is it?" I say. "You can tell me."

"Last summer . . ." She smudges a tear from her face. "Oh my . . ." Her hands are shaking. Her voice trembles. "I only meant to scare her," she says.

It takes me a minute to understand what she's saying. My ears start to ring. "Wait . . . Diane . . . You mean—?"

She nods at me, her face crumpling. "I'd just had it!" she says in an angry rasp. "She had pushed us and pushed us and pushed us! But I didn't intend to hurt her, Bess! And I hadn't planned it! I just happened to be on Whippoorwill that day, and when I saw that ridiculous truck . . . I just wanted to scare her," she says, shaking her head quickly from side to side. "That's all I wanted to do."

"Does Bradley know?" I say.

"Of course." She grasps the cup of tea in front of her, as if she needs something to hold on to. "Thank God nothing happened to her, because otherwise . . ." She puts her hand over her mouth like she's about to be sick. "I never would have forgiven myself." Her eyes dart to mine for a split second before she looks away. "I don't know what came over me."

"It's okay," I say, reaching out my hand to hers. She wraps hers around mine and holds it, tight.

"So you understand now?" she says. "Why all this nonsense with the inn is so upsetting. Why everything she does . . ." Her voice trails off. I can feel her hand shaking in mine.

I stand, the chair scraping the floor as I do, and go around the table to embrace her.

And she lets me.

THIRTY

Susannah smiles when she sees me. She is so good at it, the sunny morning-talk-show-host grin, so *easy* with it. It's frightening, actually, to realize how simple it was for her to manipulate me.

She is wearing black silk pajamas, sitting on the couch in the office with her legs stretched out on the cushions, an old paperback copy of *The Great Gatsby* splayed open on her lap, a needlepoint pillow under her feet.

"We need to talk," I say, my heart racing.

Her face falls as she comprehends my mood, the smile disappearing from her face like a flower wilting in the heat. "Cindy, you can leave us," she says.

The door closes with a thunk.

Susannah looks at me, her chin jutting forward. "This is about yesterday, I assume? At the festival?"

"No," I say, as calmly as I can. "It's not about yesterday."

"Then what?" she says, her brow knitted, as if she couldn't possibly fathom why I might be angry.

"This is about everything, Susannah," I say.

"Everything?" She laughs like the word amuses her.

"Everything you've told me over the past several weeks. All the lies."

"Oh, *this* again?" she says. "You're still mad I didn't tell you about the resort?"

"This is insulting," I say, dropping my bag. I pull the chair away from the desk, turn it to face her, and sit down. "But sure, why don't we start with that? This whole story you've told me, about Teddy leaving you with nothing. I don't believe it anymore. It isn't true, is it?"

She gasps like she's choking on something, her spindly hand gripping the front of her shirt. "Of course it's true!"

"But I've been thinking about it, Susannah, and it doesn't make any sense. There are so many other routes you could've taken. What about all your wealthy friends in New York? The people you socialized with? Couldn't they help you out?"

She starts to laugh. "The people I socialized with were only my friends *because* I had money, Bess. Because I was Teddy Lane's wife. Once he died, they were done with me. I may as well have died, too. Trust me, this is a world you know nothing about."

"I find that hard to believe, but okay," I say, nodding efficiently. "Then let's talk about some of the other things you told me. Teddy, for instance."

"What about him?" she says, picking the paperback up off her lap and knocking it absentmindedly against one of her legs, like all this bores her.

"I believe what you told me about how he controlled you, but you also had him believe that you and Bradley were somehow involved," I say, repeating what Diane told me this morning. "And you didn't come back here all those years because Teddy wouldn't let you. Is that right?"

I can see her jaw shift behind her closed lips, the subtle way that it clenches.

"I told you," she says, her voice a coarse hum. "He was terrible to me."

"You didn't help the situation, though, did you, Susannah?"

"You don't know what it's been like for me," she says in a broken whisper, her eyes wide as saucers. "You would understand if you knew."

"Okay, then." I cross my arms over my chest. "Explain it to me, Susannah. That's why I'm here. I want to know why you've wasted all this time lying to me, just to screw my family over in the end."

She scrunches her face up. "I haven't lied to you, Bess!"

"Oh, give me a fucking break," I say, starting to stand. "Do you think I'm an idiot?"

"No, no!" she wails. "You have to understand, Bess. I've told you the truth. I just left out the . . ." She shakes her head like she's trying to will it all away. "It was devastating, what they did to me!"

"Who? What *who* did to you?" I say, exasperated.

"Bradley and Henrietta!"

I roll my eyes. "My God!" I rub my hands down my face. "You are seventy years old and still pining over a teenage romance. Why, Susannah? *Why?*"

She looks down at her lap, her cheeks hollowing out like she's sucking on a mint. "Have you read this?" she says, lifting the book.

"Years ago, in high school," I say, frustrated by her crazy whims. *I'm going to be here all day trying to get to the bottom of this.*

She runs her hand over the cover. "This is Henrietta's copy."

"Henrietta's?" I say. "Okay, what does it have to do with—"

"I stole it from her. Well, I stole it from her house. On the day after she died, when I went to see her father. I went into her room and I took it, along with the ribbon I showed you."

"Why?" I say.

"She and Bradley used to read this to each other, passing it back and forth. We would sit out on the green in front of Draper while we ate our lunch, on a blanket that Henrietta would bring from home. We had all read it, of course, for school, but the two of them were enthralled by it. I would lie between them, my head on Bradley's lap, listening to them read to me. It felt almost . . . parental, in a way. Comforting. But you know what?"

"What?" I say sharply, wanting her to wrap this up.

"When I stole the book, I was taking it for a memento. That's it. But after I got it home, I discovered that there was a note tucked in the book, from Bradley to Henrietta, where he professed his feelings to her. It was proof! They were making a *fool* out of me!" She lifts up the book, stabbing it into the air. "I swear, it was almost like she left it there for me to find!"

I take a deep breath. "Susannah," I start. "Listen . . . listen closely. I'm *done* with all your bullshit about the past. I want to know why you've been harassing my in-laws all these years. I want to know why you've been lying to me, luring me in with your stories only to hurt us with this resort. That's why I'm here. I have no interest in your teenage heartbreak, do you understand?"

"But it's all related, Bess," she scolds, her eyes piercing mine. "Be patient! I'm getting there!"

I raise my eyebrows. "Go ahead. But I'm not going to sit here all—"

She flips through the paperback, fanning the pages. The book falls open so easily in the spot where she's stopped that I can tell she must have looked at it dozens of times. She holds it up next to her face and begins reading.

"'I hope she'll be a fool,'" she recites, her voice loud and round like a teacher standing in front of a classroom. "'That's the best thing a girl can be in this world, a beautiful little fool.'"

"And?" I say.

"That's what everybody thinks I am! That's what they thought I was!"

I start to laugh. I can't help it. I want to hurt her.

Her eyes fly toward me, and what I see when I look at her watching me laughing at her is the hopeless, lonely girl she says she's always been. She is so sad, a stunted woman, really, who's let herself live her entire life according to her relationship to these people who maybe didn't care that much for her, her fixation leading her astray like a mouse trapped in a maze, every path leading nowhere. As much as I could hate her right now, after everything I've learned, the truth is that I do feel sorry for her. At least, for the teenage girl she was, alone and duped by the only people she says accepted her.

She reaches across the coffee table, pushing the book at me.

"What?" I say, taking it.

"Flip to the back," she says, pointing to the book. "The last line is the one I always loved most."

I turn to the back. The cover is tattered, so fragile it is barely holding on to the pages. I read the last line: "'So we beat on, boats against the current, borne back ceaselessly into the past.'" I drop the book and look at her, waiting for an explanation.

"Let me tell you something, Bess," she says, and I notice she is flushed to her collarbone. "Share a bit of wisdom, now that I've lived my life. Fitzgerald was spot-on when he wrote that. No matter what you try to do in your life, no matter where you go, your past *never* leaves you."

"You really believe that?" I ask.

"I do," she says, her mouth a thin pink line. "For better or for worse, I do. That's why I'm back here, Bess. It's exactly what I told you the other day. I am here to redeem myself, and to absolve myself of what happened here."

"Absolve yourself—" I start. "Susannah, I'm not understanding. I thought you just said that Henrietta and Bradley did horrible things to you . . ."

"Oh, they did," she says, nodding. "I meant every word of that. But I know *why* she did it—I know why she tried to take him from me."

"Why?"

"Because I had made her miserable, Bess. I was so jealous. Of everything she had. You know, some of the kids made fun of her because she was poor. Everyone said her mother was crazy because she hanged herself. But you should have *seen* the way her father doted on her. Do you know what that was like for me to watch?" Her eyes start to well up and she squeezes them tightly, willing away the tears. "To see how, despite the fact that she was poor and motherless, she had *everything* I never could? Her father adored her. We used to go to her little house and sit in her backyard, and I would watch the two of them. He taught her how to plant tomatoes, how to fix the sink, change a tire. She could do anything. He'd pinch her arm gently when he teased her about some comment she made. He talked to her. He so clearly *loved* her."

"Okay, so you were jealous of her. But what does that have to do with what I'm asking you now? What does that have to do with the way you've treated Bradley all these years? If you came back here to redeem yourself, like you say, then why are you so hell-bent on doing things that are only making you more enemies?"

She sniffs. "On the day that Henrietta died, she and I had an argument, like I told you. She asked if she could catch a ride with me and Bradley up to the Cliffs. We always rode together, the three of us, but in my state of mind, I lost it. I knew that once we got to graduation, the two sure things I had in my life—Henrietta and Bradley— were going to leave me."

"You told me the other day that Bradley took off after her that night, which I know is a lie. You insinuated that he had some role in her death."

"No," she says, the corners of her lips pulling down as if on strings. "He had nothing to do with it. I was angry the other day. I felt like you had me pinned in a corner, Bess. I shouldn't have said it."

"Then tell me the truth. This is your last chance, Susannah. This is it."

"Bradley picked me up to go to the party. We went on to Henrietta's house, even though I'd told her we wouldn't, and I dragged her out of there, even though she didn't want to go anymore. It wasn't even seven o'clock and I had already drunk at least a third of the bottle of brandy that I had hidden under my bed. The plan had been to sneak it to the Cliffs that night for everyone to enjoy, but after my fight with Henrietta, I started early and didn't stop. And then my best friend wandered off. When I told you the other day that Bradley ran after Henrietta, I was lying. Henrietta wandered off on her own. It's just like everyone says."

"You think it was just an accident?"

Her lip trembles. "I don't know . . . I was so drunk. But like her father said, she could have walked these mountains blindfolded. And she hardly touched alcohol. She hadn't had a drop that night." She shrugs. "I've never been able to forgive myself for the way I treated her that day. All these years, yes, I wanted Bradley back in my life. Being with Teddy . . . it made me see what kind of man your father-in-law is. But I think I also felt like if Bradley accepted me, if I could just have his stamp of approval, then the weight of my guilt would be lifted. But then, when I got back here, I realized that Bradley was never going to help me fix what people here thought of me. I'd dug my own grave with the way I'd behaved toward him all those years, and I was just going to have to live with the consequences. I just wanted . . ."

"What?"

She shakes her head.

"You just wanted his attention?" I say. "You were like a child, not getting what you wanted, so you kept acting out until you did?"

She nods. "I guess so . . ." She presses her fingertips to the corners of her eyes. "Bess, I know you won't believe me, and I don't blame you, but I really do care about you. I value how you've listened to me. You've let me tell all my old stories, remember the few good memories I have."

"Well . . . ," I say, taking a deep breath.

"I don't blame you for hating me."

I nod.

"Tell me what I can do to make it better. I promise, I'll do anything."

I look to the far wall, to the Magritte painting, the lovers and their shrouded faces. She always said it reminded her of someone. Now it makes my stomach turn, realizing that she'd likely meant Bradley.

"I have an idea, Bess," she says. She scooches herself to the edge of the couch and leans to face me, with her elbows on her knees. "I know you hardly owe me any favors, but . . . now that I'm really thinking about it . . ."

"What?"

"I'll drop this whole resort idea."

"Oh, really?" I say. "As easy as that? Susannah, you told me the other day that if you didn't follow through with it, you wouldn't have anything."

She raises a palm to me, as if taking an oath. "I can find another way," she says. "I promise, Bess. And I'll leave your family alone, once and for all."

"I don't know if I can believe you."

"There is a catch . . . ," she starts.

I stand up to go. "Of course," I say. "Of course there's a catch."

"This is the only way I can think of to finally free myself," she says. "I want you to write your story. But I want to tell you something first, and I want you to include it."

I walk across the room for my bag. "You've got to be kidding me. After everything, you want to bribe me into writing something flattering about you in a major newspaper?"

She stands, walking across the room to meet me. "Please,

Bess!" she pleads. "Please! Just sit down. Let me explain. Let me tell you one last story."

"Susannah, I—" I start for the door.

"Bess, just hear me out."

"I can't believe you—"

"I'll drop this thing with the house, I really will."

"Susannah . . ." I take a deep breath, weighing whether I even want to know whatever it is she wants to tell me. "I'm not making any promises. . . ."

"Okay!" she says, clapping her hands together. "Now, please, sit. This might take a minute."

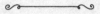

Later that afternoon, when I get home, I dial Noelle's cell.

"Sorry to bother you with this on a Saturday," I say after she answers. "But I need to talk to you about this story. I think we need to take it in another direction."

"Don't apologize," she says. "I'm in the office. What's up?"

"Well," I say, pausing to take a deep breath and settle my nerves. "I hardly know where to start."

THIRTY-ONE

"Did you see it?"

"Oh, yes, I saw it! I've read it four times."

"Can you believe it?"

"No, I can't. I swear, my jaw is on the floor."

THIRTY-TWO

⁓———⁓

WASHINGTON POST MAGAZINE
"A Daughter's Homecoming"
SUNDAY, NOVEMBER 11, 2018

Susannah Greyhill Lane—or Cricket, as she's known to some around here—has come home. Just over a year ago, following the death of her husband, the billionaire Teddy Lane, Susannah shocked everyone in this town of barely seven hundred by announcing that she was returning to Esperanza, the once grand home where she was raised. It overlooks Greyhill, Virginia, the charming Shenandoah Valley hamlet that she was away from for more than five decades.

Esperanza means "hope" in Spanish. And Ms. Lane, now seventy, says hope is all she has left. And in fact, it's why she's returned.

"I came back here because of my father," she says, revealing a secret she hasn't shared with anyone in her adult life, including her husband of nearly fifty years.

"The mayor?" I ask, referring to former mayor Wallace Greyhill. According to Susannah and most everyone in town,

Mayor Greyhill and his wife, Amelia, essentially left her to fend for herself throughout her childhood.

"No," she says, a smile spreading across her face. "My real father."

In Susannah's home office, originally the sun room, is a trunk. One side of it is occupied by Ms. Lane's diaries—gold, crocodile-skin-covered journals she used to order in bulk from the Smythson shop on Madison Avenue in Manhattan. On the other side is a box teeming with photographs: old black-and-whites from decades ago, Polaroids and shiny color Kodak prints from the 1970s and '80s. To pore through them with Ms. Lane is to witness the incredible life she's led. There are photos of her as a child with her late sister, Margaret—as toddlers in Easter dresses, in green velvet next to the Christmas tree. There are photos of Susannah with her famous husband in St. Tropez, Barcelona, Hong Kong. And there are photos of parties —so many parties—and the parades of famous actors, authors, and dignitaries she has hosted in her homes.

"Ah," she says, straightening up. "Here it is."

Ms. Lane declares that this is her most treasured photo. She keeps it encased in a small envelope, pale pink, from a card her husband gave her one Valentine's Day. The photo itself is small, a three-by-three square, and upon first glance it looks like a throwaway. The photo is yellowed, overexposed, and blurry. It features an image of a man standing on parched grass. He is tall and rugged, in a wrinkled buttondown shirt with the sleeves rolled up and the kind of pants a man wears to work when his work involves getting dirty. The man is not smiling. In fact, he looks troubled, almost angry, which makes a lot of sense, once you learn who he is and what he's been through.

Of all the men Susannah Lane has known over the course of her life—her father, the mayor; Teddy Lane, the famous husband—it is this man, a man she hardly knew when he was alive, who is responsible for all the choices she's making now, in the twilight of her life. The man, whose reputation is well-known in Greyhill, is Timothy Martin. He is the father of Henrietta Martin, Susannah's best friend from childhood, whose tragic death when she was just seventeen shook this small community. But the fact that he was her best friend's father is not what makes him so important to Susannah. What makes him so treasured is that this man, Timothy Martin, was actually Susannah's father, too.

She discovered the family secret when she was just fourteen, and now, at seventy, Susannah Lane says she feels compelled to reveal who she really is, in large part because she believes that doing so will help close the rift that began between herself and the community after Henrietta's tragic death.

"My mother had an affair with Mr. Martin when he was doing some work on our house," she explains, holding the picture in two cupped hands as gently as if it were a robin's egg. "When I discovered that he was my true father, I was desperate to tell somebody, especially Henrietta, who had always been more of a sister to me than my own, but my mother threatened me and told me to keep it quiet."

She discovered the secret while snooping in the back of a

drawer in her mother's bedroom. She found there a love letter from Mr. Martin dated the year of her birth. A letter, she
says, that she was amazed to find still hidden in her mother's
things when she came back to the home last year. "I know we
can't be together," it reads (see photo, page 17). "I know that
this is my only choice . . . just know that I will love you, from
afar, for the rest of my life. We will always know the truth,
and hopefully the brief time we've had together—hopefully
it will be enough to sustain us."

Ms. Lane confronted her mother about the affair immediately after she discovered it. "You have to understand, the
news was a boon for me! At least initially. All my life, I'd felt
like an outsider in my own home. My mother treated me like
I was a blight on her life, my father completely disregarded
me. Now I knew why. I'll never forget the look on her face
when she saw the letter in my hand," she says. "Mother sat
me down and told me everything. As far as my father, the
mayor, and Mr. Martin knew, I was the mayor's daughter.
She hadn't told either of them the truth about me—at least,
that's what she claimed, though from the disdainful way my
Greyhill father looked at me, I don't doubt that he knew the
truth. Mother said that if I ever told anyone, she'd make me
regret it for the rest of my short life. She said that nobody
would believe me anyway, which was true. Nobody would
have had the nerve to doubt my mother, who was a fixture
at the Methodist church in town. She was hardly the type."

"And Mr. Martin?"

"He quickly become my obsession," she says.

Her mother's threat kept her from ever revealing the

truth to Mr. Martin or her best friend, Henrietta—her half sister, she now knew.

"I know it's unbelievable. But I just couldn't. Despite how I hated my mother, I still wanted her approval. It's only natural. And something about this secret, twisted as it was, bound me to her in a way that I couldn't give up."

Mr. Martin led a life marred by tragedy. His wife committed suicide when their daughter, Henrietta, was just an infant, an event Susannah believes might have been related to Mr. Martin's affair with her mother. And then, at just seventeen, Henrietta was killed by a fatal fall during a graduation party, ostensibly after drinking too much and wandering off.

Ms. Lane left Greyhill just weeks later, a fact that has led many to believe she is responsible for her friend's death. In a way, Ms. Lane says, she accepts the accusation, but she says the real reason she never returned was that it was just too painful. "People want to believe that something far more sordid happened—that I pushed her or something ridiculous like that—but the truth is that we had had an argument just before she ran off. I had said horrible things to her, things I had never revealed. And I told her who my real father was. And I said—I didn't mean it," she says now, tears falling from her face. "I told her that her own mother died because of me."

She left Greyhill racked with guilt.

Timothy Martin, meanwhile, spent the rest of his life trying to convince the local community that there was something more to his daughter's death, but the mayor—

Susannah's presumed father—wouldn't hear of it. Mr. Martin, along with dozens of other members of the community, mostly the rural residents who make up the town's working class, protested this for years, begging the local government to investigate Henrietta's death. When they wouldn't, something in Greyhill changed.

You wouldn't know it, of course, strolling the quaint downtown. A perennial fixture on those "America's Best Small Towns" lists, bucolic Greyhill draws hundreds of day-trip visitors from surrounding cities each year.

But if you look beyond the cobblestone streets and quaint shops in the downtown business district, you'll discover that the legacy of Henrietta's death is an unfortunate fracture between the town's haves and have-nots. Those who live in town—the shop owners, teachers, doctors, and town council members—seem to prefer their insularity, even referring to the rural members of the community as "Others," a coarse term that came into use soon after Mr. Martin began his crusade to discover the real cause of his daughter's death.

"I didn't know the true extent of what he was doing—he even went so far as to implicate me—until my mother called me to tell me he'd died," Ms. Lane says now.

"I remember the phone call like it was yesterday. I was standing in our apartment, in front of the big picture window in our bedroom that overlooked Central Park. The lights had just gone on at Wollman Rink, and from where I stood on the fifteenth floor, the skaters looked so tiny. We had just had the first snow of the season. The first snow always made me feel a little melancholy because I knew what it signaled: the deep settling in, months and months of cold and gray, dark descending on the city. Winter.

"It had been years since my mother and I had spoken. She asked me how things were in the city, as if we were accustomed to chatting regularly. She was calling to relay the news. That's how she put it: 'I am calling to relay the news that Timothy Martin has died.'

"I asked her about his memorial service, and she stumbled. My mother had never once faltered with her language, that's one thing—maybe the only thing—I admired about her. Her speech was so elegant and effortless that it was always as if she was reciting a script. I wanted to attend, but of course that was impossible. It would have made a spectacle of things. My mother then—she did something shocking.

"She told me she was sorry. That infuriated me. It was what I'd wanted to hear my whole life, but once it was out there, I couldn't take it. I'd already lived with the weight of regret for so many years, but when this happened, it was as if somebody was doubling the load on my back. Why hadn't I taken the time to tell him that I knew that he was my real father? Why didn't I tell him what I'd said to Henrietta right before she died? He deserved to know. He would have been so much better off. We all would have."

When Ms. Lane decided to return to her hometown after her husband's death, she anticipated that her homecoming might not be smooth—and she was right, though she might have underestimated just how unhappy the townspeople would be about her return. When she announced that she would be selling off much of her family's land, over three hundred acres that surround the city limits, many residents balked, worrying how the potential buyers might change the fabric of the community.

But in the midst of making these decisions last summer, Ms. Lane was injured in a car accident outside of town. "My return hasn't been what I had hoped it would be," she laughs. She says she's now begun to reconsider the sale of the land, and that she plans to take the property off the market. "I'm hoping that by sharing my story, and by announcing that I am going to forego the property sale, at least for the time being, the community might begin to regard me with new understanding.

"I left Greyhill because of the pain of losing my best friend," she says. "And later, I stayed away because I lost the father I never knew. I know I've been gone a long time," she says. "But as the only living Greyhill—in name, anyway—and as Timothy Martin's daughter, I feel a responsibility to every member of this community to reveal myself as I truly am. Greyhill is a wonderful place, and I want it to make all my ancestors proud. I hope Henrietta is looking down on me, along with our father, and I hope they can see a happy future for all the people here. I hope for that more than anything you can imagine."

THIRTY-THREE

Bess

By the time I pull the roast out of the oven, I realize I'm a little drunk. I put the pan on top of the stove and shut the oven door with my foot.

"It needs to rest, Bess," Diane says, turning to me from the other side of her kitchen, where she's sprinkling parsley over her potato dish. "The foil's in that drawer beside you."

I know, I say to myself, and reach for my wineglass. *I know, Diane.*

"What time did you say you're meeting William for dessert?" she says.

"Not until eight," I say.

"Good," she says, walking to the sink and wiping her hands on a dish towel. "That will give you time to sober up." She gives me a look.

"Now, now," I say, smiling. "No need to micromanage me."

She laughs. "Okay, okay," she says. "You're right."

I put my glass down, winking at her as I do, and start out of the kitchen. "Where are the kids?" I say, sitting across the couch from Bradley. "And Cole?"

"I think they went out back," he says, his eyes pinned to the football game on the television.

"Bradley," I say, fortified by the wine, "what did you think?"

"Think about what?" he says, his eyes still on the game.

"You know," I say. "The story."

He sniffs hard, like he has a cold.

"I hope it didn't make you uncomfortable," I say, lowering my voice.

"Nah," he says, reaching over to pat my hand. "Like I told you when we talked, I'm happy to put all this behind us. I'm sorry you got roped into it, is all. I know it's not the kind of thing you wanted to deal with when you moved here. Although, now you're a local celebrity. That story is all anyone's talking about in town."

"For better or for worse," I joke, thinking of how I've been received around Greyhill since the piece came out. Everywhere I go—the grocery store, William's, pickup at Draper—people pepper me with more questions, wanting to find out what else I know. *The stuff you couldn't fit in the article*, some have said, sidling up next to me. "I'd almost prefer that everyone go back to snubbing me."

"Oh, it's all for the better," Bradley says. "Definitely for the better."

"Well, thank you." I study him for a moment. "Susannah told me what she thinks really happened. Up on the Cliffs that night."

He nods, his eyes back on the TV, and I get the sense he wishes I hadn't said anything.

"She thinks Henrietta really did just wander off. She apologized for what she said to me, trying to pin it on you."

"Well . . ." He sucks in his bottom lip, his eyes gazing to some far-off place. "Susannah's a very fragile person, as we all know by now. I should really apologize to you. For not warning you what you were getting yourself into." He looks toward the kitchen. "You don't think she'll keep going with this accident stuff, do you?" he whispers.

"I don't think so, Bradley," I say. "I really don't. I think she wants to let everything rest, once and for all."

"Good," he says, and then suddenly he claps, the Cavaliers having made a play he's pleased with. He takes a sip from his tumbler of Diet Coke. He's done with this conversation, I can tell.

I hear Cole and look out the window. His arms are in the air, and Livvie's are, too. She's jumping up and down, a gleeful smile on her face, pumping the football in her hand over her head. "Touchdown!" Max yells, running across the yard.

"Bradley?" I say, reaching over to pat his arm. "Maybe someday you can tell me what she was like."

"Who?"

I raise an eyebrow.

He smiles, his eyes twinkling from the reflection of the TV. "She was one of a kind. Never let anyone get to her, you know?" He winks at me. "Never let anyone tell her who to be."

I look up and see Diane leaning against the threshold of the door.

"Elizabeth, come on," she says, turning back toward the kitchen. "This dinner's not going to cook itself."

THIRTY-FOUR

A couple of weeks after my story is published, I'm home alone on a Saturday afternoon. Cole's at the inn, and the kids arc out at Lauren's farm with some friends from school, celebrating her birthday. I'm tinkering around the house in my socks, half-heartedly writing out a menu for the holidays, something to look forward to now that the story is behind me, especially because my parents are coming to visit.

I hear a thump on our front stoop and go out to see what it is. A small manila parcel rests on our top step. I pick it up, bring it inside, and sit cross-legged on the couch with the envelope in my lap, glancing up at CNN to a shot of a reporter standing outside the Capitol building. It is a beautiful, blue-sky day, and I feel a stab of envy, watching her. But it's not for the reasons that would have dragged on me just a few months ago, when I would have pined for her hustle and purpose. Now, I just envy the fact that she is there. That she gets to run along the Potomac, eat at my favorite Ethiopian place on Ninth Street, walk among the lit-up monuments at night.

The fact is, I still miss DC, I always will. But it's not enough to go back. There's no going back now. Greyhill is home.

I flip the package over in my lap and notice there's no return address. In fact, on second glance, it looks like it wasn't sent
through the mail at all. *Did somebody drop it off?* I close my eyes,
trying to remember whether I heard a delivery truck or someone's
car . . . I tear the tape off and reach inside, and when I do, I gasp
out loud. It's like I have a grenade in my lap.

For a minute or two, I can't move at all. I sit there, staring at
it, my hands on either side of me, braced against the couch like
I might tip over. Like all the rest of them, the journal is gold, the
cover engraved with SGL.

I open it up, and find when I fan through the pages that there
is only one entry, just two pages long. It isn't dated, so it's impossible, at first glance, to know when it was written, whether it was
recent or years ago. Her penmanship looks just like you'd guess,
elegant and feminine, and once I start reading, I realize that just
like her, this is far more complicated than it appears.

> *Sinking, sinking, it starts. That's how I feel. All day,*
> *all night, when I thrash in the sheets, wondering when*
> *you're going to let go. All this time later and I still feel*
> *just like I did on the day you died, like I have an itch*
> *coming from deep inside the marrow of my bones, and the*
> *only way to make it better is to make it stop. Make myself*
> *stop. End it.*
>
> *On that morning I got in the truck, it was exactly a*
> *year to the day after Teddy's heart attack. It's surprised me*
> *that nobody has made that connection. I thought what I*
> *was doing would be obvious. I thought there would be a*
> *big to-do about it. I thought people would know. "She must*

have been so distraught over his death." "She couldn't live
without him!" "Now at least they're together again."

But no! Nobody seems to understand what I was trying
to do. Nobody seems to understand how badly I wanted to
die that day. I don't anymore, but it is still so difficult to
be alone. Nobody has ever understood it, the unbearable
loneliness I've suffered, the ungodly solitude I've endured.
I want to be done with it now, Henrietta, but things didn't
turn out the way I intended. I didn't get my wish. And
so back I go, back to New York, to my gilded cage, still
without the one thing that has always eluded me: love.

This is my punishment, isn't it? This is the price I pay.
There is nothing more pathetic, or dangerous, than a lonely
woman. That's what it all comes down to. That's the crux of
this whole thing. It's what I see crawling all over this place.
It's what killed Henrietta, and her mother, and it's what
was supposed to kill me.

Do you know what? Right before you died, I could hear
you yelling for me. Worse, I could hear the worry in your
voice, and Henrietta, I'm sorry: it thrilled me.

It's amazing how much I remember from that night,
considering the state I was in and the amount of alcohol I
had consumed. I'd gone off to get another beer, and when I
looked over at you and Bradley, leaning against his car, you
were laughing. It was the kind of laugh that lovers share.
Intimate and easy, in on the same joke.

I was convinced that the joke was me.

Was it?

To this day, Bradley says he can't remember.

But that was it, I decided. That was the moment. I launched myself up the hill and into the bramble. I drank the beer, guzzling it down, and then smashed the bottle into a tree. I was crying then. Sobbing. Nobody saw me. People were too busy celebrating. That's what I remember: the sound of celebrating. Laughing and whooping and music. It was an impossible sound, so far off from what I was feeling.

When I got to the clearing, I stood with my back against a tree and looked out at the lights of the town beneath me. I thought about what a prison this place had been, and how the only thing that had brought me any happiness over the course of my seventeen years of life had been you. And Bradley. But you were both discarding me now, too.

I tried to think of the best scenario. I really did, Henrietta.

I told myself that I was imagining what was going on with you two, and that Bradley and I would stick to our plan. This place beneath me, these lights in the distance were my future. I would marry him and raise his babies. I would make it work.

Or if what I was seeing between the two of you was real—if you were truly in love—I would accept it. Take it on the chin. I could run off, like you planned to and like I soon did. I could find a new life somewhere else.

I told myself all this, Henrietta, trying to make it better. I tried to make another choice.

I took a step back, but then I heard the two of you. I

couldn't bear it. I couldn't bear another minute of feeling the way I did. That's when I stepped out onto the ledge.

I don't know what it was that brought you and Bradley to me at just that moment. Call it fate. Call it serendipity. Had you been a second later, I swear, Henrietta, my plan would have gone off without a hitch and it would be you writing to me now instead of the reverse.

I put my hands out to the sides—a swan dive, I suppose—and then I heard you scream my name.

Oddly, when I turned and saw you and Bradley standing there, the fear in your eyes, my first thought was not that you had come looking for me. My first thought was that you had come up to that secluded spot, away from the party, to be alone. Together.

I turned back toward the edge. The view of the town, the lights, seemed to be pulsing. I took another step. Your voices. And then I felt your arms around my waist, barreling around my middle, willing me back, the two of us falling backward, safely on the ground

I should've just surrendered then, Henrietta. I should have been brave enough to face all the pain I felt. But I didn't, did I? I had to keep going. That's what Bradley was always admonishing me with: "You take things too far, Susannah!"

I stood up, and you stood up with me, and your arm was pulling my arm, and I was pulling away, and then Bradley was trying to pull us apart and his hand was your hand and your hand was his and it all happened so fast—

There was a scratch. Pebbles underfoot. A whoosh. The

crack of tree limbs. And then Bradley and I were staring at each other, our horrified eyes trying to will the other's to say that what had just happened had not happened. But it did. It did, Henrietta.

"I didn't mean to—" he said, his hands clawing at his cheeks. "I don't understand how—"

"I know," I said. I didn't let him finish. "I know."

My hands are shaking when I finish reading. There's a note tucked into the back of the journal, between the blank pages. "There are more," it says. "Lots more, if you want them. *Lots to write about, Bess . . .*"

I reach for my phone on the coffee table.

"Elizabeth," Diane says. "Good afternoon."

"Hi . . . Diane?" I cough it out, the phone shaking in my hand. "Sorry to bother you, but quick question: a package was left on my stoop this morning but I didn't happen to see who left it, and there's no note and no address. Did you by any chance notice if someone stopped by our house?"

"As a matter of fact," she says, "I was moving my Christmas cactus into the living room this morning—it needs more light if I expect it to bloom at all this season—and I saw a car, but I didn't recognize it. It was a teal color? Virginia license plates. They parked right in your driveway, but I couldn't tell if it was a man or a woman. Whoever it was had on a big, puffy coat with the hood pulled up. Now that I think about it, I'm thinking it was a woman—a very petite one, actually, too small to be a man. She seemed in a hurry."

"Okay, thanks," I say, picturing Cindy's frame. "That helps."

"What was the package, if you don't mind my asking?"

"Oh, nothing," I say, searching my brain for an answer because I know that won't satisfy her. My eyes land on the *National Geographic Kids Almanac* on the coffee table. "It was a book that Max is borrowing from a friend. I just wondered which friend; his mom forgot to include a note. Anyhow, thanks again!" I hang up before she has a chance to respond. The diary is next to me, threatening me, like it's alive. I put a hand to my chest, feel my heartbeat pounding beneath my palm, pick the diary up, and read it again.

THIRTY-FIVE

⁓——⁓

Six Months Later
Draper Hall Parking Lot

"I heard Eva and David are moving up to Washington."

"To do what? Pursue his political future?"

"Who knows. Who cares! But you know what else? Someone said Cole was joking at that guys' poker night about running for mayor."

"Cole Warner?"

"Mm-hmm."

"That actually makes sense. I can see that."

"Can't you, though?"

"Yes, but what a twist! Bess as *First Lady*!"

"Well, she knows a thing or two about that role, doesn't she?"

"Ha! I actually heard she's working with William."

"Yes, I think the inn is going to add a catering business."

"Just what she needs, to be surrounded by food all day."

"You're terrible."

"Just honest. Actually, though, she'll probably do a good job with it, if what she's done with the inn is any indication. Have you seen the lobby?"

"Gorgeous, how she decorated it!"

"To die for! Diane was going on and on about it at the hair salon. She said the color scheme was her idea."

"Interesting! But speaking of Bess, did you hear about Susannah Lane?"

"Selling Esperanza. I saw Martha Brown taping the listing up in her window yesterday."

"The Warners should buy it. They could actually turn it into a resort, the way everyone said Susannah wanted to. I wonder what she's doing back in New York."

"Working with someone on her memoir, I heard."

"*Memoir!* That should be something."

"I know. Whether it's truthful or not, I'm sure I'll read it."

"Me, too. I'll read it cover to cover."

"Everyone will."

"It will be the talk of the town."

"You know something has to be."

"Truer words, my friend."

"Mm-hmm."

ACKNOWLEDGMENTS

I am incredibly fortunate to have now written three books under the guidance of my wonderful editor, Emily Griffin, and my agent, Katherine Fausset. Emily's sharp insights helped shape this story in so many crucial ways, and I am beyond grateful for our easy, collaborative rapport. Katherine always expertly navigates our sometimes complicated industry on my behalf, and has taught me so much in the process. It is a joy to work with them both.

Thank you to the entire team at HarperCollins: Amber Oliver, Suzette Lam, Mary Sasso, Falon Kirby, Julie Hersh, and Andrea Guinn. From start to finish, it has been a pleasure to work with you.

Special thanks to my husband, Jay, and our girls, who understand when I have to disappear for a few hours (and sometimes the occasional weekend) to write, and cheer me on even when I'm grumpy. Your support means the world to me.

This book features a few women who don't necessarily do the best job supporting each other, and I would like to acknowledge the many women in my life who have done the opposite for me. I am occasionally asked whether my relationships with other female writers are competitive, and I am always delighted to report that they are, in fact, some of the most extraordinary, supportive people I have met in my professional life, and I am so proud of how we rally around each other. Finally, thank you to my network of close girlfriends who do so much for me on a daily basis—the phone calls, the emergency childcare, the comic relief, the long talks, and lunch dates. Life would be far more difficult, and not nearly as fun, without you.

About the author

About the book

Insights,
Interviews
& More...

Read on

Meet KristynKusek Lewis

© Magin Urdanick

KRISTYN KUSEK LEWIS is the author of *Save Me* and *How Lucky You Are*. A former magazine editor at *Glamour* and *Child*, Kristyn has been writing for national publications for nearly twenty years. Her work has appeared in the *New York Times*; *O, The Oprah Magazine*; *Real Simple*; *Reader's Digest*; *Glamour*; ▶

Self; *Redbook*; *Cosmopolitan*; *Marie
Claire*; *Parents*; *Allure*; *Good
Housekeeping*; *Cooking Light*; *Health*;
Men's Health; the *New York Daily News*;
and many more. Kristyn is a graduate of
the College of the Holy Cross and the
Vermont College of Fine Arts, where she
earned an MFA in creative writing. She
lives in the Washington, DC, area with
her family. ∾

A Conversation with
Kristyn Kusek Lewis

What was the inspiration for Half of What You Hear?

MY STORIES HAVE always started with a character, but with this book, I also knew that I wanted to write about a small town. I have lived most of my life in and around major cities, but I harbor serious country-mouse fantasies, in part because of the childhood summers I spent near Shenandoah National Park in the Blue Ridge Mountains. I just love this part of my home state. I feel like my blood pressure drops twenty points the farther I head into the country, and after several visits to the Blue Ridge Mountains and the somewhat more posh areas in and around Middleburg, I started crafting the idea of Greyhill.

I also had an inkling that I wanted to write a story about a woman who is in her early forties and feels fairly established in her life, but then gets plunked down into something entirely new. When I started working on the story, I had just moved back to the Washington, DC, area, which is where I was mostly raised, after living elsewhere for over twenty years. My advantage over Bess is that my move was a homecoming—but in far less dramatic fashion, I was going through a similar ▶

5

A Conversation with Kristyn Kusek Lewis
(continued)

adjustment, finding my way in a new environment, and using a geographic move as a clean slate to really think about what I wanted next for my life and my family.

Which of the characters in this novel came the most easily to you? Which did you struggle with, and why?

IT IS ALWAYS fun to write about somebody who is badly behaved, so I quite enjoyed writing about Susannah, even after she began to show some of the demons that have haunted her throughout her life. One of the first scenes I wrote about her is the one where she is revealing some of the ways she exacted revenge on the women who were threatening her marriage, and it came from a murky memory of a story I'd once heard about somebody who'd hidden a dead fish behind someone's radiator. I wanted Susannah to have this dark, almost cruel side, because particularly with older female characters, we don't always see the full range of the person, and I wanted to write about somebody older who was not the mild-mannered, grandmotherly type. That said, I didn't want her negatives to be negatives for their own sake—I wanted to show the reasons for her behavior, to show that she's really lived a life, and make her sympathetic. To show that like in real life, nobody is entirely good or bad. Bess was tough at first because so much of her experience in the story is reactionary: she's reacting to the way the new community views her, to her mother-in-law's expectations, to the struggles she sees her daughter having, to her husband's relative ease, all while knowing with some certainty that people have already made up their minds about her. She had a tricky path to navigate in the story, and as badly as I wanted her to succeed in her new town, I almost felt like the experiences she was having meant that I had to simultaneously be the hand on her back pushing her forward, and the one setting obstacles in front of her.

Livvie and Max feel like very realistic teenagers. Are they based on your own children?

As EVERY PARENT knows, kids grow up at lightning speed, and just when you think you have something figured out, your kids have moved into a new phase, with entirely different challenges. My kids are younger than Livvie and Max, but I know what it feels like to mourn the stages that your kids have moved past. I wanted Bess to be reexamining her life as a mother as her kids are ▸

moving out of their grade-school years, when it could feel like they are reaching the age where they no longer need her as much. Of course, she discovers by the end of the book that they very much still need her, but I thought that with Max and Livvie in this tween place where they have one foot in their childhood and one foot in their teens, Bess would question what her life as a mother has looked like and what she wants it to look like going forward, in her "new life" in Greyhill.

I also wanted Livvie's experience in town to echo some of Bess's teenage struggles, just to mess with her a little more and give her more to grapple with as she adjusts to her new reality. And given how she spends so much time thinking about Susannah's experience as a teenager in Greyhill, I wanted her to have a present-day scenario to give some relevance to her anxieties about how the town works.

How did the process of writing this novel differ from the process of writing How Lucky You Are ***and*** Save Me? ***Why did you decide to include an element of suspense?***

I WISH I COULD say that the decision came consciously, but as I began writing about the characters, the suspense element revealed itself to me. Though it's not necessarily fun while you're writing it—it can be maddening, in fact—it's fun to look back and see how a story progresses and changes from draft to draft. For instance, in the earliest version of this novel, Susannah and her husband, Teddy, were very much alive and married, and Bess was Susannah's caretaker as she recovered from her accident.

It's hard to compare the experience of writing each novel I've published because they're each so different. When you're writing fiction, you're really immersing yourself in the world you've created, and comparing each experience is nearly as difficult as trying to compare completely distinct places on the globe. Each book has its own unique makeup. That said, I knew after writing *Save Me*, which is a story very much inside the head of one character, that I wanted to write something with more exterior action and more moving parts, which is why the idea of a town felt so appealing.

What are you working on next?

EACH OF MY books has had a central subject—the growing pains of long friendships, marriage, life in a small town—but the common thread, I've discovered, is that I write stories about identity, and how women think about ▶

A Conversation with Kristyn Kusek Lewis
(continued)

themselves in the context of the choices they've made and the people they surround themselves with.

My next book is in that same vein, but it's a story about a family. At its heart is a woman who's stumbled into a career as a bestselling "happiness expert" but isn't actually all that happy herself. It's about how the person we present to the world—whether through our daily interactions or our jobs or our Instagram accounts—is often dramatically different from who we are deep down. That could sound like a bummer, but the book has some comic elements that have been really fun to write—partly because these well-meaning characters, including a zookeeper husband and a college-age daughter, have a propensity for making really bad decisions despite their best intentions. It's that whole car-wreck scenario: you hate to see it happening, but you just can't look away. ∽

Reading Group Guide:
Discussion Questions for *Half of What You Hear*

1. Does Bess's move to Greyhill feel like an escape from her humiliation in Washington or a proactive move for her family? What would you have done in her shoes?

2. Do you think Bess deserved to lose her job at the White House? Is "venting with a coworker," as Bess describes her behavior, ever acceptable or is it always a bad idea?

3. In what ways is Greyhill a typical "small town"? Does it seem like the residents make a conscious effort to keep out outsiders, and if so, do you think this is true of small towns in general? Would you ever live in a place like it?

4. Does Cole owe it to Bess to help her feel more comfortable in Greyhill because it's his hometown, or is it better for her to have to carve her own path?

5. What does Susannah owe the residents of Greyhill? Is it fair for her to sell off the land even if it ▶

Read on

means a fundamental change in the town's character? Is change inevitable?

6. How do the flashbacks to Bess's high school years reflect her current-day experience with the other mothers in Greyhill? Is Cole right that she's projecting a bit? Or is Livvie's experience trying to find friends in their new town similar to hers?

7. Susannah is a layered, complex character with many secrets. By the novel's end, how had your initial impressions of her changed? Did you feel more or less sympathy for her?

8. Henrietta Martin has taken on an important symbolic significance for the residents of Greyhill. What does she represent for them? How do you think they'll change their opinions about her and her death now that Bess's article has shed some light on the incident?

9. Diane is, in some ways, a typical mother-in-law, but she surprises Bess by the end of the book. Did you have to revise your earlier impressions of her, as Bess did? What do you think their future relationship will be like?

10. Does gossip serve any positive purpose in this novel? Have you ever had an instance in your own life when gossiping helped a situation, or do you believe in the old adage that if you can't say something nice, then you shouldn't say anything at all? What do you think of people who are described as gossips? ∽